DECEPTION IS OUR REMEDY

DECEPTION IS OUR REMEDY

Alexandra Gavranovic

Published by Dumetella Press in the United States of America.

Identifiers:

979-8-9891651-0-0 (Paperback)
979-8-9891651-1-7 (Ebook)

To Booboo,

who nearly deleted this story several times

ONE

THE IDEA OF A BIRTHDAY, of being celebrated just for existing, isn't one I'm familiar with. In fact, most of the time, I doubt my existence. What's the purpose of a life full of nothing? I once read an old saying: "Live every day as if it's your last." But I don't think that saying can apply to me. No one would be able to tell which day was my last, as every day I live the same. Yet I do have one thing—one person, rather—that makes my nothingness feel like something. My best friend, Reginald. And ironically, today is my "special day."

"Happy birthday, Cal!" Reginald calls out.

The sun is hanging just above the horizon, and a light breeze fills the air. Our special place, the fields of Neighborhood 33, has never felt more like home. I watch in bewilderment as Reggie opens a bag he brought with him, pulling out a book with a leather cover and no words written on the front. Handing it to me, he grins.

"It was my birth mom's," he says. "She used to journal in it. She left it behind when she left me last year. My adoptive mother suggested it would be a good gift. I wanted to get you something since I haven't been able to for so many years. So I ripped out the used pages."

I glance down at the book now in my hands, gently rubbing my fingers over the soft brown leather. It isn't customary to give gifts for anything where we live. Birthdays are usually not even recognized. I'm surprised but thankful for the present. My eyes travel back up to look into his.

"Are you sure you want me to have this, Reggie? I don't want to take an important piece of your mom from you."

He simply nods in response, and I gently open the front cover. Inside, the name Eina Gray, in fancy penmanship, has been crossed out and replaced by the name Callista Tieron in Reggie's messy attempt at script. As I flip through the pages, empty white sheets face me with endless possibilities. I close the book and stick it into my bag. I adjust myself into a kneeling position, then lean over to hug Reggie.

"Thank you," I whisper into his ear.

He hugs me back, then pulls away to look into my eyes. A gust of wind comes and pushes my hair into my face. He reaches his hand up to brush it away, tucking the strand behind my ear. I bite my lower lip nervously. His eyes drift down for a second, then move back to mine. We continue to look at each other, as if we could read each other's mind. He's my best friend, the only person I've ever been able to rely on. He means everything to me, and I know I mean just as much to him.

The fleeting moment is broken by the crunching of leaves from my right.

"Callista, come home now. It's past curfew!"

I fall backward onto my hands and push myself to my feet. Grabbing my bag, I take one glance at Reggie, then turn to run toward my mother, Alina. I sense his eyes on my back as I start walking home with her.

Gathering my courage, I speak quietly. "I'm sorry I missed curfew. Reginald wanted me to go out with him, and I didn't realize how late it was."

She doesn't even respond, and I lower my shoulders. *What did I expect?*

We continue to walk down the road until we turn onto our street. The sun has fully set by the time I reach the steps of my home. It looks dull, like every other house on the block. Alina walks inside, leaving the door open for me to follow. The familiar scent of flowers greets my nose.

"Shower and go to bed. You don't get supper, as you made me come find you past curfew." She throws the command over her shoulder, then stops and turns to face me with a sigh, her tone softening slightly. "I know you and Reginald are friends, but you're seventeen now, Callista. I expect you to know better. It seems that each year, you become increasingly rebellious. I don't want to have to separate you from him, but I will if I have to."

She doesn't even give me the chance to respond, as she walks into the kitchen as soon as she finishes speaking.

A frown spreads across my face, and my stomach rumbles. *What am I going to do? Reginald is my only friend. He's the only one who exists here that I can see. Our Neighborhood is so big, but so empty. And I still don't know why. I'm just trying to find some way to break up the monotony of life here.*

Knowing better than to try to defy my parents and their strict belief in the 3R's restrictions, I quickly head upstairs to my bedroom. I throw my bag on my bed as I enter the bathroom, then turn on the shower faucet. I undress, thinking about what I want to write in my new journal. The possibilities seem endless. I could write about how out of place I feel in my home, the distance between me and my family, or about my best friend. Or I could finally get out all the feelings I have toward my parents for once. Maybe I could just write about my experiences. They could serve as a way for me to feel like what I deal with matters, and perhaps one day, they could help the future generations of children forced to live out a life like mine.

My mind swirls as I contemplate what I should do. The steam from the shower quickly fills the space, bringing me back into reality.

When I finish dressing and preparing for sleep, I flop onto my bed.

They don't even love me. I'm nothing more than a responsibility they have to upkeep to look good. Why was I cursed with such awful parents? They tell me nothing, then wonder why I ask so many questions. If they just shared, maybe things could be different. Maybe then I'd understand and obey the curfew more, and I would listen. But they don't even try to explain.

My mind wanders with progressively angrier thoughts. Before they can get too unbearable, I flip to my side, staring at my door. Unusual talking echoes through the floorboards from below. I know I could get severely punished if I'm caught sneaking or disobeying my parents. Yet the opportunity to learn something, anything, wins over my logic.

Creeping out of bed, I slowly tiptoe to my door. I press my ear against the gray wood. The words I hear are broken and unclear.

"Soon ... plan ... will be ... taken ... no time ... death ... Eclium ... REM ..."

The talking stops, and I assume my parents have either moved outside to speak or are now whispering so I can't hear.

An eerie chill carries across my body at the cryptic words, and I return to my bed and grab my bag. I lean over to my single bedside table and open the drawer to take out a pen, then lean back against my pillows and open my bag. I feel for the leather book and slowly take it out, opening it to the first blank page. It doesn't surprise me that my parents have secrets. They don't even look like me, let alone have any personality traits similar to mine. I can't think of a single instance where I have felt truly loved by them.

Today, Alina showed a brief glint of her humanity. But her punishment negates that glint. I'm forced to respect them, even though I'm not so sure they respect me. With this in mind, my hand travels to the left side, and I begin to write.

December 16th, 2103.

My parents have just had the strangest conversation, and although I couldn't hear all of it, two things stuck out to me: Eclium and REM. I don't currently know what these words mean, but my gut tells me they're important. This world I live in is governed by a low-profile government that most refer to as 3R but whose true name is unknown. The area in which I take residence is divided into Neighborhoods that range from numbers 30-39. My neighborhood is 33. I have constant nightmares about the same thing, yet I'm unsure of their meaning. I always see a girl. I see demons. I hear screams. It scares me. And I have no one I feel I can tell.

The words come out messily, my hand not used to writing, especially about myself. I debate whether it's even important. After all, who's to say that anyone would care about my experiences?

Footsteps outside my door make me freeze, and I quickly put the book and pen underneath my pillow, then press the button on my headboard to turn off all my room lights. Finally, I maneuver under my blankets and close my eyes.

Moments later, my door creaks open and then slowly closes again. I let out the breath I was holding and decide it would be best for me to sleep. My brain clouds as I drift off into my slumber.

"Don't hurt them, please!" My cries fall on deaf ears as my mouth doesn't even move. Dark shadows fall limp in front of me as other figures inject them with an object. In the corner, the outline of a small girl stands with the shadow of a man holding her arm. I hear whispers in my ears.

They tell me I'm powerless. I reach out, using all my strength and will, trying to save her. I have an inexplicable urge to be by her side. I feel drawn to the shadow girl.

A sharp pain causes me to cry out. I'm grabbed roughly as the girl seems to get farther and farther away. Another shadow of a man holds my arm tightly, and I watch as the small girl and I are dragged away from the scene, away from each other. I scream in agony and despair, but no sound comes out. The darkness swells, and the whispers grow louder. And then it all stops.

I wake up in a cold sweat. My heart races in my chest, and I feel like if I close my eyes, I might be stuck in an endless void forever. I throw myself out of bed and move quickly toward the bathroom to splash my face with water.

I wish I knew what these nightmares mean. My vision moves up to my mirror, and I stare into the blue eyes of the girl looking back at me. *I want them to go away.* I'm snatched out of my thoughts by Alina's voice as she walks into my room.

"Callista, you best be getting ready. You know you have an appointment today, and I took off work for you!" She stands with a hand on her hip, staring at me from the bedroom.

Not as if it's my choice. I simply nod in reply, preparing myself for the day. I manage to get ready in ten minutes, and she stands watching me from the same place the whole time. As always, she won't give me privacy.

At last, without a word, she walks out of my room and toward the stairs, leaving me to follow. My father sits downstairs watching the daily Neighborhood broadcast directly from 3R headquarters. There's a fresh diffuser on the coffee table emitting the fragrant smell of roses. The news reporter is discussing how there will be a new food introduced to the 3R Catalogue: freeze-dried cake pops. An image of a bright-pink ball on a stick flashes across the screen with text below it that reads, "Order now to be one of the first consumers!"

I scoff. *It probably tastes just as awful as everything else. Why does he even bother watching that junk?*

Alina taps her foot on the hardwood floor, clearly irritated with my lack of speed.

"Alright, I'm coming," I say with a groan, following her as she exits the house.

She moves urgently down the road, and I drag my feet behind her. We pass several homes identical to ours, the only difference being the number on the mailbox. Half of them have their lights off. The only sign of life from the rest is the brief, shadowed outline of someone in a window. *Everyone must be preparing for work.*

As we pass the postal office, Alina sighs. "I bet your father will be ordering those cake pop things. I personally don't think they look very good. I won't be surprised if he brings them home when he picks up our week's food supply tomorrow. I suppose we should be grateful that our government is trying to provide us with a larger variety of goods." She glances back at me, and I nod ever so slightly.

"I still don't understand why our food is always dry," I comment, trying to keep the exasperation out of my voice.

"You learned that in school, Callista. You know that the Great Climate Crisis War has caused it to be extremely difficult to send out fresh produce. That's why we're supplied freeze-dried food. It lasts longer and is more sustainable. Our government is doing its best."

You mean the school I'm not even allowed to attend anymore? I go silent, knowing that if I continue to push, she'll just scold me for asking too many questions and "not appreciating the generosity we've received."

I grow nervous as we get closer to the only doctor's office in the Neighborhood. We pass several more houses before we arrive at the dreaded steps. I pause for a moment to look at the building, and Alina continues inside.

Why do I even have to come here? Alina says it's just to make sure I'm healthy, but I always feel worse after my appointment. I debate running for a moment. There's no one in sight, no one to stop me. Yet I don't move. I know I can't. I wouldn't make it far, and I have nowhere to go. *I would rather deal with this than be stranded without food and shelter. And I don't know how dangerous the outsiders actually are.*

I gulp and push back my fears. I've never truly considered trying to leave. Especially not after I was punished when I was six for playing too close to the Neighborhood gates. I made a game out of seeing if I could spot any other human beings on the other side of the tall, menacing gates. But I couldn't. There were only trees, broken apart briefly by the road that leads to what I can only assume to be other Neighborhoods. When the guards stationed there noticed me, I ran away. I thought I got away free. But I must have been reported, because Alina told me off for being "too curious" and "too nosy." I was prevented from leaving the house for three days as punishment. That situation was one of many that started my never-ending questions and doubt.

I take hold of the cold metal door handle and pull. A rush of chilled air wisps through my hair, causing goosebumps to prick up on my skin. I step inside, letting the door shut with a bang behind me. The natural sunlight vanishes behind me, the only light source being the bright white lights that line the ceiling. The unwelcome smell of chemicals and medicine clouds my senses, making me even more uneasy.

Alina is facing the counter and speaking through a window to the Neighborhood physician, Dr. Isaac. When he spots me, the tall, pale, and eerily slim man smiles.

"Ah, Callista. You're finally here!" he says. "It's been some time."

I wish it was longer. I force a thin smile onto my face. The urge to make a retort bites at me, but I know better. Talking back gets you punished. Asking questions gets you punished. And I'm pretty sure I'm reaching my parents' limit of patience for my questioning. Who knows what they'll do if I keep pushing.

"Let's just get this done." My tone is more clipped than I intended, earning me a scowl from Alina. I try not to focus on her and instead prepare myself for the upcoming discomfort.

"Of course. Follow me," the doctor says, then he exits from behind the counter and comes into the waiting room. He holds open the door for me to come through, and I glance at Alina. Her expression is neutral, lacking any sympathy. I know she won't tell me that I don't have to go, no matter how much I want her to.

With my head held high, I go through the door and follow the doctor toward the back of the building. We pass a few empty offices, then enter the examination room.

Even though I've done this so many times, it never gets easier. The room is too small, the near silence too unsettling. The dull bleakness is the same as it always is. A small clock hangs on the wall, ticking as the seconds go by. A dark metal cabinet with several drawers sits just below it.

The doctor ushers me to lie down on the long metal bench in the middle of the room, and I hesitate before doing as instructed. He grabs two of the needles from a drawer and walks over to me. I'm not sure if I'm imagining it, but one of the needles seems slightly larger than usual.

"You know the procedure. Sit still," he says. His face is firm, lacking any form of expression.

I close my eyes and think of Reginald, as a sharp pain travels up my arm and a moment of dizziness hits me. Seconds later, he jabs the second needle into my arm, and I swear I can feel him take the blood out of me. I swallow back a wave of nausea, biting hard on my cheek.

As soon as the feelings pass, I swing my feet off the bench. When I still feel a pulsing pain in the first injection site, I look down at my arm. There's a red patch as usual, but I notice with rising alarm that there are also small maroon lines spreading outward.

No one likes to give me straight answers. But he can't deny something as obvious as this. "Doctor Isaac, I can still feel the pain," I comment, my voice uneasy.

He looks up at me from his crouched position next to the cabinet. His eyebrows rise in confusion as he stands to move closer.

"That's strange. I'll order some pain medication so it will be here next time your family picks up your supply from the mailer."

I frown, unconvinced and mildly irritated by his nonchalance. "What are these lines?"

"You must be having some sort of allergic reaction. We started using a new protein in our shots that's made to keep your vitamin levels balanced. I'm sure it'll go away soon." He waves his hands, then moves to open the door. "I have some paperwork I must do now."

My frown deepens, and I say nothing as I move to go back toward the lobby. *He's hiding something. Why is the shot suddenly different? It makes no sense.*

Alina is waiting for me, staring mindlessly at the television on the corner wall, which is playing a pre-recorded episode of *The Neighborhood and You,* an awfully boring series depicting our government's history in a "comedic" way. It's one of the only five shows that ever play and is equally as dreadful as the rest.

"I'm finished," I say, making sure to hide my upset. I try not to focus on the pain in my arm, not wanting to give any hint that something is off.

Alina snaps her head to me, smiling in as close to a loving way as she can get. "And you didn't cause any trouble?"

I shake my head. "Of course not."

She stares at me for a moment too long, reading me to see if I'm lying. When she's satisfied, she stands. "I meant to tell you earlier, but your father and I have a work friend coming over tomorrow night for dinner. Reginald's mother is also coming. I hope for your sake that you're home on time. I don't like having to punish you."

I nod.

Wordlessly, Alina exits the building, and I follow suit. We exchange few words on the way home, and as soon as I arrive at our doorstep, I hurry past her and into my room.

I flick the switch to the bathroom, then lift my shirt sleeve to look at my arm in the mirror. The pain has dulled, and the lines are gone. *Were they ever there in the first place? Or am I just going crazy?* I blink several times, but nothing changes. *If these appointments are supposed to be keeping me healthy but, in fact, harm me, am I actually safe? What's REM? What's Eclium? And why do I feel like I don't even know my own home?*

I hurry to my bed and pull my journal and pen out from underneath my pillow. I sit at my desk, hovering the pen above a clean page.

Then, I begin to write.

TWO

THINGS THAT DON'T MAKE SENSE.

> *Eclium/REM—What is it? Who is it? Why were my parents discussing it so secretively?*
> *Dr. Isaac—Why was I given a different shot, with no explanation? What's the purpose?*
> *Alina—Why does she hate my questioning so much? Doesn't she know that if she just gave me straight answers, I wouldn't ask so many things?*

I pause when I hear Alina talking to someone. I strain to make out the words, trying to identify the other voice. When I have no success, I sigh and close the journal. *I can't let them find this.* So I place the book and pen underneath my mattress, hoping no one decides to randomly search my room. Then I swing open my door and exit into the hall. I'm now able to recognize the strange voice as Reggie's.

Why is he here? I quickly go down the stairs to see what's going on.

When Reggie sees me, his eyes light up. "Cal!" he exclaims. "I wanted to see if you wanted to hang out."

I look to Alina, and she nods.

"I'd love to." I grin at him, eagerly moving to the door.

"Just don't forget about curfew," Alina calls as we exit the house. I don't bother responding, glad to have an excuse to do something other than worry about all the things being kept from me.

The sunlight beams down on us, keeping us relatively warm in the winter air.

"I got a surprise for you," Reggie says slyly.

"Another one? You spoil me."

"You'll see. It's at our regular spot."

I pout. "Won't you give me a hint?"

He shakes his head. "Then it wouldn't be a surprise. We're almost there."

In the near distance, I can make out the shadow of the big tree that marks our spot. I picture its dark wood marked with age, an *R* and a *C* carved into the bark. Reginald suggested we carve our initials after I had a fight with my parents about the children who left. It wasn't always just me and Reggie.

When I was little, I would ask my parents why there were no other children at school even though other children lived here. They simply responded that the government decided it was better for children to get individual educations. I remember occasionally seeing a young face in a window, only for the curtains to cover it moments later. Or seeing two children in the distance playing together, only for them to run away when I approached.

There was one girl in particular who stood out though. I never got to speak to her, but I used to see her looking at me through her window each day when I was on my way to the field. Sometimes we exchanged small waves. One day, I cried to my parents and said I wanted to meet with her. They exchanged alerted expressions and told me that I shouldn't be interacting with anyone except Reginald. I complained and threw a fit. This led to them reprimanding me and not allowing me to leave the house for a month. I never saw the girl again after that, so I asked more questions, and received more unsatisfactory answers. Then the other children began to disappear. By the time I was five, they were all gone, except for Reggie. Only adults remained. I asked once more and was told that "most families leave the area to seek better education for their children." I was convinced that meant we should leave too, but my parents insisted that they believe "the education provided where we live is the best."

I was unsatisfied by their responses, but I knew I couldn't do anything. I was too young. A few years later, I dared to bring the topic up again, hoping they would provide me with more insight, since I was older. I was wrong, and our conversation ended up in a fight that ended with me storming off to meet with Reggie. He assured me he would never leave my side and that the strength of the tree bark represented the power of our friendship. He said our initials served as a reminder of this. His words comforted me, but they didn't make me forget what had happened.

"You're going to love this," Reggie says, bringing my focus back to the present situation. We climb the final few paces up the small hill to our spot. He walks behind the tree and bends over to grab something I can't see. I lean to the side, trying to catch a glimpse of whatever he has.

"You better not be trying to peek!" he calls, and I laugh.

"I would never!" I sit down against the tree, leaning my head back and staring up at the sky. The gentle movement of the wind through the barren trees puts me at ease. When Reggie joins me with a large picnic basket in his hands and a blanket under his arm, my eyes widen. He has one hand firmly placed on top of the basket, almost as if he's trying to keep something inside.

"I thought it would be nice for us to have lunch together," he says. "I took some extra food from my house for us."

I smile wide at Reggie as he sits beside me, laying out the checkered blanket. "Thank you," I say.

"That's not all." He smirks at me, and I hear a faint noise come from inside the basket. "Open it."

I look at him with suspicion, then quickly open the basket lid. Suddenly, a small black ball of fur leaps out, letting out a loud meow. My mouth falls open as I watch the little kitten pounce at the edge of the blanket.

"How did you—"

"I may have met someone who got her for me to keep, but we can share her. I know your parents don't allow pets in the house. Feel free to give her a name."

Overwhelming joy fills me, and I pick up the kitten to stare into her green eyes. "Emmy? I feel like it's fitting."

He nods and replies, "Emmy it is."

I move to sit atop the blanket, holding Emmy in my lap. She crawls out of it and walks around, pouncing on leaves that blow over every once in a while. I take out a sandwich from the basket, and Reggie does the same. The bread is plain and the meat is dry, but I wouldn't ask for this moment to be any other way. I tear off a piece of the meat and give it to Emmy, who eats it up eagerly.

"At least someone seems to enjoy the taste," I joke.

Reggie chuckles. "You don't like it? I personally find it to be extremely tasty."

I look at him with astonishment. "You're joking."

He quirks an eyebrow. "Am I?"

Shaking my head, I relish the rare feeling of genuine joy.

We spend the next couple of hours together, and for once, I'm not eager for time to pass. The only part that I relish about my life is that my parents work during the day hours, and they've permitted me to spend my time at the fields so long as they don't need me elsewhere.

The sun is setting once more, and I sigh, knowing I'll have to return home soon. My earlier joy has now made way for my regular unease. *Reggie is my only friend. I trust him, but I'm not sure if I can tell him what I know.* Although I realize he's likely as clueless about the answers to my questions as I am, I still find myself needing reassurance.

"Can I ask you something?" I finally say.

He turns and tilts his head at me, pieces of his dirty-blond hair falling in front of his eyes.

"You're always honest with me, right?" I watch Emmy sleeping in a ball on the blanket, nervous to see his reaction to my question.

He reaches out and takes hold of my arm. I meet his gaze, searching it. He seems to hesitate for a moment, his eyes flicking away and back so quickly that I wouldn't have noticed if I'd blinked. His eyebrows crease in concern before he speaks.

"Callista, I would never hurt you. Is something wrong?"

I notice he didn't directly answer my question, and I frown. *Why is he deflecting?* His lack of a straight response assures me that I can't tell him about what I heard my parents talking about, at least not yet. *I should get more information before I bring this up.* He's always felt like someone I can trust, but paranoia from the eerie conversation I overheard blocks any sense of reason I may have.

I turn my glance back to the fluffy black ball of fur on the blanket and force a small grin. "No, nothing is wrong."

"Are you sure?" His voice is gentle, and his concern gives me pause.

"It's nothing." My tone comes out clipped, and Reggie pulls his hand away. The sun is setting in the distance, alerting me that I must be on my way. I stand from the blanket, looking down at Emmy and Reggie. "Thank you for today, Reggie. I'll see you later."

He looks up at me, his lips pressed in a firm line. Then he says, "See you around."

I frown, then turn to leave. *Why did I have to ruin the moment?* I mentally scold myself as I head down the hill and onto the street that leads me home.

When I arrive at my doorstep, the door swings open, and my father looks down at me.

"Nice to see you home on time, Callista. Your mother wanted me to check to see if you were on your way, but I see there was no need." He motions for me to come inside, and I do so briskly, forcing a smile on my face.

"What's for dinner?" I ask as I head to the dining room through the kitchen, nodding at Alina as I pass her.

"Meatloaf," she responds as she carries three plates of what can only be described as dry, odorless bricks of meat to the dining room table. I groan inwardly. The food does nothing to raise my appetite, and the visual appearance of the meal irks me. Regardless, I plaster on my most satisfactory smile and thank Alina when she places the food in front of me.

Once we've all gotten settled, Alina pulls out our government-issued tablet. She presses a few buttons on it, and a projected image of the 3R symbol appears in front of her. It floats in midair somewhat ominously.

"I'm thankful for our government providing for me," she says, then she slides the tablet toward my father.

"I'm thankful for our government's successful economy." He slides the tablet over to me, moving the projection to sit in front of me.

I pause, trying to think of something. *It's not as if I can say I'm thankful for all the secrets that are kept around here.* My parents glare at me, and I stutter out a response. "I'm thankful for, uh, our government's technology!" I quickly swipe my hand across the tablet, closing the projection.

Alina lets out an exasperated sigh. "Callista, it's not a good habit for you to be so hesitant with our daily thanks."

"We have so much that we've been granted," my father remarks.

"I won't do it again," I reply. *Even though I probably will.*

"Very well," Alina responds, turning to look at my father. "How was work today, Tiber?"

"It was good, very busy. I saw John as I was leaving the Neighborhood. He told me to say hello to you."

"I'm surprised he was on guard duty. He usually has the night shift."

"He said that Callum had to switch shifts with him. Oh, I almost forgot. The boss wanted me to remind you about our meeting tomorrow."

As my parents get swept into their typical discussions about their accounting work, I tuck some of the pale meat from my plate into my pocket. *Emmy will like this.* Then I push the rest of the food around so my actions aren't too obvious. Too engrossed in their own conversation, my parents don't seem to notice. I force myself to take a few bites of the meatloaf for some energy, coercing the dry lumps down my throat with water.

"Can you pick up the food for me tomorrow, Callista? I'm afraid I won't have time with work and Laurence and Adeline coming over," my father asks, his voice coming out sternly. He words it like a question, but I know it's more of a command.

I wipe a drop of water from my lip and meet his gaze. "Of course." *After all, I have nothing else to do.*

"Thank you." A smile spreads across his face but doesn't meet his eyes.

I turn toward Alina. "May I be dismissed?"

She nods. "Just clean up your dish first."

I stand from the table, my plate in hand. My parents start discussing what we should serve for dinner tomorrow as I turn on the kitchen sink. Cool water pours across my hands as I scrub the plate's spotless surface. *I don't understand why we even bother cleaning our dishes; our food is always so dry that it doesn't make a mark.*

Once I've finished with the plate, I quickly clean my silverware and place all of it beside the sink to dry. I dry my palms on my pants, then head upstairs and into my room. I flop onto my bed, staring up at the ceiling. My body is energized, but my mind is tired. I feel so useless, like I have no purpose to my life. Something is missing, but I can't figure out what. I may be used to my routine, but I don't enjoy it. Despite everything I wish for—a free life—I don't know that I can do anything. There are too many regulations. Even if I have doubts about how safe I am here, I'm stuck. And I could never leave Reggie. With that demotivating thought in mind, I close my eyes. I don't even realize when I drift off to sleep, eventually traveling into the land of my nightmares.

I awake to the sound of rain pattering against my window. The sky outside is dull—not a single ray of sunlight passes through the clouds. I lean over to check the clock on my bedside table. Just before noon. My parents are at work, leaving me alone in the empty house. And with the bad weather, I won't even be able to go to Reggie and our spot.

I let out an irritated sigh, then force myself up from the bed. Shuffling through my drawers, I pull out an oversized sweater and leggings, then quickly change. Once I've finished getting ready, I drag my feet down the stairs. *I might as well go to the mailer now. It doesn't look like the weather is going to get any clearer.*

I slide on my sneakers, then grab an umbrella from the basket beside the front door. As soon as I step outside, I'm met with a brisk wind that creates goosebumps on my arms. *Let's just get this over with.*

The cloudy overcast creates a dull atmosphere that lacks any joy. Each house I pass seems to be weeping as the rain drips from the rooftops and hits the ground with a splat. There are no lights on now. Everyone has gone to their respective jobs. I could visit Reggie's house, but after the way we left off yesterday, I don't feel like seeing him. I have too many thoughts in my head, and I need more time to collect myself.

When the monotonous rows of houses break to make room for the small brick building, I let out a huge breath. I open the door and am instantly embraced by warm heat. Directly ahead, a short, round woman with bobbed hair sits behind a long countertop. When she hears me, her head snaps up from her computer.

"Hello, Opal," I say. "I'm here to pick up." I fiddle with my umbrella, struggling to shut it. Water drips from its fabric, creating a small puddle on the floor.

She looks at the mess distastefully, a frown on her face. I toss the umbrella to the side, brimming with embarrassment and frustration. "Sorry." I step up to the counter, forcing a small smile to my lips. "My father asked me to come today. He's busy, and we have company coming over later."

She looks me over, then lets out a loud sigh. "Very well. Let me fetch your order."

I shuffle back and forth as she turns and walks over to a stack of boxes. She moves a couple of them around, muttering something under her breath.

Other than the boxes, the building is fairly barren. It smells of wood and paper. The walls contain a single television screen and a few advertisements for different foods available. Most of the advertisements are clearly old, their edges torn and the words faded. The only one that looks new is the one for the cake pops. Besides that, nothing else is of note. I've been here only twice before, and each time I've been filled with unease. *I can't imagine working here. It seems so dull.*

My attention snaps back to Opal when she places a large box on the counter in front of me. She reads off a piece of paper.

"Twenty-one standard breakfasts, twenty-one standard dinners, forty-two waters, one set of cake pops, and painkillers. Here you go." She slides the box forward, and I pick it up. It's relatively light for the amount of supplies inside, and I can carry it with ease.

"Thank you." When I turn to leave, I realize with a sinking feeling that I won't be able to keep myself dry and hold the box. I let out an audible groan. *This is going to suck.*

"You can keep the umbrella!" I shout as I swing open the door and step out into the pouring rain.

THREE

I toss the soiled box onto the ground as soon as I step inside. My clothes are drenched, and my shoes leave wet footprints behind me. I hurry upstairs to change, wincing at the trail of water I create. *I have to clean this up before my parents get home. They won't be pleased if the place is a mess before their guests come over.*

As soon as I put on the dry clothes, I feel instantly relieved. Throwing the soaked items in the dryer, I grab a nearby towel and set to work drying up every spot of water I created. I can still hear the rain outside. Its earlier pattering has now slowed to a gentle tap. *Of course I got stuck in the worst of it.* I try my best to not let my irritation swell, but it's increasingly difficult.

"I shouldn't even bother with this," I murmur, but I continue wiping up the spillage anyway. Once I've finished, I turn to deal with the box.

It's so completely drenched that I'm able to tear it open with my bare hands. Luckily, the packages inside are covered in their own individual wrappings and haven't been affected by the rain. *If the food got damaged, I wouldn't hear the end of it.*

When I take out the painkillers, I eye the box with suspicion. The pain is gone. But I still don't know why it was there in the first place. And Dr. Isaac was too quick to just throw pills at me.

I place the box aside, planning to bring it upstairs later to hide. *My parents don't share with me, so I won't share with them.* I then resume gathering up the remaining boxes to bring to the kitchen. My stomach growls. I sigh and decide I should eat. As I put the food away in the cabinet, I hold on to the cake pop box.

I remove the plastic and take a knife from the drawer to cut through the cardboard. Inside, three large perfectly designed pops are laid next to one another. An intense air of extreme sweetness infiltrates my nose. I cringe. They don't look particularly appetizing, but I have no interest in eating my usual mediocre meals.

I pick up one of the freeze-dried desserts and place the rest into the cabinet with everything else. Then I sit at the kitchen table and turn on the television. *What boring show can I mindlessly watch today?* I flip through the limited channels, deciding on *Prey: The Enemies Before,* a dramatic documentary series about the people and governments that supposedly used to live where we do now. There hasn't been a new episode in ten years, and I know practically every fact by heart. Regardless, it's more entertaining than the rest of the shows that excessively promote the 3R lifestyle.

I take a bite of the dusty cake pop as I ingest the show. It's all about the third world war and great climate crisis that made hundreds of species extinct. The show heavily emphasizes how evil everyone is, except for those living in the East—the New America, where the Neighborhoods are. Even though it's the only history I know, I can't help but want to know more about what really happened. There isn't much information given about the other factions in the war. Most of the show is just a large dramatization about how sad it is that all of these unique species are gone. Without the dramatics, it would be ten times more boring. It also heavily plays on the depressing fact that we no longer have seasons due to the war. I'll never know what life in that type of environment was like. That's why the Neighborhood region is in a permanent chill, similar to the temperatures of what used to be known as winter.

The show's strategy works. A distinct memory of crying when I first watched this episode creeps into my mind. I couldn't fathom how so much death could occur, and I was so distraught that I didn't even question the accuracy of the information. My parents attempted to comfort me, assuring me that the outside evils that caused so much suffering were long gone. They also used it as a way to keep me inside the Neighborhood, explaining how the "outsiders" are "corrupt" and "dangerous." They convinced me that if I ever managed to leave, I would get hurt. This worked up until now as a way to keep me inside.

Now I'm not sure the inside is any safer.

Several hours later, as I'm mindlessly flipping through an old school textbook in my bed, I hear the front door open.

"Callista, we're home! Laurence and Adeline are on their way, so please come down here!" Alina calls, and I sigh. Another useless day is almost over.

"I'm coming!" I toss the textbook onto my desk and drag my feet downstairs. When he sees me, my father half-smiles.

"Did you pick up the food?" he asks.

I nod, motioning to the cabinet. "It's all in there."

Alina gives me one of her rare genuine smiles. "Thank you for still going despite the storm. I honestly thought you wouldn't bother."

I have an urge to scoff. *If I didn't, you would punish me. I didn't really have a choice.* Instead of stating my thoughts out loud, I just incline my head. Alina doesn't push the subject. She just opens the cabinets and pulls out one of the boxes. I notice her hesitate, and when she turns to me with the open cake pop box in her hand, her earlier smile is gone.

"I know I told you I didn't want these. But I realized they would be good to give out tonight. That doesn't mean you can just eat them. Your father ordered these for our guests and for us. Not for you to put your hands all over."

"I was hungry," I respond nonchalantly. *I won't get away with this. I should have just starved.* My stomach churns as I wait for my inevitable punishment.

"And you could have had one of the breakfast meals. Do you really not think about anyone other than yourself?"

My mouth drops open, and my anxiety is replaced by anger. *Is she serious? She's the one always doing things that benefit her.*

Just as I'm about to retort, there's a knock at the door. When it swings open, Laurence and Adeline are standing there with large smiles on their faces.

Alina instantly smooths over her expression. "Adeline, Laurence, I'm so glad you were able to make it!" As she passes me, she quietly whispers for me to go sit. I roll my eyes but comply. When she reaches the door, she wraps each of them in a quick hug, then motions for them to follow her over to the dining room. "Please, take a seat!"

"You look lovely as always, Alina," Adeline comments. She sits across from me, grinning. "Why haven't you come over recently, Callista? You know you're always welcome in our home."

Laurence sits beside her, directly across from my father, who has taken a seat next to me. "Oh, you know, they're always sitting in that field! Even in the cold," my father says, then he chuckles, leaning back in his chair.

I tighten my lips, disliking being under so much attention. Much to my relief, Laurence changes the topic.

"I still can't believe we're getting a new CEO," he says. "Marge has worked at the company for so long!"

Adeline sighs dramatically. "That's what happens when you age. I hear she's going to be moving up north to the richer neighborhoods with all the industry plants. Settling down with some young man who's a doctor."

The single telephone propped against the wall buzzes, breaking up the meaningless chatter. Alina appears in the kitchen doorway with several packages in her hands. "Tiber, can you get that? I want to bring dinner to our guests."

"Of course, dear." I watch as my father stands from the table, grabs the phone, and steps into our small living room.

I wonder what that's about. Not wanting to be forced into further conversation, I stand. "I have to go to the bathroom. Please excuse me."

Alina shoots me a disgruntled glance but doesn't stop me as I hurry up the stairs. I open my bedroom door and close it, making sure the sound is audible. *He never takes calls during meals. Especially not with guests. Something's off.*

I crouch low to the floor and make my way down the stairs. I avoid the spots I know are creaky, holding my breath as I pass the conversing adults in the dining room. When I'm just outside the living room, I push myself against the wall and strain to listen in to my father's conversation.

"We can't have another join us now. Not when it's almost her time. It might create a distraction, and she might lash out. You know she's already too inquisitive. Remember 3041? She considered her a friend even though they never met. Who knows how she would react to having another child here, even if there's an age gap." He pauses, and when he continues again, he's clearly irritated with whoever he's speaking to. "Don't you remember a few years ago? When you were transporting one of the children, and she saw them? She wouldn't stop questioning. Don't bring anyone else yet. She's almost gone. We can wait a little longer. There are plenty of other Neighborhoods. I'm in the middle of dinner, so I'll be hanging up on you now. Goodbye."

Distinct shuffling comes from the living room. My heart nearly stops in my chest. *Crap! He's going to see me.* I consider my options. I could try and go back upstairs, but he would likely see me, as our living room is quite open. That's too risky. Or I could pretend I just came downstairs. I quickly settle on the latter, swiftly positioning myself closer to the staircase. As my father leaves the living room, I take a deep breath and proceed to the dining room.

"Callista? What are you doing away from the dining table?" he asks.

I stop at his question, forcing my most convincing smile. "I had to go to the bathroom."

He glowers at me, looking skeptical. After a moment, he nods. "Very well."

I let him walk past me, then I enter the dining room right behind him. Alina shoots me a glance but continues conversing with Laurence and Adeline over their food. As soon as I sit in front of my plate of dried-out tomatoes, chicken, and broccoli, I process what I heard my father say.

Was he talking about me? He had to be talking about me. I can clearly remember when I saw the child in transport on the road outside the gates. And I ask a lot of questions. But why was he talking about me? And to whom? What other child did he not want coming here? And what did he mean that it's "almost her time" and that I'm "almost gone"? Is he going to send me somewhere?

I start fidgeting with my fingers anxiously. I want to ask my parents what's going on, but I know they won't give me any answers. And part of me fears that if I do ask, I'll get punished. Punished worse than I have before. I don't know if my parents are evil necessarily, yet I don't think they're kind. They're unpredictable in how extremely they may react to something they view as unruly.

I don't even realize that Alina is talking to me until I feel someone smack my arm. I blink, refocusing.

"Listen to your mother when she speaks to you, Callista," my father says beside me. I realize he must have been the one to smack me, and I scowl.

Then Alina says, "Callista, Laurence was just saying how he knows about a job opening for eighteen-year-olds that will be available next year. It's at our workplace, so you would be able to get there by transport with me and your father. You would be an assistant to the marketing team." She smiles at me, seeming friendly. But I can hear her hidden words: don't be rude around our guests.

"Yes! I really think you'd be a good fit," Laurence adds.

Worried about what I overheard my father saying, I can't stop myself from retorting, "That sounds great and all, but I'm not sure I'll be available." *Since apparently I'll be "gone" soon.*

Instantly I realize my mistake. Laurence and Adeline exchange worried glances, clearly off-put. Not wanting to give my sleuthing away, I scramble to fix my mistake. "It's just that I was really hoping to work with Opal at the mailer. When I was there earlier today, I couldn't help but be intrigued by the, uh …" I pause, trying to think of a convincing reason. "The great access to all the wonderful items our government provides."

"I suppose that's an option as well," Alina comments.

I hope my compliment of our government didn't seem too out of character and doesn't create further suspicion.

"Well, I sure hope you'll consider it," Laurence says, taking a bite of his food.

"I will." I let out a silent exhale when the conversation is over and the adults begin discussing politics. I force the dull food down my throat, then sit back and resume dissecting my father's phone call. *Are my parents going to send me away somewhere? Does this have anything to do with what I heard them talking about the other night? Am I safe?*

I make a spur-of-the-moment decision to try and get information out of my parents, and I'm hoping it doesn't backfire. I wait for my parents' conversation to pause, knowing better than to interrupt them.

"Laurence," I say, "I was thinking about what you said. Do you think I could come visit your workplace in a few months so I can see how I mesh with the environment? I wouldn't want to agree to something without experiencing a part of it first."

I don't miss the startled looks my parents give me, or Adeline's uneasy shift in her seat. *I got them. They're definitely hiding something.*

Before Laurence can even respond, Alina chimes in, her voice uneasy. "I don't know, honey, our job has very high security, so it may be difficult to get you in if you're not working there."

Honey? She rarely, if ever, calls me that.

"Surely you could ask?" I say with false hopefulness. "I think the opportunity sounds interesting. I'd love a more hands-on experience."

Alina says, "I don't know—"

"What your mother means to say is, we'd be glad to inquire, but it likely won't happen," my father says, giving me a soft smile. "We all appreciate your eagerness though." He looks at Adeline and Laurence with a pointed stare.

Adeline grins. "Of course! I wish Reginald would show this much interest in learning about his potential work."

Laurence inclines his head. "We need more youth like you, Callista. Kids just don't have drive these days."

"Okay," I say, and I fake disappointment by drawing it out. Then I sigh as Alina stands from the table, gathering everyone's empty or mostly empty plates.

"How about some dessert?" she asks. "It's getting late, and we do all have work tomorrow."

"Sounds great," my father responds.

I sink down in my chair, returning to my thoughts. Even if part of me wishes that I just misheard that phone call, it's clear to me now. Something is going to happen to me, big or small, and I don't think I'll like it.

After some time, I've finally compiled a comprehensive list of all the inconsistencies in my life. Somehow, someway, they must all be related. The painful shot, the strange words my parents said, the lack of children. The most pressing issue being how I'm confident my parents are planning on sending me somewhere sometime before my next birthday. The only benefit of all this is that it has kept my mind busy enough to make my nightmares somewhat less frequent. The only evidence that my sleep is still sometimes fitful is that I still wake up in cold sweats, even when I can't remember what I dreamt of.

My parents have also become increasingly antsy in recent weeks. I think Alina has been attempting to be kinder to me, but I don't think she realizes this only makes me more suspicious. She has taken off from work several times now to spend the day with me. Every time she does, it's been dreadful. I'm used to my regular routine of spending time with Reginald, even if it can become boring. More than that, having Emmy around has added a new excitement to my day-to-day routine. I frequently bring her leftovers, which she devours with haste.

I had my doubts after the small fight Reginald and I had over whether I could trust my best friend. But I realize I was just being paranoid. After all, I can't believe everyone here is against me. As further evidence of his loyalty, he has brought picnics and little cards to me five times when we've met up. He's also profusely apologized for ever causing me to doubt him. I've had to assure him that he didn't do anything wrong. Needless to say, our relationship has recovered from our spat.

When Alina is home, she forces me to walk around our Neighborhood, past the duplicate homes, and try to "bond" with her. She even ordered me my own box of those dry, dusty cake pops. But she still enforces curfew and will punish me if I'm late. So, even though she tries to act differently, I don't really feel like anything has changed.

Today my father is the one staying home, as Alina must go to work for some important project. I don't bother to hide my frown as I head into the living room, where he's waiting. He sits on our uninviting pasty-white sofa with a cup of water in his hand.

"Callista, please take a seat. I think we're long overdue for a conversation."

Just great. More attempts to make up for the lack of attention they've given me the past seventeen years. I'm sure they're just trying to distract me or give me false hope of a normal life.

I take a seat beside him, turning my body so we're face-to-face. His chin is lightly stubbled, and I notice unfamiliar dark lines under his eyes.

"I know your mother and I can be harsh sometimes. But please understand that we are only doing what's best for you. In this world, you need to learn to respect the rules to succeed. Our government wants the best for its citizens, and we just want you to realize that."

I huff. *I wish they'd stop trying to make me a servant to our government.* But then I say, "I know this. You both tell me frequently."

I catch a brief flicker of irritation in his gaze. "What I wanted to say is, I know you feel you're unable to do anything. But you have great things in store, and your purpose will be fulfilled soon."

"And what purpose is that?"

"To contribute to our society."

"How?" I push, wanting to make him squirm. I'm tired of sitting and waiting for answers that won't come. *I know he's hiding something. I don't know what I'll do when I figure out what, but I won't just obey anymore. He's kept too many secrets. I can't trust him.*

He replies smoothly, as if anticipating my question. "By getting a job."

"Of course." My response is clipped and dismissive, causing my father's smile to turn into a deep frown.

"Why do you insist on being so blatantly disrespectful to me and your mother?"

I squeeze my hands into fists, anger bubbling up inside me. *I've tried to be obedient. But why respect and obey someone who doesn't respect me?* I take a deep breath to calm myself. *I can't keep reacting like this. I can't give them any sign that I'm trying to figure out their secrets.* I relax my hands and exhale. "I apologize. I've just been dealing with a lot. Getting older is quite terrifying. I've never had a job before."

His frown softens, and I watch as he hesitates for a moment, then awkwardly places his hand atop my own. I fight my instinct to pull away, not wanting to escalate the situation once more.

"It will be okay," he says. An uncomfortable silence passes between us. We avoid eye contact, and he pulls away his hand. "Do you want to watch television together?" he asks.

I'd rather be with Reginald or trying to put together your secrets. But I know I can't do either of those things. Not if I want to keep up appearances.

Through tight lips, I respond, "Sure. You can choose the show."

He grabs the remote and puts on *The Neighborhood and You.* I force back a groan, leaning my head onto the couch cushion.

This is going to suck.

Midafternoon, my father gives me permission to go and meet Reginald. He uses the home phone to contact Reggie's house and let him know. I'm not allowed to use the device to contact my friend ever. The government doesn't permit those under the age of eighteen to make phone calls for a reason neither my parents nor I have a good explanation for. It doesn't make any sense. I suspect it's just another form of control.

As I slide on my shoes at the dining room table, Alina comes in through the front door. I look up, startled. *She's home early.*

"Oh, going somewhere, Callista?" she asks.

"I was just going to meet with Reggie for a bit. Don't worry. I'll be back before dark." When I mention my best friend's name, her eyes light up in recollection.

"I almost forgot. I saw Adeline today, and she asked me to notify you that she and Reginald will be leaving our Neighborhood tonight."

FOUR

I STARE AT ALINA, DUMBFOUNDED. "What do you mean? How is that even possible? Where is he going?" I nearly shout at her.

"Watch your tone, Callista. Adeline received an offer to work directly with the government, so they'll be moving somewhere that will better suit her new position. She was unable to give me any further details."

Before I can stop myself, I swing open the door and run to our meeting spot, hoping to find my best friend there.

Behind me, I hear Alina shout, "Don't just run away when I'm speaking to you!"

Alina is going to kill me for leaving before she dismissed me. Her nice act won't stop her. I push the thought aside. *There are more important things right now.* My brown hair flows through the wind, and I make it to our hill faster than I ever have. Reggie is already there with Emmy. I hike up with labored breaths, pausing at the top. I gasp for air as my adrenaline wears off.

"I guess you heard." He looks up at me, his brown eyes glinting in the sunlight.

I finally catch my breath and yell, "What the hell, Reginald? You know I have no one but you, yet you're just going to accept this?"

He looks at me with genuine sadness, and I soften, lowering my voice. "I just don't know what I'll do without you." I take a seat next to him, staring off into the grass. "Will you ever come back?"

Emmy is sleeping in his lap, and he makes sure not to make any sudden movements that might disturb her.

"I don't think so, Cal." My heart plummets to the lowest depths it's ever been. He turns his head to watch my face, and tears well up in my eyes. "Hey, maybe we can write to each other?"

I frown and struggle to hold back my brimming tears. "How would we do that? No one is allowed to use the mailer to send things out. We can only take things in."

We stay silent for a few moments, and then I feel him shift next to me. "I know," he says. "I'll escape from the car when my mother and I are going away. I'll find a place to make a camp, and I can live there. I don't know how, but I'll figure out a way for us to meet up. It'll probably be a while. I'll need everyone to think I died so no one finds my hideout or is suspicious of you." He speaks rapidly, his breaths coming out short and quick.

I think about his proposal, then shake my head. "That's reckless. As much as I wish it could work, there's no way. There are too many guards. And based on the security around here, you probably won't be able to get out of the car. Even if you did, how would we meet up? I can't even get close to the gates, let alone close enough where I could speak to you."

I pull on the grass beside me anxiously. My tears begin to fall, unable to be held back any longer. The thought of never seeing my best friend again is too much to bear. *This is the worst thing that has ever happened to me.*

He moves his hand on top of mine and turns my head to look him in the eyes. Gently wiping the tears from my face, he says, "You're right. It's impossible. So sneak away with me. When I'm past the gates, I'll find a way to disable them for you. I'll set a trap or something. I'll try to get whatever I set up to go off around midnight. But you can't come tonight. I need time to prepare. I'll set something up. I'll figure something out. And tomorrow, you can come after me. We can find each other in the forest. I'll be near the closest water source. And then we'll be together."

He looks so sincere, so genuine, so confident about this likely impossible plan. I know it would be stupid to follow it, but I also don't care. I'm confident that I'm no safer here than I would be out there. Whatever outsiders they may be—all the people my parents warned me about—they can't be any worse than the liars surrounding me. And I know Reggie would take care of me. He isn't like my parents, like the doctor, like anyone else. He's my friend. We belong with one another. And I would do anything to stay with him.

"Fine. Let's do it." My voice is stuffy but full of resolve.

He grins so wide that my heart melts. We stare into each other's eyes for several moments, neither of us speaking. Then he pulls away.

"I leave at midnight tonight," he says. "I'm sorry I can't give you any help escaping. But I know you can do it."

I nod. "No matter what happens, I won't regret anything."

"Neither will I."

I fall back onto the grass and look up at the sky. Reggie does the same, placing Emmy on top of him. We lie in silence, and at some point, he wraps my hand in his. I will finally be leaving this place. All of these years, I put up with these strange rules and restrictions because I knew I would at least have one person beside me. And I know now that my destiny is a ticking time bomb that may explode at any second, causing unknown destruction. There's nothing left for me here. Even though part of me wants to stay and try to figure out the mystery, I could never live with myself if I passed on the opportunity to stay with my lifelong friend.

I squeeze his hand in mine and close my eyes. The cool breeze allows me to imagine a place where there aren't so many secrets, and where I could be truly free. The thoughts calm my anxious heart and allow me to drift into a blissful rest.

When I awake, the sun is already setting. I sit up swiftly, looking to my side instinctively to question why Reginald didn't wake me. He's not here. Instead, a page from my journal sits tucked underneath my bag, and Emmy is in his spot. The journal is on the ground, along with the pen.

Cal, I was notified that I must prepare for my transfer. I didn't want to wake you. I wish I could make your journey easier by taking Emmy, but my mother told me last minute that our new place doesn't allow pets. I don't know why she bothered allowing me to have her in the first place if this was going to happen, but that doesn't matter now. I trust you'll be able to take care of her. Don't come after me until tomorrow. We'll meet again. You just need to be patient. Once I run, I can't turn back, and you won't be able to either. Don't forget that.

~ Reggie

I scoff at his note and stuff it in my backpack, then proceed to scoop up Emmy and tuck her in the pack's largest front pocket. *This is going to be difficult enough already. Now I have to make sure to keep Emmy safe as well.* She lets out a soft meow, and I grin before returning focus to my mission.

I turn to look at the sun, noting its place on the horizon. I then proceed to check my holo-watch: 17:00. I curse under my breath, racking the calculations in my brain. *The sun should set in approximately ten minutes, and curfew begins in five. My parents will be wanting to know where I am, especially after the scene I made earlier.*

I start toward my home, walking swiftly. Emmy peeks out of the pocket, and I rub her head lightly with my finger. "Stay down,

Em," I whisper to the small kitten. She meows in response, and I give her head a tap, causing her to duck down into the pocket.

The light around me grows darker as the moments go on, and I continue checking my watch each time I feel a minute has passed. 17:03, 17:04, 17:05. At 17:05, I arrive at my doorstep. *Right on time.*

I quickly tuck my bag under a bush in the yard so my parents don't see Emmy. I silently pray she doesn't run off. I'll bring her to the field tomorrow before we set off at night.

When I twist the doorknob and enter the house, I'm faced with two pairs of glaring eyes. Luckily, Alina doesn't seem to notice that I'm no longer wearing the backpack I was wearing this morning.

"You shouldn't have run off," she says, frowning.

"We've been trying to be more respectful of your time as you've grown, but you need to be respectful of us as well," my father adds, his tone stern.

I push off my shoes, fighting to keep my nervous energy in check. *I can't slip up now.* I say, "I'm sorry. I won't do it again."

"You apologized this morning yet rudely ran off hours later. How do you explain that?" my father asks.

"As your father just said," Alina adds, "it was incredibly disrespectful for you to behave this way. You keep becoming more and more rebellious. We want to treat you like a peer, but your actions force us to treat you like a small child."

I bite my lip to stop myself from retorting. I can't act too well-behaved, as that would be out of character. But I can't let them know how much distaste I have for them. I settle on saying, "I'm not becoming more rebellious, but I could have asked for permission to leave earlier. I was just afraid I wouldn't be able to see Reggie again."

Alina sighs, her anger relaxing. "Let's have dinner, and we can talk."

I nod, then move to the dining room with my father. *Thank God she's letting me eat,* I think as I sit. *Once I leave, I don't know how hard it will be to get food. That, and I need to feed Emmy. I need to stock up for the coming days.*

Alina brings out three sandwiches. Each one consists of two bread layers, dried-out meat, and cheese powder. Although its texture isn't at all appetizing, it's one of the better meals offered to us. The smell of aged cheese makes my stomach grumble as she places the plate in front of me.

After she sits, we do our usual thanks to our government. I just rotate between the same nonspecific things each week. Today I'm "thankful" for our food. Yesterday I was "grateful" for our protection. *I have my own lies too.*

Once we've finished, I pick up the sandwich to take a bite.

"Before you eat, let's talk," my father insists.

I groan, reluctantly placing the sandwich back on my plate. Alina looks at me across the table. Her expression is hard to read, edging on disappointment.

"I know you're attached to Reginald," she says. "That's why I made sure to finish my project as soon as I could so I could come home to tell you. I knew you would react strongly, so I wanted to give you a chance to process so that you didn't lash out. But you did anyway, so I'm not sure I should have bothered."

Strange. That almost seems considerate. I feel a part of my heart warm, the smallest bit of me still yearning for parents who care for me. But deep down, I know it must be too good to be true. *It's too out of character. I shouldn't trust it. More than likely, she just didn't want to deal with me when I'm angry. She doesn't care about my relationship.* Unsure of anything kind to say, I fumble with the corner of my sandwich.

"We know he's your only friend here, so this must be difficult. But the good news is that when you join the workforce, you'll meet plenty of others. So it doesn't matter much," my father adds with a clearly practiced cheeriness.

Rather than give me comfort, his words anger me. All my effort to stay restrained flies away. My fury over all the darkness I've been kept in mixes with my nerves regarding tomorrow's plan.

"First of all, you can't just replace a friend," I reply. "I'm sure you would know that if either of you cared about your own relationships." I stand, tossing back my chair. My voice rises in octave. "Secondly, how dare you act like you suddenly care about me? You can't seriously expect me to be understanding when you have yet to give me a genuine explanation for anything that has occurred to me during my life. You've given me no reason to trust you, to believe you, to see any of your actions as genuine!"

I angrily grab my sandwich from the table, then turn to stomp upstairs to my room.

"Get back here right now!" Alina shouts, but I shut out her voice as I slam my door behind me. I crawl into my bed, the sandwich still in my clenched fist. My anger turns to despair, and I begin to sob. As my tears fall, I shove bites of my dinner into my mouth to keep quiet. The cheese powder spills out onto my tongue, slightly tangy but also sweet. I would enjoy it more under other circumstances.

Once I've eaten half, I toss aside the rest to save for Emmy. I continue to cry for what feels like hours until my eyes dry up. I know there's no way my parents will forgive me for my behavior. I haven't lashed out to this extent since I was fourteen. Back then, I'd just been told I would never return to schooling. I was furious to learn this, as school was my only pastime and activity, and I felt it gave me more insight into the world I lived in. Without it, I knew I would no longer have a safe space to ask questions. After I screamed and raged at my parents that night, they forbade me from seeing Reggie for a month. They even had the guards come by every hour to make sure I was home while they were at work. I was incredibly depressed during that time and had little motivation to eat, shower, or get dressed. All I did was sit in my room, dragging my feet to meals when I was forced to. Now that Reggie is leaving, they'll have to find a new way to punish me. And I'd be lying if I said I wasn't afraid. Hell, they may even come up to my room now. I'm not allowed a door lock, so it wouldn't be hard to reach me. Even worse, tomorrow is Sunday, the only day they aren't required to work. If they don't come up tonight, they definitely will then. I know they won't pass on the opportunity to scold me. They may even be suspicious of me now, since they know I don't trust them.

Whatever it is, I'll be fine. I'll only need to tough it out for the daytime. My eyes blink sleepily, overwhelmed by all the emotions I've experienced today. *One more day.*

"Wake up, Callista. Now." My father's voice booms from the other side of my door, his fist pounding against the paneling. Before I can open it myself, he flings the door open. I quickly get up, standing firmly. I stare at my father eye-to-eye, trying to hide my unwanted fear. He stares down at me. The space around us is so silent you could hear a pin drop. Then he roughly grabs my wrist. "You're coming with me," he says.

I'm startled by this, causing a slight panic to set in. "Your grip is too tight," I say through gritted teeth.

He frowns, then loosens his hold on me. "Come." His tone softens slightly. He pulls me from my room and down the stairs, moving at a swift pace. Then he leads me to the living room and lets go.

Alina sits on the couch, her legs crossed. My father points for me to take a seat on the floor as he sits beside her. I do so cautiously, making sure to put distance between myself and my parents.

My father clasps his hands, sitting up straight. "We've been nothing but honest with you. I don't know where you got the idea that you shouldn't trust us. We've given you this house, let you hang out with your friend, and provided you with a good life. We've given you explanations when you ask your many questions, even if you aren't satisfied with them. You live in a place that many envy. Our government, this lifestyle, is something that many strive for and few receive." He looks to Alina with a nod. I can feel my insides twist.

"I've had a lot of time to think about how to punish you for last night," she says. "After much discussion, your father and I have decided to ground you for an indefinite amount of time. The length of your punishment will be determined based on your behavior in the coming weeks. We need you to be in good shape if you're to come and work with us at some point, and it's clear you're too emotional right now." Alina looks almost smug as she delivers my sentence.

My mouth falls open. *So I'm a prisoner? A prisoner inside a double-walled cell.* Normally, I wouldn't accept this so easily. Not that I would have much of a choice, but I know I would likely lash out again. Yet I feel somewhat calm. *Tonight I'll be free of all of this, one way or another.* Then, I have a sudden realization. *If I can't get outside, how will I feed Emmy? What if she runs away?* I chew on my lip. *I have no choice but to hope she stays put until tonight. I know my parents will be watching me like hawks.*

They wait for me to respond, likely expecting me to blow up. But all I do is let out a long, apathetic exhale. I stare at them blankly. "I have no reason to go outside anymore anyway," I say.

They exchange surprised glances. Alina purses her lips, then says, "Very well. You can go back to your room now. You may not come out until dinner. Breakfast is for children who behave well."

I say nothing as I stand and drag my feet back up the stairs. As soon as I'm in the privacy of my room, I let out a breath I didn't realize I was holding. I raise my wrist, checking my watch. It's 9:00. If Reggie was able to set his trap, I need to make sure I'm at the gate by midnight. Everyone should be sleeping by then, except for the guards. That means I just have to survive the next fifteen hours. Then I'll be free.

I take out my journal and pen and sit on my bed. Sunlight streams through my window, providing me with a comforting heat. I lift my pen above a blank sheet, then set to work. I have to make sure my escape plan is flawless.

It all starts with dinner. Usually, we eat at 17:35. Assuming it's the same tonight, we should finish our meal by 18:00. Normally, I would then either reread old schoolbooks or watch the television until I feel tired. But tonight, I need to go straight to bed. I likely won't be very sleepy, but I'll need to get some rest before I set out.

I decide to set my alarm for 23:30, giving me thirty minutes to leave the house and reach the gates. I'm hoping I'll be able to reach them in twenty minutes, but I need to prepare for potential mishaps.

Once I reach the gate, well, I don't know what will happen. I'll just have to hope for the best.

I write out my plan several times over, committing it to memory. When I feel confident I know what to do, I close my book and place it to the side. I'll have to remember to bring it with me when I leave later.

Without anyone to keep me company, boredom sets in quickly. I lean over to my bedside table and open the top drawer, pulling out one of my only storybooks. It's battered and torn, but the cover is still readable. *Scarlet's Fabrics.* There's a picture of a little girl behind a machine that has detailed fabrics spitting out of it. The story is strange. It's about a girl who makes clothes for her friends and the adventures that the clothes go on. As a child, I asked my teacher why the story focused on the clothes and not the friend's adventures. She just said it was one of many "pre-Neighborhood nonsensical stories" and that "the book should be banned, as it isn't educational." The book was never banned though, likely because it doesn't contradict the government's principles or feed "unsafe" information to children. Regardless of its disarranged nature, I've always found it somewhat entertaining and humorous. Having such limited media at my disposal, it has just been nice to have one thing that isn't about our government.

I fiddle with the worn edges, then open up to the first page. Relaxing against my pillow, I become absorbed in the familiar tale of the girl and her clothes.

After reading several more old schoolbooks, I'm finally summoned to dinner. When I arrive at the table, my parents barely acknowledge me. Tonight we're eating meatloaf again. You'd think that with how "great" and "powerful" our government is, we'd get more variety. But we only have four different options.

I drone through mealtime as quickly as I can, making sure to do and say the right things. I can't tell how suspicious my parents are of me. They behave as if nothing has changed, even though something clearly has. Work is the topic as usual, and I'm ignored. I tell myself, *As long as they don't stop me tonight, then none of this matters.*

As we finish up the meal, a sudden realization hits me. This will be my last meal with my parents. In a strange way, the thought bothers me. Sure, we've never been explicitly close, but they've kept me alive all these years. But on the other hand, they've also kept an excessive number of secrets from me and never shown me much kindness. Their punishments are cruel. I never got gifts from them. They rarely compliment me. And the limited praise they do give comes only if I follow their rules. I don't have any particularly good memories with either of them, so I don't think I'll miss them. I won't miss this house, this Neighborhood. I suppose what bothers me is the thought of what could have been.

I'll be free soon. Then I'll put all this behind me.

FIVE

"CALLISTA, PLEASE WASH THE DISHES and then go to your room. No television tonight," Alina orders.

I say nothing, gathering our plates and bringing them to the kitchen. When I've finished cleaning them, I head to my room. I stop halfway up the stairs, peering down to the dining room, where my parents still sit, conversing about how someone got promoted at their job. *This is the last time I'll be seeing them. Hopefully.*

A sudden feeling of queasiness rumbles in my stomach. As the clock ticks forward and I approach my escape, I become acutely aware of how dangerous my mission is. So many things could go wrong. But since the only other option would be to stay here, to be a prisoner in this deceitful world, I have no choice but to risk it all. I'll never get the answers I want, but maybe I'll at least find some sense of happiness. If I can do that, it will all be worth it.

I finish the climb to my room and check the time: 18:05. I grab one of my heavy jackets to prepare for the chill air later in the night. Then I tuck my journal and pen into the biggest pocket. I snatch some necessities from my bathroom and a change of clothes from my drawer. With my backpack still outside, I'm forced to try and fit everything into the jacket. I manage to squeeze everything tightly into the pockets, even the leftover sandwich from the night before. They're so full that if I make a wrong move, something will fall out. *Probably not the best idea if I'm going to be running*, I tell myself. *But I have no other choice.*

I set the alarm on my watch for 23:30. I'm not tired whatsoever. *This could be my last time to shower. I should take advantage.* I pull out a long-sleeved gray top and navy pants from my dresser, then place them on my bed to change into after I've cleaned off.

I step into the bathroom and turn the faucet, taking one last look at myself in the mirror. I look as anxious as I feel. My hands are clenched, and I can't stop shifting on my feet. *It's going to be okay. I'll shower, then I'll sleep. Then it will be time.*

I smile at myself, but it looks unnatural on my face. Shaking my head, I look away from the mirror and prepare myself for the evening ahead.

A beeping noise awakens me, and for a brief moment, I'm overwhelmed by fear. I swiftly sit up, scanning my room. Everything looks fuzzy, so I blink rapidly to shake myself out of my groggy state. My mind clears and refixes on my current goal.

It's time.

I creep out of my bed, then tiptoe over to my desk to put on my coat. I quickly slide on my shoes and head to the window. It's different from the one I had when I was little. My parents replaced it after I snuck out to meet Reggie in the fields past curfew. Our home security cameras had spotted me running off and instantly alerted my parents. I didn't make it far before some guards stopped me and my parents dragged me back to the house. They forbade me from going anywhere for two weeks.

Thinking back now, I realize I'm even more of a prisoner here than I thought. *Limiting my meals and keeping me trapped. I can't wait to leave.*

I scan the window's edges for some sort of latch. When I can't find one, I pull up on the bottom. It doesn't budge. There's no obvious lock, but I know there must be some way to open it. I never even thought to check out the windows for a new system, which I now regret.

A small voice carries to my ears. "Please state the password. You have one attempt before authorities are notified."

I startle, stepping backward. *This is new. Is it a security system? This wasn't here before.* I mentally scold myself for not automatically assuming my parents would add further security to the house after my little escapade. I rack my brain for possible words. *What would they know that I wouldn't?* I almost laugh at myself for even thinking it would be so simple. They keep practically everything from me, so it could be anything.

My heartbeat increases as I begin to doubt myself and worry about what the authorities or my parents would do to me after I've already caused them so many problems. *Come on, think!* It takes me several moments before I think of a word. Something my parents wouldn't expect me to know. Something that's such a secret that they waited to discuss it when they thought I was asleep.

REM.

I take a large gulp and quietly mutter the word. Several painstaking moments pass, then the window beeps and a green light blinks. Then there's a sound of something unlocking. I try the window again, and it opens smoothly, causing a smile to spread across my face.

I look down and grimace, realizing why my parents had the tree in front of my window chopped down. I reprimand myself once more for not thinking this through. The only option is jumping. Sweat trickles down my spine, and I hesitate for several moments. Then I hear footsteps behind me. *Just my luck. My parents must not be asleep! This is my only chance.*

My bedroom door handle squeaks with the sound of someone opening it. I count down from three, then jump down onto the grass, landing in the prickly bushes below my window. I roll off them and wince in pain, looking down at my now scratched, bloody hands.

Above, my room light turns on. Fresh blood drips in a thin trail down my palms. I push away the stinging sensation emitting from the cuts and force myself to my feet.

My legs move faster than I ever thought they could as I round the corner of the house. When I spot my backpack, I hastily grab it. I take a quick peek inside, and my heart sinks.

Emmy is gone.

I frantically glance around the area, pushing aside leaves and scouring the ground in the limited light. I don't even care that my wounds are getting dirty as I shuffle through bush branches. Finally, just as I fear I must leave her behind, I note a small black heap underneath one of the bushes. I reach out and touch it. Two small green eyes blink up at me as Emmy wakes from her nap.

I don't have time for this, I think as I quickly scoop her up. She lets out an annoyed meow. I ignore it and place her roughly in my backpack, then toss it over my shoulder. Then I take off once more, fear propelling me forward.

As I run, I feel movement against my back and realize Emmy might be trying to escape. I move over to a tree near my path and duck down, pulling my backpack to my front to check on the kitten. She peeks her head out and looks at me inquisitively. I give her a small pat and push her back down.

"Please just stay still," I whisper. I hear her meow as I throw my backpack over my shoulder and resume my sprint.

Several other house lights turn on as I pass them, and I note that my mother must have alerted the authorities to my disappearance. The speakers lining the street buzz to life, and I speed up to the point that I'm nearly tripping over my feet.

The border is directly behind the fields, so when I see the spot under the tree, a small wave of relief washes over me. I don't slow down, and the speakers behind me become alarms. Lights flash in my peripheral vision as I make it to the opposite side of the hill, using it as a cover.

I find a large tree nearby and crouch low behind it. In the near distance, a van is pulling up to the gate. The gate's massive walls open with a loud buzz, allowing the vehicle passage. When it pulls through, two figures step out. They're covered in shadow as they approach the night guard.

My watch glows a soft blue light, and I check it, realizing it's already 23:55. *It's almost time.* The night guard separates from the other two figures and enters the van. It proceeds to drive off, swiftly passing the exit checkpoint. The gate doors shut behind the vehicle, causing my heart to drop. *How am I going to escape if the gates aren't even open?*

The two figures step into the light, and I note that they look slightly different from the night guard. They're wearing formal black suits, not the typical navy ones the regular guards have. The entire area is bleak, full of muted colors. The station's white concrete walls are lit only by the surrounding lamps and the flashing red of the emergency signals.

Sitting here, waiting for some unknown signal, I become increasingly afraid. I don't know what happens if someone tries to escape. I don't know if anyone has ever attempted it. I don't know anything except that it has been made clear to me that I'm not to break the rules. And rule breakers get punished.

I shake my head, trying to stay focused on my mission. My jacket is oversized and completely black. It would be enough to cover me if I snuck through the exit—if there weren't so many lights on. And if the gate was open.

I sit back against the tree and exhale, feeling hopeless. My throat thickens as my eyes become bleary. *I can't do this. I have no clue what I'm doing.* I force my eyes shut, searching my brain for any ideas, just as I hear a sudden commotion.

I pick up one of the men speaking, and I listen in.

"Crap, power went out. Thirty-four, please turn it on so we can continue our search. I'll watch the gate."

I hear the buzzing of the gate opening, and I register that it must have been connected to the same power source as the lights.

I check my watch, and it reads back 00:00. *Reggie must have done this. I don't know how, but he has given me a way out. This is my only chance! If I get caught, the punishment can't be any worse than the one I'd get if I return home.*

My mind swirls with anxiety and fear. I remember the nightmares that I don't understand, all the secrets my parents keep from me, and the lack of love in my family. I don't know what's going on—only that I've been confused my entire life and never felt like I completely understood where I live. I think of my best friend, waiting for me alone in the forest, and a sudden burst of adrenaline hits me.

I readjust my backpack as I stand and prepare to sprint. My chest rises and falls as I take a breath just before I launch forward on my feet.

The alarms continue to blare in the background. I thank them silently for covering up my footsteps. As I approach the open gate, I'm finally able to just barely make out the two men. One is inside the guard station, and the other is fiddling with a flashlight.

"Thirty-four, is there another flashlight in there?" the second man calls, angling his body toward the small building.

I take the chance to scurry behind him. When I pass over the gate's threshold and am no longer surrounded by its foreboding walls, I nearly collapse in relief. But I know better than to rejoice yet. Abruptly, a light turns on, and I freeze. I look over my shoulder and notice lights starting to flicker on one by one.

Panic rises in my chest as I sprint faster than I ever have, scattering away from the light's reach. I hurry toward the forest, craving the protection of the trees. When I reach it, I'm swathed in darkness. The only illumination comes from the dim glow of the moon.

My breath comes out in short, shallow spurts, and I feel slightly lightheaded. I tread slowly deeper into the forest so I won't be found as quickly, then I collapse behind one of the many trees. My hands burn with pain, and I look down at them to see the bleeding has stopped. But the wounds are still very open. The dried blood is mixed with dirt. I hope it doesn't get infected. I find a sharp stone next to me and cut off two slices of fabric from my shirt, wrapping each one around my scratches so they won't get any more exposed.

I look down at the small screen on my wrist and am alarmed. *What if my watch is somehow giving information to my parents or someone else?* I never even considered the idea before, but after everything I've witnessed, I wouldn't put it past them. The notion that I could be found causes me to rip the device off and smash it with the stone. I relax as I observe its broken remains.

Emmy makes noises from inside my bag, reminding me of her presence. Careful not to irritate my scratched hands any further, I slip the backpack off and open the pocket to let her out. She slowly climbs into my lap, rubbing against my arms. I pull out the remains of the sandwich from my jacket pocket. In an instant, she's nibbling on the leftovers. She must have been starving after not eating for so long.

I lean my head back against the tree and allow myself to catch my breath. I can faintly still hear the alarm, an unwelcome reminder that I can't stay here long. As Emmy finishes up her last few bites, I hear voices in the distance.

"I think I saw something over there!" someone shouts. Then I hear the crunching of leaves.

I mutter several curses under my breath. *They're coming.* My surroundings are dark. I have no sense of which way I should go. I place Emmy back into the bag, but she makes it difficult, trying to push out as I close the seal.

I force myself to take a deep breath and stumble to my feet. I'm extremely dehydrated and exhausted, but the sound of nearing footsteps drives me forward. I have to take several steps before I grow steady on my feet. I determine the direction the voice and noise are coming from and start off directly opposite it. I can only hope I make it far enough that they drop their search.

I'm not as fast as I was before, and I keep having to take short breaks to catch my breath. Dread rises in me when I realize they may discover the remains of my watch, allowing them to know where I was. I try not to dwell on that fact and push my feet forward.

I'm filled with comfort when moonlight finally shines down through the trees, allowing me to stop stumbling in the darkness. When I can no longer move, my feet sore and my vision blurry, I halt. I still hear shouting, but it isn't as close as before. *Maybe they went a different direction.* I don't know the protocol for searching for escaped residents, but an eerie feeling settles over me at how easy it was for me to run. They could have very well overpowered me. It's not as if I was armed or dangerous.

Then a chill goes down my spine. *What if they know exactly where I am but want to give me false hope?* I shake off the thought, dismissing it as a side effect of my dehydration. My world seems to spin, and I struggle to keep my eyes open. I want to continue running, to guarantee I'm safe, but my body is too worn out. I reluctantly allow my lids to close and my breathing to steady. The rhythm of my heartbeat serves as a soothing repetition that distracts me enough that I drift off into an unsteady slumber.

The sunlight shining on my face wakes me, and I swallow. My throat is parched and my head aches. I glance around at my surroundings, my eyes landing on my backpack.

I forgot to let Emmy out! I swiftly open the zipper, grateful that I didn't seem to have closed it all the way. The small kitten doesn't hesitate to jump out. I swear she's glaring at me, her tail twitching with irritation.

"I'm sorry," I whisper, reaching out my hand for her to sniff. She pauses, then slowly approaches my finger. She seems to contemplate whether she should trust me. "I won't put you in there again. I promise." As if she can understand and believe me, she rubs her face against my outstretched hand. I take the opportunity to pet her, and she expresses her pleasure through a soft meow. Once she's satisfied, she starts walking around, stopping every few inches to sniff at the ground.

I don't know what time it is. All I know is that I still seem to not have been found. Either I got far enough from the entrance or they gave up. There's no good reason for them to do so, but I resolve to think of it as a blessing rather than something sinister.

I push myself off the ground, slightly unsteady on my feet. Emmy is now stretching, and I take the chance to scoop her up and cradle her in my arm. I use my free hand to sling my bag over my shoulder. With a strong desire to survive, I set off to find Reggie, deciding that my best bet would be to look for a nearby water source for myself and Emmy.

He probably also looked for a water source. I don't know how far he went, but this is the best place to start.

SIX

THE FOREST IS VERY DENSE, and I have to meticulously avoid several thorny bushes. Even though I can see where I'm going, my lack of water and food makes it extremely difficult to navigate the terrain.

I never thought to consider how laborious locating my best friend would be. Having sat around most of my life, I'm not used to this level of physical exertion. *I'm weaker than I thought.*

It's strangely empty in the trees. There are no sounds other than the crunching of the ground below and wind drifting through the branches. After several hours with no sign of water, I start to lose hope. Emmy seems just as dehydrated as I am. Every so often, she starts to pant. Without her, I might have given up at this point.

When I finally hear the distant sound of water, I feel a boost of adrenaline. I readjust Emmy in my arm and pick up my pace. As I get closer to the sound, I start to run, beyond excited for the refreshment and the hope that I'll find Reggie. Emmy squirms in my grip, and I pull her closer.

The trees finally part, revealing a wide riverbed. I'm overcome with elation as I near its side and put my small kitten down. She cries and looks at me as I crouch to scoop up the crisp liquid. I splash my face, instantly refreshed as the water hits my skin.

"Cal, is that you?" a voice calls from across the river.

I squint, trying to make out whoever it is. I'm slightly blinded by the sun reflecting on the water's surface.

"Reggie?" I shout back.

The figure moves closer to the edge of the water, allowing me to see them. When my eyes land on my best friend, completely unscathed and safe, a wide grin spreads across my face.

"Follow me!" He moves swiftly down the riverbank, and I lift Emmy to follow him on the opposite side. When we reach a calmer part of the river, he stops.

"You can cross over here!" he calls out.

I look at the water, my stomach twisting. "I don't know how to swim. And I don't want to drop Emmy!"

Much to my surprise, Reggie doesn't hesitate to wade across. Only his feet get wet as he crosses because the water is shallow.

"Take my hand," he says, reaching out.

I hesitate, then wrap my free hand in his. The water goes up to my calves when we step in. It's ice cold, causing a shiver to go down my spine. He guides me gently, making sure to point out any rocks hiding beneath the surface. When we finally reach the opposite side, I'm beyond grateful.

"Thank you." I pause, considering him. "Why did we have to cross?"

He turns and points toward the direction he came from. "I started setting up a camp there. You must be thirsty. Follow me."

Camp? How does he know how to set up a camp?

As I follow him, my shoes slosh, water spilling through the small holes in their fabric. When a gust of wind passes by, I pull my jacket closer around me and Emmy. Luckily, it doesn't take long for us to reach Reggie's camp. All he has done is make a simple campfire. The distinct woody smell is powerful but not unpleasant.

He motions for me to take a seat on a log beside its warmth. There's a large backpack beside it. Once I'm seated, I place Emmy in my lap. She shivers and opens and closes her mouth. I hold her close to my stomach.

"Emmy needs water more than I do," I say.

"I brought two of the empty ration containers I had at home," he tells me. "I've been using them to heat the river water to kill any bacteria. I can go get some for both of you now."

Reggie heads toward the water's edge, only to return moments later with two full metal containers. He puts on a pair of gloves and then wraps his hands in several layers of what looks to be fabric. I watch in awe as he holds the first container above the fire, waiting patiently for it to start to bubble. As he performs the process, I find myself wondering how he learned to do it. These aren't skills we were taught in our limited schooling. We're expected to live in the Neighborhood forever, so why would we know how to survive outside it?

Reggie sets the first container aside and starts working on the second. "It should only take a few minutes to cool off in this weather," he says. "Then it will be safe to drink."

"Shouldn't we talk about what happened over the past forty-eight hours? And how do you know how to do all this?"

He looks up at me, his eyebrows creasing. "I just thought you could use some refreshing first. I'm sure you've been through a lot." He pauses, seeming to ponder something. "I learned some basic survival skills from an old book my dad left behind. It looked to be from before the Climate Crisis War. I probably wasn't supposed to read it, but I was too curious."

Adeline mentioned once how Reggie's father had been a highly influential politician. I determine that must be how Reggie got access to so many pre-war items.

After he finishes boiling the second container, he sets it down and unwraps his hands. "First one is probably done now."

I raise an eyebrow at him, then move Emmy to the side and lean over to pick up the container. Just as he said, it's no longer hot. The surface is still warm but not scalding. I take a large sip, relishing as the liquid travels down my dry throat. Then I offer it to Emmy. She takes several moments to realize what it is, but when she finally does, she laps up the water vigorously. I smile down at her, glad she's going to be okay. Then my stomach grumbles.

"What are we going to do about food?" I ask. If I'd had more time to plan, I would have stolen some of our food supplies.

Reggie grins at me, then walks over to the backpack perched against the log. "Since we were moving, no one questioned why I had such a large backpack. But instead of clothes, I filled it with all our meal storage. We were just going to leave it behind because our new home apparently has some other food plan." He unzips the bag, revealing rows of the familiar metal containers. "There's at least twenty days' worth. Even more if we use it sparingly."

I jump to my feet and wrap him in a hug. "You're a genius," I say. I pull back, looking him deep in the eyes. "Thank you for setting up that trap. I don't know how you did it, but I wouldn't have escaped that awful place without you." We stare at each other for several moments, and my heart flutters. Then I drop my arms. "Let's eat and catch up. Then we can figure out what's next."

He nods, bending over to pull out one of the meals. "We can split this into three parts. The meals will last longer that way."

I look to see which dinner he has picked up and groan when I see that it's meatloaf. "Come on," I moan. "Can't we at least have the sandwich tonight? I had the meatloaf yesterday."

He laughs and says, "Alright."

Once he has divided up the sandwich into three parts and I've gathered more water, we sit around the firepit. The sun is going to set soon, which is evident by the decrease in light coming through the tree foliage. I separate the meat covered in cheese powder from the sandwich and place it in front of Emmy, who gobbles it up greedily.

Even though I'm dirty and tired, I haven't felt this comfortable in a long time. As Reggie and I eat, I fill him in on everything that went down after he left. From my parents grounding me to almost losing Emmy to nearly being caught. I keep out the part about the window and the password. Even though I trust him, I have no interest in getting into mysteries of the past.

He listens eagerly, encouraging me to share every detail. I relish in the sensation of being around someone who genuinely finds value in what I say.

"And then I found you," I say as I finish the tale. "I really feared for a while there that I would never see you again. How did you even disable the power in the first place?"

"Well, it's a bit of a story," he says without elaborating.

I roll my eyes. "So was mine, and I told you! Spill."

He sighs, looking off into the distance. "Not much happened until we were driving out of the Neighborhood. I didn't have much time to plan, so I had to improvise. Once we'd just passed the gates, I made the driver stop, telling him that I left something important at our house. I begged him to let me go get it, but he insisted that I stay in the car. So he unlocked the door to get out and ask someone to gather my 'important item.' But as soon as he hit the unlock button and I heard a click, I was out of there. I grabbed my bag and sprinted toward the woods."

It was that simple? I'm surprised that worked. With the high security in the Neighborhood, I would have thought they wouldn't give anyone the chance to leave.

I frown. "That seems too easy."

He shrugs. "Maybe they were lenient because of the position my mother got."

I guess that would make sense. If Adeline was going to work with the government, she would be given more freedoms. "How did you set the trap?"

My question seems to excite him. He leans forward, staring intensely at me. "When I was running, I was scanning the gate walls for any sign of something I could use to my advantage. And then I saw it. There was a thick power line stemming directly from the gate's opening. I kept its location in mind, then set out to find a river. I didn't sleep at all that night. I discovered this place, set up camp, and waited. When it started to get dark, I retraced my steps to the wire. When my watch hit midnight, I used the knife I kept for meals to cut the wire. I wasn't sure it would work, but I'm so glad it did. As soon as I cut the wire, I ran off again, afraid I would get discovered. Since you said the power came back on, they must have had some backup source."

He speaks so calmly, as if none of what he did was a big deal and he could do it a thousand times over. His nonchalance irks me. I was terrified, and it took me hours to find this river. *How could he have possibly done all of that in the span of under forty-eight hours?* I never noticed a wire outside the gate, but then again, I was fleeing for my life. I scold myself mentally. *All the dishonesty at home has created some serious trust issues in me. Reggie would never lie. He's my best friend.*

"That sounds like a lot. I'm just glad we're both safe," I say as I scan the ground, accepting somewhat begrudgingly that it's going to be my bed for the night. Emmy has already made herself comfortable in my lap. When Reggie places his hand atop mine, my eyes travel up to meet his.

"Thank you for doing this. It won't be easy, but at least we're free now," he says.

"I didn't want to be there anymore anyway. I wanted to stay with you." I frown, realizing how selfish I am. "I'm sorry. You probably would have had a good life if you stayed with Adeline. I'm sure families of government workers are treated like royalty. Now you're stuck with me in the middle of nowhere."

He smiles gently at me. "Don't apologize, Cal. This was my idea. And that life wasn't for me. The only place for me is by your side."

I scoot a bit closer to him, lean my head on his shoulder, and gaze into the burning embers of the fire. "We should follow this river and see where it goes tomorrow," I say. "Maybe we'll find a place we can call home."

"I like that idea."

We sit in silence, the only sound being the crackling of the flames. A strange comfort wells up inside me. I'm finally free of my prison. I no longer have a curfew, annual shots, mysterious parents, or a fear of what's going to happen to me. I'm in charge of my own destiny now. And I get to live it out with my best friend and closest ally.

We spend the next several days following the riverbank. It's a strangely straightforward path, and our scenery doesn't change much. Whenever it starts to get dark, we set up a small camp for the night.

Emmy takes turns perching on bags, going between mine and Reggie's. She manages to stay firmly in place even when the terrain is uneven. Sometimes, when the path is clearer, we let her run on her own, something she clearly enjoys. It's nice being able to laugh about something. At home, it was a rare occurrence. When she pounces on leaves or tree roots, I can't stop myself from smiling. I can't say, though, that I've gotten used to sleeping on the cold, hard ground. My body still cramps up every morning. The only good part about my lack of sleep is that I think it's why I haven't had any dreams or nightmares. I'm never deep enough in the unwelcoming world of my mind to experience them. It's a blessing and a curse. Since I'm not used to eating so little and moving so much, I find myself becoming tired much faster. Regardless, I push on.

The sun is halfway through the sky when I spot a clearing in the woods to the right of the path of the river. "Reggie, over there!" I say, pointing toward the opening. "What do you think it is?"

"Only one way to find out."

We approach the clearing cautiously, aware that we aren't safe even if we're out of reach of any guards. As we get closer to the opening, I make out the familiar pavement of a road. I stop dead in my tracks. Reggie pauses beside me, and Emmy lets out a small meow from his backpack.

"That doesn't look good," I say. "We shouldn't—"

He places a gentle hand on my shoulder. "What if it isn't what we think, and it's a road to freedom?"

The idea hadn't even passed through my mind. We've been walking for quite some time. It wouldn't be completely unfathomable for us to have exited the reach of the Neighborhoods and the surrounding community. Yet I have an itching feeling that we haven't gone far enough.

"I don't know. What if it isn't? Do you really want to risk it?" I chew on my lip, unsure.

He seems to contemplate my words, his eyebrows creasing. "How about we just look? If it seems unsafe, we can easily go back to the river."

I sigh. "Fine. But only for a second."

He takes my hand, and we walk together toward the opening. A bit of curiosity sparks inside me, even though I'm terrified. *This could be it. This could be our way to a new world.* I focus on the potential positive outcomes as we get closer. When we finally have enough view to see through the trees, my heart stops.

The road isn't one to freedom. Instead, it leads to an eerily familiar gate.

"That's ..." My voice drops off, my stomach queasy.

"Another Neighborhood." Reggie finishes.

I step backward as I see a van pull up to the gates—a van identical to the one I saw that child get taken away in so many years ago.

"Let's get out of here," I whisper sharply.

He doesn't argue. We hurry quickly back toward the river, toward where we came from. My breaths come out sharply. I didn't realize how afraid I was of going back to that place until now. I know I'm not safe there anymore, but I didn't expect to grow so used to being away from it so fast. My senses are on overload. I barely register what's going on around me.

When we finally stop, my hand brushes against soft fur, and I hear a gentle meow. My head snaps to Reggie. He's holding Emmy next to me, looking down at me with concern.

"I'm sorry," he says quietly. "I shouldn't have pushed it. I really thought we made it far enough to be free of that place."

I take Emmy from his arms and hold her tight against me. Her presence calms me, allowing my mind to refocus. "It's fine. You couldn't have known."

We stand in an uncomfortable silence for several moments.

"Do you want to keep going?" he asks. "We still have some time before it gets dark."

"I guess. I'll hold on to Emmy."

I'm still shaken by what I just witnessed. I knew other Neighborhoods existed, but I'd never seen one before. I find myself wondering who's on the other side of the gate. *Is that one of the places all the kids moved to? Or is it one of the wealthier Neighborhoods my parents sometimes mention? How come it looks so similar to my old home?* I wish I had someone to answer my questions. Yet once again, I'm left wondering, with no one able or willing to give me what I want.

"Reggie, who do you think lives in there? More kids like us?"

Reggie looks back at me, his expression thoughtful. "That would be nice. I wonder how different life is in there."

"Me too."

That night, we settle down beside a fallen tree. Few words pass between us, both of us distracted by what we witnessed earlier in the day. After seeing something reminiscent of the life I recently left behind, I find myself disturbed. *Have the guards given up on locating us? What do my parents think? Did they realize that I left with Reggie? Have they met with Adeline? Or do they not even care?* I laugh to myself, earning a confused glance from Reggie. *Who am I kidding? They never cared about me. If they had, they would have been honest with me from the start.*

Wanting to break the uncomfortable silence, I stand and walk over to sit beside my friend. "Do you think we'll find our road to freedom soon?" I ask.

He tilts his head, his lips twisting down into a sad smile. "Honestly, I'm not sure. But as long as we keep going, we'll find it someday. And at the very least, we're together."

His words bring me some solace. "And we have Emmy," I add.

"Of course. I could never forget her."

I look admiringly down at our sleeping kitten, who's currently snuggled up in my coat on the ground. "What do you want to do when we find it?"

"I want to buy you the most luxurious house we can find," he says.

I chuckle, smirking at him. "Oh? And how will you afford that."

He feigns indignation, raising his eyebrows in mock shock. "How could you even ask that? I'll obviously be the wealthiest man just by saying my name. Everyone will be dying to pay for my time."

"Now, how did you come up with that one?"

"I may be too confident because I have such a great supporter."

He winks at me, and I punch his arm. "Seriously though," I say. "What would you want to be? To do?"

"I'm serious. Somewhat. I would like to find a nice place to live with you, for us to be able to find some sort of passion and be happy together."

He looks so sincere that it gives me pause. *Does he mean like a couple?* The thought causes my cheeks to redden. *That's stupid. He probably just means as friends, like how we are now.*

"I'd like that too," I finally reply. "I'd like to be away from all this fear and misery. I want to find a place without so many limitations, where we're free to be who we want and do what we please. If a place like that even exists."

"I'm sure it does, somewhere."

I meet his eyes, lost in the moment. Then a breeze passes through the air, causing a shiver to pass down my spine. I instantly wish I hadn't given my coat to Emmy.

Sensing my discomfort, Reggie leans in closer to me, wrapping his arm around my side. "I'll keep you safe, Cal."

My heart flutters at his words, a strange feeling tickling inside me. I find myself smiling more next to him. I can laugh without worry. I've never doubted that he cares for me greatly. And I care for him too. *Maybe I should just forget about everything that happened. Move on. It no longer matters now anyway. My parents can't touch me, the government no longer controls me. I don't need to understand any of it because it's no longer my life.*

I determine right then and there that I won't let all my uncertainties weigh me down anymore. I'm now free and in a new chapter. *It'll be better this way.*

"We should go to bed. Another long day tomorrow," I say with a yawn.

When Reggie tilts his head to place a kiss on my cheek, a sudden burst of excitement shoots through me. His green eyes glint with the flickering of the fire's flame. "Won't you be cold?" he asks.

"I'll be fine," I say, but when he pulls away, I instantly miss his heat.

He smiles coyly at me. "Are you sure?"

Exasperated, I sigh. "Fine. I'm freezing. But I don't want to wake Emmy, and I can't get too close to the fire. So I'll have to deal."

"Or you could sleep with me?"

My mouth nearly drops open. It wouldn't be the first time I've slept next to him, but I've never slept with him. I debate whether all of his sudden advances mean he likes me or he's just being extra kind. *It doesn't matter. Who knows if he'll act like this again, so I should take advantage of it.*

"I—if you're okay with it," I stammer.

I watch as he stands, finding the smoothest spot he can. He motions for me to join him after he lies on the cold ground. I crawl over to him somewhat hesitantly. We both lie down facing the fire. As I stare at the flame, I hear rustling behind me. I nearly jolt as Reggie presses up against my backside, wrapping his arm around me and squeezing me against his chest.

"Is this comfortable?" he whispers, his words tickling my neck. The leaves below barely provide any cushioning, and I know I'll be sore once again tomorrow. But none of that matters now, not with my best friend so close to me.

"Yes," I respond, my voice quiet.

"Goodnight, Cal."

I close my eyes, embracing the warmth surrounding me. My nerves are at ease, and I feel safer than I have in a long time.

"Goodnight, Reggie."

SEVEN

I**T'S AFTER ONLY TWENTY-FOUR** hours that I once again see a clearing in the distance. Once again, it's off the river's path. Except this time it looks different. I don't spot any road. Rather, I see a bright field of luscious greenery. It looks warm and inviting, and it's a welcome change from the overbearing bounds of forestry.

Reggie and I exchange a meaningful glance.

"It's just like our place," he whispers.

"But better," I reply with a grin, filled with a wash of excitement.

He reaches out and grabs my hand, giving it a tight squeeze. We keep our hands interlocked as we approach the clearing, a newfound energy evident by our quickened pace. Once we break through the trees, I finally have a full view of the field. There are wildflowers spread throughout its grass, and it seems to stretch for miles. A few trees interrupt its nearly seamless emerald sea, but otherwise, it seems like it was perfectly placed here just for us. In the Neighborhood, flowers were scarce. I always thought that, due to the colder weather, I would never see one up close. But now that I've seen them and know they're able to live in our climate, I find myself questioning why my old home had none. *Probably because they would interrupt the unity of everything,* I think scornfully as I let out a sigh. *But I need to remember that I'm leaving that all behind.*

Reggie drops my hand and walks farther into the greenery. "This is incredible," he says.

I place Emmy on the ground, and she bounds off after Reggie. "It really is," I call after him. Wind rushes through the trees, causing my hair to fly around. It normally would be chilling, but with the bright sun beaming down on my skin, it feels more like a welcome embrace.

I follow Reggie as we go farther into the grass. As he walks by a patch of wild blooms, he bends over and plucks a vivid purple flower with an orange center. Its colors shine vibrantly under the sun's gaze.

He lifts it to his nose, taking a whiff of its scent. "You should smell this." He holds it out to me as I join his side. When I take a deep inhale, my nose is overwhelmed by a sweetness I've never experienced before. Reggie grins.

I pull away, frowning at him. "What?"

"You just looked genuinely happy. It's nice to see." He stares at me a moment longer, as if pondering whether he should say something else, then deciding against it.

"Here," he says. He moves closer to me, and my heart starts to race. But rather than approach my face, he gently pushes back a strand of my hair and tucks the flower behind my ear. When he pulls away, he's beaming at me. "You look beautiful, Cal."

My cheeks flush, and I avert my eyes from his. "Thank you," I reply. I chew on my lower lip, scanning our surroundings for something to break the tension. My eyes land on Emmy, who's currently biting on the stem of a white bloom. I laugh, bending over to scoop her in my arms. She lets out an annoyed cry as I place a kiss on her forehead. "You can't eat that, silly!"

Reggie steps away from me, and when I look up, I see that he looks somewhat dejected. I'm about to say something when his expression shifts back to a cheery one. "How about we race to the end of the field? Whoever gets there last has to prepare the camp!"

I quirk my eyebrow at him. "Are you sure you want to challenge me?"

He smirks. "You don't even stand a chance."

"Whatever you say, Reggie. Just don't come crying when you lose! Give me a moment to secure Emmy." I kneel and slide my backpack off my shoulder, opening it up to place my kitten inside. She meows unhappily. "Sorry, girl, it won't be for long," I whisper. I close the zipper, leaving just enough room for her to breathe. Just as I'm standing back up, Reggie sprints away. "Cheater!" I yell.

"It's not cheating if we never made rules!" he calls, not even bothering to look back.

I groan and take off after him. He already has an advantage due to our height difference. I'm nearly a foot shorter than him. The air rushes past me as I move my legs as fast as I can. I know I have no chance of winning. Reggie has already become a distant vision. Still, I don't slow down my pace. I channel all my strength into pushing my body as far as it can go. But it doesn't take long for my limited sleep, food, and water intake to catch up with me. My vision spots slightly, and my head begins to pound faintly, so I reluctantly relax my speed.

"Slow down!" I call into the woods, then hear a distant voice shout back.

"You'll just have to run faster!"

Jerk! I'm no longer excited by the prospect of this race. I didn't realize the field would extend this far. Furthermore, I can feel Emmy bouncing around in my bag. Not only am I not physically able to run, but I also don't want to disturb her anymore. I squint, trying to make out Reggie in the distance. But instead of seeing the outline of a person, I see trees. The seemingly endless field isn't so endless after all. Rather than continuing farther, it abruptly collides with the forest. *We were supposed to go to the end of the field. But I don't see him anywhere.* My surroundings are eerily quiet, and a shiver travels up my spine.

"Reginald?" I call out uneasily. I pause in front of the entrance to the forest, maneuvering my backpack so it's sitting on my front. I check on Emmy to see her looking at me with wide eyes. I reach down to pet her, hoping to calm myself and her. I glance around, and the trees seem to be filled with darkness watching me. I push back my growing panic as much as I can before it consumes me. *He must have gone into the forest. Maybe to try and scare me or something.*

I take a deep breath, then step back into the deep foliage. I continue to call out my friend's name, my nerves on edge. As I move, the ground below me starts to grow steeper. *What's he up to? Why did he just disappear?* Trees creep on my shoulders, barely any sunlight traveling through their leaves, until I eventually see a small light up ahead. I speed up to reach it as fast as possible. The sound of water rests in my ears, getting louder the closer I get to the light. When I finally reach it, I spot Reggie staring at something. Filled with anger and fear, I shout at him.

"What the hell, Reginald! Why didn't you wait at the end of the field?"

He ignores me, pointing in front of him. "Before you get mad, just look!"

I scowl but move closer to look at what he's pointing to. A cliff stands in front of us with a very large, strong river about fifty feet below. In the background, tall mountain peaks seemingly touch the sky. My gaze travels to directly in front of the cliff edge, where a diamond-shaped object sits, hovering without movement. It's both magnificent and foreboding, like nothing I've ever seen before.

"What do you think this is?" he asks.

I struggle to focus and stay irritated with my friend as the object's presence pulls for my attention. "How would I know?" I spitefully spit back. I want to yell at him more for abandoning me and ask how he was even able to run when we're so malnourished. Yet those issues seem so insignificant compared to whatever is before us. The oddity pulls me in, absorbing my attention. *What is that?*

My instinct tells me I need to make sure Emmy is secure. I pull my bag toward my front and peer at her small figure through the small gap in the zipper. She's fine. I then position the bag onto my back again and tighten the straps.

The peculiar object begins to glow and flash, and then a slow hum comes from it. Something inside me sparks a heavy curiosity, and I step toward the strange diamond. It's at least four times my size, and its iridescent color is captivating.

"Cal, I wouldn't go any closer if I were you. We have no clue what this is!" Reggie says, but I barely hear him as I feel a sort of trance come over me. Continuing to move closer and closer, I reach out to try to touch this strange object, and I slip. Snapping out of the trance, I scream as I slide rapidly down into the river.

"Help!" I cry, desperately trying to find something to cling to.

I faintly hear Reggie say something, but I'm unable to make out the words as I close my eyes and brace for impact. But much to my surprise, I never hit the deadly water below. Instead, a blinding bright light glows and pulls me back toward the diamond. The strange pull brings me to a hovering stop in midair, slightly out from the cliff and only a bit above the ground. I watch as a triangle of sorts forms directly in front of me. Once the triangle stops growing, an image of a city appears. It's almost as if it's a window to another place. It doesn't look like a mere photograph, but rather something I could reach out and fall into.

"What's going on?" I ask. My chest tightens with anxiety, and the backpack shakes around. Emmy must be just as terrified as

I am. It feels extremely unnatural for me to be in midair, and seeing the world below causes me to become nauseous. I try to move back toward land, pushing my body forward. I swing my arms, attempting to create some type of momentum, but I manage to move only an inch. Before I can get any farther, I'm pulled tightly back to my spot.

"Do something!" I cry out while tears prick my eyes.

Static starts to come from the diamond, along with the hum. Some sort of robotic voice speaks as the object turns from its white shade to a light blue.

"Hello, Callista Tieron of Neighborhood 33. My name is DETA, also known as Diamond Excellence Tortus Animosity. I'm an AI sent here to bring you to your new home. Don't fret. You won't be hurt. However, you have no choice in this matter. I can also sense Reginald Gray here. Don't worry about him. He'll be taken care of. You may feel sick during this transportation process, but it shouldn't last long after you arrive."

The static ends, and the hum grows increasingly louder as I watch Reggie running around saying something. He looks at me, and I sense a slow movement coming from where I am. I look away briefly only to see that I'm being pulled closer to the strange triangle faster and faster by the second. In a moment of panic, I reach my hand out to Reggie. He takes a leap to grab it, and I hold on with as much strength as I can muster. The speed increases so fast that my hair and skin feel as if they're about to be ripped off.

"Why are you so heavy!" I manage to sob, struggling to speak as he starts to slip from my grasp. The words he mouths in response are inaudible over the humming in my ears. Just as I'm about to lose all grip, the speed increases all at once until I can no longer see. The static buzzes in my head once again with a final sentence I won't forget.

"Callista Tieron, Number 3265, Welcome to Eclium."

EIGHT

I REGAIN CONSCIOUSNESS, ONLY to feel my head pounding with pain. My vision is spotty, and I'm slightly queasy. Shock and confusion fill me as I blink to regain my full vision. Once I do, I see I'm on a long, paved highway. I sit up slowly, wary of further injury, and notice the outline of a large city in front of me. *The buildings are so big. Why are they so big?* Behind me, the road stretches for miles, its surface dull and eerily smooth. It goes straight into a light fog with what looks to be water far beyond it. *The ocean?* The sky glows a light pink mixed with blue, and I search for a clue as to where I am. *Am I dreaming?*

Suddenly, the events that just occurred flash back to me in a second. The wave of information causes me to panic, my breathing quickening along with my heartbeat. My vision begins to spot again, then I force myself to take deep breaths. *Where's Reggie?* My fear grows strong again, and I look around, hoping to see him appear. When he doesn't, my mind races. *Could I have dropped him and killed him?* Various emotions course through me, and I start to shake. Tears prick at my eyes as I think of all the things that could have happened to my best friend. *I never even got to tell him how much I care for him, or how desperately I wanted the future he spoke of to come true.*

The air is eerily silent until I hear a small sound come from the bag on my back. *Emmy!* The sound brings me back to reality, and I take another deep breath, wiping my tears. *That thing said he'll be "taken care of." It could mean he either died somehow or is safe. I want to find him. I need him. If he somehow got hurt, I couldn't help but feel responsible. Maybe this is all some crazy nightmare. Maybe he's still at home.*

I quickly take off my backpack and bring Emmy out of the bag. She looks disoriented and frightened, her small eyes frantically glancing around before landing on me.

"It's going to be okay," I whisper, although I'm not sure that it is. Everything around me is fuzzy, and I struggle to make sense of everything. Holding Emmy in one arm, I attempt to stand, only to stumble onto my knees. The world spins for a brief moment. I decide I must have hit my head harder than I thought.

A sound creeps into my ears, and I listen as it gets louder and closer. Its intensity only increases my head pain, and the noise rings in my ears. Just as I turn my head, a large, long metal vehicle of some sort zooms past my left toward the city. My hair blows into my face in the gust of wind, and I shudder. I have no clue what's going on—only that I don't think it's good.

I squint, noticing a massive diamond object floating in the sky above the city. *That DETA thing. Why is it just sitting there? What does it want with me?* It looks much smaller now that it floats in the distance, its large triangular frames reflecting its surroundings. I manage to find some sense of calm, but my anxiety doesn't dissipate.

If I'm going to find Reggie, I first need to think back to what happened. Maybe that DETA thing gave me a clue. I struggle to think back on everything the freakish object said. When I replay its message in my head, I fill with horror. *It said, "Welcome to Eclium." That's the same word my parents mentioned. But why? Did I never really escape them? Am I still unable to move on from my past?*

I know if I harp too much on my fears that I'll get nowhere. If I want to know what's going on, I need to find information. Even if I'm nearly petrified. Even if my own body is against me. If not for myself, then for Reginald.

With my new situation facing me, I focus on staying calm and holding back my emotions. My muscles are twitchy, and my mouth is incredibly dry. I feel more unsafe than I did in the Neighborhood. *I need to get out of here. I'm too exposed.*

I place Emmy back into her pocket, and she cries again, attempting to jump out.

"I'm sorry, Emmy, but we have to move again."

She continues trying to jump out, and I continue pushing her back in until she eventually gives up and settles down.

The sun above seems to be halfway in the sky, and I realize with a sinking sensation that I'm already running out of time. I push myself once more to my feet, steadying myself before I stumble back down. I'm sure I shouldn't be moving with all my dizziness and head pain, but I don't have much of a choice. With no desire to go into the foreboding fog, I head toward the city.

Not long after I start down the long road, footsteps echo behind me. There was no one there when I checked my surroundings. They must have been hidden. *I knew it. I'm not safe.* My muscles tense, and I increase my speed. I instantly regret my choice as my balance becomes even more unsteady.

"Wait! Stop running!" a gruff voice calls out, but I push myself to continue. *Why is someone chasing me?* Much to my dismay, my body fails me, and I sway to the side, falling to the ground. I barely manage to stop my face from hitting the hard pavement. My hands, knees, and arms sting painfully. *I'm screwed.*

"Are you okay?" the voice asks, now by my side.

I force myself into a sitting position and raise my arms protectively. I look up, surprised to see a boy. He's much taller than me, with short black hair and an appearance that seems to scream he isn't to be messed with. He has a muscular build, one that suggests he's used to being physical. All of this creates an intimidating, albeit attractive, image. But not enough for me to be any less defensive.

"Sorry, I didn't mean to startle you," he says. Then he reaches out a hand, and I hesitate before grabbing it reluctantly, letting him hoist me up.

I take a moment to steady myself. "Well, what did you think would happen?" I ask as I glare at him.

"I didn't expect you to run. I wanted to see if you knew anything about where we are. I've been wandering down this road for hours. You're the first life I've seen."

I shrug and look away from him to check on Emmy. His eyes follow my movements, and I try to ignore him as I swing the bag over my shoulder and open the pocket to see the little kitten, who's in a ball, looking up at me.

"Good girl," I whisper. I readjust the load on my back and turn my gaze to see the boy watching me. "What?"

"Nothing. I'm just surprised you have a pet."

"My friend got her for me."

"Where are they now?"

"He—" I pause, an ache pulsing in my heart. "He didn't come with me."

The boy seems to know what I mean, as he doesn't press any further. I resume my path toward the foreboding structure but stop when he doesn't follow me. *He could be the only life I see for a while. Maybe we should stay together. But I can't trust him. He could be dangerous.* I'm mildly afraid that this could be a mistake. Yet I don't seem to have many options. I do know I don't want to be alone. With this boy as my only potential companion, I don't have much of a choice. I take a deep breath to settle my new anxiety, then pivot to motion at him.

"You coming?" I ask.

His eyebrows shoot up as he catches up quickly. I resume walking, and he follows next to me.

"When'd you get here?" he asks.

His easy manner loosens up my nerves a bit. "Today. How did you get here?"

"I assume I arrived here the same way you did." His long arm stretches out to point at the diamond hovering above the city.

"Do you know what that thing is?"

"Only that it refers to itself as DETA."

I frown. *This is too weird. Why were we both brought here? I should get to know him. If he has more information, he won't share it unless he trusts me.*

"We should probably exchange names since we could be spending a lot of time together," I finally say. "I'm Callista, but Calli is fine too." He doesn't respond, and I look over at him as we continue walking. "Do you have a name?"

His demeanor turns cold. "Sharing things like that is pointless. It gets you attached to someone," he mutters.

I raise an eyebrow, confused as to why his personality shifted so suddenly. *Something's up.* I lift my gaze back to the city in the distance. We're about halfway there already. The boy doesn't say anything else, and I don't try to get him to talk. There are more important things to focus on right now.

When we finally approach the place where the empty land and city break, the size of everything takes my breath away. Having been raised around cookie-cutter homes with no differences whatsoever, I find it enthralling to see a new environment. It's strange how the buildings start so abruptly. The road just extends straight into its walls, nothing getting in its way. I suppose the

Neighborhoods were designed similarly, although they at least had woods surrounding them.

As we walk deep into the city, I note how quiet it is. The buildings stretch for miles, yet they seem incredibly empty. I peer inside windows as we pass. There's no sign of abandonment. Everything looks fully furnished. I see hints of office spaces, lobbies, and countless other spaces that I've never been exposed to before. It reminds me of the photos I used to see in school, except more fantastical.

I look around at this strange place with wonder and a new fear. Then I realize something. This city is just like the Neighborhood. Although there are differences inside, all the buildings are identical in size, shape, and color. The thought sends a chill down my spine. *Is this just a more lavish version of the prison I escaped?* These walls could hide things I wouldn't want to see. I find myself wishing I had my friend here to experience this with me. *He would know how to comfort me. He always did.*

I try not to worry about Reggie and reoccupy my mind with something else. *I need to choose a place to take shelter,* I tell myself. The sun is now nearly set, and any light coming from it is covered by the towering buildings. I shiver in the now cold air and wrap my arms around my chest, looking around for somewhere we could possibly sleep. When I turn to ask my new companion which building we should go in, I see him walking off.

"Where are you going?" I yell after him. A light turns on a block away, and I rush toward it. It's glowing from inside one of the lower levels of a large building, and the boy stands inside. I scowl at him. "You could have told me you were going to find a place," I say.

"Well, I'll keep that in mind for next time." He scoffs as he adjusts the pillows on one of the two couches in the middle of the room.

Jerk. Where did the friendliness go? The building seems to be a hotel lobby, but there's no sign of anyone having gone through it in ages. Dust coats all the furniture, but other than that, there's no sign of damage.

I walk over to the adjacent couch and dust it off. The pillows are soft and create a nice, plush area for me to rest my head. Just as I'm taking off my backpack and gently retrieving Emmy to place her on the couch, the lights shut off, and I let our a startled yelp.

"Geez, do you have to be so loud?" the boy asks.

I bite back a retort and sit on the couch next to Emmy. *Hard to say much when I don't even have a name to call you.* I sigh, leaning my head down onto the pillows as I place Emmy on my chest and lift my feet onto the couch. The cushions are a welcome respite from the cold, hard forest floor.

"Could you at least give me something to call you?" I ask.

"Just call me K." I hear the couch nearby shift with his body weight on it.

I wonder what that's short for. Knowing I'm going to need rest, I close my eyes and drift asleep to the gentle feeling of Emmy's purr.

"Rosalie and Elijah, do not fight, or this will be more painful than it needs to be."

A large dark figure stands in front of two smaller figures on their knees. Behind them, another shadow creeps up with some sharp object in its hand. It has a large toothless smile—one that seems to be an endless pit that could swallow me whole. The object glints, and the shadow twists it in its fingers.

I sense the presence of another being. They're beside me, holding my grip. I try to see their faces, but I'm unable to make out any physical details. Something starts to tug on me and the other being, dragging us farther and farther away from the terrifying beings in the front.

I detect an itching beneath my skin, and red-hot pain burns me. I try to free my hand so I can figure out where the pain is coming from, but the grip on me only tightens. The being seems to be trying to comfort me, but I squirm away as my limbs tremble. My mouth opens, and I scream. But I hear nothing as my vision turns completely dark.

I'm awoken by violent shaking, and I open my eyes, only to stare directly into K's. "What the hell was that for?" I slap away his arms and eye him warily.

"You were shaking and mumbling something, so I woke you up." He gives me an indiscernible look, then turns away. "Don't worry. Your cat's safe. I moved her when you were shaking so she wouldn't get distressed." He picks up Emmy from the floor nearby. She meows as he brings her over to me. I readjust to a sitting position on the couch and take her from him.

"Thanks," I mutter quietly. My headache and nausea seem to have subsided significantly, likely aided by the night's rest, even though I had more nightmares.

He turns again and walks over to the couch, shuffling through a small bag. When he moves away from it, the sun glints on something shiny in his hand. The knife startles me as he walks toward me, and my heart races. I instinctively grab the pillow and raise it to throw at him, but he lifts his hands in surrender.

"Chill. I was just going to give you this dagger so you can protect yourself. I found it and another in an abandoned truck when I first got here. We'll have to work together if we want to figure out what's going on. Just don't use it on me."

He slowly lowers his hands and resumes walking toward me, more cautiously this time. When he gets close enough, I let him hand me the dagger hilt first. It's nothing like I've seen before— sleek and sharp, unlike the kitchen knives I was occasionally allowed to use at home. The sight of it sends a chill down my spine. I'm uncomfortable with it in my hand, having never used a weapon before. I lightly touch the side of the blade, tracing it. I know I couldn't use this to harm if I had to. But I doubt K would let me give it back to him.

Knowing I have no choice, I place it next to my left leg and move Emmy to my right, then lean over to grab my backpack. When I open it, I notice the journal Reggie gave me. I quickly pull it out and store the sharp weapon in its place. Leaning back, I open the leather cover and trace over Reggie's writing. *I'll find you. I hope you're okay.*

K goes back over to his area, seemingly deep in thought. I slowly flip the first page and am faced with my first entry from a month ago. I read it over quickly. *Eclium. I still have no clue why my parents knew about this place.* My eyes travel up to K. *Should I tell him about this? Maybe he can help me figure this out.* I bite my lip in contemplation. *I should risk it. It'll be better to go at this with someone else.*

"K, I need to share something important with you." My voice snaps him out of his thoughts, and he walks back over to me, then sits to my left. Our arms brush briefly, and I tense slightly before showing him the book. "I wrote this journal entry a month ago. My parents mentioned the same word that DETA did when I was brought here."

His bright gray eyes trace the words on the page quickly.

"It must be the city name," he says. "I assume DETA also said, 'Welcome to Eclium,' before it brought you here?" I nod and he continues. "So, based off what you wrote, your parents must know something about wherever we are, and they were trying to keep it from you."

Obviously. Does he think I'm stupid? I force back my annoyance, nodding once more. "I agree. They must have been hiding something, but I don't know what." I pull the book away, close it, and drop it into my bag.

"We should go search for more people. They might be able to help us get answers." He stands and walks out the door. My hands move quickly as I kiss Emmy on the forehead and place her in the backpack's front pocket. I stand up and hurry after him, trying to keep up.

As we walk, an idea comes to my mind. "I remember seeing a train of sorts pass by me when I first got here," I say. "If we can find where it leads, we're sure to find others!"

K stops walking and turns toward me. "Where is it?"

I ponder the question and shrug. "Well, it was to the left of wherever I was, and since we've been walking straight this whole time, going left is our best bet."

He turns left and walks through an alley between buildings. I loudly exhale and follow him. *Why doesn't he tell me before he takes off?*

The alley is dark and still quiet, but the small amount of sunlight allows me to follow K. The path isn't too long, and we soon arrive at one road that goes to the right and one that continues straight. We follow the straight road without any discussion.

After ten minutes of walking, my stomach growls loudly. A flush travels up my neck and onto my cheeks, and I frown.

K turns to me, crossing his arms. "Hungry?" he asks.

Embarrassed, I respond quietly, "I guess so." I realize I've completely forgotten about my personal needs, and along with the hunger comes a wave of fatigue. *It probably doesn't help that I haven't eaten a full meal in days. Emmy is likely starving too.*

"If we're lucky, we'll find food soon," he says. "But don't count on it."

"I know."

We continue moving, my pace becoming slightly more sluggish. I try and focus on other things to distract me from my growing hunger. *I haven't had nightmares for so long. At least not ones I can remember. But I finally did last night. Who are Rosalie and Elijah? Why was I in so much pain? And why were those shadow figures back? What does this all mean?* Recalling the nightmare creates a faint, echoing pain reminiscent of the one I imagined. I wince, trying to push the thought from my mind. With no success, I become increasingly unnerved.

"K?" I ask, my voice unsteady.

He looks back at me over his shoulder. "What is it?"

"Can we talk while we walk? I can't stand being in more silence."

When he doesn't respond, I scold myself. *Idiot! Why would he do that? You aren't friends.* Yet much to my surprise, he replies, "Sure."

A small wave of relief washes over me. "What was it like where you came from?"

"It was very …" He pauses, his voice drifting. "Isolating. Everything looked the same, and we were kept in by towering walls. I never understood why. My parents said they were to protect us from intruders."

"Wait. Did you also live in a Neighborhood?"

K stops dead in his tracks, turning to me with a serious expression. "Yes. How did you know?" I catch a hint of suspicion in his tone and carefully decide my next words.

"I lived in a Neighborhood. We weren't surrounded by walls, but extensive gates. And all the buildings were nearly identical."

We stand there, staring at each other, unsure what to make of the information. *What are the chances he also came from a Neighborhood? And how come he had walls around his? This can't be a coincidence.* Although I'm unnerved by the realization that something must be going on here, I'm more at ease with my new companion. *He's like me. I should still be careful, but I think I can trust him.*

"I hope for both our sakes that we find someone with answers," K states as he resumes walking.

I'm slightly put off by his words, uncertain whether he thinks I'm lying or is just generally hard to read. I can tell he doesn't plan on answering any more of my questions, so I resign myself to following him in silence.

NINE

AFTER WHAT FEELS LIKE several hours of walking, we eventually reach a break in the road. Nearby, the sound of bustling people fills the air.

"Do you hear that?" I ask, excited and skeptical about the prospect of meeting others.

K nods. "Let's check it out. Carefully."

We cautiously move closer to the sound, and it grows increasingly louder with each step. Eventually, a building comes into view, just a short block away from a track. It towers like the rest, but it almost seems like the upper levels are just there so it matches the other buildings surrounding it. Inside, lights are on, illuminating figures sitting and chatting. A large sign with fluorescent neon-pink letters reads, "Lee's Diner." The smell of food travels from inside, and although it would normally be comforting, something about the place feels wrong.

K and I peer inside, observing the crowd. Against my will, my stomach growls once more. *I'd love to eat something, but it seems too convenient for there to be so many people here when everywhere else is deserted.*

Before either of us says a word, a man appears in front of us in an apron and shoots us a toothy grin. He has bulging muscles, emphasizing his frame. One of his eyes is unmoving, and I note it must be glass.

"Hello. Name's Lee. Why don't you two come inside? You must be starving."

K and I exchange glances and shift uncomfortably. I signal to him with a shake of my head that I don't think it's safe.

Just as K opens his mouth to speak, the man interrupts him. "Wonderful! So glad you both have decided to join us." He reaches over and grabs our arms, tugging us inside with ease.

My apprehension grows as the man drags us to the counter in the middle of the diner and motions for us to sit. No one around seems to notice our forced entry, and they all continue to eat and chat as if we didn't even exist.

"So! What would you kids like to eat?" Lee asks.

Neither K nor I take a seat. I take a step backward, my mouth twisting into a frown. "Sorry, but I'm not hungry."

"Come on, don't you at least want a small bite?"

The smell of the food is intensely tempting, especially considering I've had freeze-dried meals all my life. I hesitate and glance at K, who seems annoyed by the man's insistence.

"Fine," K finally says. "Two sandwiches. Make them hot. We won't be eating them here."

The man's grin widens, allowing us to see the full set of his teeth. When he goes into the kitchen, I frantically turn to K.

"I don't like this. We should go while he's distracted." I start toward the door, only to be stopped when a brooding man with deep-black hair and sharp eyes appears in front of me.

"You and your friend need to trust me right now," the man says.

I widen my eyes and step backward, bumping into K.

"Who—"

I'm cut off by a loud bang and shouting.

Voices yell, "There they are!"

My head spins to see a group of five men standing at the door, pointing at me, K, and the stranger beside us.

"Shit, we didn't get here fast enough," the dark-haired stranger mutters. Then he grabs our arms. "You two need to trust me, okay?"

"I don't know who you are, but we aren't going anywhere with you," K says as he jerks away from the strange man, his face contorted in an angry scowl. I do the same, wanting now more than ever to get out of this building.

When the man starts to speak again, he's abruptly cut off by a loud noise. I watch in horror as the stranger falls to his knees, an intensely red patch on his leg.

"Grab on to me!" he cries through clenched teeth.

I don't move, my body freezing up. Another shot fires, hitting him square in the middle of his chest. The man hits the floor, unmoving.

When K grabs my wrist and whispers in my ear, I'm taken out of my shock. "Do you see any other exit?" he asks.

I snatch my gaze away from the lifeless man. My heartbeat picks up as spots dot my vision. *That man is probably dead. I could be next.* "No, only the door," I barely manage to respond.

In the midst of all the chaos, I realize that I'd failed to notice that the people who were once eating and talking have disappeared. Only K, the man on the floor, the five men standing at the door, and I remain.

The one in the front seems to be listening to a radio in his ears. "Boss says we should take them now," he says to the rest of his posse.

"These two must be new recruits," a shorter man with a large scar across his face comments. "They haven't activated. Shouldn't put up much of a fight."

I realize they must be talking about K and me. *I won't let them take me anywhere.* My defenses rise, and I reach to pull over my backpack slowly, my hands shaky. In my peripheral vision, I notice a glint come from K's hand as he takes out his dagger. The men start shuffling around, filling their weapons with bullets. Just as they turn to move toward us, I throw myself over the counter and open a cabinet, quickly grabbing my dagger from my backpack and stuffing the pack inside the cabinet to keep Emmy as safe as possible.

"Stay here, Em. I'll be back. I promise." The kitten lets out a quiet meow as I shut the door, locking her in. I know I have to move fast. Otherwise, she could suffocate. As I move away, I tense, my muscles uncomfortable with the blade in hand. *I'm not a killer. What am I supposed to do with this?* Another loud bang comes from the other side of the counter, and I flinch, praying that K didn't get hurt.

I creep around the corner, holding my dagger in an awkward position in front of me. I watch as K fights two of the men at once while another one lies on the floor with several slashes across his chest. The oozing gash makes me sick, and I look away, only to see the other two men heading in my direction. As they approach, my desire to live takes over, and I throw out my leg, successfully tripping the first man. My second attacker doesn't react fast enough and falls on top of his comrade.

I take the opportunity to jump over them and rush toward K. He has successfully knocked out one of his attackers. Realizing that I should go help him, I start toward him as he fights the third one. But I'm interrupted when something strong hits the back of my head. I fall forward, managing to throw my arms out to protect my face from impact and dropping the dagger to my side in the process.

My vision spots and my ears ring. I manage to lift my head, only to see the world spin as a foot pushes my head back against the floor. I dizzily look over to see K being restrained by two men, with another aiming the gun at him. I try to push myself up to regain my footing, only to be slammed down again.

"You aren't going anywhere. Your group needs to know this is our place," a man says.

I hear a bang in the direction of where I last saw K. My fear turns into despair as I close my eyes, unable to keep them open anymore with the intense pain in my head. *This is it. I'll never see Reggie again. It's over.*

The surrounding darkness consumes me until a small orb of light shines in the distance. I feel a need to reach out, and I will myself to bring it closer. By luck or sheer will, I manage to do so, and my shadow-filled mind becomes lighter and brighter as the orb nears me. Once it's right in front of me, it disappears at the same time the sound of shattering glass comes from above.

My senses refocus, and I open my eyes, only to see the room I'm lying in filled with darkness, the only light being a dim glow coming from outside.

I'm no longer dizzy, although my head still aches and my ears have a slight ring. I push myself off the floor slowly to regain my balance and stand, only to sense my mind pulling at me. I close my eyes for a moment. Then I see the light in my head bounce around and vanish once again.

Confusion fills me as I open my eyes to see the area around me lit up by some unforeseen source. I notice glass lining the floors. When I look up, I realize that all the light bulbs are gone. *Am I imagining things?*

In the newfound brightness, I notice that the men who attacked me are on the floor, their heads bloody and gashed with glass sticking out of the wounds. The blood makes me nauseous. I feel heavy, and my stomach churns. *I'm going to be sick.* I look away quickly, not wanting to stare too long at the gruesome image. But that doesn't help.

I turn to see K on the floor with a gash in his arm from what I assume to be the bullet and a few cuts on his legs from the glass. The other attackers lie nearby, just as damaged as the first batch. The urge to throw up the remains of whatever food may be in my stomach washes over me, and I put my hand over my mouth to try to hold myself together.

As a distraction, I observe the rest of my surroundings. The windows that lead outside are also shattered from some form of impact, and a brief ray of sunlight lines the road far away. Then I spot the source of the light. It's the orb, the same one I saw in my mind. I spot it floating mere feet before me, its presence ominous.

This doesn't make any sense. What is that thing? I stumble backward, unnerved. But when I move, so does the orb. With each step I make to get farther away, it moves a step closer. *I must be dreaming.* I pinch my arm and wince at the pain that shoots through it. *I'm not dreaming. This, whatever this is, is very real. And it seems to be connected to me. Did it cause the lights to shatter?* I gulp. *If it did, that means I caused all this wreckage. Even if it wasn't intentional.*

I watch the glowing sphere with suspicion. Then I close my eyes, praying that when I open them, it will be gone.

I wait several moments, then open them. The orb is gone, as if it had never been there in the first place. Then I do it again, except I wish for it to appear. I do this several times, the orb blinking in and out of existence as I will it. It doesn't physically feel as if there's something on me, but I can sense the presence of the light. It makes me uneasy and more anxious than before. I never once would have thought it possible for light to take a physical form like this, and I definitely wouldn't think it would be connected to me.

I don't want this. I will the light away, telling myself that it's just a side effect of everything my body has been through. *It isn't real. I have no desire to be attached to something against my will.*

I remember the small kitten hiding behind the counter, and I rush to the cabinet to grab her. When I open the backpack, she looks at me with terror. I pick her up gently while shushing her. "Emmy, it's alright, girl. I'm sorry," I whisper to her. I pet her for a few moments, allowing the texture of her soft fur and the vibrations of her purring to ease my tension. Then I reluctantly place her back in my backpack and sling it over my shoulder.

As I start to stand back up, footsteps echo from the doorway. I slowly peek over the counter and see a young woman with light-brown hair walking inside, talking into a walkie-talkie.

"Tyrus and the boy are here, along with the attackers. Doesn't look like backup is needed. Seems the girl's power has awakened. The attackers are unconscious. I don't think they'll wake anytime soon. The girl is nowhere to be seen."

She steps cautiously around the bodies and glass as she heads toward K and the other man, who I assume to be Tyrus.

I shift on my feet, and the floor below me lets out a creak. *Crap.* I don't have time to search for an exit before the woman moves toward my side of the counter with a knife in her hand.

"Whoever is there, come out, and I won't hurt you," she says.

I tense up, and my heartbeat increases as I slowly stand up with my hands raised.

"Oh, it's you." She casually repockets her knife, walks over to me, then laughs. "Put your hands down. I won't hurt you."

I do as she says and stand still, trying to figure out her intentions. I don't want to fight anyone else. I can't.

"My name is Tessa," she says. "I'm here to help you and your friend. The other man on the floor over there is my brother Tyrus." She pauses, eyeing me up and down. "Your name is Callista, correct?"

I nod slowly, unsettled that she knows my name. My hands tighten beside me, ready to defend myself if I must. *How does she know who I am? I don't trust this.*

She turns and motions over to where K lies. "I'm guessing you know Kieran?"

I purse my lips, furrowing my brow. "He told me to call him K."

She holds back a grin and nods. "I used to be partners with his sister a long time ago. Anyway, Tyrus and I aren't your enemies. We're a part of a group of people like you and K over there."

"What do you mean 'like me'?" I eye her with confusion.

"Have you really not figured it out yet? Do you think those lights just exploded on their own?"

I step back, frowning. "Are you saying I hurt these people?" I already guessed as much, but I really don't want it to be true.

Her expression softens into one of understanding. "It's okay, Callista. It was out of your control. Don't blame yourself. They weren't good people anyway." She steps toward me, approaching me as if I were a wounded animal. She seems to mean well, but instead of feeling comforted, I just feel more on edge.

Crossing my arms, I frown. "I don't want it. I never asked for any of this."

"Unfortunately, you don't have much of a choice."

The words hit home, and, for a moment, I picture Alina saying them. *I never have much of a choice.* I take a deep breath and force a laugh. "I'll play along, for now. What can you do?"

A smile spreads across her face, and she grabs my wrist, closing her eyes as she holds tight. I move to pull away, but her grip is too strong. Her eyes shutter closed, and a cooling sensation comes over me as the pain in my head seems to fade away. I look down and notice the cuts on my palm have healed too. When she lets go and opens her eyes, I flex my hand, amazed and slightly terrified by the absence of pain.

"I'm a healer. My brother's a teleporter. Sadly, the doofus wasn't fast enough to get you out of here." She sighs and glances downward, then starts to move back around the counter.

My eyes widen. *This is impossible. Healers? Teleporters? And I can control some light or something? How did any of this happen?* I want to believe this is all part of some greater joke, but it's hard to ignore what I've witnessed.

"Wait," I say. "So, can you help K and your brother?"

She nods slightly. "Well, I can heal the bullet and stab wounds, but I can't get rid of any toxins inside. Don't worry though. The bullets were only filled with a sedative that should keep them asleep for a few more hours." She kneels down next to them and lays her hand on Tyrus's chest.

"None of this makes sense. How is this even possible?" I ask. I look at her suspiciously, unsure of her intentions.

"You'll understand in due time. For now, try not to worry too much."

"Why can't you tell me anything now?"

"I wish I could, but it's not time," she says.

"You keep talking about time, but it seems like now is a really good time to tell me more about this life-changing information."

"You really do like to ask questions, don't you."

Her words once again remind me of my parents and their constant displeasure over my desire for understanding. Any further retort falls flat on my lips, replaced by a sinking feeling. *Why does no one ever want to tell me the truth? Is it really that difficult?*

"Will you be staying here?" I ask, wanting to change the line of conversation. I inch closer to her to watch her work.

She turns and frowns at me. "I can't. At least not yet. There will be a time."

What is all of this nonsense about time? I hold back an irritated scoff.

All of Tyrus's wounds have healed, so she moves over to K's body. "I trust you can handle this guy," she says. "His sister was my best friend. I'd hate to leave him in the wrong hands."

I stare at K's sleeping face and exhale. "We'll be fine." But we'd be even more fine if she would tell me something instead of beating around the bush.

She finishes up with K's wound, then moves over to Tyrus and hoists him up. A buzzing comes from her walkie-talkie as a tall, inconspicuous man blinks into my vision. *Another teleporter?*

"Callista, I'm sorry." Tessa moves toward the tall man. "This is my ride. I promise we won't leave you two for too long."

I open my mouth to ask what she means just as the three of them blink out of existence.

I'm left with only the smell of blood and K's sleeping body. I'm at an utter loss as I look around the diner, carefully avoiding looking at the wounded men. *So in this unfamiliar place, there are people with strange abilities. And I'm one of them.* The thought feels unnatural. My jaw clenches. *I can't believe Tessa just left me here to fend for myself when she clearly had resources and answers as to what's going on.*

I slam my hand on the wall, letting out a frustrated cry. *Why can't I have something go my way for once?* With no idea of what to do next, I decide it's best to stay busy. I go back behind the counter and into the kitchen. Placing my backpack on the counter, I open the pocket and allow Emmy to free roam. I then grab a broom from the corner and return to the main area of the diner to sweep away the glass to clear a path.

Once I finish, I hoist up K as much as I can and drag him back into the kitchen.

There could be more of those guys. So I decide we should probably leave as soon as K wakes up. If we were to be attacked, we would easily be overtaken.

I find myself in denial over this apparent power I've suddenly been given. I don't want to mess with something that has the potential to destroy. *Too much of my life is out of control. I don't need something else creating chaos.*

The fridge sits directly to my right. I walk over and slowly open the door. Much to my relief, a small package of pale meat sits next to a small loaf of bread. Both items seem off-color, likely not fresh. *I guess the smell earlier wasn't real. Or maybe I imagined it.* The meat doesn't even look natural. It seems to be extremely processed. But I take out both, deciding that it's worth the risk to try the food.

Emmy crawls over to me, smelling the meat in my hand. I tear off a small chunk and place it on the counter for her, then I rip off my own piece of meat and hunk of bread. I create a makeshift sandwich and bite into it. The bread is stale and the meat flavorless. *Tastes like home.* The thought is bitter, but I can't deny that it's nice to finally be eating something.

When I finish the bland meal, I'm overcome with thirst. The faucet beside me turns on when I twist it. I stick my head underneath to drink. Emmy also walks over, and I pick her up to let her lick from the flowing stream.

The room is dark other than a dim light from a broken nearby window. I pick up Emmy and walk over to K's resting body, then sit down against the nearby wall. Emmy's contented purr relaxes me, and I push away all other thoughts.

"What are we going to do, Em?" I whisper to her, wishing now more than ever that I had Reggie by my side.

TEN

I WAKE GROGGILY, SURROUNDED BY almost complete darkness. The only light source is faint moonlight that barely makes it through the single window. *How late is it?* Emmy is fast asleep on my lap when K wakes up.

After I finish my explanation, K's frown deepens. "I do recall my sister mentioning knowing a Tessa once," he says. "Although she never told me much about how they knew each other. Whoever she is, she never lived in my Neighborhood."

It must have been nice having a sister. I look at his expression longer, watching as he seems to think about something. "Are you going to be okay?" I ask.

"None of this makes sense. I mean, how did we get here? How do you have some 'power'? How is it possible for anyone to have powers? And why didn't Tessa tell me anything? Why didn't my parents say something? Did they know?" He pauses. "Never mind."

"I'm just as frustrated and confused as you are. I don't know why I'm here. I don't know why I have this orb thing. I don't even want it. I never wanted any of this."

An awkward silence wraps around us. Having met so recently, there's an unseen limit to how much we can share. I think we both want to open up but are afraid. *I don't even tell Reggie everything. So why do I feel like I can tell this stranger?* But I know this much: Both of us are in similar situations. Neither of us knows what's happening or what to prepare for next. And I know I'm terrified. Based on what I experienced earlier, I reluctantly start to realize that I may have to rely on this strange power. The only option I can think of for us to start moving is to utilize the orb. *I don't want anything to do with any of this. But we're just sitting ducks here. I don't think I have a choice.*

I close my eyes, picturing the fluorescent sphere in my mind.

"Wow, you weren't lying," K says.

I shoot open my eyes, glaring at him. "You thought I made this up?"

"Not really. I also saw that guy teleport out of nowhere, and I know I was injured. I just didn't expect this." He points to the orb floating mere inches before me.

"Yeah, well, I wish I had lied. I don't like this thing being tethered to me."

He gets up and steps closer to it, curiosity written all over his face. "Maybe this isn't such a bad thing. It seems pretty useful."

"Except it somehow shattered all the lights in here and injured those men. I don't know how it, or I, did that. But I don't want to repeat it."

"They attacked us. I'd say they deserved it."

I glower at him, crossing my arms. "Maybe they did. But I didn't want to be the one who shot the bullet."

I tap Emmy, waking her from her slumber. She stretches and lets out a small noise when I scoop her up. I grab my bag and place her inside, getting to my feet. "Let's just go." *To where, I don't know. Anywhere but here.*

K gets up after me, dusting glass powder off his pants.

"There's some water in the kitchen," I say. "Who knows the next time we'll find some, so you should take a sip before we go."

He nods, moving to follow my instructions. I go to the front to wait for him, my orb trailing right behind me. He joins me moments later, wiping droplets from his mouth.

We step out into the night and begin walking with no destination in mind. My muscles tense as I dwell on my lack of progress since arriving here. I still have no idea where Reggie is, and now I have a whole other problem to deal with. *I don't care if this orb thing is helpful. I don't want it.*

We continue walking in silence until we eventually reach a cutoff from the city. Forest suddenly surrounds us, and we see a small bridge with a flowing stream below it. *Everything here is so abrupt. Why?*

"Whoever designed this place really needs to improve their skills," K remarks.

"This makes no sense." I frown, contemplating whether we should turn back. *The buildings were empty. Maybe these woods will lead to answers.*

"We should come back to investigate this area in the daylight," I say.

K nods just as Emmy starts to scratch from inside my backpack. Confused, I lift it off my shoulders and open it slowly to check on her. But as soon as I unzip it, she jumps out. When she hits the ground, she sniffs the air, then stares at the woods on the other side of the stream.

"Maybe she has to go to the bath—" K cuts off when Emmy sprints toward the forest.

I panic and run after her. "Emmy! Come back!"

K tries to tell me to not follow her, but I ignore him. The darkness makes it harder to see her black form, and my orb won't go any farther than right beside me. Once in the forest, I lose track of her completely and fall to the ground, stifling a sob. Behind me, footsteps approach, and I don't even bother looking up. She was my last piece of family.

"We'll find her, I promise." K gently places his arm on my shoulder.

I stare hopelessly at the forest floor. "She's never taken off before." In front of us, leaves shuffle and a loud meow echoes.

"There!" I yell and quickly push off the ground, taking off once again. As I get closer to the noises, I hear a slight human cry but barely register the sound. When I arrive, Emmy is sitting on the ground with her teeth sunk into a chipmunk. Grimacing, I pick her up, and she drops the lifeless creature. I wince, pulling my gaze away from the animal's corpse. *I've never seen any wildlife before. And now the first thing I've seen has died.*

Emmy stares off into the forest, and I hear the human cry again just as K catches up to me.

"You have to stop doing that," he says.

You're one to talk.

He growls under his breath, and I ignore him as I slowly walk toward the cry. I notice the shadowed figure of a young girl sitting against the side of a tree not far from us. Emmy jumps out of my arms and runs off once again, but this time she heads toward the figure. She rubs against the girl as the girl cries softly. It seems she doesn't notice our presence. I approach cautiously, unsure of what I might find.

"Hello?" I whisper, not wanting to scare or threaten her. My orb illuminates the scene before more clearly. The figure peeks out around the tree, and I face a girl around my height with mid-length dirty-blond hair and bright-blue eyes. Slight freckles trickle across her nose. Something is strangely familiar about her, and it unnerves me.

I don't trust this. I should get Emmy and leave. "Emmy, come on." I try and get my kitten to come to me, but she acts as if I'm not even there. I step closer to the girl, bending over to quickly pick up Emmy, then stepping away. K joins my side, eyeing the girl warily.

"Who are you?" he asks, his voice low and uncertain.

"Aviana," she says. Then she looks up and stares at my orb, her face lighting as she does. "I think I'm like you." As she says that, she focuses on something in the distance, and a bluebird flies over and perches on her shoulder. "I can somehow control animals. And understand them a little too."

My eyes widen. "And you're okay with that?"

She shrugs. "I enjoy their company. I may not understand how I'm suddenly able to do this, but I'm not complaining."

I can't help having an itching feeling that she's holding back something.

I exchange a look with K. *Another person like us. I shouldn't jump to conclusions. She may be just as lost as we are. But we can't trust her yet.*

"Why were you crying, Aviana?" I ask.

"I heard you guys talking, and I was controlling that chipmunk to see who you guys were."

I frown. "So you were spying on us?"

"No, I wasn't! Well, I guess technically, I was. You're the first people I've seen since I got sent here yesterday." She shifts, seemingly uneasy. "Anyway, I clearly didn't hide well enough because your cat spotted me. When she attacked the chipmunk, I lost control of it." She drops her voice to a whisper. "It was awful. It felt like a small part of me died with it." She seems to deflate, her face contorting in pain.

Guilt washes over me. *She seems innocent. I'm just being stand-offish for no reason. I can trust her for now. She's no different than K.* "I'm sorry. Emmy has never done that before."

She shakes her head rapidly. "No, it's fine! It really isn't your fault."

"You said you arrived yesterday?" K asks, his forehead scrunched.

"Yes, sometime in the morning."

"What brought you here?"

"Something called DETA."

"Where did you—"

"Stop interrogating her!" I say, smacking K on the arm.

"Weren't you just doing the same thing?" he asks.

He's right. I sigh. "Neither of us is any better off than she is. There isn't any reason for us to trust each other more than we trust her. After all, we're still strangers too."

"Fine." He looks down at Aviana and offers her a hand. She hesitates before taking it, allowing him to hoist her off the ground. "It sounds like your situation is almost identical to ours," he says.

"If you don't mind me asking, what's your ability?" she asks K.

He visibly stiffens.

"I have none. But I don't need one, nor do I want one."

That's a bunch of lies. If he doesn't want one, then why was he so curious about mine? I don't say anything, not wanting to add tension.

"Oh, I'm sorry," Aviana says timidly.

"There's nothing to be sorry over," he retorts.

I give a tight-lipped smile to Aviana. "My name is Callista, and this is K. Do you want to join us? We're trying to figure out what's going on and why we all were sent here."

"Are you sure? I don't want to burden you."

Before K can respond, I shake my head. "You aren't a burden. I think it would be good for us to have extra company."

K sighs and nods. "Just make sure to keep up."

We walk back toward the flowing body of water together.

"I can use the birds to find us some shelter," Aviana says.

"Go ahead." I nod at her approvingly, watching as she closes her eyes and takes several steadying breaths. I notice her body visibly relax, and I find myself impressed by her control over her ability.

It doesn't take long before she's refocused on us, pointing us in a direction. "The city continues that way. There might be an open building."

She starts forward, and K and I follow, trudging in our exhaustion. The wind pushes at my loose hair, and I hug Emmy to my chest tightly. It's much colder here than at home.

It doesn't take long for us to be surrounded by the vaguely familiar towering buildings. We try several of them, only to find each of them to be locked.

I let out a frustrated groan. "I guess we have to sleep outside."

K steps backward, the hilt of his blade in his hand. "Not if we force our way in. Stand back."

Aviana and I back away swiftly and watch in shock as K throws his blade directly at a glass door's handle. The glass shatters upon impact, making enough room for K to stick his hand through and unlock the door from the other side.

"That was reckless," I remark, staring at the glass shards lining the ground. *What if he got hurt? We don't have any medical supplies.*

He shrugs, opening the door for us. "Would you rather have slept in the cold?"

"Thank you," Aviana says as she cautiously enters the building.

I give K side-eye as I enter after her, and he keeps his expression neutral.

The building's interior is bland. There are no sofas, only a reception counter and several tables surrounded by tall chairs. Still, it's better than the alternative.

"Thanks for doing that," I say, giving K my most sincere smile. Then I make my way to one of the corners and sit down, placing Emmy on the floor. She doesn't take off this time. When I've settled my position, I take note of the orb bouncing in the air beside me. I almost forgot that it was here. I cringe, bothered by the thought.

Its light spans far enough to briefly illuminate most of the floor. Aviana has made herself a spot beside the reception desk, and K is underneath one of the tables. No one says anything to each other, and I have no desire to break the silence.

Leaning against the wall, I pull out my journal and pen. Emmy curls up beside me, her body gently moving with every breath she takes. I look down at the journal and open it to a fresh page. My hand hesitates above the paper. *There's just so much to say. I don't know where to start.* I flip the page back to the list I made. Then an idea pops in my head. I turn back to the blank page and rewrite my list.

Things That Don't Make Sense.

Eclium
REM
Dr. Isaac
Alina

I then draw a connecting line between Alina, Dr. Isaac, REM, and Eclium. From there, I draw several more lines extending from Eclium and label them Reggie, DETA, The Orb, and Abilities. In small print, I add short descriptions of the significance of each thing. By the time I've finished, I have a clear start of a web illustrating the connections between everything.

Now I just need to figure out why there's a connection. I yawn, overcome with exhaustion. The eerie silence surrounding me seems to echo, not providing any sort of comfort. *I should rest. Who knows what tomorrow will bring.*

I place my journal and pen back in my bag, then remove my jacket and fold it up to use as a pillow. As soon as I lay down my head, I close my eyes, allowing myself to succumb to sleep.

"Sissy, why was Mommy crying?" A small girl tugs on my dress, her eyes wide and filled with worry.

I frown down at her and open my mouth to respond. But no words pass my lips. She continues to pull on my clothes as I try to speak.

"Sissy, why? What's happening?" Her expression becomes more pained, her voice increasing in octave.

I'm overcome with sadness, with the desire to wrap her in my arms. But I can't move. I can't talk. I can't do anything. The girl starts screaming, her voice echoing in the endless shadows. I feel myself torn from her, dragged away as I watch her crumble to the floor in despair.

ELEVEN

M Y EYES SHOOT OPEN, AND I frantically scan my surroundings. Emmy is sleeping on my chest, and Aviana and K haven't moved. There's light pouring in through the glass windows, and my orb is still floating in place next to me. *Nothing has changed. It was all in my head. But who is that girl in my dreams?*

With an unsettling feeling in my chest, I gently lift Emmy from my body and place her on the floor. She emits a meow, seemingly bothered that I disturbed her sleep. My body is incredibly stiff and sore, making it difficult for me to stand. I have to get up slowly, and once I'm settled on my feet, I slide on my jacket and pick up my backpack. Emmy squirms as I place her inside the bag's pocket. The orb follows each movement, making me uncomfortable. *I don't want to deal with this right now.* I close my eyes and am filled with relief when I open them and the orb is no longer in my sight. *Maybe I can just forget about it for a while. At least until I have more answers.*

I catch movement in the corner opposite me and notice Aviana waking up.

"Hey," I whisper.

She pushes herself off the floor and moves to join my side. "I wanted to thank you again for allowing me to join you guys," she says. She looks to me with such a genuine expression that I once again am overcome with shame over my earlier animosity.

Unable to meet her gaze, I focus on a leaf on the floor. "Of course. You're like us."

She half-smiles, then looks over to K. "Should we wake him?"

I nod. "We don't have time to waste."

Aviana shifts uncomfortably on her feet, and I realize she doesn't want to be the one to disturb him.

I sigh. "I'll do it," I say.

She smiles gratefully at me as I near K. He looks strangely peaceful. I tap him with my foot several times, hard enough for him to notice but light enough that it shouldn't hurt. When he wakes, he looks momentarily confused. As soon as his eyes fill with recognition, he sits up and stumbles to his feet.

"Have you been awake for long?" he asks as he follows me back over to Aviana.

"No. We just got up. I don't want to waste any time though. We should head back to the forest. See if we can find anything."

K stops mid-step. "I was thinking about that. Why would there be information in the forest? Shouldn't we investigate the buildings first?"

I pivot to stare at him. "But they're all locked."

"Clearly, not all of them are locked. We were able to find an open one the other night." He moves his arms around, gesturing to our surroundings. "We could even explore this building more. I just think it's too soon to give up on the city."

"It's not giving up," I scoff.

"If I may interrupt," Aviana says hesitantly. "I think K is right. I didn't personally go far in the woods, but I saw a lot through the animals. And all there was were trees."

I stare at her, and when she smiles, I can't find it in myself to be angry. She's right. We haven't explored here enough. It would be stupid to move on so soon. I sigh, crossing my arms. "You're right. I'm sorry."

K looks surprised by my response, his eyebrows raised. "Well then. The door behind the reception desk has a faded sign. I'm unsure what it says though. There might be a staircase or something back there."

I nod, letting him lead Aviana and me to the back of the building.

Just as he guessed, the door opens to a solid-white staircase that seems to extend upward for miles. We wordlessly exchange a look before setting foot on the stairs. After two flights, we're faced with an unlabeled door. Cautiously, I step forward to open it, revealing a large office space. It smells of old air and stale dust. There are dozens upon dozens of desks covered with computers and scattered papers. There's a large, empty meeting room on one side, towering file cabinets on the other. Each wall is lined with large glass windows that illuminate every corner of the space.

"I wonder why whoever worked here left in such a hurry," Aviana remarks.

K huffs. "Whatever happened, it affected everyone around here. None of these places looks like people expected to leave."

"Let's split up, search the area for anything of note we can find," I suggest.

Neither Aviana nor K argues back, each of them taking off in different directions. Aviana heads to the meeting room, and K forges toward the file cabinets.

I walk to the closest desk and sit in the empty office chair. The desk is dark oak, its surface holding a faint stain that resembles the bottom of a mug. I move aside some of the papers, revealing the keyboard connected to the computer monitor. Searching for some sort of on-switch, I drag my fingers across the bottom of the screen. When I feel a slight indentation, I push.

Nothing happens. I try it again, only to get the same result. *There's no power. I won't be able to start it.* I resign myself to searching through the papers instead. My eye catches on a small rectangular card with a picture of an island lit by a sunset. I pick it up, inspecting it. There seems to have once been words on it, but it's unclear what it said. Liquid must have been spilled on it at some point; there's a large mark that has removed half the image. I flip the card in my hand. In scrawled handwriting, one word has been thoroughly crossed through, and beside it, the writing reads "Eclium."

Is this a photo of what Eclium used to look like? As I'm pondering the strange card, my thoughts are interrupted by a loud thump. I jump, peering over to see what the sound came from.

"Sorry," K says, standing off to the side of a fallen filing cabinet. "The handle was jammed. I must have been too aggressive with it."

"Geez, are you okay?" I ask, stepping away from the desk to move toward him.

He raises his arms in front of him as if pushing me away. "I'm fine, don't worry."

"What happened?" Aviana calls, peeking out from the meeting room.

"Nothing. Don't worry about it!" K responds, seemingly frustrated.

I roll my eyes and return to the desk. There isn't any other information of note on any of the papers. Half the sheets are illegible, the other half are only discussing things such as profit margins and other business lingo I don't understand. I find myself disappointed by the lack of information. *This is only one building. And I at least found something.* I go around to the other desks, but none of them contain anything new.

"Did either of you find anything?" I call out, turning toward the meeting room, where Aviana lets out a loud sigh.

"No, nothing about abilities or anything of note," she says.

"Nothing here either. Did you?" K asks, joining my side.

I hold up the card. "Only this card. I think it's a picture of Eclium."

I hand it to him and watch as he observes both sides. "So we're on an island," he says.

Aviana scowls. "DETA teleported us."

"Do you think we should try the other levels?" K asks.

I shake my head. "I have a feeling this is all we're going to find here. We should try another building."

"Alright. Let's get out of here." K nods toward the stairway we came from, then strides forward. He stuffs the card in his pocket.

I speed up to join his side. "Hey! I wanted to hold on to that. I found it."

He side-eyes me. "Fine."

I watch as he grabs the card and hands it to me. I grip it firmly, sliding it into my jacket. *If things go south, I need to be the one with the information.*

"Callista, why do you keep Emmy locked up in your bag?" Aviana asks. "She doesn't like it."

I stop mid-step, looking at Aviana as if she has two heads. "She seems to be used to it to me. It's the only way. I wouldn't want her to run off."

"But she wouldn't run off."

"How do you know that?"

"I can sense it. She doesn't like being trapped on your back all the time."

At this point, K has also stopped, and we both stare at Aviana. I'd almost forgotten that she can feel what animals do

"I …" I say. Still unsettled by the idea of abilities and unsure what to say, I fidget with my backpack strap. *Should I risk it? What if she can't keep up?* But I slowly peel the straps off my shoulders, then open up my backpack. Emmy jumps out, clearly eager to be moving. She lifts her gaze to meet mine, then lets out a small, joyful meow.

"She's happy now," Aviana says quietly.

I don't know if I'll ever get used to this.

"I hope you're right about her not running off. I don't want to have to chase her again," K mutters as he resumes his path to the lobby, with Aviana, Emmy, and me following.

Emmy struggles going down the staircase, her body much too small to make each jump swiftly. I end up having to carry her down, but once we reach the ground floor, I place her back down. I'm surprised when she's able to keep up with us, although I can tell she'll be getting tired quickly.

When the sun has already begun to set, I notice Aviana becoming sluggish. I'm also becoming weaker, my mouth dry and my stomach gurgling. Even K doesn't move smoothly on his feet. Emmy lies down, panting.

"Can you use your ability to find us some food?" I ask with a groan.

K stops, his breath labored. "Callista's right. I don't think we'll be able to go much farther without some food and water."

"I can try." Aviana closes her eyes, furrowing her brow. She seems to be struggling to reach anything, perhaps because we're no longer close to the woods. After several long, drawn-out moments, she stares ahead. "It looks like there are some old residential buildings farther down. I was able to briefly connect with a rat eating something. It could have just been eating out of the trash though."

"I'll take it." I lean over to scoop up Emmy with shaky hands. She doesn't resist, and I'm momentarily filled with worry that she won't be able to handle the lack of sustenance much longer.

K says nothing as he charges forward. I drag my feet behind him. Luckily, the building Aviana mentioned is only a few blocks away. It's just as huge as the rest of the structures, but its walls are concrete instead of glass. There are multiple balconies protruding from it, and the entrance is marked by a faded gilded sign. A few letters are missing, but it isn't difficult to make out the words: Apartment 736. The doors aren't like the ones on the other buildings either. These don't seem to have any locks. There are only two simple rusty handles on the glass frame, one of which K doesn't hesitate to pull on.

The door gives some resistance but eventually swings open with an echoing creak. My stomach groans once again, and I hurry into the building. We're instantly faced with a lobby not unlike the other buildings, except it contains a massive carpeted staircase that extends upward in circles. The room smells faintly of mildew, causing my nose to twitch in disgust.

I stare at the looming staircase. K approaches its base, staring upward. "The rooms must be upstairs, where those balconies are."

"Well, what are we waiting for?" I hold Emmy close to me, her body still moving rapidly with every pant.

K gives me and Aviana a look, then heads up the stairs. I allow Aviana to go ahead of me, earning a grateful smile from her.

As soon as the stairs break off to the first floor, we all nearly sprint for the first door we see. It isn't locked, and it swings open to reveal an extensive dining space, living room, and kitchen. The space is only dimly lit by the window, and when K looks at me expectantly, I groan. Reluctantly, I close my eyes and summon my orb.

An unwelcome jolt of energy travels through me when it appears, lighting the space. I can now make out a hall branching off from the living room, likely leading to more rooms. The air is stale, the floors grimy. On the wall, there's a picture of a little boy holding a baseball bat. Beside it, there's a framed certificate titling someone named Kimmy Jones as the scientist of the year.

A family lived here. And they had to leave. But why? My attention is dragged away from the wall by the sound of the refrigerator and cabinets being swung open. I turn and watch as Aviana and K search for any food they can find.

"There's nothing in the fridge," Aviana says.

I want to comment that it's already obvious there wouldn't be, as anything sitting here would be too old. But I keep my mouth shut.

K tosses a few boxes of some sort of cracker onto the counter. Then he stops, a grin spreading onto his face. "I think I just hit the jackpot." He eagerly pulls down several sets of sealed cans, each with a different image on it. One set contains pictures of various fruits, and the other, meats. My mouth waters at the sight. *There's no way this will be any worse than the food at home.*

He opens one last cabinet, and I'm beyond overjoyed when he takes out four water bottles. Aviana gathers several bowls piled up in the sink and brings them to the dining table. I take one of the water bottles, then go to the table and pour it in a slightly stained bowl for Emmy. Gently placing her down, I allow the small cat to vigorously lap up the liquid.

I then head back to the kitchen to help K bring all the food over to the table. Once the table is full, we each grab a bowl and dig in. I take a box of the crackers, a can full of peaches, and a can of chicken. Popping open the seal, I pour the peaches into my bowl. I expect them to be stuck together, dried up, something like at home. But a rush of orange liquid and cubed fruit pours out instead. I salivate at the sight. I don't hesitate to lift the bowl, pouring the juice and fruit chunks into my mouth. It's delectably sweet, almost as if it was picked just yesterday. I finish it up so quickly that I barely have a moment to enjoy it.

"This is the best meal I've ever had," Aviana comments as she wipes her mouth with her sleeve.

"Same here. I don't even care how old this food is. At least it isn't dried out." I grab the box of crackers and tear it open.

K adds, with food in his mouth, "Why didn't they serve this at the Neighborhood instead of those awful meal kits?"

I don't even wince when his spit flies across the table. I'm too overcome with a rare sense of happiness to care. "Probably because of some hidden agenda, like everything else that goes on there," I comment.

K lets out a grunt of what I assume to be agreement, and Aviana inclines her head. Emmy cries once she has finished her water, so I open the can of chicken and pour half of it in her now empty bowl. Once again, my expectations are surpassed. Rather than being a chunk of dried chicken, the meat is shredded and covered in a creamy sauce.

I grin as Emmy fervently eats, then I serve myself some of the mixture. Although it isn't heated, the meat isn't cold either. The sauce is slightly chunky, but when I lift it to my mouth, I barely notice it. The meat isn't flavorful, but the sauce tastes of cheese and spice. It combines flawlessly with the chicken, creating a balanced burst of flavor and perfectly satiating my hungry stomach.

I finish my meal with a few crackers, all of which are perfectly salted and unlike the dry bread from home. I lean back in my chair, placing a hand on my stomach. I don't know the last time I truly felt full. *I don't think I've ever felt like this.* I can tell the others feel the same. K has gone through two cans of the meat, and he has a faint food stain on his cheek. Aviana lets out a loud belch. She instantly covers her mouth, muttering a sheepish "Excuse me." For some reason, that causes me to laugh. She starts to giggle too, and I even hear K let out a chuckle.

"You know, we still haven't learned anything to explain everything that's happened," Aviana says. "But right now, I don't think I care."

Out of the corner of my eyes, I glare at my orb. "You might be right, Avi, but I do hope we learn more soon." I surprise myself when I call her by the nickname. It feels oddly familiar on my tongue. She doesn't seem to mind, her face shifting into a joyous grin.

Outside the nearby window, there's only a faint bit of sunlight left. The day seems to have gone by so fast. Yet, as Avi said, we don't know anything new that's of significance. The fact makes me antsy, eager to get moving again. I abruptly stand from the table, no longer entranced by the meal before us. "Let's investigate this apartment, then we can stay here for the night."

"But we'll have to stick together. You're our only light source." K stands, his chair screeching against the floor as he pushes it away.

He's right. I exhale and nod. We don't bother cleaning off the table. It's obvious no one lives or comes around here anymore. Together, we head down the hall.

We pick the first door on the right, and I have to shove it with my side to get it to open. Inside is a quaint bedroom with deep-blue walls that have several areas where the paint has begun to peel. There's a small twin-sized bed covered in a blanket with toy trucks on it. Colored blocky letters on the wall spell out the name Kyle.

This must be that little boy's room.

Avi squeezes by me and squats in front of the small bookshelf in the corner of the room. K approaches the child-sized desk stacked with papers and coloring supplies. I fidget with my fingers uneasily. *It feels wrong, being in this child's room, even though it's evident no one lives here anymore.* I never had such a kid-friendly bedroom. I never had toys either. I can tell, just based on the furniture, that this child was loved by his family. *I wonder what that's like. Being a part of a family who loves and supports you unconditionally.*

K and Avi must also be uncomfortable, as they don't touch anything and quickly return to the hall.

"I don't think we'll find anything important in there," Avi says. K nods. "Yeah. Let's look somewhere else."

We wordlessly move to the next door, which reveals another, much larger, bedroom. This one must have belonged to the kid's parents. Although bland, it looks well lived in. The bed is still made, although there are a few stains on the sheets from something lightly dripping from the ceiling.

I approach the desk in the corner and pick up the single piece of paper sitting on it. My eyes travel ravenously over the words, hoping for something that will be of use to us.

To the citizens of Oswia,

A formal address. This paper must be important.

I have unfortunate news. I know our island home consists of some of the brightest technological minds, and we are perfectly safe. The current Climate Crisis War is tragic. Our planet is being destroyed by the very people it permitted life. But there is nothing we can do. Unfortunately, it is too late to save it. This war has created many tragic circumstances. And we are the victim of one such circumstance. I have recently been privy to the information that we are positioned in the middle of a high-flood-risk zone. As the water levels continue to rise, more and more land is being sucked under. And I'm afraid we are next. I have already confirmed that there is no way to stop this. Citizens, we all will have to evacuate. On April 15, 2046, an alert will sound. When you hear this alert, you and your family must drop everything you are doing and head to the docks. There will be several ships waiting there to transport you and your loved ones to safety. I am trying to do everything I can to make this as seamless as possible. As we face this tragedy, we must make sure we stay far away from the conflict. We will not be taking any sides. Our pride is our advanced technology and business opportunities. I will not let that be taken from us. Even if it is destroyed in this terrible flood, we will still have our minds. And with that, we can still thrive. I apologize for any pain this causes you.

Sincerely,
President Min

TWELVE

I READ THE LETTER OVER AND OVER, trying to make sense of the information. I barely notice K and Avi joining my side and taking the letter from my hand to read it.

Avi bites on her lower lip, deep in thought. "Oswia? Is that what Eclium used to be called?"

"It seems so," K says. "They were told to evacuate. But if they knew ahead of time, why does it look like everyone left in such a hurry?"

"You're right, K," I say. "It doesn't add up. There must have been something else that happened." I ponder the letter and its meaning. *This wasn't just a place for people to visit. There was a country here, an entire society thriving on these lands.* "Do you think the flooding occurred sooner than they planned for?"

K looks at me, considering my words. "That would be the most logical conclusion."

"It's kind of sad to think about," Avi says. "There were families here, and they had to just up and leave their entire lives behind because humankind was too greedy."

Avi's words give me pause. "It's kind of like us, in a way. I mean, I chose to leave my home, but I didn't choose to come here." When she looks at me with confusion, I frown. "What's wrong?"

"What do you mean you chose to leave home?"

"How did you even leave the Neighborhood?" I ask her. I look at Avi, then at K. "I thought you two did too. Isn't that how you found DETA? Above a river away from the Neighborhood?"

They exchange a look, and I realize I assumed incorrectly.

"DETA appeared in my neighborhood. Right outside my house. My parents wanted me to pick up our meals, but it took me before I could," K explains.

Avi turns to him with her mouth hanging open. "You're kidding. The exact same thing happened to me." Then she looks back at me, her mouth twitching. "Can you explain?"

I nod slowly, then tell them everything, from my time with Reggie to his sudden departure and us running away together, to me being sent here. Bringing up the past causes me to realize I haven't thought about Reggie in a while. Guilt sinks low in my chest. *He would understand. There has been so much happening. Of course I haven't had the chance to think about him. I still have time to find him.*

When K and Avi don't say anything, I fear they think I'm lying. But my fear is put to rest when Avi places a gentle hand on my shoulder.

"I can tell you cared about him," she says.

"I did," I whisper.

"So, did we all have only one other person our age in our Neighborhood?" K asks. Avi and I nod.

"Wait. What about your sister?" I ask, confused.

He freezes. "She didn't live with me. It's complicated. I don't want to get into it now."

Avi looks between us curiously but doesn't say anything. I bite my lip, deciding not to push the topic.

K shakes his head and refocuses on us. "Then almost everything about our lives was the same, except for how we got here."

He turns to me, an unreadable expression on his face. "Callista, do you think your friend knew about DETA?"

I stare at him, shocked he would even suggest such a thing. "There's no way. DETA must have found us out there. If it can teleport people, I'm sure it has some sort of tracking system as well. Plus, if you two also had a friend, why don't you think they might have set you up? It's all the same."

He doesn't seem convinced but doesn't press the issue. An awkward silence fills the air, only to be broken when Emmy trots into the room. She lets out a small yawn, relaxing my tension.

"Emmy's got the right idea. We should rest up. Who knows what new information we'll find tomorrow," Avi says. Then she stifles her own yawn and stretches out her arms.

"You two can take the bed. I'll sleep on the couch." K gives each of us a nod and then exits the room before either of us can argue.

How can he even see where he's going? As if answering my silent thought, I hear K give a muffled yelp as something hits the floor.

"Are you okay?" I call, not wanting him to be injured, even though I'm mildly irritated with him.

"Fine!" he shouts back.

Avi eyes me hesitantly. "Do you mind sharing? If you want, I can take the floor."

I shake my head. "No, it's fine. I'd rather share than have anyone be forced to sleep on the cold floor again."

Avi shrugs and crawls into the bed. I scoop up Emmy and lie on the opposite side, sliding off my worn sneakers and allowing them to hit the floor. I stare up at my orb, studying it as it floats above my head. *Why me? Why can't you go bother someone else?* It doesn't move, and I feel stupid for thinking it may have the capability to communicate.

Closing my eyes, I push the light away and allow the room to become enclosed in darkness. I lie here stiffly. Struggling to quiet my busy mind, I recall some of my favorite moments with my friend. How we dreamed about our future, how he would hold me close to keep me warm. The memories mellow my roughened heart, putting me at ease. *I'll find you again, Reggie. I'll get my answers and find you so we can finally reach our future together.*

A couple of days pass by, and I still have no explanation for the happenings of Eclium.

Avi, K, and I have been using the apartments as a base camp. We've explored multiple different complexes, but none of them provide any new information. At the very least, they offer comfortable shelter and food. A few of the apartments have also contained old clothes, which I was more than grateful to change into. Today we've decided to branch out from the complexes and try another one of the office buildings.

Even though the sun beats down on us, the chill in the air prevents me from being hot. One of the things I've noticed after being here for almost a week is that even though all the buildings are identical, they seem to be divided into sectors. All the apartment complex buildings are next to each other, and the offices are grouped together as well.

As we round the corner and enter the office sector, I zone out, my mind analyzing the recent events in the hope of finding some sort of explanation. Each day I'm more and more confident that this is some sort of setup. I don't know that whoever placed me and the others here means harm. But this is too strange to be a coincidence. Everything that led up to this point feels connected; I just need to figure out how. My parents have always had secrets. What is the chance that I'd be coincidentally forced into a scenario that's clouded in mystery? I still don't like that I was pushed into this. I'm still frustrated and scared. But I can't deny that it's nice having other people around me, especially ones who come from similar backgrounds.

I'm forced back to the present when a sudden gust of wind passes behind me and a soft tap hits my shoulder. I let out a squeal, stopping and turning only to be faced by a handsome man with a spine-chilling smile. My scream alerts my companions, and K steps in front of me, pushing the man away.

"Can we help you?" K asks in a low growl.

The strange man smiles widely, and goosebumps crowd my arms.

He looks over at me and stares at Aviana. Then he lands his gaze back on K. "You can't help me, but I think I can help you."

"I'm sure you can. Now go." K scoffs and spits at the man's foot.

I'm mildly surprised by K's aggression, but I can't help but be thankful. This man gives me the creeps.

The man clucks his tongue, not backing down. I tense, preparing for another attack. Instead, he pulls out a high-tech device of sorts from his jacket. He taps it a few times, seemingly typing something, and a hologram appears before us with an image of a large building.

"This is Remedy Academy, a place for people like you three," the man says.

K backs away slightly, a look of confusion on his face. My orb is currently in its hiding phase, and it isn't obvious that Avi has any sort of power. K, on the other hand, hasn't shown any sign of being different. I haven't thought much about it, but now I realize it's strange he doesn't. *Yet another inconsistency in this situation*, I think. Then I decide it isn't a priority at the moment and push the thought to the back of my mind.

Our lack of response annoys the man, and he sighs. "My name is Victor Leon. I'm an admin at this Academy, which serves children like you, who have, let's just say, unique abilities."

"We don't know what you're talking about," K snarls.

"Oh? Well, I may be mistaken, but I promise you it will be worth your time to consider my words."

"How can we trust you?" I speak up, and K shoots a glare back at me. I ignore it.

Victor smiles at me and nods. "Very good question. You all can decide if you want to trust me once I show you the Academy. If you don't like it, you can leave. No strings attached."

I contemplate the offer and notice Aviana and K doing the same.

"No thanks," K says. Then he turns and pulls us away. I stop in my tracks, releasing his grasp on me and shooting him a glare.

"He obviously knows something. Maybe we can get some information out of him!" I hiss at the stubborn boy in front of me.

Heated fury seems to wash over him, then he responds. "He acts as if I have an ability, but we don't even know if I do. I don't like that he knows you two have abilities in the first place. Plus, what if he's scamming us and there's no way out? We could be trapped and die."

His very negative attitude isn't unfounded. *He has a point. But this is the strongest lead we've had since arriving here. And I'm desperate to know why I have this stupid orb following me.*

"Look, if he tries to separate the three of us, we'll leave instantly," Aviana chimes in.

"If we get trapped, we'll find a way out together," I say, nodding, even though part of me feels we shouldn't take this deal. I know that not everyone is to be trusted. But at the moment, our ragtag group has nowhere to go. And if I can get some form of an answer, I'll do whatever I need to get it.

"Fine." K reluctantly turns back to Victor and scoffs again. "We'll follow you."

It takes about an hour to arrive at the Academy, and when we do, it's even more massive than the hologram suggested. It's situated way past the office and residential sectors I've become familiar with. Yet it still has its own towering buildings surrounding it that look similar to the ones we left behind. There seems to be one main building with what appears to be hotel rooms or apartments on the sides. About five lines of kids who look to be ages fifteen to eighteen are outside the Academy, seemingly waiting for it to open.

"The opening ceremony starts soon," Victor says. "I have to leave you all now. Just hop into the line, and when the headmaster is ready, follow everyone else inside!"

Before I can ask Victor any more questions, he's gone.

"Well, that's just great," K growls.

"Guess we should get in line, then, and hope to find him and question him later," I say. Then I slowly move toward the crowd. Chills prick at me as soon as I step inside the gate to the Academy, and I make sure to always have sight of Aviana and K.

As we move slowly toward the crowd, I observe everyone around me. They all seem to be normal kids like us. I wonder if they have any powers too. There are around forty people here, and the large crowd makes me nervous.

"I don't understand how there are so many people here when everywhere else is empty," I note.

"Maybe the Academy is newer, so not many people know about it," Avi says. "Or this area has only recently been populated after whatever happened to its former residents."

"It's possible, Aviana, but it's still strange. We have to make sure we're on guard," K says, his expression stern.

"K's right. There are too many potentials at play. Let's just be careful," I comment, keeping my eyes on the people in front of us.

"I just hope this doesn't take long," K mutters.

After we've stood for what seems like hours, the Academy doors finally open. The sun has already started to set, and the skies have turned pink. We follow the crowd, only to be stopped at the door.

"Please place your hand here," a scruffy man in a black uniform commands. He's standing beside a medium-sized device with an indentation shaped like a hand.

I exchange a look with Avi and K, then reluctantly do as the man said. I feel nothing when I touch the cool surface and watch in a mix of awe and fear as a blue light travels across my palm. When it disappears, the man waves me through the door. I pass through nervously and wait for K and Avi on the other side.

"I wonder what that was about," Avi says.

I'm not given a chance to respond as another man ushers us forward. The area is bustling as we take three seats toward the back of some kind of amphitheater. I've never been around so many kids my age, and the nervous energy excites and overwhelms me.

We're some of the last to arrive. Not long after we sit, the doors shut loudly. I sense K tense next to me, and I squeeze his hand. There are men and women in suits spread out along the periphery of the room, watching us. Their eyes make me uneasy. *This is just a test. I need to get information. I may not want my ability, but I do want to understand why I have it.*

We seem to be in a main hall of sorts, as there are stairs on each side of the massive room leading up into hallways and what I assume to be more smaller rooms, possibly classrooms. In front of us is a hall to what could be the cafeteria, and possibly links to tunnels that seem to lead to the apartment buildings. A smell of warm honey envelops the space, which is surprisingly calming, unlike the rest of the atmosphere. K and Aviana are silent beside me, observing the building too.

Eventually, a loud boom of a microphone comes from a balcony between the tops of the stairs, and the lights turn off—except for the ones directly above the speaker. The sound shushes everyone inside the room.

"Welcome, welcome!" An older man is speaking into the microphone. "I'm so glad to see all of these lovely faces in our Academy.

You all are our sixth group of arrivals this semester! I'm sure all of you have many questions, such as why you have your abilities and how you even got here in the first place. All of those will be answered in due time. Today, I would like to encourage you all to consider why you should stay with us. Here at Remedy Academy, we'll provide answers and help controlling your newfound power. We have lovely dorms, a massive cafeteria with a great selection of food, and many activities to fit all your interests!"

Whispers echo around the room, and I look at K, who seems to be fixed on the man. Aviana watches intensely, and I turn back to listen.

"Our only rules here are that you must not be out past curfew, you can't leave the premises, you must wear your uniform, and, most importantly, you must attend your classes. We have all sorts of learning opportunities here, which our other students are currently attending. You can learn how to channel your abilities and maximize your potential. Failure to follow our rules, however, will result in punishment!"

I eye the man with suspicion. Something is telling me that there are hidden rules not mentioned. *Maybe I'm being too judgmental. This could be a good thing. If it isn't, I won't hesitate to run.*

The man continues to talk about what classes they offer, and I tune it out to talk to K. As I tap his shoulder, he turns to look at me. "K, what should we do?" I ask, my voice brimming with concern.

He contemplates my question before responding. "I don't trust this place. I don't. But after thinking about what you said, I think you're right. We could probably get some useful information about what we are and how to get home."

"What if we stay only until we find the information we want, and then we leave?" Aviana suggests.

I think about her words before agreeing that it's our only option. "Alright, let's do it," I say. "We have to make sure we stay together." They both nod in agreement. With a nervous exhale, I turn my attention back to the man speaking.

"Now that all of the formalities are done with, I'm your headmaster, and I would like to welcome all new students to Remedy Academy!"

Clapping sounds echo from all around the room as I take a final look back at the front door before accepting my new fate.

THIRTEEN

*"*M*Y LITTLE SOL, MOMMY AND DADDY can't stay with you. You need to listen to the men. I'm sorry, sweetie."*

The figure before me is dragged away with tears in their eyes, and I watch as it morphs into a familiar person—someone I distinctly recall as my mother.

"Mom, please come back!" I cry, reaching out to my mother, only to be pulled back by a strong arm. Another little girl cries next to me, reaching out for what I now see is my father being dragged away by a man with a bright red R on his shirt. The man pulls out a sharp object, and a wicked grin spreads across his face. My parents try to pull away, and I scream. But no one hears. No one does anything as we're forced to watch the man drive the object down. They stop moving. Then, darkness.

I sit up quickly as I wake, breathing heavily. Shaken and frustrated by the dream, I grab my pillow and toss it angrily to the floor. My breath comes out heavy as I look around. Emmy cries, disturbed by my movement. We were initially told she couldn't stay with us, but Avi managed to convince the guards that Emmy is here to help her train her ability. I place a comforting hand on Emmy, not wanting her to make a bunch of noise. She rubs against my fingers, then curls back up in a ball on top of my pillow. Avi sleeps soundly in her bed, right next to mine. There's another girl in a twin bed next to hers.

The thin cotton sheets are unfamiliar as I roll out of bed, noting the dim light coming through the windows. My brand-new lace nightgown drags on the floor as I walk to the bathroom. I stare at my reflection in front of me in the mirror. *This nightmare felt more real, more substantial than it has ever before. I know it's more than a dream. It's a memory.* My heart sinks as the realization settles in my stomach. None of it makes sense, but I know deep in my gut, with complete certainty, that this much is true.

My real mother and father are dead. I trace the outline of the mirror slowly with my finger as an emptiness crashes over me. *Who were those people I thought were my parents? Why don't I remember my real parents? Or am I going crazy?* I frown as I wonder what else in my life was a lie. I stare at myself in the mirror. The girl who looks back at me looks like a stranger. *I just want answers.* A single tear rolls down my cheek, then another. I don't know how I feel. In this new, strange situation with new friends, I'm more confused than ever. I'm pained to think about what might have happened to my birth parents and why I don't remember them.

Then a terrifying thought hits me. *If my parents weren't real, was my relationship with Reggie real?* I shove the thought away. *No. He was always there for me when my parents weren't.* My chest tightens as I acknowledge how I've been continuously putting other things above finding my best friend. *How could I ever think he was a liar? I hope he understands. If he really is alive, if my hope isn't unfounded, I'll tell him everything.*

Then my mind drifts to K, the enigmatic stranger who has become a sort of friend. I don't like that he isn't with Avi and me. He's not allowed to be in the same dorm as us, so he's instead in the room that connects to the other side of our community bathing area. Avi and I wanted to fight the arrangement, but K insisted we not draw attention to ourselves.

A figure flashes into view in the reflection. I squeal and jump at the sight, but when I turn around, I see that it's only my new roommate, Melissa. I frantically wipe the tears from my face, embarrassed.

She blinks at me and giggles. "Chill, girl, it's just me. I have a muting ability."

I scowl at her as she pushes past me toward the bathing area.

"Then, can you please not use your muting ability when you're walking up to someone?" I hiss after her, not wanting to wake Aviana.

She just shrugs as she walks into the bathing area and shuts the door behind her.

Is this what it's going to be like being around here? And why do I feel like I'm the only one who doesn't want anything to do with this? I sigh and turn back into our bedroom.

Avi is now spread out on her bed, snoring. I don't know how she can sleep so restfully. I wish I could. I notice a sheet of paper sticking out from underneath our door, and I walk over, bending down to pick it up. It's a letter.

Hello, students!

As you may know, today is Monday, which means it's your first day of our Academy! I know you all just arrived yesterday, but we do not hesitate here. Other students have been attending classes for months, and now that you are here, you must as well. Do not fret. Today will be a half day so that you all are able to adjust. You will have lunch and every class after on your schedule. You should have enough uniforms for every person in your dorm sitting on top of your dressers! Remember, uniforms are mandatory. You and the other students who arrived in your recruitment group will be attending classes on similar schedules but broken up into four

My eyes travel down the letter, landing on the schedule written at the bottom.

C1) Breakfast 9:00
C2) Power Basics 10:00
C3) Training I 11:00
C4) Lunch 13:00
C5) REM 14:00
C6) Training II 16:00
C7) Break 18:00
C8) Dinner 20:00
C9) Curfew 21:00

I stare intensely at the name of the fifth class, remembering hearing that word before from my parents. Fear jolts down
my spine. *If my parents knew about this class, then I can reasonably
conclude they must have known about my abilities.* I frown, wishing I
knew the significance of this realization. I notice small writing
below the schedule:

*Note: REM is a solo class that will be daily, even on weekends. Solo
class means that only one student will go daily. You will be notified
when it is your turn.*

My gut twists and my insides turn. For a moment, I contemplate keeping the information to myself, then decide against it.
*I may not be able to trust many people, but K and Avi are like me. Out
of everyone I've ever known, they understand this situation the most*

and are in as much potential danger as I am. But first, I need to write this down.

I scramble over to my bedside drawer, take out my backpack, and remove my journal. I scribble new connecting lines and add descriptions, noting the revelation from my nightmare. Seeing everything on paper does little to ease my nerves. I take a seat on my bed, placing my head in my hands. *How could I be so foolish? Why am I even surprised that their lies go so deep?* I mentally scold myself for caring. *They clearly never loved me. I already knew this. I need to focus on the bigger picture.*

I hear shuffling from the bed behind me and look over to see Aviana waking up. I slowly stand and walk over to the dresser to set down the letter. The clock above reads nine forty-five. I open the cardboard box sitting on top to find three packages and three pairs of white shoes. Each package has a name written on it in dark ink. I take out mine and Avi's, leaving Melissa's in the box. Tossing Avi's package to her, I hold mine and turn to walk into the changing area.

"What's this?" she asks, turning the package over in her hands.

"Uniform, I assume. There's a letter you can read on the dresser."

I continue walking into the changing room connected to the bathroom, then shut the door, clicking the button that activates the magnet lock. After I rip open the plastic package, I pick out the contents, pulling out long navy socks, a frilled navy skirt, and a white blouse top with an *R* embroidered on the shoulder. I tense at the symbol, recalling it from my nightmare. *This place is connected to my parents as well?* My head starts to ache from all the unknowns. I once again find myself longing to be anywhere else, in any other situation but my own. As the image wavers in my mind, I remember a word: *Sol.*

My mother had a special name for me. My earlier sadness resurfaces, and I use all my will to push it back, refocusing on the uniform.

The outfit fits snugly on my body as I braid back my brown hair. I step back into the bedroom area and notice Aviana dressed, pulling her pair of shoes out of the box. I do the same, then sit down on the edge of the mattress to put on the white shoes.

"I read the letter. That REM class seems strange," Avi says.

No kidding. I nod and stay silent, afraid that someone is listening to us.

Once Aviana and I are dressed, we sit on our beds. I stare at the hologram on the wall. It lists our schedule and how long we have until class, along with a small Academy news projection on the corner. I find myself intrigued by the newscast and swipe my finger on the screen to enlarge the picture. As soon as I do, the broadcast's audio emits from the screen. A boy and a girl— both dressed in full uniform—stand in front of a podium, their postures studious.

The girl—looking to be about my age, with flat chestnut hair and bright eyes—proudly speaks with a friendly smile. "Good morning, fellow students. And warmest welcomes to our tenth recruitment group of the semester! We're happy to have you here. My name is Dia, and I'm a flame-bearer."

The boy is nearly a foot shorter than her and seemingly younger too. He speaks next. "My name is Tungsten, and I'm an air-weaver. As you can see, here at Remedy Academy, there are students of many different ages and abilities. We're constantly working to discover more talented people and hope you feel happy to make this your new home."

Dia resumes, tilting her head as she stares head-on. "We know that having an ability can be scary and confusing, but that's what we're here for. Don't hesitate to ask for help if you have any questions or concerns!" She pauses, moving a paper I hadn't previously noticed in front of her.

I stop paying attention when she starts discussing the current weather patterns, as I'm too focused on the pair's appearance.

They look happy. Giddy, almost. Seeing such a genuine display of glee is unfamiliar to me. But I can't deny that it provides some form of comfort. *Maybe this place isn't as bad as I thought.* Then I recall my nightmare and the *R*, which instantly takes me back to my thoughts.

Moments later, Melissa walks out of the bathroom with her ebony hair hugging her face. "Let's go," she says. Then she turns and walks to the door, opens it, and leaves us in her dust.

"She's so kind," I mutter. I hear Aviana chuckle a little.

Not bothering to follow our roommate, we wait outside our door for K to come out of the room next to ours. When the door handle next to us creaks, we move, coming face-to-face with a tan black-haired boy.

"Oh, sorry!" he says as he maneuvers out of our way, then walks down the hall toward the cafeteria. Aviana and I exchange glances before another boy comes out. This one walks with much more confidence. He has short brown hair and caramel eyes. He grins at us as he exits the room, extending a hand to me.

"Hello, my name is Brayden Phillips. I'm a psychokinesi." I shake his hand, observing his face. He then lets go to shake Aviana's hand and steps back. "What are you ladies named?" He stands expectantly, and I freeze. Deep laughter comes from the boy's room, and I turn my attention to it, watching as K comes out with a grin.

"Alright, man, that's enough," K says. He turns to Aviana and me, tilting his head and causing his hair to fall across his forehead. He wears a uniform that's similar to ours, with navy jeans, white shoes, and a white top with a navy tie. The same *R* sits on his shoulder. "Sorry, Callista and Aviana. This guy is a fool."

I raise my eyebrows, surprised at the level of comfort K is exuding. I guess they got to know each other quickly. Maybe too quickly. Regardless, I'm glad to have the change in the atmosphere. It's so different from how it has been the past few days.

"It's fine," I reply. "Brayden, my name is Callista, and I—"
I pause, trying to think of a word for my ability. "I don't know.
I have some light orb, and I think it manipulates electricity. It
kind of confuses me. Honestly, I'd rather not have it."

Brayden shoots me a kind grin, and it settles my nerves.

Avi speaks up. "My name's Aviana, as K said, but you can just
call me Avi for short. I can control animals."

Brayden continues grinning as he listens to her, just as static
comes from above.

"Students, this is your headmaster speaking. Please head to
the cafeteria pronto. You don't want to be late on your first day!"

I stiffen and motion for the others, then we head down the
hall to find the cafeteria.

"So, is everyone here just as lost as I am?" Brayden asks in a
lighthearted way.

I scoff. "You can say that again. This place is unnerving."

No one comments.

"So, where do you all come from?" Aviana questions.

"I came from a Neighborhood," Brayden says. "It's some
strange, kind of messed-up place that's utterly lonely. Well,
almost lonely."

When he responds, I halt, causing everyone else to stop as
well. "You also lived in a Neighborhood?" I ask. We all stare at
one another. *I don't know why I'm surprised. It seems like everyone
with an ability did.*

We take turns describing our former homes in detail. Each
Neighborhood sounds like a cookie-cutter copy of the next, other
than the apparent differences in the barriers surrounding them.
Brayden describes his Neighborhood to be like K's, surrounded
by a wall, which is unlike mine and Avi's, which had gates.

"I really don't like this," I groan. The others murmur agreement.

Aviana adds, "I have so many questions. I hope we get some
answers."

"Brayden, how long ago did you come here?" I ask, looking at him.

"Maybe, like, three or four days? I'm not sure. I didn't see a single soul until I arrived here though."

My mind turns as it processes this new information, trying to form connections. *Every new bit of information makes less and less sense. And each piece further confirms that there must be some greater reason we were all sent here at the same time.*

"It can't be a coincidence that our situations are so eerily similar," K says.

"You're not the only one who thinks that, K," I add. A bell rings, causing me to jump. We all look at each other with unease, wary of our surroundings. "Keep on the lookout. We should talk more about this another time," I say, continuing toward the cafeteria.

The cafeteria is larger than I expected. It has two floors and dozens of tables bustling with students coming in and out from their lunch periods. It smells like a mix of dozens of spices, overwhelming my senses in a pleasant way. As we stand huddled and dumbfounded, a patrolling guard approaches us.

"New students?" she asks in a flat tone. We nod unanimously, then she huffs and says, "This way." Then she directs us toward an empty circular plastic table with a large button in the middle.

I scan the room, unsure where the food is. Before I can ask, she places her hand on the round object. A holographic screen appears above it, displaying dozens of food options. "It's simple," she says. "You place your hand on the button, and it scans your handprint. Then you can pick and customize a meal from the hundreds of choices offered. It will be delivered to you through these spaces in the table. Keep in mind, you can use the button only once per meal. It won't allow you to order extra food." She points out the indentations that I hadn't previously noticed on the table's surface in front of each of the six seats. "Understood?"

We all nod once again. As she retreats to her post, I let out a breath I hadn't realized I'd been holding.

As we all take a seat, Brayden nominates himself to go first. No one argues, and we all watch curiously as he places his palm on the button and the hologram moves to face him. He scrolls through the food choices, and I strain to make out the images from my seat. Almost seconds later, the indentation slides apart, and a plate appears with a steaming piece of what I recognize to be pizza. I've never had it before, but I recall it from old pictures of food offered before the Climate Crisis. I'd always wished the Neighborhood offered it, but I don't imagine it would have tasted very good if they had. Unfamiliar but pleasant smells waft through the air, and my mouth waters.

Brayden stares at the slice for a moment with wide eyes, then lifts it and takes a bite. I lean toward him anxiously. It doesn't look dry at all. Its surface shines with the fresh tomato sauce. He swallows his bite and smiles, and we all relax.

"It's delicious," he says. "I think this is the freshest food I've ever had."

"Can I go next?" I ask, and the others nod. I debate between a sandwich and the same thing Brayden got, then decide on the sandwich. *I want to see just how different it is from the Neighborhood's food.* I see the option to pick a dessert and eagerly press it, selecting a slice of chocolate cake. When my food arrives, I eagerly dig in. I can't deny that it's superb. Rather than tasting dry or powdery, it feels like the ingredients were just made. The meat is juicy, the lettuce and tomatoes crisp, the cheese creamy, and the bread soft and warm, like it just came out of the oven.

No one speaks as we eat our food, too engrossed in the pure bliss of having a true meal for once. I lower my shoulders when I finish, wishing I had more. But when my eyes land on my slice of cake, my posture straightens eagerly. Avi has also just finished her slice of pizza, and she eyes my cake hungrily.

"I should have ordered that too," she says softly.

Somewhat reluctantly, I push the plate between us. "We can share."

Her eyes light up as I split the piece in half, placing one part on her plate. "Thank you," she says.

When I bite into the cake, I'm overwhelmed by the chocolate melting in my mouth. *I could eat like this every day.* I don't know how they send the food so fast or how they have so many options, but it seems so inconsequential in comparison to everything else.

This is delicious.

After lunch, we head to class together, everyone in a lighter mood after enjoying the delicacies. We have to go down several connecting halls until we arrive at the proper classroom. Inside, Melissa and the boy who exited K's room are already waiting. There are three rows of paired desks lined up in front of a blank hologram. I take a seat nervously, looking around for our teacher.

When the next bell rings, a tall and foreboding woman with lengthy black locks strides in.

"Hello, class. My name is Ms. Fern, and you shall call me such."

She takes her place in front of the hologram, touching it with her palm. It comes to life, displaying six blank profiles.

"In my class, you'll be learning how to use your abilities outside the combat setting. Since it's your first day, I want to go through each of your profiles so I can be aware of your power. This information will be shared with your other teachers as well."

She swipes on the screen, selecting the first profile. Then she points to Avi. "State your name and your ability. Then rate your comfort with it so I know how much we need to work on."

Avi stands, smiling uneasily at Ms. Fern. "My name is Aviana. I have the ability to see as an animal and control them. I think I'm pretty comfortable with it, but I'd like to learn more."

Ms. Fern nods and swipes her hand across the hologram. I watch in awe and horror as it fills in with a picture of Avi seemingly taken just now, along with the information she just said. Ms. Fern doesn't waste a moment, motioning for Avi to sit, then pointing at me.

I stand with feigned confidence, staring directly at the hologram instead of Ms. Fern's cold eyes. "I'm Callista." I consider my next words carefully. "I only have a light orb. It seems pretty useless to me. I could do without it." *I don't want to give away all aspects of my ability. Who knows if I'll ever have to use it in self-defense.*

Ms. Fern raises an eyebrow at me but says nothing. She stares at my face for an uncomfortably long moment, then looks away, adding the information to the new profile. *What was that all about?*

I retake my seat, biting on my lower lip. After having Melissa and the strange boy I now know to be Alec talk about themselves, she finally turns to K.

"You."

FOURTEEN

K VISIBLY STIFFENS. *How will she react to him not yet knowing his ability? Or the possibility that he may not have one at all?*

"I don't have an ability," K says. He keeps his tone level, but it doesn't hide the tic in his jaw.

"No ability? That's impossible." Ms. Fern's frown forms deep lines on her face.

"It is possible. I'm living proof."

"Don't talk back to your instructors," the teacher says. K scoffs, earning a glare from her. "It's perfectly fine that you haven't activated your ability yet." She pauses, looking him up and down. "I wouldn't be surprised if you're subconsciously suppressing it."

One look into K's eyes tells me that he wants to spit back another retort but thinks better of it. *Good. We can't already be under tight watch.*

"The good news is that the Academy is the perfect place for you to discover your potential. I'm sure you'll know your talent in no time," Ms. Fern says.

Once all the profiles on the screen are filled, she smiles tightly at us. "For the rest of class, I'll be briefing you on the topics we'll discuss this school year."

Melissa groans, earning a chuckle from Brayden.

It's going to be strange being taught again after so many years.

The rest of class passes quickly, almost too quickly, and before we know it, we arrive at break time. I take the opportunity to pull Avi and K to the side.

"Hey, so I wanted to tell you something. That REM class. My parents mentioned that word before. I wasn't supposed to hear them say it. It must be important to them as well. They made it the passcode to unlock the window in my bedroom. I guess it's possible they didn't know I would gain an ability, but if they knew this much, I wouldn't be surprised if they did." I keep my voice to a low whisper.

"That doesn't make any sense," Aviana says, frowning.

"I never heard my parents say anything about it, but I tuned them out most of the time. I wouldn't be surprised if they also knew about it. Whatever *it* is," K adds.

"It feels like more things are connecting, but at the same time, there are even more possibilities," I say, exasperated and tired of the overwhelming unknowns.

"Should we ask a teacher about it?" Aviana asks, causing K to jump in right after her.

"No way. If Callista's parents knew about it but never told her, then we probably aren't supposed to question it."

I shake my head. "I don't think it's necessarily a bad idea to ask. But at the same time, it could put a target on our backs. Or maybe I'm just overthinking this. All I know is that we need to be cautious."

"We don't know enough now to make any conclusions," K agrees.

I debate telling them about my nightmare, how my parents aren't my birth ones, and how the distinct *R* that matches the one on our uniforms were all in my dreams before I even saw them. But despite my desire to talk about it, the wound is too fresh and unfamiliar. *Maybe after we get settled in here. If there are no obvious signs of danger, I'll tell them. But I should keep some cards to myself. In the greater game, I need to hold on to some information. Even if I can trust them, if anything were to happen, I don't want there to be a risk of this knowledge getting out.*

Stillness stretches between us, broken by Aviana's chipper voice. "Want to spend our break outside? We may be less likely to be heard out there. And it could be nice to have a change of scenery."

I shrug, and K nods. We then make our way to the yard. After sitting in the sun in contemplative silence for some time, I start fidgeting with my shirt. I can tell I'm not the only one feeling antsy, as K is glancing around, and Aviana is bouncing her leg.

"Let's skip dinner. I want to explore more around the Academy, maybe get some more answers," K suggests.

"What if we get caught?" Aviana asks with concern.

"I'm sure it'll be fine," K says. "It's just dinner. Plus, it's not like we're prisoners. We decided to come here of our own free will. They can't control us." He stands, dusting the dirt off his pants. "We should go now, though, before they try and force us anywhere."

I hope he's right. I bite my cheek and stand, causing Avi to follow reluctantly.

We sneak back in through the side door we exited and head toward the dorm hall nearby. The corridor is eerily quiet without the bustling of students, and I notice a shadow at the end of it that I hadn't noticed before. I'm about to mention it when I feel a hand on my arm, twisting me around.

A guard stands in front of me. Another two are behind Avi and K. They all look like they could easily take us in a fight, so I try and stay as pleasant as possible.

"Were you all trying to skip dinner?" the one holding me asks. In unison, we all shake our heads, and the guard smiles. "Good!

I wouldn't want you to starve. You want to be able to learn more about your powers, don't you?" We all nod simultaneously, and they let us go, pushing us toward the cafeteria. "Go on now!"

We quickly shuffle toward the cafeteria as my heart pounds in my chest. *Why did that seem like we were escaped sheep being herded?*

The large, open space greets us, with the welcome smell of food pleasantly flowing in the air. We find the table that Melissa, Brayden, and Alec are sitting at, and we join them.

"Well, I guess we're stuck here," I comment with a broken laugh. Melissa, Alec, and Brayden look at us curiously, not understanding. I stiffen under their attention and force a smile.

"Doesn't the training teacher look like a toad?" Brayden says, breaking the tension. We all giggle, and conversation starts.

"How did you all come to be here?" I ask as I select a pork sandwich from the hologram menu.

"I don't know. It was really sudden," Melissa replies. She plays with the food on her plate and twists her lips in disgust.

"Let me guess. You approached a strange object, and then, poof, you awoke here," Brayden says.

Melissa's eyebrows rise. "How did you know, Brayden?"

"That's what happened to the rest of us." He shrugs, shoving an entire bread roll into his mouth. I find myself admiring how easily he's able to interact with others. He doesn't seem to have an ounce of suspicion toward the other students—something I struggle with. Even if they all seem to be like me and I want to trust them, I know I should be cautious.

"Well, I for one say good riddance. I never liked my home. The only other kid my age was this stuck-up brat who always had her nose in some old textbook or another." Melissa pushes her plate away and leans her elbows on the table.

"Are you going to eat that?" Alec asks, and when she shakes her head, he takes the plate. I look at him curiously, and he seems to shrink back. "What? I'm hungry." His words come out in almost a whisper. Not wanting to make him uncomfortable, I turn back to Melissa.

"That's another thing we all seem to have in common," I say. *And another strange thing. Why were we all practically isolated?* "I can't be the only one who thinks that something maybe—I don't know—darker is going on here," I say, my thoughts too consuming to keep to myself.

Melissa shrugs. "It is weird, but coincidences do happen. I wouldn't worry so much." Her comment ticks me off, and I struggle to keep my irritation to myself.

If only it was that simple. I half-smile. "Yeah, you're probably right. I'm just paranoid."

As we continue eating, we all share a little more about ourselves. My hypothesis that every student here comes from a Neighborhood seems to be true, as the others confirm that they grew up in one. None of us come from the same place, which makes it even stranger. We all saw other kids around but were never allowed to speak with them. Yet we all also had only one other kid our age around. Stranger, we all had to go to yearly appointments with a cause unknown to us. It's almost as if we all lived the same life. *How many Neighborhoods are there? What's the chance that we're all so similar by accident?* Even though our conversations make me more uneasy, I can't deny the certain warmness that covers my body from having so many people around me that I can actually talk to. *Reggie was great company, but I always longed for more.*

"I know there's still a lot for us to figure out, but I could get used to life with the rest of you." Aviana addresses us fondly, earning smiles from everyone at the table. I embrace the moment and look warmly upon what I hope to be my first true group of friends.

The next week arrives quickly after we spend our first week acclimating to the new school environment. I haven't had much time to try and snoop for information. Whenever we have free time, we're closely watched, and I'm always too exhausted by the end of the day to try and think about anything other than sleep. K hasn't shown any sign of his ability, a fact that he pretends to not mind. I, on the other hand, have been grateful that I've yet been called on to use my orb. But this new day brings a sinking feeling in my gut. *Our power basics teacher, Mrs. Brighton, said she would be going in-depth about each of our abilities on a rotation starting this week.*

"I'm glad we'll finally be learning more about why we have these abilities today," Avi comments as we're getting dressed for the day.

I half-smile, sliding on my shoes. "Yeah. I just hope she explains how we got them, not just how to use them."

"Did you ever think that maybe we just won the genetic race?" Melissa says, tossing her shiny black hair into a messy bun.

Avi laughs. "That sure would be nice."

"I know it's not that simple," I reply, my tone more clipped than I intend. Avi and Melissa exchange an uncomfortable glance, likely unsure how to respond. I let out a sigh, standing from my seated position on my bed. "Sorry. I'm just tired of being held back from information."

"I understand, Callista. It's okay. We're all going through this together, remember?" Avi speaks gently, placing a steady hand on my shoulder.

How is she always so kind and collected?

The moment is broken by the dinging of the bell, alerting us it's time to get to class. I tug restlessly on my uniform's collar as the three of us exit to the hall and join K, Alec, and Brayden.

Mrs. Brighton greats us cheerfully at the class door, waving to other passing students on the way to their respective classes.

Then she ushers us inside, and we all take a seat at the large communal table in the center of the room. Her voice booms across the room when she speaks.

"I hope you all are excited for today. There was a slight change of plans. The higher-ups have recommended that, as I delve into each of your abilities this week, I test to see if you have any …" She pauses, seeming unsure what to say. "Mutations, I suppose? Although that makes it sound quite negative." She chuckles, waving her hand in the air as if dismissing the idea. "Anyway, I shuffled all your names around to choose the order we'll be going in. And the lucky person who was picked as our first is …"

My hands clench and unclench nervously under the table as Mrs. Brighton pulls a piece of paper from her pocket.

"Callista!"

I'm unable to stop the groan that escapes me. "Can't someone else go first?" I ask.

"Now, dear. I'm afraid I simply can't do that. Trust me. This will be fun!"

K leans closer to me, whispering in my ear. "I know you don't like having an ability. But just think. You might be able to learn what we want to know faster this way, and then we can leave sooner."

He has a point. I slink back in my chair. "Fine. What is this 'mutation' test?"

"Very good!" Mrs. Brighton chirps. "It's quite simple. For you, since your ability manifests as light, we'll test and see what other forms of light it can create. For example, electricity creates light, so we'll test to see if you have the electrical ability as well."

Her words create knots in my stomach as I recall the broken lights in the diner. *I don't want the teachers to know if I have any other abilities. Hell, I don't even want to know.* Not wanting to give myself away, I plaster a neutral smile on my face.

"How will we do that?" I ask.

Mrs. Brighton stands and goes to her desk to grab a container full of wood and metal. She brings it to the table and places it in front of me. "Everyone else, please stand back. If the test works, I don't want anyone accidentally getting burned or shocked!"

Burned? Shocked? My eyes widen, and I look to Avi and K for solace as they obey Mrs. Brighton's orders. K surprises me by squeezing my shoulder, an action that reassures me slightly.

Once everyone, including Mrs. Brighton, has backed away, I'm told to summon my orb. I hesitate, then I close my eyes to call for the light. I haven't seen it since before arriving at the Academy, not wanting anything to do with it unless absolutely necessary.

"Now what?" I ask, my voice shakier than I'd like.

"Pick up the metal rod and place it on the table."

I do as ordered, lifting the silver metallic cylinder and gently placing it down.

"Now close your eyes and imagine your orb. But instead of seeing it creating light, see it making sparks. Visualize power going into the rod."

I take a breath and close my eyes. Then I pause. *Should I listen and risk giving away my only potential advantage?* I follow Mrs. Brighton's instructions but try and think of anything other than placing electricity in the rod. Yet by telling myself not to think about it, my mind constantly travels to the image my teacher painted. And when I hear startled gasps around the room, I snap open my eyes, shocked by the scene before me.

The rod seems to be vibrating, with small colorful sparks appearing every few seconds. Against my better judgment, I reach out and touch it but feel nothing but a faint warmness. The electricity travels onto my skin, and I discern a buzz throughout my body. I'm overcome with energy, feeling stronger than I ever have before.

"Incredible. Absolutely incredible!" Mrs. Brighton's voice interrupts my focus, and the electricity disappears, along with the pleasant sensations. I continue to stare at my hand, not sure what to think. *Did I really do that?* I'm barely given a chance to cope before Mrs. Brighton is telling me to do the same thing again, but with the wood as I'm imagining fire. I wish I could deny that I'm impressed with myself, with the fact that I have two abilities and may be stronger than everyone else. Absorbed by the moment, I don't hesitate to follow her instructions. I visualize my light orb in the darkness of my mind. Then I picture it as a burst of flame instead of a simple light. It takes a few moments before I'm overwhelmed by heat. It's not painful. And when I open my eyes, the log is nearly crisp, consumed by a bright-orange fire.

This is unbelievable.

I can't keep my burning question to myself. Turning away from the quickly dying flame, I stare doubtfully at Mrs. Brighton. "How is this possible?" I wave my hand around for emphasis. "No one has explained how any of us have abilities."

Avi pipes up. "Yeah, and why did we only get them when we were sent here? Do you know what DETA is?"

I look at her with a slightly annoyed glare. *We shouldn't give them too much information. They could use it against us.*

Mrs. Brighton's expression doesn't show any sign that she recognizes the name DETA. Looking at Avi, she frowns. "Sorry, dear. I don't know what that is." Then she turns to the rest of us, replacing her frown with her typical cheery grin. "As for your other questions, I understand your confusion. I don't have the proper resources to explain the history. But in short, you all have always had your abilities. They're just now being awoken. We've yet to discover how some children have abilities and others don't, but we're currently trying to discover that as we meet more and more students like you."

How were they awoken? And why now? Her words make some sense, yet they still don't explain the connection between REM and my parents. *I guess it's possible that she doesn't know, since she isn't a part of administration.* Reluctantly, I nod.

With a sudden movement, Mrs. Brighton joins my side, clasping her hands around mine. "Callista, I hope you know how wonderful this is. You're a light-, fire-, and electricity-bearer. There are so many opportunities for you, and I'm so proud to be able to teach you!"

I'm uncomfortably warmed by the genuine excitement in her brown eyes. I smile at her nervously, gently pulling my hands from hers. I hate that a part of me is also thrilled by this new discovery. The sensation of creating energy and flame still buzzes inside me, making me antsy. I anxiously rejoin my peers, fidgeting with my fingers.

"That was impressive," Brayden whispers to me.

"Thanks," I mutter back. He shoots me a wink, and I glance away, uneasy.

In the remaining class time, Mrs. Brighton tests Avi, Alec, and Melissa. Much to the disappointment of each of them, none of them possess any other abilities. K stays silent the entire class, never once mentioning anything about what occurred. Avi, for her part, apologizes to me for mentioning DETA, explaining that she thought it would be a good time to ask and that "Mrs. Brighton doesn't seem nefarious."

I avoid eye contact with our teacher as we exit the classroom, swiftly maneuvering the hall. There was some error with assigning our class a training teacher, so we were exempt from the class the first few days. I hoped this would be the case for the remainder of our stay. But this morning on the hologram in our bedroom, Melissa, Avi, and I found out we would be combining with another class. Avi said it's an opportunity to make more friends, but I personally don't see any benefit.

K places his hand over the handle leading into Room 364, our new class. When he opens the door, the room is already full of another class of students and an instructor. Six additional desks have been shoved inside for us, and they're all positioned extremely close together in the back of the classroom. At the front of the class is a massive lectern, likely the professor's. I exchange a worried look with Avi, who also seems somewhat hesitant. The six of us shuffle our way inside, cramming ourselves into the messily placed desks.

"Welcome. You must be my new students. You may call me Mr. Richard. I'm a new professor here at the Academy."

The instructor, a rough, brusque man with a scratchy voice, is speaking to us from the front of the class. Three of the students in front of us turn around in their desks to eye us over. I try to stay calm, still unsure about what we'll be learning in this class.

"I'll be teaching you all to use your abilities in combat situations," Mr. Richard says. "Your profiles have already been transferred to me, and I've studied up on them. This class means business, so slacking off won't be tolerated. We'll start today with basic combat that any ability-bearer should know."

"Why do we need to know how to fight?" K asks, suspicion evident in his voice.

After being attacked that one time, I would like to know basic self-defense. But I don't see why we have to learn it in school.

Mr. Richard's somewhat friendly disposition shifts to more tense almost instantly. "Well, K, you lot are gifted children who are at risk of being taken advantage of. Don't you all want to know how to protect yourself?"

Everyone in the class mutters agreement except for me, K, and a small girl hunched at one of the front desks. I eye her curiously. She seems to be writing something. Her head is down, and her dull blond hair is wrapped around her face.

"Lilac, pay attention when I'm speaking." Mr. Richard places a hand on the girl's desk, and her head shoots up.

I'm unable to make out her expression from the back of the classroom, but I manage to see her nod swiftly. *I wonder what she was writing.*

"Now that that's over with, follow me," Mr. Richard says. "We'll be going to the gym for the rest of class."

As we all shuffle out of the room, I notice a stack of papers and a thick file sitting on Mr. Richard's desk. My eye catches on the file. "Frequently Asked Questions for New Professors," I read. *I wonder what that's about.* I make a mental note of the file, hoping to have a chance to ask about it at another time.

"Come on, Callista!" Melissa calls, and I scurry away to join her.

FIFTEEN

CLASS GOES BY IN A BLUR. The Academy's gym is expansive and foreboding. There's a large tank of water that I presume is meant for water abilities, extremely heavy weights going up to five hundred pounds, various flammable substances, and lots of other various pieces of equipment. There are even two glass doors leading into a gated outdoor field.

I'd hoped, albeit reluctantly, that we would get to experiment with the fascinating items. But Mr. Richard doesn't hesitate. As soon as we arrive, he directs us to a set of locker rooms, where we're told to put on a sportier version of our uniform consisting of a loose tank top and matching shorts.

Once we're all dressed, we're instantly forced into physical drills to test our endurance, resolve, raw strength, and a multitude of other skills that we were told are "necessary."

I rarely have a moment to catch my breath. *The only thing I've learned is how incredibly out of shape I am.* Whenever I try to speak to K, Avi, or the others, Mr. Richard yells at me to stay focused.

When the bell finally rings, I fall to my knees, covered in sweat and grime. As we exit the gym, I notice Lilac split away from the group and head toward the restroom. Curious, I decide to follow her.

"Callista, where are you going?" K calls, stopping at the restroom door.

"I want to wash my face off before lunch!"

I don't bother looking back at him as I quicken my steps to catch up with Lilac. My legs are a little wobbly after all the physical exertion, but I manage to stay on my feet. Swinging open the bathroom door, I head inside, only to stop when I find Lilac standing with her arms crossed.

"Why are you following me?" she asks, her voice laced with suspicion.

I open my mouth to respond, only to realize that I don't have any good reason. "I, uh …" my mind scrambles before finally landing on the memory of what happened at the start of class. "What were you writing in class?"

She scoffs, turning away from me to face the sinks. "I don't see how it's any of your business."

"You're right. It isn't." She eyes me in the mirror, seemingly waiting for me to leave. I scramble for an excuse to get her to talk to me, spitting out, "How about you join me and my friends for lunch?"

Her eyebrows rise, and she shrugs. "I can't make lunch. But I guess I can join you for dinner. I'm not telling you anything though, so don't get any ideas."

I raise my hands defensively. "I won't ask."

I scurry out of the bathroom, mulling over our brief conversation. *There has to be something going on with her. Or am I just being paranoid? If I can get her to trust me, maybe she'll tell me more.*

"Callista, K, can we talk?" Avi asks as we make our way from our dorms to dinner.

K glances around, his eyes landing on Alec, Brayden, and Melissa talking several feet in front of us. "Here?" he asks, his voice unsure.

"Where else? Just be quiet," she responds.

I pull my shower-dampened hair into a messy bun and step closer to them. "What's up, Avi?"

"I was thinking," she starts in a nearly inaudible whisper. "What if we use Emmy to find out more information? Since I can see through animals and she's small, we can use her to sneak around and see things we may not otherwise." When I start to retort, she cuts me off. "We'll be careful, of course, and wouldn't put her in any danger. I promise."

"That's genius," K exclaims.

I stop in the hall, a deep frown crossing over my face. "How will you keep her safe?"

Avi turns to me, her expression soft. "I know we haven't known each other long, but you can trust me. I would never put an animal in danger. Especially not your pet."

K gives me as close as he can get to a sympathetic smile. "Callista, think about it logically. This could be a serious advantage for us."

Not completely convinced, I cross my arms. "What if you get caught?"

"I won't."

I hesitate, starting to move again. *It could make it much easier for us to learn more about the inner workings of the Academy.* My mind drifts to Reggie, recalling the day he introduced me to the small kitten. *She's been through so much with me already. I don't feel right about it, but I know that Avi wouldn't try and hurt her. And if it seems dangerous, I'll make her stop.*

Looking Avi in the eye, I sigh. "Alright. But you have to tell me every time you use her. And as soon as things go south, we stop."

She nods. "This will help us. You'll see. If it makes you feel better, I can practice taking control this week. Then next week, we'll send her out on her first mission."

"I like that plan," I say, reassured.

"Hey! Why are you all so far behind? You're so slow!" Melissa shouts back at us. The three of us increase the speed of our steps to catch up with the others, eager to get to dinner.

We're all already working on our dessert when Lilac finally joins our table. I scoot closer to Avi, allowing the newcomer to sit between me and K.

She seems somewhat disturbed. Her face has dirt smudged on it, and her eyes look tired. "Sorry. I had to make up some work," she says.

"It's no problem," I respond, giving her as friendly a smile as I can muster,

Melissa eyes her curiously. "Why do you look like that?"

"Melissa!" Avi says. Then she turns to Lilac and places a comforting hand on top of hers. "Are you okay?"

Lilac instantly pulls her hand away, frowning. "I'm fine. I was just practicing with my ability."

"What is it?" Brayden chimes in, taking a bite of his brownie.

"I can manipulate plants." Lilac swallows, her eyes coming to life with a sudden vigor. "It may seem lame, but there's a lot more to it. There are so many things you can do with nature, from helping trees grow to manipulating vines …" Her words drift off, then she sinks down in her seat, seemingly embarrassed. Her earlier roughness returns, her expression falling flat. She turns her cool gaze on me. "Anyway. Callista, why were you being so nosy earlier?"

"When did you speak to her?" K asks her, confused.

"She followed me into the bathroom after training," Lilac responds, crossing her arms.

Put off by her changing attitude, I shift in my seat. "You just piqued my curiosity."

"Well." She softens, a strange look crossing over her face. "Thank you for allowing me to join you all for dinner. My roommates are incredibly standoffish. They barely acknowledge my existence."

I find myself even more intrigued by the strange girl and her constantly shifting emotions. "It's nothing. You can sit with us anytime."

"You're one of us now!" Avi says with a cheery grin.

I catch Alec glance at her for a brief moment, then return his gaze to his meal.

"Where do you come from, Lilac?" Brayden asks.

"Brayden, was it?" she replies, and he nods.

We all observe her as she hesitates. *It seems she doesn't like to share much one minute, but then the next, she's open. If she continues this way, I probably can get information out of her.*

"It was a large place. But very empty."

In unison, Melissa and Avi ask, "Was it referred to as a Neighborhood?"

Lilac's eyebrows shoot up, and she seems momentarily startled. Then her tone turns dark. "Who told you that?"

Alec, normally quiet, speaks up. "We're all from Neighborhoods too. I believe every student here may be." He keeps his tone even and calm, and it evidently works to ease Lilac's tension.

"I don't understand ..." Her voice drifts off, and I exhale.

"We don't either," I tell her, keeping my words short and simple, not sure if I should share anything else. *We need to feel her out more before we tell her what we know. Even Brayden, Melissa, and Alec don't know everything.*

The conversation comes to an awkward end when the bell rings, signifying it's time for us to go to bed. Lilac says her goodbyes, and we invite her to join us for meals again.

Exhaustion hits me once we're back in our dorms, and I fling myself onto my bed, jostling Emmy from her nap. I pull her close to me, petting her soft fur. As she purrs, I close my eyes. *With Emmy's help, we'll hopefully learn what we want to know soon. Then we'll be able to leave and forget all of this nonsense.*

A slight chill passes over me when I realize that I'm not as strongly against having an ability as I once was. I can't deny the strange comfort and thrill I felt today, and the thought frightens me. I force it out of my mind, focusing on sleep.

"Sissy! It's your birthday! Wake up!"

I shake a small girl wrapped in blankets. Her head lifts quickly as she blinks up at me with sleep-ridden eyes.

"Sissy?" she says, wiping her face with a closed fist. I can't make out her facial features; her face is a dark shadow. All I can see are short blond locks peeking out from atop her head. It's evident the moment she registers my words. "Can I open my presents now? Can I? Can I?" She throws herself out of bed, running to her door. I chase after her, giggling.

"Mama said she made you your favorite strawberry pancakes for breakfast, and you have to eat first."

"Pancakes!" she screams cheerfully, pulling open her bedroom door and rushing into the hall. We sprint down the stairs, the smell of fresh berries and butter wafting to my nose.

A woman with a gentle expression places two full plates of pancakes in front of each of us once we've sat at the table. She places a kiss on the little girl's head, humming softly. "Happy Birthday, dear. Do you feel like a four-year-old yet?"

The girl bounces up and down, stuffing her mouth full of the fluffy delicacies. "Yes! I'm a big girl now, just like Sissy!"

There's a knock at the door. Something screams at me to tell the woman to not answer it. To beg her to stay. But I can't speak. I watch helplessly as she stops, turns to the noise, and smiles back at me and the girl.

"I'll go answer that. You girls stay here."

The girl continues to eat happily, oblivious. When the woman reaches the door, the scene around me falters, falling into nothingness. The last words I hear, faintly echoing in the distance, are the sounds of two girls begging.

As the next few days of classes go by, I start hearing rumors in the halls. Students speak of other students dropping out of class, or of hollow ghosts roaming the halls after curfew. I barely focus on the chatter.

None of that has anything to do with my goal. It's just baseless chitchat.

It is break time in our third week. The sun is setting in the distant sky, and students bustle about as they make their way to their schedules' places. Mrs. Brighton has officially tested every student, and I'm the only one who possesses multiple abilities. She has made a large show of honoring me as if I'm some unique specimen that everyone should be grateful to have the chance to be in the presence of.

I can't deny that I enjoy the pride my position has given me. At first, I was resistant to the challenges in my training classes. But each time I call to my flame, my light, or my electricity, I'm a bit more comfortable and a little less scared. Where my arms once tensed up each time I activated my skill, I'm now usually able to do so with a steady hand. I still don't have a solid control over it. I still have moments when I'm unsure and wish that none of this had happened. Yet in other ways, I see my abilities as a chance to defend myself if things go south.

K has yet to discover his ability—something I can tell has been weighing on him. He doesn't talk to me or the others much, preferring his own solitary comfort. I've had little time to focus on him, as Avi and I have just begun utilizing Emmy.

I hold the kitten close under my blouse, praying she won't make a sound. Avi is waiting in our dorm for me to send her out. Today is our fifth attempt at directing her. We weren't sure where to send her for information. That is, until I remembered the file I saw on Mr. Richard's desk. There's a ventilation shaft between his room and the hall. Our hope is that there will be some stray papers around that Avi will be able to see through Emmy's eyes. Or even better, that we could somehow get into that file. Our first four attempts were unsuccessful, as I backed out at the last second when I ran into one guard or another, afraid to get caught. But I can sense that we'll have our breakthrough.

Walking as inconspicuously as I can, I weave through groups of students until I finally reach a hall corner with a vent. Using the moving crowd as cover, I bend down and unlatch the ventilation sheath. Gently, I take out my small kitten and place her on the floor.

"Stay safe," I whisper, nudging her forward. Just when she starts to move away from the opening, her body freezes. *Avi must be in control.* I watch as Emmy goes, with somewhat unnatural movement, into the vent and disappears from sight. I close the vent quickly, then fade into the rest of the students as naturally as possible.

I did it. Now it's up to her. It takes every ounce of my willpower to not sprint back to the dorms. I practically throw open the door when I arrive. Avi is on her bed, her eyes closed. She almost looks to be sleeping, but I know better. There's a faint twitch in her fingers every time she uses her ability. Melissa is out of the room, and we told the boys that we're taking a nap. I'm left to wait in elongated silence for Avi to wake.

When her eyes finally flutter open, I jump to my feet. "What happened?" I ask.

"She's at the vent. Hurry and get her before she gets lost."

I don't hesitate for a moment. The halls have fewer students now, so I don't have as much protection. Instead of being stealthy, I move as quickly as I can. None of the guards seem particularly bothered by me, and I hope it's because they think I'm late for class. When I finally reach the vent, I remove its cover in one quick motion.

Emmy comes crawling out, her black fur covered in dust. But other than that, she's unscathed. I scoop her up in my arms, placing kisses all over her small body. She meows, looking dazed. *I should get her back to the dorm quickly.*

Within minutes, I'm back with Avi, and Emmy is eating from her food bowl on the floor. My breath comes out quickly, and I have to take a seat on my bed to calm myself down. Avi comes and takes a seat next to me.

"It was there. The file, I mean. It took me a while to get to it, but as I was looking around, I spotted a way up. I'm glad Emmy's so agile. Otherwise, I wouldn't have been able to get up there. It took several attempts, but I was eventually able to open the file." Avi explains what occurred in one breath.

Then, she meets my eyes, a strange glint of hope forming in her ocean-blue pools. I wait eagerly for her to continue, my nerves on high alert. *This could either be a reason for us to get out of here as soon as possible, or a reason for us to stay longer.*

"I think this place might not be as dangerous as we thought," she says. "There were a lot of words, and most of them were fuzzy. But I made out this much. Apparently, the REM class is just a personal trainer class. It's like our other courses, but more one-on-one. It's supposed to allow us to receive more intentional teaching or something. There's also apparently a common confusion between REM and REHM, since they sound the same. REM, offered at the Academy, is just short for Remedy. REHM stands for Radical Embassy of Housing and Municipals. It's some group that has taken over the former US and promotes a specific set of ways cities should be run. They're apparently trying to branch out to other areas, even Eclium. Maybe that's what you heard your parents talking about. We must not be the only ones who were wondering about these topics, as it was in an explanation to the teachers."

I blink at her several times, absorbing her words. My mind scrambles, somewhat shocked by this new information. *This place isn't dangerous? I still don't understand why I have an ability, or how we got here.* I can't help but feel there's more to all of this. But this information does ease me somewhat. It would be nice if we could settle in for a bit, if only until we get our remaining answers.

"I don't think we should stay here longer than necessary, regardless of what you learned. We can't risk it," I say firmly.

Avi bites her lower lip and slowly nods. "I guess you're right."

"Thank you for keeping Emmy safe, Avi."

"Of course. I promised you." She fidgets with her fingers. "Should we tell K?"

"I think we should. He's been through all of this with us so far. We can trust him." The words come from my mouth easily, yet I find myself doubting. *He's been acting weird lately. I wonder if he'll even talk to me.*

"Do you want to? Or should I?" she asks.

"I will," I say, standing. I give Avi a half-smile as I head through the communal bathroom to the boy's dorm. I knock before opening the door and am surprised to see K alone on his bed.

"Hey," he says, not glancing up from a textbook on his lap.

"I need to share some things with you." When he still doesn't fully acknowledge me, I let out an irritated sigh. "What's been going on lately?"

Finally, he looks up. "Nothing."

I roll my eyes, crossing my arms. "Clearly, something has been. I know you don't like to share, and I'm not a big fan of it either. But we're all we have. If you're going to act all aloof, at least give me a good reason for it."

He raises his eyebrows, and I note a faint frown on his lips. "You wouldn't understand. You're the chosen one, after all."

I take a seat on the edge of his bed, my irritation melting. "Is that what this is about?"

Shrugging, he closes the book and places it on his night-stand. "I don't know. I thought I would have an ability by now. I feel useless."

I study his face with consideration. He seems to be holding something back, something he doesn't want to share. But I know better than to push. He's already been more open than I expected, admitting this much.

With a small smile, I meet his gaze head-on. "You aren't useless, K. You and Avi have both been incredibly valuable in helping me navigate. If you never approached me that day, I would have likely still been alone. And even if I hate to admit it, I can't stand being by myself." I pause, shifting in my position. "As for being the 'chosen one,' this is all scary for me. I didn't ask for any of it. And as you know, I would rather be a nobody. That's why I need you guys."

I realize this is the first time I've had a genuine conversation with K. For once, we aren't arguing or just chatting with a group. It's also the first time I've truly been honest with myself and acknowledged that I enjoy my new company. *I trust K and Avi. We're in the same boat.*

K inclines his head, a strand of his hair falling into his face. "I hadn't considered it that way," he says. "Sorry. I'm … I'm not used to sharing."

"Neither am I. But it seems like there are a lot of new things for us to get used to!"

The tension between us eases as K's expression turns to one of curiosity. "What did you want to tell me?"

"Oh. Avi and I sent out Emmy and found something."

After I explain what I've just learned, K's brow furrows. "So, this Academy isn't as bad as we think? It still doesn't explain a lot of things though."

"That's what I said. Avi is hopeful, but she agreed we shouldn't stay longer than necessary. If it is true, at the very least, we can be a little less on guard. It's better than being in the Neighborhood. We aren't alone here."

"You can say that again," he grumbles, and I chuckle.

"What do you think our next step should be?" I ask.

His expression turns thoughtful, and he purses his lips. "We try and acclimate to life here and behave as other students would. You and Avi should continue to work on becoming skilled with your abilities. If something happens, it will be useful to have something to fight back with. No one will suspect us if we act like everyone else. Then, once we feel we have enough information, we leave."

I consider his words. "Alright," I finally say. "That sounds like a plan."

SIXTEEN

THE NEXT DAY, LILAC FINDS me on my way to my dorm. Her skin seems paler than usual, and wide-framed glasses sit on the bridge of her nose.

"Hey," she says. "Do you want to come over to my dorm? I want to show you something." Her olive-green eyes shimmer with hope.

I raise an eyebrow, confused by her sudden approach. Even though she has been eating with us the past few days, she hasn't said much. The first day she sat with us was the most she ever spoke. Ever since then, she's barely uttered a word.

"Yeah, I guess I can."

She grabs my hand and starts pulling me down the hall. I become increasingly concerned every moment, uneasy with her urgency. When we reach her dorm, she looks both ways, then pushes me inside. She shuts the door behind her when she enters, letting out a sigh of relief.

"Sorry about that. I just wanted to make sure we weren't being followed." Reading my apprehension, she frowns. "I kind of stole something from a kid in my class. Real stuck up. He's a metal-bender. He made this really neat spiral thing, and I couldn't help myself. I wanted to see if I could get vines to grow around it and crush it, like those old snakes did to their prey. You know which ones I'm talking about? Since you're also from a Neighborhood, I assume you've seen the documentaries. Anyway, he wasn't very happy when I took it. Now I think he's out to get me. So I wanted to see if you could take it and hide it until I need it."

She speaks quickly, much like she did during that first meal we had together. When she's finished, she takes a long, deep breath, then looks away bashfully. "I did it again," she whispers almost inaudibly.

My mind spins as I process her rapidly spoken words. *This girl is so strange.* I attempt a smile to make her feel less embarrassed. "Show me," I say.

She looks at me with surprise, then turns and hurriedly moves to one of the beds. I take a moment to observe her dorm. It looks identical to mine, except for its pungent floral scent and the traces of dirt piled in its corners. My nose twitches, the smell a bit too strong for my liking.

She rejoins my side holding a long metal spiral. It's incredibly smooth, but nothing else about it stands out. "This is it," she says. "He doesn't know who you are. If you have it, I can tell him that I never took it. He'll have no proof. I won't get in trouble that way."

"And how long do you want me to hold it?"

She bites her lip. "Just a few days? Until he stops asking about it. When he has moved on, then I'll take it back."

I sigh, reaching out a hand to take the object. "Fine."

"Thank you." Her expression shifts once again, this time to one more apologetic. "I don't have much experience talking to people. So don't take anything I say personally."

She must be warming up to me. I nod. "I'll see you at dinner."

"Yeah, now get out of here!" She pushes me lightly out the door, then closes it when I reach the hall. *I don't understand her.* I toss the spiral between my hands, then hide it under my shirt. When I round the corner on the way to my dorm, I come face-to-face with a boy of about fifteen. His dark skin glows with sweat, and a scowl sits on his face.

"Have you seen a girl around here?" he asks. "Messy hair, nerdy glasses? Looks up to no good?"

This must be the kid Lilac stole from. I feign my most innocent smile. "No, sorry."

He stares at me intensely. It takes every ounce of my willpower to not avert his glare. After several long, excruciating moments, he scoffs. "Whatever," he mumbles, pushing by me.

I feel the spiral slip from my shirt, but I manage to catch it before it hits the ground. *That was close.* I move even faster to my dorm, not wanting to encounter the boy again. When I open my door, I bump into Melissa.

"Ow! Watch where you're going, Callista!" she shrieks.

"I'm so sorry," I say, moving to the side. "Are you okay?"

She takes several breaths before looking at me. "I'm fine. Just be more careful next time. I'll see you at dinner."

Before I can say anything else, she has pushed past me and is halfway down the hall. I wonder where she's going, but my attention is once again snatched away when Brayden taps my shoulder. I jump and turn on him, glaring.

"Were you trying to scare me?" I ask.

"Maybe a little," he jests, a smirk playing at his lips.

I roll my eyes. "Why are you even in my dorm?"

"I heard Melissa shriek and was curious." His eyes travel down to the metal object in my hands. "What's that for?"

"Just something Lilac wanted me to hold on to for her."

He raises an eyebrow but doesn't push. "Well, K and the others are in the library. I was just on my way to meet them. Do you want to come with?"

"Sure, let me put this down first."

Brayden moves aside, allowing me to enter my dorm to place the spiral in my drawer. Once I have, I rejoin him, and we make our way together to the library. The halls around us seem increasingly less unwelcoming each day. As we walk together, the walls glow with the reflection of the evening sunlight. My abilities are present only in the outer edges of my mind, and they're not as threatening as they once were. Smiling to myself, I keep my head forward, determined to learn what I can so I can finally find the freedom I've always craved.

Two weeks go by smoothly, and I adjust to this new lifestyle. Although teachers are somewhat secretive, the lack of anything bad happening makes the Academy seem like a safe place. I still have suspicions, but I can't ignore how being here has helped me hone my abilities and make new connections. K, Brayden, Avi, Melissa, Alec, Lilac, and I have all become closer.

Lilac has slowly opened up after regularly eating with us. She still claims that boy is after her, and she hasn't asked for the spiral back yet. I find the whole situation silly. *Aren't there dozens of things she could use to practice her ability? Why does she want to use a piece of metal so badly?* Regardless of my confusion, I still hold on to the object for her.

After attending for two weeks, we're permitted to leave campus one break per week. This opportunity is extremely welcome, even though there isn't much to do around the city, since most of the buildings are eerily empty. When I asked one of the professors about it, he simply dismissed it. All he said was that the city is functionally like a historic college town, the ones we've read about in our history books. He wouldn't provide any further information.

As a result, we have to find fun by hiking through the forest where I met Aviana. We discovered a small area with a waterfall that we often bring snacks to and chat around. Melissa always utilizes her ability to muffle our speech so we get more privacy, which has been helpful and reassuring. Alec has also shown to be impressive with his memorization. Apparently, his ability is an iron-clad recollection. He has utilized his skill to allow us to know when the guards patrol. Unfortunately, we're not permitted to go far, and there's always a guard within a hundred feet of us.

Through this time together, we've bonded over our shared experiences. The fact that we were all raised identically is still something we've yet to explain. All of us have tried to find out more information, but the adults always dismiss us or give us a half answer. But as days go by and nothing changes, our search becomes less important and isn't at the forefront of our thoughts anymore.

It is dinnertime. As we all order our food, I take note of one person missing from our table.

"Where's Lilac?" I ask.

Avi and Alec exchange a look. Melissa shrugs and says, "Maybe she got tired of eating with us?"

I shake my head. "No, that can't be it. She would have said something. If not out of courtesy, then because I'm holding on to something for her."

"She acted normal in class," Brayden remarks.

Something in my gut doesn't sit right. "We should check in on her."

"I agree with Callista. It doesn't hurt to check." K's support furthers my resolve.

Melissa huffs. "I'm sure everything's fine, but if you all insist, we can ask around tomorrow. Curfew's after dinner, and I personally don't want to find out what happens if you break it."

Brayden and Alec murmur agreement. I look to Avi with pleading eyes, and she nods. I drop the subject, not wanting to start an argument. As soon as dinner is over, I pull Avi and K aside outside our dorms.

"Let's use Emmy," I say. "I know where Lilac's dorm is. They turn the lights out when we're all sleeping, so no one should see her."

"Are you sure?" Avi asks, unconvinced.

"It's our best chance," K comments.

"I'm sure," I reply. "I don't want to risk wasting any time."

"Do you really think something bad happened?" Avi asks.

I look at Avi, her face contorted in worry. "I don't know, but I want to find out."

With that, we make a brisk plan. Working quickly so we can get Emmy in the hall before doors are locked, I draw a brief map of where Lilac's dorm is. K is forced to stay in his own room, separate from us, as to not draw suspicion from the others.

Avi and I set everything up while Melissa showers, not wanting her to comment on our plans. I hand my messily scrawled map to Avi, and she takes a moment to memorize it. As soon as she looks up and gives me a nod, I scoop up Emmy into my arms.

"Please stay safe," I whisper into her fur, placing a kiss on her head. She lets out a soft meow as I put her into the hall, shutting the door so she can't come back into our room. Hearing the shower turn off, I tuck myself into bed. Avi already has her eyes shut. *Now I just have to wait.*

I close my eyes, but my mind doesn't rest. The only sound I hear is Melissa making her way to her bed. When she shuts off our room light, I open my eyes once more. I stare at the ceiling, fidgeting with my fingers under the covers. Time seems to drag on forever. When fatigue starts to set into my body, I hear sheets ruffling nearby.

"Callista!" Avi whispers harshly, making her way to my bedside.

I look frantically to Melissa, only to see she hasn't stirred. Rolling to my side to stand and face Avi, I start to panic. She has a frightened look on her face.

"What happened," I ask, afraid to hear the answer.

"I made it to Lilac's hall. But one of the patrolling guards somehow saw me. I tried to run and met a dead end. I didn't want to make Emmy fight out of fear of how the guard might react. I lost my connection with her after the guard scooped her up. I'm so sorry."

My eyes widen in horror, then pain. Images of Emmy's sweet face appear in my mind, her soft meows echoing in my head. *What are they going to do to her? It's all my fault. I was too quick to act.*

I back away in quick, jerky steps. When I see Avi's face ridden with guilt, I come to a halt. Seeing her despair, I approach her and gently pull her in for a hug.

"It's not your fault. Don't blame yourself." Even if Emmy was my cat, Avi also had her own connection to her. I wouldn't doubt she feels the same gut-wrenching pain I do.

We stay there, finding a strangely familiar sense of comfort in each other's arms. I dismiss the ease we hold each other with as due to our shared sadness. When I finally pull away, Avi's face is twisted.

"What about Lilac?" she asks.

"Tomorrow. We'll look tomorrow. For both of them."

She nods, slowly crawling back over to her bed. I flop onto my bed, lie on my back, and close my eyes. *I'm so sorry, Emmy. I shouldn't have sent you out there. Please be okay.*

I'm not sure if my emotional distress causes me to pass out moments later or if it's my desire to make it to the next morning. Either way, I don't stay awake for long and am soon swept away into a fitful sleep.

During Mr. Richard's fight-training class the next morning, Avi is called to the front office. When I attempt to go with her, figuring I could ask about my cat and Lilac when I'm there, Mr. Richard forces me to stay.

"The administrators only permit one student at a time. And you don't have a pass to skip class," he says.

I manage to refrain from scowling, giving Avi as hopeful a look as I can muster. Once she's left the classroom, I turn to my teacher, deciding to direct my burning question at him.

"Where has Lilac been? She usually eats dinner with me, but she wasn't there last night." I scan the classroom, my gut twisting as I spot the empty seat. "She's not here today either."

K, hearing our conversation, joins my side. Mr. Richard looks unbothered. "She's sick, resting up in the medical ward. Nothing to worry about. Now stop interrupting class time." He turns away, dismissing me with his movement.

"We can ask Rena. She's Lilac's roommate," K whispers.

I sigh, then make my way with him to my desk in the back. Luckily, I sit just behind Rena, so when we all stand to make our way to the gym, I grab her hand and pull her back. K stays away, and I silently thank him. *If we both confront her, she'll be more suspicious.*

"What are you doing?" she squeals, and I shake my head at her.

"Stop making so much noise!" I whisper. "Stay back with me on the way to the gym. We need to talk."

Rena looks at me with distaste but doesn't argue. As we head for the gym, I move close to her, keeping my voice low. "When did you last see Lilac?"

"Oh, so that's what this is about? I'll tell you if you leave me alone."

"Deal."

With a dramatic sigh, she looks off into the distance. "She was called to go to her REM class before dinner yesterday. Haven't seen her since."

My face contorts in shock. "And that doesn't concern you?"

She shrugs. "We got an alert this morning that she's recovering from a sudden fever in the medical ward."

I purse my lips. *How likely is it that she would get sick right after going to REM? What happened in her supposed personal training?*

"Thanks, Rena."

"It's nothing. Now, if you'll excuse me." She pushes past me and joins Indy, her other roommate, farther down the hall.

K joins my side, giving me a knowing look. "Something's off?"

"As always. Apparently, Lilac had her REM class yesterday. Rena hasn't seen her since, but she's said to be in the medical ward. Just like Mr. Richard said."

"Then you should go."

I raise an eyebrow at him. "And ditch class? I don't exactly want to find out what our punishment might be."

"That's why I said *you* should. I'll make an excuse for you."

I consider his idea, nodding. "Thanks. Let's hope she's there."

Without a moment's hesitation, I separate from K and make my way to the medical ward, which is in the front office, where Avi was called. *Maybe I'll be able to see her as well.*

I'm not stopped on my way. When I reach the two cold white doors, I try to stay as calm as possible. Pulling on the handle, I step inside the medical ward and am instantly surrounded by the smell of medicine. My nose twitches in discomfort, unused to the chemical scent.

The walls are barren and cold, and the room is chilly. The nurse is nowhere to be seen. There are six beds lined with blue covers. But all of them are empty. *She's not here.*

A button on the wall is labeled "Sign In." Glancing over my surroundings once more, I move over and push it.

A hologram appears with two columns. The one on the left is labeled "Sign-In," and the one on the right is "Sign Out." I study the names and dates listed carefully. *The most recent student left three days ago. No one has been here since.* A sickening feeling sinks in my gut. *I need to find Avi.*

I nearly sprint to the front office, fear driving me forward. When I see her walking out of the main office doors with tears in her eyes, I skid to a stop. She spots me and starts to sob.

"Callista, I … I'm so sorry," she stutters as she approaches me.

"What happened?" I nearly shout, my heart rate increasing.

"Emmy. She's gone."

I stare at her dumbfounded. "What do you mean she's gone?" My voice escalates even further. Seeing Avi's guilty expression instantly makes me feel bad, so I take a breath in an attempt to calm myself. "Please, Avi, tell me what happened."

She reaches her hand up to wipe her tears. "I will. Just not here. Follow me."

We move down the hall, avoiding the gaze of passing guards. When we reach one of the several restrooms scattered throughout the Academy, Avi pulls me inside. Thankfully, the space is empty, giving us a moment of privacy.

"What happened to Emmy?" I ask again, anxious. I can barely stop myself from grabbing her, my impatience growing each moment.

"I was told that since I 'can't keep control' of Emmy and Emmy has to 'follow curfew too,' she's no longer allowed to live with us. Apparently, they sent her to live with a retired teacher in the apartments outside the Academy. We aren't even allowed to visit."

Her words come out broken, and I can tell she feels the entire situation is her fault. Her eyebrows are pinched, her head low.

My mouth hangs open, no words coming forth. I can barely hold back my desire to cry. Letting out a hard sigh, I close my eyes. "Don't blame yourself. I … We'll get her when we leave this place. Which might be sooner than we think."

She looks at me with confusion, and I explain what I learned about Lilac. Once I've finished, she asks in a shrill voice, "So she just disappeared? And the teachers lied about where she was?"

I nod, biting my lip in uncertainty. "We need to get into her dorm. If we go to class now, I might be able to convince Rena to let us in. Lilac might have left something behind."

She takes several deep breaths. "Good idea."

Having a new goal seems to keep both of us busy so we don't worry about Emmy. Within no time, we're in the hall outside the gym, arriving just as the Academy bell goes off. Avi and I stand as nonchalantly as we can, waiting as students exit the gym. When K comes out, he looks to both of us, and I wave him over.

"No time to explain," I say. "We need to get into Rena's dorm."

He frowns. "She's already there. She left a few minutes ago to pick up a textbook she left behind."

I exhale, becoming increasingly more nervous by the minute. "We'll miss lunch. Let's just hope no one notices."

SEVENTEEN

Knocks hard several times on Rena's door. No one answers. I do the same. Once again to no response.

"Do you think she left already?" Avi asks, a hint of worry in her voice. Neither K nor I reply, instead banging our fists on the door once more. Finally, we hear a voice from inside.

"Geez! I'm coming. Calm down!"

I let out a sigh of relief. When Rena opens her door, her lip curls down. "You again. What do you all want now? I have to get to lunch."

"So do we," I tell her. "But I need to look in your dorm."

Her eyes widen as she crosses her arms. "Hell no. Why would I let you do that?"

I blow out a breath of irritation. "Listen. I think something happened to Lilac. She wasn't in the medical wing. She never was. I just want to check her things."

She looks us over suspiciously. "Ugh. Fine." She points to K. "But he stays. I have a no-boy policy."

K starts to speak, but I place a hand on his arm and give him a hard look. Then I turn back to Rena with a smile. "Thank you, Rena."

She rolls her eyes as she moves to the side and lets Avi and me inside. "Be quick. Her bed's the one closest to the window."

I make haste to Lilac's bedside table as Avi approaches the dresser. When I slide open the drawer, I face a stack of papers. I pick them up, shuffling through them carefully. Each piece has an intricate drawing of different plants with every part labeled. *Was this what she was working on that day in class?* The papers are dated, and I realize they become less refined as the dates progress.

The final sheet at the back of the stack is blank. Seeing its empty surface, I rub the back of my neck. "I don't understand," I mutter.

"Have you found anything?" Avi asks.

I stuff the papers back into the drawer. "No. Just some drawings."

"I haven't found anything either."

"She probably just decided to leave the Academy," Rena says.

But it doesn't look like that. And if she did, why would the teachers lie about it?

Accepting that we won't find anything important here, Avi and I make our way into the hall. I feel defeated and like I've let Lilac down. K looks at me expectantly, and I look down to my feet, shaking my head.

Rena joins us, letting out an exasperated sigh. "If I find out anything, I'll let you know. Now stop worrying so much! It's exhausting to be around." With that, she strides away, her hair swaying behind her.

"I can't believe there's nothing," I say.

"Why would our teachers lie? Why did they have to take Emmy from us? I don't want to be here anymore," Avi cries, and I grab her hand reassuringly.

"They took Emmy?" K asks.

I nod. "I'll fill you in later. Even though I'm worried about her, I at least know she's alive. I'm most concerned about Lilac.

If the teachers claimed she was in the medical wing and she never was, then she must be somewhere we aren't supposed to know about."

"Or it's somewhere we know about, but that place isn't what we thought," K suggests.

I look at him, his silver eyes telling me he's thinking the same as me.

"REM," I say.

"He doesn't know what he's gotten himself into. We had a plan, and now he's let the power get to his head."

A familiar woman and man are speaking to each other as I play with a set of dolls on a wooden floor.

"Innocent people might die, Rosie. It's not safe here any longer."

The conversation is intense. But I can't understand its implications. All I see are my dolls. The chatter is mere background noise. Suddenly, my doll starts to melt. Its pretty face contorts into a painful one, creating a terrifying picture. Then the man and woman are now in front of me, their faces identical to my destroyed doll. I scurry backward, tears pouring down my face. I try and scream, but nothing comes out.

Then everything, everyone, everywhere is melting. And I'm alone.

I sit up quickly, sweat beading on my forehead. The sun is just rising, its light barely illuminating the room.

Avi and Melissa are still sleeping. My hand shakes as I reach over to my nightstand and open my drawer, pulling out my journal. I use my other hand to wipe away the sweat. *Those people. They were the same ones I've seen before. They were my parents. I know it.*

My stomach turns in knots as I scrawl restlessly in my journal. Each word steadies my hand as I collect my thoughts, my feelings, my fears. There are so many connections that I never expected, and so much more I've yet to explain. After I've written everything I can, there are only about a dozen empty sheets left. Once a comfort, the filled pages now leave me with a sour taste in my mouth. *I got too comfortable. I should have known there was more to this place than what those papers claimed.*

Frustrated, I toss my journal to the end of my bed and turn over in my covers. I'm restless. *Are we even safe here?* I find myself missing the familiar comfort of Emmy's soft purrs beside me. The bed feels empty without her, my last piece of normality. I stare up at the ceiling, willing myself not to dwell on my nightmares. I can hear a clock ticking in my mind. *Ticktock. Ticktock. Ticktock.*

Unable to stand myself any longer, I throw the suffocating blankets off my body and make my way to the bathroom. I turn on the shower, desperate to wash away all my thoughts and emotions. *The others will wake up soon. At least I have privacy this way.*

When I'm changing into my uniform after leaving the hot shower, I hear a shriek come from the bedroom. Quickly, I run in, only to see Avi sitting on the bed with fear on her face as she stares at the hologram on our wall. I turn to see what shocked her and notice a message in dark-crimson font:

Aviana #6707: Please meet Professor Cline tomorrow in the cafeteria after lunch so he may escort you to your REM class.

Goosebumps prick my arms, and I rush over to Avi, grabbing her shoulders to look her in the eyes.

"You don't have to go! We can leave today." Tears prick my eyes as I hold her. I've never thought to worry about this class until something happened to Lilac. Now, not knowing if she's safe, I refuse to let anything happen to anyone else I know.

"This would be the easiest way for us to learn more about Lilac." Avi speaks softly, her voice filled with resignation. As I look into her icy-blue eyes, I see her holding back tears. I regain composure just as Melissa walks into the room.

"What's going on here?" she asks, brushing her hair. Before we answer, she notices the hologram and scoffs. "Are you all seriously crying over that? I heard they use that class to teach students 'special skills' or something."

I stare at her, dumbfounded. "Who told you that?"

"A professor." She shrugs and turns just as I speak up again.

"How do you know they weren't lying?"

She rolls her eyes and turns back to us. "Look, I don't. But we might as well assume the best situation because it's not as if we have much of a choice anyway. Plus, have they lied to us yet?"

"Actually, they have," I say. "Lilac wasn't in the medical wing, which is where Mr. Richard said she would be. And the last time she was seen was right before she went to REM."

Melissa's mouth falls open. She seems conflicted, unsure what to say. Her normally snobby attitude fades into a concerned one, and she walks over, touching Avi's shoulder gently. "I'm sure you'll be okay, Avi. Just like I'm sure Lilac's okay. We'll all be here for you when you're done, and life will continue."

Avi sniffles and nods slowly, forcing herself to believe the words.

If only it were that simple.

A distant voice echoes in my head: *It'll be okay, dear.* I push away the whispers and stiffen. Melissa walks away again. Avi and I take a seat on her bed, a silence passing between us.

"We can still leave, you know. It's not too late," I tell her.

"I don't want to. I wouldn't feel right leaving without knowing what happened to Lilac. And the best way to do that is by going to the same place she did."

I wish I could convince her otherwise, but I know she's right. We've tried all our other options. If we want to find out what happened to Lilac, we have to go right to the potential source.

We sit there quietly till the speaker above buzzes and a bell rings. Jumping up, I hurry to finish getting ready. I pull back my hair in a ponytail and glance in the mirror, then I move out into the hall.

Breakfast passes silently after we fill in K and the others about Avi's situation. Brayden, Alec, and Melissa seem concerned, but not to the extent I am. K is hard to read, and I know Avi is worried. Our usually lighthearted conversations are nonexistent.

Training class approaches quickly, and I pay special attention. If it comes to it, I'll fight to help Avi. I'm still not an expert, but I'm much more confident in my abilities than I was when I first arrived here. I also fully believe I can defend myself. I know how to blind someone, electrocute them, and burn them. I haven't practiced on living people, but based off the shape the training dummies are in after I face them, I know I'm a force to be reckoned with.

K's ability still hasn't shown itself, but he manages to hide the fact by blending in with the crowd of students. Initially, I was surprised that the teachers didn't question him. I even once asked the teachers if they knew why, and I was assured that the "Academy is watching" and "K hasn't been awakened."

Suddenly, it's already the end of the day, and we're all sitting together in the dorm common area, comforting Avi about tomorrow.

"Hey, Avi, I don't know what will happen, but we're all here for you," Alec says as he lays his hand on hers and they stare into each other's eyes.

"I have an idea that might cheer you up," Melissa says as she stands, motioning for Brayden to follow.

The rest of us trail after them, only to watch Brayden scare some hall monitors by using his ability to move paintings lining the hall and Melissa mute the sound so the guards are surprised. Before they spot us, we take off, giggling.

As we turn a corner, I pause. Just a few feet away is one of the classrooms with a wide glass window into it. I look at the others with a devious smile. Inside the room, a professor sits at her desk, sorting through papers. I reach my hand out and call toward the lights lining the ceiling. It takes me a moment to focus, but once I do, the lights shut off. We all peer around the corner and watch as the professor stands up, irritated. She goes to the light switch, but it doesn't work. When she goes to the door to leave the room, we all fall back and hold in our laughter.

"We should do this more often," Melissa says.

"No way. We would totally be screwed over," Avi says with a laugh.

Not wanting to get into too much more trouble, we head outside. We find a small clearing near the small school garden and sit. Brayden uses his ability to pluck some flowers, and I watch in awe as they float over toward Avi and land on her lap. Melissa seems mildly perturbed by this but doesn't say anything. It's easy for us to forget for a moment any doubts we have, enjoying the simple moments together.

"We're so lucky we didn't get caught," I say.

The others nod.

"Or maybe we did and they just haven't mentioned it yet," K suggests.

"I sure hope not!" Avi adds with a half-smile. We spend the rest of the break making fun of our professors and other classmates. By the time it's curfew and we have to sleep, Aviana has a wide grin on her face.

Back in the dorm, Avi approaches me. "Callista?" she says.

"Yeah?"

"Thank you for being my friend." She grins at me sadly.

I try to laugh it off and say, "Avi, you aren't dying, so don't act like it."

She doesn't smile, and I sigh. "Let's just go to sleep, alright?"

She slowly nods, and I move over to shut off the light, not bothering to wait for Melissa to come in. I stare at the wall and eventually drift off, thinking of all the ways I may be able to help Avi.

"Aviana, Callista, you two aren't like the other children. They're going to take you from Mommy and Daddy, and you have to promise us you won't forget one another. You may no longer have us as family, but you'll always have each other."

My mother's sweet embrace as she holds a small girl and me in her arms is comforting. But the moment doesn't last long, as she dissipates into dust with a chilling scream.

All that's left is me and the girl, who turns to look at me. I stare into her eyes, blue like mine, and her dirty-blond hair as she follows my mom and turns into dust, saying, "Help me, sissy."

My eyes shoot open, and my breath catches. My heart pounds in my chest faster than it ever has. Everything looks foggy as I scan my surroundings, only to see that I'm alone in my dorm.

Aviana is my sister? How is that possible? I shake my head, not believing it. Yet at the same time, it doesn't seem completely unfathomable. I can still see the blurry remnants of past dreams in which I had a sister. I never saw the girl's face, but something inside me knows it was her.

It was Avi.

Wrapping my head around this new information isn't an easy task. It feels as if some chain has been broken in my own mind, and a new form of affection for the younger girl washes over me. I'm overcome with the sensation of being squeezed, like an intense pressure is pushing on me.

My eye catches on the hologram in front of me. A small note written in delicate lettering sits on it: *Sorry, Callista, but I had to go out early! Catch you at breakfast. ~ Mel*

Next to the note, I realize the schedule shows that lunch is almost over. I blink to see if I read it wrong, but it doesn't change.

Crap, I'm late! Why didn't they wake me? They're taking Avi now!

The sudden urgency snaps me out of my ruminations. I quickly jump out of bed and rush to change into my uniform, not bothering to tie my shoes. As I finally run out of the door, the bell goes off, announcing the end of our lunch period.

As I enter the cafeteria, I bend over, out of breath. It's completely deserted. I stifle a sob. *I want to see my sister. This is too much information to process alone.*

A guard notices me and walks over before I can run off. "You have to talk to the headmaster later due to you missing class. Please ask a guard to take you to his office after dinner. You have permission to leave your meal early so you can make it in a timely manner."

I nod, too afraid and emotionally distraught to argue.

"Also, please wear this wristband so no one questions why you're eating early." He pulls a white band out of his pocket and motions for me to put out my wrist. I oblige warily, and when he clips it onto me, I feel a sharp sting of pain from where it sits. I try to move the band, but it's too tight and doesn't budge.

The guard doesn't give me a chance to ask him any questions. When he sees that his job is done, he walks back to his post, and I turn, deciding it's best for me not to search for Avi alone. I rub my wrist and tighten my lips. *It just pinched my skin.*

I go to class begrudgingly.

The day passes slowly, and I meet up with the others during break time in our dorm. When I see that Aviana isn't there, my stomach churns.

"Maybe she had to do something afterward and couldn't make it here," Melissa says uncertainly.

"I doubt it. Lilac still isn't back. I knew she shouldn't have gone. We should have done more to stop her." My tone is clipped, my resentment over not forcing Avi to leave souring my mood. "K, can we talk for a moment?" I pull him to the side and whisper. "We should tell them everything we know. They all came from Neighborhoods, too, and were brought here without explanation. They deserve to know more."

Much to my surprise, he doesn't argue. "I agree." He moves back to the group, and I follow. He takes a few moments to fill them in on everything, including what I heard about REM from my parents and the strange healer girl from the diner. The others seem a bit more concerned now that I have a story to put behind my worries. I notice Brayden doesn't seem to be completely surprised by the information. This doesn't sit right with me, but I'm unsure if it's just the tension in the moment getting to me. Regardless, I can't ignore his reaction.

"Did you already know about this, Brayden?" I ask, trying not to sound too accusatory.

"What do you mean? I only knew as much as you'd told me before," he responds, slightly defensive.

"Callista, let's just focus on finding Aviana," K says. "I know you're stressed. Don't take it out on Brayden."

I'm appalled by this, having expected him to notice the same thing I did. But when he meets my gaze, I relax. I'm not sure what he's trying to tell me, but I resolve to trust him.

"I have to meet with the headmaster later too," I say.

"Can you ask him what happened to her?" Alec asks quietly.

"I will, but I doubt he'll say anything truthful."

K seems to ponder my words before shaking his head. "I'm going to follow you there."

I grab his hand. "I'll be fine. I don't want you to get in trouble."

Before he can argue, the bell rings, and we all stand. I wave to my friends behind me and head off to the cafeteria alone to quickly eat. They have to wait ten minutes for the first dinner wave before they're allowed to go eat, but I go early as the guard told me to.

The walls seem narrower as I move swiftly, feeling slightly dizzy. I push back the sensation and continue to move toward my destination, not wanting to miss out on my meal. When I arrive at the cafeteria, I scan my Academy ID and use the holographic screen to choose a quick meal of a sandwich and carrots. The system receives the order quickly, and I move to my designated table just as the serving tube connected to the ceiling delivers my food.

As I bite into the sandwich, I'm more nauseous than before and decide not to finish it. *I don't feel good about this.*

I stand, swaying slightly on my feet. I grab the table edge to balance myself before moving toward the trash bin to throw out my barely touched meal.

I walk over to one of the guards lining the cafeteria walls. "I'm scheduled to meet with the headmaster for my, uh, punishment." I stutter slightly and shake my head to snap out of the sick fog I'm in.

The man uses his hologram scanner to pull up my student ID, comparing it to me, then nodding. He then walks off, and I realize he wants me to follow him. When we reach the end of the main hall, he stops and motions for me to do so as well.

"Did you notify any others of this encounter?" He speaks in a low, pronounced whisper.

I freeze and tense, debating if it would be safe to lie. Deciding against it, I frown. "I was not told that I wasn't allowed to share."

In response, the guard simply scowls. "Ah, that idiot!" he says. "Now this will be much more difficult."

Before I even get the chance to ask what he means, I'm overwhelmed with fatigue. My body goes limp as I fall to the floor, hitting it with a thud and blacking out.

EIGHTEEN

THE SHINE OF THE CEILING LIGHT gives me a headache as I open my eyes. When I do, I realize that I'm on a couch in an unfamiliar room.

Startled, I sit up and look around. Two guards stand at each wall, and they don't even look at me as I glance around the room in a panic. Eventually, my eyes land on a desk with an older man behind it. The man notices I've awoken and grins.

"Ah, Callista! Welcome to my office."

I stare at him with bewilderment. "Headmaster?" I cough as my voice comes out hoarse.

He lets out a deep chuckle that sends shivers down my spine. "Sorry about that. Side effect of the drug."

My eyes nearly pop out of my head. "Drug?" I try to shout, but the attempt only results in more pain.

"Yes, I couldn't have you know where my office is located, so I had one of my guards give you a memory-erasing drug."

I struggle to hold back my anger. "When? I never saw that happen."

"Oh, in your band of course! When he put it on you, a micro-scopic needle inside the band injected it into you."

My eyes travel down to the cuff-like item still sitting on my wrist, and my lips curl down. When I look back up, I stare at him in a mix of shock and rage. My anger is momentarily lessened as a question pops in my head.

"Why not just blindfold me?"

"Well, that has a higher risk of you being able to gather information."

I frown. "Why are you telling me this then?"

A smile plays at his lips. "Oh, simply because you'll only remember what I let you. You see, my team has created a tool that lets me selectively delete memories in conjunction with the drug you've been given. All you'll remember is that you got scolded for being late to class."

"But then what's the point? Why tell me this at all?"

He tsks and shakes his head. "Asking questions. You do that a lot, I hear. I understand you want to know more about the REM classes, correct?"

I'm unable to stop myself from perking up. *How did he know?*

He grins. "Well, Callista, if you want to know more, then perhaps you should become one of our head students. It's a new program I want to create, and it will give you access to top-secret information. You would have to do what I say, of course."

"And why would I do that?"

"Everything comes with a cost."

Not sure what to say, I wait.

He starts speaking again, almost as if to himself. "Yes, yes … perhaps she would be a good fit. But for now …" He leans down and presses a button, and my mind fogs up at the same time my eyes shut. Moments later, I open them again and look around in confusion. *Did he just try to wipe my memory? But I can still remember everything.* Not wanting him to know his plan has been foiled, I play the part he wants me to.

"Headmaster, how did I get here? I remember walking here with a guard, but I don't know what happened after that."

He grins, clearly thinking he was successful. I smile inwardly. *He doesn't know that I have my memories.*

"You passed out, but my guards safely brought you here. You must not have eaten enough! It's important that you keep your body healthy."

I nod and fake a perfect student attitude, hoping it doesn't come across too fake. "Yes, sir, I'm sorry. Why did you want to see me?" I tilt my head like a curious puppy. Inside, my stomach twists. *If I slip up, who knows what he'll do.*

"I would like to warn you that if you're late again, you risk suspension."

I frown and feign guilt. "I'm sorry for my absence today. Thank you for letting me know."

He nods in approval of my response. "Very good. Now, any questions?"

I take this opportunity to take a risk and ask about Avi. "What is REM, really? I have two friends who have gone recently and haven't returned."

The question takes him aback, and he shakes his head. "It's only a personal training class. Your friends are likely deep in their work. They'll come back eventually." He fumbles with something on his desk. "I'm afraid I have no more time, so you must leave."

As soon as the words leave his mouth, I'm hoisted away by guards who render me unconscious once more.

This time when I wake up, I'm in the infirmary. The window shows complete darkness outside, and a nurse sleeps at the desk. I stand up slowly, not wanting to wake her up. Tiptoeing out the door, I shut it and exhale. *That was terrifying. And it just confirms that something darker is going on.* I turn to walk to my room, assuming it's past curfew. A finger touches my back, and I turn only to be face-to-face with K.

"Where did you come from?" I whisper.

He shushes me and pulls me into a nearby bathroom. "I awakened my ability! I can control darkness and shadows."

My mouth falls open in astonishment. "How'd you find out? How were you able to awaken it so suddenly?"

His smile falters, and he glances around nervously. "I was following you and the guard who escorted you when you passed out. I needed to know where they were bringing you, but the dim lights around exposed my shadow. I don't know how, but before I knew it, the shadows around seemed to cover me in a blanket of darkness, and I noticed no nearby guards could see me when I tried to get their attention."

He stops, giving me a moment to absorb his words.

"So it was triggered by your desire to be hidden."

"I think so. I followed you all the way to the headmaster's office but didn't manage to get in there with you. Then I kept watching you as they brought you here."

"That's incredible. I'm so—" The sound of footsteps echoing from inside the infirmary interrupts me, and I tense.

Then K grabs my hand. "We need to get out of here," he says.

I barely nod in response as he pulls me down the hallway. Before I know it, we seem to be in a blanket of darkness. I can't see a thing, and I close my eyes briefly to summon my orb as he guides me. The area around me becomes brighter, but I don't see any sign of light. I'm still unable to see my surroundings, as my light seemingly can't break through K's shadows. K moves through the dark easily, and I note that his ability must also allow him some kind of night vision.

As we maneuver through the halls, I hear the guards talking around us, seemingly oblivious to our presence. Eventually, K opens a door, and a gust of cold wind hits me. I become aware that we're no longer inside the Academy. Rather, we're outside in the chill night air. Guards shout around us, but K moves, unfazed. I hear the guards' footsteps retreat to where we came from.

"They must have noticed the door, right?" I ask in a low whisper, resulting in K nodding. We continue to move forward until I stop, forcing K to stop too. "When will you tell me where we're going?" My mind wanders as I think of any place other than our dorm where he could be taking me.

"We're leaving, Callista."

His words send shivers down my spine. I stiffen and step back. As I do, the surrounding shadow fades, and I realize I'm moving out of the reach of his ability.

"I'm not going to leave Avi." I pause and think before speaking more. "Nor would I want to leave Lilac, Alec, Brayden, or Melissa. They need us, I don't know what exactly is going on here, but we can't leave it to them to find out. We don't even know what they've done to Aviana or Lilac."

He frowns and shakes his head. "I agree with you. But we don't have enough information to give us an upper hand. We need to find outside help or get more supplies. Something to give us more of an advantage. We can come back for them."

I process his suggestion, considering his words carefully. "We made a promise to stay together. That promise included Avi. I have a lot to tell you about what happened with the headmaster. I think we may be able to find out more if we stay. Trust me. I do think there's something bad going on. But I want to know why."

Something flickers across his eyes but disappears too soon for me to discern it. "You might be right. But it's too dangerous to stay here, even if the danger is just a potential risk and not a guarantee. I don't want anyone to get hurt. We know what we need to know about our abilities, and everything else isn't important right now. I know you have questions, and I do too. But after all the time I've spent thinking about it, there are too many unknowns here. It would be more logical for us to leave and make a plan for how to get answers another way. We aren't leaving Aviana, Lilac, or the others behind. If we only get one attempt to save them, don't you want to be fully prepared?"

K won't back down. I think he has a good point, and I can't deny that there may be a risk to us staying. I sigh and reluctantly agree. I feel wrong leaving my friends behind as I walk forward into K's shadow. *It's okay. I'm coming back. I won't leave them for long.*

He pushes his shadow away as we approach the extremely tall gate to the school.

"Looks like we have to climb," I mutter.

We step forward and position ourselves on the bars, pushing upward. As soon as we reach the top and lift our legs over the colossal fence, a shock shoots through me, and I fall backward, slamming my head on the hard ground with a loud crack. Another shock shoots K back even farther, and I scream out in pain as my head throbs from the impact. I reach my left hand back and feel a warm, thick liquid coat my fingers. Pain shoots through my right arm as I move my body slightly. I try to move the limb but fail.

The world fades in and out of the darkness around me as time seems to slow. I hear screaming and am unsure if it's from me or the boy lying a few feet from me. Everything is spinning. I can't manage a coherent thought, all my senses frazzled. Footsteps echo around me, increasing my head pain. Shouting occurs as another, much more painful shock shoots through my body, and my consciousness fades away.

"The girl's birth name is Callista Tyra. She was assigned Neighborhood 33, with the headmaster's son as her control. Her ability is light and electricity. Was found out past curfew last week with K Erebus, Neighborhood 38, with Mirena Rose as his control. Each was dosed with a heavy amount of the Recall. They won't remember ever having a problem with this place. They'll still have their memories but no negative feelings toward our Academy, and they'll be unconscious for another week. No, they won't have any memories of the situation either."

The words drift foggily through my mind, coming from behind a faraway door. I try to move closer, to hear more, but my body doesn't move. I'm frozen in place. This seems more real than fake, but I'm unsure why. As my efforts fail, I'm sucked deeper and deeper into darkness.

My head is throbbing when I open my eyes to the bright light shining above me. My nostrils are overwhelmed with the smell of chemicals. As I turn my head to look at my surroundings, a cold sensation comes from my head and right arm. I look over to my arm and notice some sort of marking. It looks to be a burn.

I lift my arm slowly, and a million pricks travel down it. Surprisingly, I don't feel pain. It simply is numb.

Slowly, I sit up in the bed. I look to my side and realize I'm back in the medical infirmary. *Who brought us here?* Another form lies in a separate infirmary bed, and I stand on unsteady feet to walk over and investigate. When I get close enough, I easily identify the rough face of my friend.

"K?" I say in a hushed voice, brushing some stray black hairs out of his face.

Silver eyes flutter open to look at me, and I jump back. He stays silent as he sits up slowly, touching his head in the same way I did. He doesn't seem to be injured anywhere else, and he adjusts to his surroundings quickly. When he stands, grabs my hand, and wraps it in his, I'm startled by his offering of physical touch, my body tensing uncomfortably.

"I'm sorry," he rasps. "I should have known it wouldn't be an easy escape."

I'm moved by his genuine concern.

Somewhat awkwardly, I use my free hand to pat his shoulder. "It isn't your fault."

We stand there in silence for several moments before footsteps come from our left. Quickly, we move back from one another and stare at the nurse who just entered the room.

"Good. You're both awake," she says. "I have to check your vitals, and then you can head to your dorms for break time."

I exchange a glance with K, then speak up. "What day is it? Who brought us here?"

She scribbles something on the notepad in her hand, then she looks back up at me.

"Good questions. Today is April 7, 2124."

My eyes widen as I calculate the amount of time we were passed out. *Just over one week. We must have really been knocked out.*

"You two unfortunately seemed to have been hit by a large object, resulting in your concussions and trauma-induced memory loss. It also caused you to be put in a temporary comatose state. One of our guards found you and brought you here right away."

A lie.

"How'd you know we lost our memory?" K asks.

I hold back my confusion at his question. *He doesn't remember anything? Yet I do? Again?*

The nurse shifts uneasily, then cracks a practiced smile. "Common symptom of having had a concussion, dear. Now, please follow me into the other room so I can check your vital scans."

She doesn't wait for us and walks back into the hall, expecting us to follow. I do so reluctantly, with K trailing. *Did they try and wipe our memories, but it only worked on K? Am I the only one resistant? Just like in the headmaster's office?*

The nurse walks inside a small room a few halls down, and we step inside after her. She shuts the door and motions for us to sit. We comply with her demands as she pulls out an object that seems to be a scanner and hovers it across each of our bodies.

Seconds later, a hologram appears with a picture of each of us. The nurse studies it and nods. "You two are perfectly healthy."

I stop her before she can continue. "Can you explain more about what happened?"

She frowns sympathetically. "You two were found outside next to a piece of the Academy's foundation. It must have not been secured properly and unfortunately fell on top of you both."

I raise my eyebrows and exchange a look with K. *But that isn't what happened.* Not wanting to give myself away, I feign resignation. "I hope you fixed that problem so no one else faces the same fate."

She smiles. "You can be assured that we did. Your uniform should be in your dorm. You're free to leave."

I realize I've been in a nightgown this whole time and flush with embarrassment. Standing, I walk out the door and wait for K in the hall. When he follows me out, he seems distracted. We walk out of the infirmary section of the Academy and head to our dorms silently, not wanting to let anyone hear the conversation we're waiting to have.

NINETEEN

WHEN WE STEP INSIDE MY DORM, I shut the door behind us and exhale. "Do you really not remember anything?"

He looks at me, puzzled. "I can only remember going outside with you. Everything else … it all seems so fuzzy. What that nurse said, it seems right, but also wrong."

I bite my lower lip with hesitation. "K, she lied." I take the chance to fill him in on my conversation with the headmaster and how he tried to alter my memories. "I think the nurse tried to do the same thing. It didn't work for me, but I guess it worked on you. We tried to escape, remember? It wasn't a piece of the foundation. We tried to escape, got electrocuted, then knocked out."

He furrows his brow. "I don't know what to say. I can't remember what happened, even after you explain it. It's like there are missing pieces in my mind that won't let me form the complete picture. Why didn't it work on you?"

Considering his words carefully, I chew on the inside of my cheek. "I want to know the same thing. But I'm confident now. We aren't safe here."

He nods. "Let's change and meet back here after. I'm guessing Alec, Mel, Brayden, and Avi are out somewhere else."

He walks into his dorm from our adjoining bath and common area. I grab my uniform from atop my bed. As I begin to undress, I freeze, and a chill goes down my spine. *What if Avi still hasn't come back this past week? Or Lilac?* I shake away thoughts of the possibility. *I can't think like that now. Not yet. Not until I can take action. The others might know something about it.*

The uniform feels dreadful as I slip it on over my fair skin. It slides easily over my wounded arm. As I'm putting on my shoes, the door handle to the room jiggles. I pause and try to think of who it could be. Realizing that K wouldn't come through the front door if he just went through the common area, nervousness settles over me. But before I even have the chance to freak out, the door opens and Melissa walks in. It takes her a moment to notice me, but when she does, she runs over and hugs me.

"Callista, you're finally back!" I hear slight pain in her voice. "What happened?" Concern fills me as I hug her. She pulls back, and I notice that there are dark bags under her hazel eyes and her usually neat black hair is messily tied back.

"Besides the fact that you just disappeared for an entire week, Aviana and Lilac still haven't returned," she says. "Brayden asked several guards, and they each got increasingly irritated and defensive at the question and its implications. Alec is in the library right now and has been every day past break time, trying to get more information."

The news causes my world to crash down around me, and I well up with emotion. Sweat breaks out on my skin as my eyes shut and senses narrow. *This is all my fault. If I hadn't broken my promise and tried to leave, I might have saved her by now.*

Someone shakes my arm. "Callista!" A familiar voice shouts nearby, snapping me back to reality. I blink open my eyes, looking at K. I watch, motionless and completely silent, as his lips turn down. "Brayden told me. I'm sorry."

I stare at him in disbelief. As I throw my hands in the air, tears spring to my eyes. "That's all? You're just 'sorry'? You don't even want to bother trying to save her?"

He looks conflicted and seems to choose his words carefully. "It's not that I don't. It's just they already tried. There's just no point in wasting our time trying the same things over and over again."

I scoff, and Melissa moves away from me. Fury fills me as I stand. "What did you even do? What did you try?" I shout angrily, my pulse speeding.

"We asked around! Brayden even tried to get his REM class early so that maybe he could see Aviana or find Lilac. That just made them more mad. Nothing has worked. There's only so much we can do without putting ourselves in danger!" Melissa says, her voice rising in volume.

"So you gave up because you're too selfish and only worried about your own life?" I asked. "I know Avi would have done anything to save you all."

Melissa takes several deep breaths, her expression softening. "Please, Callista, there's nothing left to do. We've had to keep our heads down these past few days because more guards have been watching us. It's clear that our curiosity isn't making us look good. We've done our best. At this point, anything else could make one of us end up in an even worse situation."

I shake my head. "Well, that girl is my sister. She's the only other person I believe is alive from my birth family. Not only that, but she's also my friend. So is Lilac. And I won't give up on my friends."

All of them look at me in shock, surprised by my revelation. I storm out the door, ignoring K as he calls after me. I walk down the hall with no particular destination in mind, eventually finding myself on the low floor of the Academy near the bathrooms. As I lean against the wall, my eyes well up with tears, and I sob. *This is pointless. There's no way I can do this alone.*

Desiring to let out my pain, I close my eyes and summon a flame to my hands. When I reopen them, I see the orange curls of fire dancing in my palms. I watch them, falling into a trance-like state until someone coughs nearby. I turn to see Brayden looking at me with a bag slung over his shoulder.

"I can help you," he says.

I raise an eyebrow at him. He motions for me to follow him into the bathroom. I follow him inside uneasily, not sure what he has planned. A million questions flash through my mind as he reaches into his bag and pulls out a small snake. It slithers around his arm, seemingly harmless.

I ask, "What—"

"Aviana has a connection to animals, as you know," he says abruptly. "I believe this snake can help us find her. I discovered it outside and thought that its strong sense of smell could help us."

I raise one eyebrow in question and lift my head to stare into his brown eyes. "I thought she could only control them, not that they can connect to her randomly."

He shakes his head. "Just like a hound, any animal that sniffs something belonging to her can find her location. At least, I suspect as much. It's our only chance."

I look at him suspiciously. "How do you know all of that?"

He shifts uncomfortably, obviously debating how much he should tell me. "I'm afraid I can't tell you right now."

The answer doesn't satisfy my suspicions, but I note that now isn't the time to push the question. *He wants to help. I should trust him. I may not have any other opportunities.*

"What's your plan?" I ask.

"We go back there and convince the others to work with us."

I tense, then I nod slowly in agreement. He places the snake back into his bag, muffling its slithering noise.

"So that's the plan we have so far," I say as I talk to Alec, Melissa, and K.

They process the information, and emotions flash across each face. Melissa is the first to speak, a wide grin forming on her lips.

"I'm totally ready to use my ability on some of those dumb guards. I know I said I didn't want to put us in any more danger, but this plan seems pretty solid. I'm in." Her easy agreement makes me feel a bit of hope.

Alec ponders the situation before speaking up. "I'm in as well. I can use my ability to memorize a map of the Academy so we'll remember what direction to go to find Aviana."

I turn hopefully to K, and he stares into my eyes. Without him, our mission would be nearly impossible, as everyone would see us. I watch as a brief glint of sadness crosses his face and he sighs. "I'll do it."

I grin widely and run over to him, gripping him in a hug. "Thank you!"

He stiffens at the contact but doesn't pull away. Slowly, he lowers his arms and hugs me back.

When I finally let go, Brayden walks in the room and says, "Get ready. We'll leave at midnight."

I can barely stay still as midnight approaches. It seems like years pass before the holographic clock next to me finally hits 00:00.

Jumping out of bed, I hurry to the common area. Melissa is right behind me, and I feel my heart race. K, Alec, and Brayden arrive in the room about the same time we do.

K looks at each one of us before exhaling. "Alright, quick review of the plan. Brayden will open our dorm door and use his ability to knock one of the window plants on the floor, temporarily distracting the guards. Right after he does that, Callista will shut down the electricity. As soon as the lights turn off, I'll cover us with my shadow ability, and Melissa will use her ability to mute our footsteps. Alec and I will stay with the snake in the front, and he'll be using his ability to compare our direction with the map he memorized so we remember where the REM location is. Got it?"

We nod in unison, then Brayden breaks off to take our first step. We watch him as he creaks open the door and reaches out a single palm, flicking his wrist quickly. Seconds later, a crash sounds, and I run over to the door as he moves away. I stare out into the hall and close my eyes briefly, pushing my ability out. The sound of glass breaking comes from the ceiling as the light bulbs shatter. I exchange a glance with Melissa as she whispers the single word that activates her ability.

"Silence."

As the word escapes her mouth, K swipes out his arms, and darkness completely covers us. Alec and K run to the front of our group and walk out the door with the snake. It moves swiftly, although we're still faster. The rest of us follow closely behind, and I let out a sigh of relief when I can't hear our footsteps against the hallway floor.

During private practice sessions they've apparently been having without the rest of us, Brayden discovered a way for K to allow another person to see while inside his ability. For our plan to work more smoothly, K gave this power to Alec.

Our movements are fast as we follow the snake. I hold on to my ability in case I need to use it against anyone. I'm unsure of what direction we move in, as it seems we're turning down halls every minute. Adrenaline allows us to move quickly, and soon enough, we reach a set of stairs. Carefully, I feel with my feet for each step as we move up. Once at the top, the pace quickens again until we eventually reach a hard stop.

"It's just a wall with a coded lock," K mutters.

I run my hands through my hair, racking my brain for any potential code.

"What's the headmaster's last name?" Melissa asks in a hushed whisper.

We all shrug except for Brayden, who speaks up. "It's Gray." The word rings a bell, and I try to remember where I've heard it. Then I freeze. *That's Reginald's last name.*

"What does that have to do with anything?" K questions.

"People often use their child's name or birthday as a code," Alec says.

Brayden squints, then looks between us eagerly. "I think he has a son named Reginald. I heard one of the guards talking about him just last week."

I freeze again, and a chill travels up my spine. "Reginald? Reginald Gray?" My voice comes out in a choked whisper as a wave of emotions travels over me. *I've been so preoccupied that I totally forgot about him once again. How could I be so thoughtless?*

The others look at each other. Brayden nods, turning to look at me, and says, "That must be his name." He looks back toward our group. "Now, do any of you know his birthday?"

A thousand thoughts rush through my mind as I shake my head in denial. *It's just a coincidence. My friend would never be involved in something like this.*

K shoots me a glance and frowns. "Callista, didn't you tell me about a boy named Reginald you were friends with before coming here?"

I look up and narrow my eyes at him. "Yes, but it must just be a coincidence. The Reggie I knew wouldn't ever be involved with this place."

The others exchange glances. Then Melissa speaks up. "It could be a coincidence, but why don't we try?"

Alec shakes his head. "We might only get one chance before the guards are notified."

"Well, do we have any better ideas?" K asks.

No one speaks up. I exhale. "His birthday is September 5, 2106."

As Alec types in the code, I find myself hoping it doesn't work. But when the final number goes in, the red glow from the keypad turns green. I hear the wall start to slide open. K looks back at me with a sympathetic expression, then he moves through the door.

Time seems to stop as I rack my brain. *He probably doesn't know his dad is the headmaster. That must be it. It's just an awful coincidence, nothing more.* The answer provides temporary satisfaction for my rising emotions as I follow the rest through the door.

"There's a long hall with several branches lined with doors," K reports to the rest of us. "No guards in sight currently. I'm going to lower the effectiveness of my ability so you all can see a bit more."

The darkness surrounding us becomes a bit more transparent, and I notice the doors he was mentioning. The snake turns down the hall to the right, and we follow it. I notice small holographic plates next to each of the steel doors. Each plate lists a different name, along with a description of some kind of ability and a button for more information.

"Whose names do you think these are?" Melissa asks quietly.

I shrug, as no one else responds, and we continue to follow the snake. The hall goes on for ages, and I wonder if it even has an end. K and Alec come to an abrupt stop in front of one of the doors. It's open, but I can't see inside.

"There's a holographic plate. Lilac was here," K says.

My heart starts to race. "Do you see her?" I whisper eagerly.

Alec replies shakily, "The … The door's just open. The room is empty."

My heart drops. "Is there anything else on the plate?"

"Yes. Come closer. You might be able to make it out," K suggests.

Melissa, Brayden, and I inch closer to K and Alec, and we're just barely able to read the text on the plate.

Lilac Kent, 16
AB: Plant Manipulation
Percent Extracted: COMPLETE

"What does that mean?" Melissa asks, voicing the question on all our minds.

Brayden exhales. "It can't be good."

"We need to find Avi. Now. If Lilac is already gone, then Avi ..." My words drift off, my heart breaking at the implication. *If something has happened to her, it's my fault.* Luckily, no one needs any convincing, and none of us hesitates to run farther down the hall.

The snake eventually stops, hissing in place.

"She's here," Alec mutters.

I turn and read the holographic plate next to the door.

Aviana Tyra, 15
AB: Animal Control
Percent Extracted: 75
[MORE INFO]

"What the hell does 'percent extracted' mean?" I ask, louder than I meant to.

My question is answered with shushing, then Brayden points out another keypad next to the door. "They most likely wouldn't use the same code twice," he says.

"Maybe they use her student ID. When she showed me the message they left her, it was included, marking its importance," Alec replies.

"None of us know it though, right?" I ask.

Alec grins and points to his head. "I took note of it when I went through the information they gave her." Moving forward, he reaches down to the keypad and types in 6707. He presses the final number, then the Enter key. An unlocking sound emits from the steel door. It slides open slowly, and a foul-smelling gust of stale air escapes the room.

K dissipates his shadow so we're all able to see inside, then we all walk in.

The door shuts behind us. We're faced with bright lights in a small room. It takes a few moments for our eyes to adjust, and when mine do, I scream in shock.

My eyes go wide as I stare at Aviana suspended in the air with thousands of small tubes connected to her body. She's unconscious, and the clear tubes seem to be separated into two groups—one carrying out her blood and the other carrying out a fluorescent substance.

A beep sounds from a screen in the corner of the room, and I look to see a progress bar move from 75 percent to 76 percent.

I stare at Avi, nearly lifeless and pale. I'm petrified as I watch my sister hang in her near-death state.

⚶

TWENTY

THERE'S A TINY DESK IN THE corner with a notepad and some other objects placed on top. A large, wide vent is positioned almost directly above Avi. The snake now curls idly in the corner of the room. I start to move closer to Avi, my hands trembling. Before I can get too close, K reaches out a hand and stops me. I look at him, my jaw clenched.

"We need to turn off the machines somehow before we can free her," he says.

Brayden and Alec search the room for an off switch, and Melissa stands in shock at the doorway. I feel hollowed out as I look at my newfound sister, pale and lifeless. I hear a beeping come from my right, and I exhale a slight sigh of relief when I notice a heart monitor.

She's still alive. The thought brings little comfort, and I recall the percentage listed outside. Putting two and two together, I realize they must be extracting some part of her through the strange tubes of liquid.

"We'll need to carry her out. She's on her last strings of life," I say as I look at the heart monitor, watching it move slowly along with her breathing patterns.

Alec gasps, and I turn to see him looking at an electric box on the wall. "Here," he says.

Before any of us can question it, he opens the box and flips the switches inside. The lights flicker above us, then all the power in the room shuts off. I will my light to appear, allowing us to see.

We walk over to Avi and debate how we can disconnect the tubes from her. Melissa points out an instrument lying on the desk, and Brayden volunteers to use it. We find gauze in the cabinet of the desk and prepare to wrap up any potential wounds that occur. Then we get to work.

The process of removing the many small tubes inside Avi is gruesome. Each of the thin cords seems to hold nearly micro-scopic wires inside it, which extend throughout her skin like a spiderweb. As Brayden removes each one, the tendrils retract back into the tube with an eerie clicking noise. It's the most terrifying sight I've ever seen, and it takes all my willpower to not throw up. I can't imagine the pain that Avi must feel.

Once all the tubes are removed, the small entry sites gush out trails of blood. We manage to bind her wounds to stem the bleeding, but her skin is so pale that it's nearly translucent, and her breathing is shallow.

Just as I think we might be able to get out without trouble, I notice a flashing red light coming from where the tubes retracted to. Before I can point it out, alarms start blaring. The sound of falling metal echoes, and when I turn to the door, impenetrable metal bars now block it.

Over the alarm, a robotic voice shouts. "BREACH IN 1915! BREACH IN 1915!"

"Shit!" Brayden mutters.

I look around in a panic.

"Guards are probably on the way! We need to get out fast!" K calls over the increasingly loud beeping.

"The vent!" Melissa yells, and I look up.

I push my light out further and squint. "There are screws holding it in place, and we can't reach it!" I cry, defeated. The beeping absorbs my thoughts and makes my heart pulse harder. I find my focus drifting off, snapping back only when K speaks to me.

"Hey," he says. "Brayden might be able to unscrew it. It's going to be okay."

I take a deep breath and nod.

"We can use the straps from the device as a holster to lift Avi up into the vent," Alec says, holding two thick bands. As our thrown-together plan starts to form, what sounds like hundreds of footsteps echo down the hall. We all exchange a look and get to work.

Brayden looks up, focused on the screws. It seems like nothing is happening at first, but then a clink sounds as the first screw hits the hard floor. A more hopeful energy passes through me, and seemingly everyone else as well. Brayden removes the last dozen screws even faster, then gently lowers the vent down.

Alec and Melissa have secured the straps around Avi's body. The vent opening is at least six feet up, causing us to have to move the desk closer to it. We decide that since K is the tallest, he'll stand on the desk. As he climbs on top of it, the footsteps that have continued to echo for the past few moments stop, along with the alarm and voice. This takes us all aback, and I look at the door nervously. Nothing happens for several moments. Then there's a loud screeching noise, and sparks fly from the other side of the bars.

"They must have completely shut the door, and now they're trying to reopen it! We have to go!" Alec says, motioning for K to continue. Melissa climbs the desk next, being the lightest. K then hoists her up onto his shoulders, allowing her to reach the opening. She doesn't move for a few seconds too long.

"Melissa! Go! We don't have time to spare!" I cry out. When I look frantically back at the door, I see a clear line where it starts to separate from the wall. *There's no way we can make this. There isn't enough time!*

Luckily, my words seem to motivate her. As soon as she's in the vent, she disappears from sight. Even though I'm the second lightest, I must go after everyone else, as I'm the only current light source. It would take too long to turn on the power. The door falls down just as Alec pulls himself up.

"Stop what you're doing now!" a guard shouts. We're now separated only by the bars, and we have to speed up. I look frantically between my friends and the guards, attempting to ignore them as they work on the thick metal between us. In only a few minutes, they'll be in here.

Brayden and K work together to lift Avi onto the desk, then they hand the straps secured around her to Melissa and Alec. I keep my back turned to the commotion at the door even as I'm yelled at by the people outside it.

It takes longer than I'd like for Avi to be securely in the vent and out of the way. As soon as she's out of sight, Melissa helps Brayden up. When I look back to see the guard's progress on the door, my heart drops. There are only three bars left to cut through.

"We need to go! Now!" I shout, scurrying up onto the desk. K exchanges a worried look with me, then raises his arms. Melissa and Brayden each take one, and, by some miracle, they're able to lift K just enough to where he can pull himself the rest of the way. I take another look at the door, only to see the final bar being cut.

"Jump! We'll get you!" K shouts as the strap that was around Avi hangs down. I take a glance at the reptile in the corner. "Leave it!" he yells.

Not having enough time to worry about the creature or the security of the strap all by itself, I jump. I hold on to the strap with all my might as my friends pull me up. The strap looks thinner by the second.

A loud clang echoes across the room as the guards burst inside. "Come down right now!" one of them yells.

I can't see them, but I imagine they're approaching me. As soon as my fingertips reach the edge of the vent opening, K grabs my shirt and hoists me up, along with help from Brayden. They make room for me in the wide opening as something quick and metal hits where I was just moments ago.

We all creep farther into the vent system, following the straight path. We move extremely slowly, as we have to drag Avi with us. Once we can no longer hear the guards' voices, I slink against the side. My neck already hurts from crawling for so long, and my heart is still racing. My light still shines around us, allowing us to see several different paths. The vent, although wide, fits only two people side by side.

"Where do we go now?" Melissa asks in a whisper.

Silence.

"We need to get Avi back to the dorms," I say.

Alec responds, "What if they come for us there?"

"They shouldn't. At least not right away," K remarks. "Those guards weren't the same ones we see in the halls. It will take them some time to identify us."

Brayden questions, "Alec, can't you try and use your knowledge of the map of the school and figure something out?"

"I suppose. I just need a moment." And with that, Alec leans his head back and closes his eyes. The silence is deafening as we wait for what feels like years for him to direct us. When he finally looks up, we exhale in relief. "I think I know where to go, or at least how to get as close as possible to the dorms." He points to a vent across from us. "If we just continue down here, after only a few turns, we should arrive."

Melissa sits up from her slouched position and says, "Let's get going."

Brayden sighs, then he and K grab the one still intact strap around Avi. Alec goes first, and the rest of us follow, unsure how long it will be until we reach relative safety.

Sweat drips down my face, and all my muscles are tense when we finally reach our destination. The vent we must exit out of is slightly smaller than the one we entered, allowing only one person to pass at a time. There's no light coming through.

"I'll try to unscrew the vent. It'll be harder since we're now on the other side," Brayden says as he moves past Alec and to the front.

No one responds. We wait in utter silence as Brayden tries to unscrew the vent. Time passes painfully slowly.

The silence is interrupted by Brayden exclaiming, "I got it!" When we finally hear the clang of the vent dropping to the floor below, we all sigh in relief at the same time. Brayden doesn't even wait a moment before he drops down. The rest of us hesitate, but when he doesn't make any noise to indicate trouble, we follow. Melissa and Alec go, then I help K lower Avi.

When my feet hit the floor, I instantly scan our surroundings. The others are stretching out their muscles. It seems we've landed in a storage closet. There's only one door that leads out into a hall. I shake out my shoulders, grateful to be out of the tight confines of the vent.

"Let's go. We have little time," K commands.

Melissa exhales loudly. "I'm going to need a shower so bad after all this."

Brayden mumbles an agreement, and she punches him lightly on the arm. I'm so concerned about getting Avi to safety that I can't laugh along.

Alec and Brayden lift Avi up between them. I open the door and peer out, then signal them that it's safe. K and Melissa activate their powers, and we exit into the hall.

I'm unable to see anything except the others once more, and I trust them to lead us the right way. I nervously fiddle with my hands. Brayden assures me Avi will be okay, and I find myself praying he's right. Even if I should be more suspicious of him and his knowledge, I can't deny that he's been helping us and doesn't seem to mean any harm. I'd like to believe that there's a good explanation for the amount of information he possesses. Since he doesn't seem to pose a threat, I decide to wait and discuss my thoughts with K at a later time.

As of right now, Brayden's an ally.

Back in the dorms, we place Avi gently on her bed. She's severely malnourished and lies limp, nearly lifeless.

"She needs to get professional help," Alec says as he examines her for any additional wounds.

"No one will help us here. She's not even supposed to be back!" Melissa exclaims.

A dizzying sensation comes over me, my skin prickling with goosebumps. "If Avi was near completion for whatever they were doing to her, what do you think happened to Lilac?" I ask.

"I ..." K's voice drifts off, his expression morphing into horror. "Do you think ..."

"She's dead," Melissa states, her voice somber.

My voice comes out in a frail whisper. "We didn't save her."

No one says anything for several grief-stricken moments. *It's my fault. Maybe, if K and I never tried to leave, we could have found her sooner.* Sickening guilt twists my gut, and I find myself falling deep within myself.

As if sensing my self-blame, K reaches out and touches my arm. "You're not to blame, Callista. It's this damn school." I see a fiery rage in his eyes, such intense emotion that it reinvigorates my senses.

"We can still save Avi. Lilac wouldn't want us to sit here and let her die too," I argue.

"But how? What are we supposed to do?" Melissa whines, desperation inflecting her tone.

I scramble my brain for anything, refusing to succumb to hopelessness. Then I remember something. "K! When we were at the diner, that girl came in and healed you and the other guy who was there. I think her name was Tessa?"

He turns to me with a solemn expression, and as he starts to respond, Brayden interrupts him, asking, "Do you know anything else about her?"

K bites down on his lip.

I ponder before answering. "Her brother's name was Tyrus."

Brayden's face lights up at the name. "I know a Tyrus."

I narrow my eyes at him. *How would he know Tyrus?*

"When I first got teleported," he continues, "this guy found me and helped me out a bit. His name was Tyrus. He brought me to this place with others like us and said I could go there if I ever needed help. I never knew a Tessa though. At some point, I decided to go explore on my own, and that's when I came here."

"Where is this place?" Melissa asks, walking over to him.

"Outside the Academy."

"How do we get out?" I ask.

Brayden shrugs. "Only way to find out is to try."

Alec, Brayden, and K hoist up Avi, then they prepare to travel outside.

Hopefully we're more successful this time. K and I can't tell them we tried to escape already. They might turn against us. I grab my journal and pen, place them into my bag, then toss it over my shoulder. Once we're prepared, we head out into the hall, hidden again under K's darkness and Melissa's power of muting.

When we reach the chill night air, the loud sound of static startles us. A sudden boom of noise comes from the speakers lining the school, and a voice sounds. "There has been a breach in Sector 84. All guards report to duty. Lockdown mode commences in two minutes."

Panic builds inside me as we sprint toward the Academy gate. A light glow emits from the gate, and an instinct tells me we need to find a way around it. The others stare at the gate, trying to find a way over it. I close my eyes, summoning my orb. When it glints into view, I observe it carefully. I look around once more, and an idea comes to mind.

"I think you need to let down your shadow," I whisper to K.

He looks back at me. "We'll be caught then."

I look to my light, and my gut tells me this is the right decision. "Trust me."

He shoots me another uneasy look, then reluctantly complies. As soon as the shroud of darkness dissipates, I direct my orb to the side of the gate farther away from us. We quickly move over to it, not wanting to waste too much time.

Once we get closer, I notice a small stone building. I hear voices inside and stiffen just as the door flies outward. Quick to action, Melissa concentrates on them, and when the guards open their mouths to speak, nothing comes out.

K steps forward and pushes out his palms, causing darkness to surround them. I bring my light orb into my hand and push all my willpower into it. A sudden burst of electricity comes forth, and I widen my eyes. I didn't expect it to work, at least not this well, as it had yet to in my training classes. The spark doesn't bother me, and I realize what I must do.

K looks at me and then back to the guards. Finally, he dissipates the shadow. Brayden uses his ability to lift the guards in the air, and I charge the electricity in my hand. Closing my eyes, I shoot my hand out toward the two men and feel it spread beyond me.

I open my eyes to the smell of burning as the guards try to scream. The sound is muted due to Melissa's ability. Seconds later, they fall to the ground, unconscious. A sickening feeling crowds my gut. *Did I kill them?* I look down at my now empty hands in terror. My vision spots as my limbs freeze up.

"One minute before lockdown."

The announcement from the speakers brings me back to reality, and I snap out of my haze. Alec is already inside with Brayden, searching through documents. I push past my shakiness, walking inside with K. I search the table on the other side of the room. A button that's labeled "IMPORTANT" catches my attention. Without thinking, I push it, and an audio message plays.

"DETA has just recently gotten a new update to keep the students in check. It will continue to monitor Eclium, along with the Recall supplement the children are being fed. Recall is going through a test phase at the moment, so if you see any students seemingly more aware that the environment is 'different,' fix them. It seems that we may have several of them around due to the still present bugs. More updates soon."

✣

TWENTY-ONE

I CLUTCH AT MY STOMACH and step back. *What does this mean?*
"I don't understand," K says.

"We've been drugged," Melissa retorts, her tone cold. Silence passes between us as Alec replays the message to memorize it.

"Thirty seconds until lockdown."

I feel my heart rate continue to increase as we frantically go back to searching. I focus on the side of the room that we haven't touched, moving objects and shuffling through file cabinets. Everything I find is useless. Sweat starts to bead on my forehead, the pressure getting to me. Time goes too fast.

"Twenty seconds until lockdown."

"Come on! We need to find this quick!" I shout, my voice coming out shaky. *Nothing, nothing, nothing!* I throw the files in my hand onto the floor in frustration. *We need to find a way to exit, or we'll likely die here.* Once I've searched everything I can, I begin forcefully moving furniture in my last, desperate attempt. K sees me struggling and comes over to help.

"Here!" Melissa yells from outside the building. I rush outside with K and see that she's holding up a controller of sorts that she must have taken from a guard's pocket. We hurry toward her, and she flips the switch, causing the gate to rise just as the speaker starts again.

"Ten seconds."

The three boys gently lift Avi up between them, and I grab my bag.

"Eight seconds."

The boys are rushing toward the opening, with Melissa and me trailing behind.

"Six seconds."

I trip due to a sudden incline, throwing my bag forward. The boys are just stepping over the threshold.

"Five seconds."

Melissa hears my fall and scatters to grab my bag. She offers her hand for help, but I motion for her to go on.

"Four seconds."

I scramble onto my feet, my heart racing. It takes a moment for me to regain my footing.

"Three seconds."

I sprint toward the others on the opposite side of the gate. My breath comes out in wheezes, and everything seems to pulse around me. As I reach the threshold, I throw myself hard out onto the pavement and hit the ground as "One" booms from the speakers and the gates shut down hard.

I exhale from the impact. My head spins, and I take several deep breaths to try to calm myself. When Melissa comes over and reaches down a hand to help me up, I take it. She then hands me my backpack.

"Thanks," I say, out of breath. I quickly take note of our surroundings. *We're out. We finally aren't trapped by the Academy's gates.* It's almost surreal being outside the towering walls of the Academy. As I allow myself a second to take in the moment, my eye catches on a spot where the ground looks uneven. Everything else is completely flat, so the small shift sticks out more.

I'm not given a chance to observe closer, as K motions for me to get moving.

It's probably just ground that was disturbed. Nothing serious. I push my aches and pains away and channel my energy into my legs. We run away from the Academy without any particular direction in mind. My light is the only brightness allowing us to see, so we have to stay in a group for it to be most effective.

Once we've reached an abandoned part of the city with no recognizable buildings, Brayden stops and motions for us to do the same. I take the opportunity to catch my breath, bending over with my hands on my knees. The boys place Aviana down gently and look at Brayden expectantly. He signs for us to be quiet, and Melissa and I comply.

K glares at Brayden and asks, "What are you doing?"

Brayden shakes his head in response, then pulls out an object I didn't notice him having before. "Contacting Tyrus." He motions for us to step away and presses a small button on the strange piece of metal.

A low buzzing noise emits from it. Then the holographic projection of a young man in his twenties appears before us. I recognize his facial features and realize it's Tyrus staring back at us.

"Brayden, this is a lot more people than we were expecting," the hologram says. "HQ won't be happy with this." Tyrus glances over us quickly, landing on my face. "Oh, it's you."

I narrow my eyes while crossing my arms. K coughs.

"I don't care what HQ thinks, Ty. These people need our help." Brayden speaks with a sense of authority I've never heard him use.

Tyrus sighs, sounding exasperated, and nods. "Alright, where's the sick girl?"

Brayden points down to Aviana, who's passed out on the ground. "I'll send over our coordinates right now. She needs help fast."

Tyrus turns away to type something just as Brayden presses the button again, and the hologram disappears. He takes out another almost identical small device, which also turns into a messaging hologram at the push of a button. "Be prepared to move," he says. "He should be here soon after the coordinates upload."

K gazes skeptically at him while Alec stares in awe at the technology. Melissa seems to be fascinated by Brayden as she eyes him with a small grin. I'm unimpressed and suspicious. I watch the screen as the coordinates upload, finishing just as the word *SENT* appears. A second later, a man's voice comes from behind me.

"I'll bring the girl first."

I twist around so fast that I lose my footing and fall backward, only to be caught by two muscled arms. In front of me, Tyrus stands over Aviana, reaching down to touch her.

"Be careful," K says into my ear.

I realize he's the one who caught me. Looking away in embarrassment, I mumble a thanks. As I readjust to stand on my own, I study Tyrus's movements.

When the palm of his hand touches Avi's skin, he closes his eyes, and they both disappear into thin air. My eyes widen just as I recall Tessa's words. *He's a teleporter.* Seconds later, Tyrus appears with a large grin.

"She's with my sister now, along with one of our other healers. They should have an update on her state within the hour. Who's next?"

"Wait," I say, putting up a hand. "Brayden. You said that you left Tyrus after he helped you. Now he just took away Aviana in the blink of an eye, and you're acting like you planned all of this. Explain. Now." I glare at him, and he frowns.

"Look. You'll get a better explanation later, I promise. But I didn't just happen to stumble upon the Academy. I went there to recruit students to our cause."

I raise my eyebrows.

"Like I said," he continued, "you'll get a better explanation later."

He doesn't say anything else, and I turn away from him angrily.

Melissa looks slightly warily at Brayden, then says, "If no one else is offering, I guess I'll go next."

Tyrus nods. "Be aware, there will be side effects."

Before she can take back her statement, he touches her, and they vanish.

I can feel Brayden's eyes on me from behind and turn just as he looks away. "Tessa's a good healer, Callista," he says. "There should be minimal damage."

His words don't help ease my steadily rising anxiety. "Minimal?" I ask. "So there will still be damage." I turn to stare at him.

He doesn't answer me, and my gut sinks. A warm hand touches my shoulder, and I look back to see K giving me a tight smile. "We'll get through this together,' he says.

He's being so uncharacteristically kind. I look up into his silver eyes and, without thinking, brush a wisp of his dark hair out of his face. As soon as I realize what I've done, I jerk my hand away. "Sorry!"

Why did I do that?

He doesn't get the chance to reply because Tyrus reappears. He looks at us expectantly, and I sigh. "Guess I'll go next," I say.

He nods in reply. I shoot a glance back at K just as Tyrus's hand touches my arm and space itself seems to falter. A mere second later, I'm inside a tunnel of some sort and smell sewer water. People bustle around me. Tyrus is already gone again, getting the next person. Melissa is nearby, eagerly chatting with a group of strangers.

As I look around the new environment, I see a girl with bright-brown hair in a white lab coat coming toward me. I recognize her as soon as I see a glimpse of her face, and my feet start moving.

"Tessa!" I yell.

She freezes at the sound of the name and turns to me as I run toward her. Her eyes widen, and I pivot to a stop just before I smack right into her.

"Tessa, where's Avi?"

She raises an eyebrow in confusion. "Who?" she asks, puzzled.

"Aviana!" I cry out in frustration. The loud conversation in the room falls silent.

Her eyes twinkle with recognition, and she frowns. "This way," she whispers uncomfortably. I feel everyone's eyes on me as I follow her a few rooms down to where a door plate sits on a wall. Aviana's name is scribbled there in black ink. I push in front of Tessa and open the door, shocked at what I see in front of me.

Avi lies on a white bed, breathing normally. She's less pale than she was before, but something seems off as I walk toward her and push back her dirty-blond hair.

Tessa walks in and speaks with sadness in her voice. "Her body is fully functional, but she will be left slightly crippled."

My eyes widen, and I turn to her. "What? I thought you healed her!" Tears prick my eyes as I wait for an explanation.

"We can heal her physical form, but we can't restore the essence of her power. Over half of her ability's essence was extracted, and it can take anywhere from weeks or months to years for her body to restore it."

I think back to the fluorescent tubes that were connected to her.

"She'll be able to function as a nearly normal human," Tessa explains. "But since she'll have a much weaker ability, it will cause her to experience more regular fatigue, dizziness, and malnourishment."

I frown as I look down upon Avi's sleeping form. "When will she wake up?"

"By tomorrow. When she does, we'll do another checkup on her vitals."

I hesitate and turn back to face her. *I should thank her. But at the same time, what if she has ill intent? I shouldn't trust anyone.* I hear shouting coming from the halls just before K bursts through the door.

"There you are!" he shouts as he rushes over to me. Then he looks at Avi. "How is she?" His eyes search mine for a glint of hope.

I frown, and tears well. Unable to hold back my emotions any longer, I lean my head into K's shoulder and sob. He seems unsure what to do and awkwardly places his hand on the back of my head. I hear footsteps, but I don't bother looking up. Instead, I close my eyes against the fabric of his shirt and finally allow my emotions to consume me. Flashes of images from my nightmares echo around me. I feel K's arms wrap around me, and the warmth comforts me. My head pulses when I squint open my eyes, only to see K looking down at me worriedly.

"You should get some rest," he says gently.

I don't respond, only nodding my head slightly. He guides me to a chair in the corner of the room, and I sit in it, gently placing my bag on the floor next to me. The seat isn't even mildly comfortable.

Sensing this, K puts a hand on mine. "I'll go see if there's a room you can sleep in."

I want to ask him not to leave my side, but he's gone before I can. I lean my head against the wall, staring at Avi's lifeless form. My eyes are irritatingly dry, and my mind is cloudy. The adrenaline high from recent events has completely crashed, and I feel almost empty. I close my eyes, trying to focus on my breathing. *She will wake up. It's not my fault.* Images of Lilac appear in my mind's eye. *At least I saved one of them. There was nothing I could do.* My heart hurts as exhaustion overcomes me, forcing me into a fitful rest.

A woman warmly cradles me in her lap as my eyes are shut. "Little sol, Mommy will make sure you're safe. The scary men won't hurt you. At some point, I can't protect you anymore. Daddy and I will have to go on a long trip to a faraway place. I know you'll keep yourself and your sister safe, my sweet Calli. Never forget how much I love you."

A man's voice calls out from somewhere far away. "Rosalie, they're here!"

The woman lifts my head off her lap and places it gently on a soft pillow.

"Calli, be careful who you trust." A soft kiss presses against my forehead before the woman moves away. I open my eyes and reach out an arm to pull her back, only to see nothing.

"Mom?" I cry out, then I shift into a ball on my side. "Come back, Mom." I want to cry, but my eyes are completely dry. I reach out and find a pillow next to me. Pulling it close, I cradle it in my arms. Footsteps sound from my other side, and I ignore them.

"Callista?"

The familiar voice rings through my ears, and I flip over, coming face-to-face with bright-blue eyes.

"Avi!" I shoot up from the bed and embrace her. She's taken aback but wraps her arms around me uneasily. I realize I'm coming on too strong and pull back. "Avi, this may be hard to believe, but I have reason to think we're sisters."

She bites her lip, her voice unsteady. "When I was unconscious, I saw brief images. But they didn't seem like just images. They felt like memories. I saw you, I think. It was as if I wasn't supposed to recall any of it. Nothing was clear."

I smile sadly at her. "I've had the same thing happening to me for months. I thought they were just dreams, but I think you're right. They're memories. I don't know why we're suddenly recalling them, but I'm hoping we'll find out." I step away, shifting on my feet. "How are you feeling?"

A small grin cracks her face, and she exhales. "I'm not a hundred percent, but I can move around fine. Tessa said my vitals were normal too and that I should only experience a few side effects for a few years. Luckily, she said they should become less severe as time goes on."

I notice her skin still has a slightly pale hue, but other than that she looks much healthier.

"I'm glad you'll be okay." I debate asking her what exactly happened when she went to REM and if she knows anything about Lilac. But before I can, someone knocks on the door. Moments later, Brayden walks in.

He looks between us. "Sorry to interrupt. Tessa and Tyrus think it's time to tell you all something important."

TWENTY-TWO

AVI AND I SHARE A CONFUSED glance and stand. "Do you need to lean on me to walk?" I ask. *I'll have to ask her about it later.*

She shakes her head. "The dizziness comes in waves. I'll be fine for a while."

I nod and wait for her to follow Brayden out the door, then I go out myself. I notice we're in a different hall than before, in an area that seems to house multiple bedrooms and small apartments. As we walk, I realize I don't know how I even got over here.

"Brayden. How long was I out?" I ask. "And what happened?" Although I don't exactly feel like speaking to him, I know he's the only one who can answer me.

He shrugs as we move. "Well, it's been a day since you arrived, but as for the other question, I don't know. You should ask the guy you fell asleep on."

Heat floods my cheeks at the implication. I look away and speed up, wanting to move faster than before.

We turn many corners and walk down several halls. Eventually, Brayden opens the largest door I've seen so far and motions for us to walk in. I follow immediately after him, moving cautiously.

The concrete walls are lined with wooden borders, and there's a small stage sitting toward the back. There are rows of seats lined up before the stage.

When my eyes fall on Melissa, Alec, and K, relief washes over me. I move to sit near them. They turn, and as soon as they see us, Melissa stands and rushes over, quickly wrapping Avi in a hug.

"I heard you were up, but I wanted to see for myself," she says.

Avi smiles, and I move away, giving them a moment to greet one another.

K motions for me to come sit next to him. As soon as I sit, I lean over to whisper in his ear. "So, what happened after I fell asleep?"

A gentle grin cracks his lips, putting me at ease. "I think you were just overwhelmed with the recent events and all the emotions they brought forward. When I came back to bring you to one of the rooms, you were already asleep, so I just carried you there."

I redden with embarrassment even more than before. "Ah, sorry. Thank you."

He shakes his head. "I understand. I was exhausted as well." He pauses, seeming to ponder. "So, you never really explained how you know Aviana is related to you?"

I smile and say, "My dreams told me." He tilts his head, but I laugh it off. "Sibling instinct."

Another flash of sadness crosses his face, and I grow confused. Just as I'm about to ask him about it, Tyrus, Tessa, and a group of five others enter the auditorium and head to the stage. Aviana and Melissa quickly run over and take a seat. The two siblings stand at the front of the stage before us, each holding a controller of sorts. I notice Brayden standing behind them amid the others.

Tyrus coughs low in his throat, then stands straight and speaks. "Hello, all. You may already know this, but my name is Tyrus, and this here is Tessa. We're like you, special individuals sent here out of nowhere, each of us possessing abilities. As you already know, I'm a teleporter, and Tessa is a healer."

Out of the corner of my eye, I see K visibly tense, his dagger-like eyes focused on Tessa. She doesn't notice his gaze as she nods to Brayden and he steps forward.

Tessa adds, "Brayden here may have seemed like a student just as you were, but that was a ruse. You see, our organization is called EMBER. We're trying to find a way to take down REMEDY Academy. Brayden was a student there two years ago. He was seventeen when he escaped, sadly with many losses along the way."

My lips flatten as my entire body tenses. *Why would they allow us to go to the Academy if they knew it was dangerous?*

Perhaps reading our emotions, Tyrus continues. "Before you all get upset, please let him explain."

Brayden moves to take center stage and smiles sadly at us. "I was placed in the Academy as a spy to get more information," he says. "They're unable to recognize me due to a special device we here at EMBER created. It distorts a person's appearance for selected groups of people, allowing you to be unrecognizable to whoever you want. Since you all didn't know me, you were unaware of this. I will say that I did tell the truth about having an upbringing similar to yours. However, I was brought months before you all. Honestly, I was surprised when you figured out so much so soon. Some of the stuff you discovered, we didn't know yet. I had to lie to you to protect the secrecy of EMBER from others."

Something about his statement unsettles me. "Why haven't you saved the other countless students who have been hurt?" I ask.

Tessa frowns, and Brayden glances at her before she takes his place. "It's not that we don't want to," she says. "We just don't have the supplies and the people to save everyone. We don't have enough power currently." She seems genuinely sad, her eyes distant.

K scoffs. "Why not tell us of your plans when you saw me and Callista at the diner?"

"That was complicated. The Academy recruiters set up the diner and the fight that occurred as a way to capture our officials to either kill or take hostage. Our spies found out about this plan, and so Tyrus and I went there to stop it. You two were caught in the crossfire, unfortunately. When we recognized you as new student potentials, we saved you. That's when we determined you would be our new spies."

"Would you just have let us die if we weren't useful to you?" I ask, barely restraining my anger and clenching my hands into fists.

"No … that's not …" Tessa stumbles over her words, clearly uncertain about what she should say. "We don't want any unnecessary casualties. Trust me."

I roll my eyes at the irony of her statement. *Yeah, like I'll trust someone who manipulated me and my friends.*

K shifts beside me and locks eyes with Tessa.

"Now, there's something else you all don't know yet," she says. "We've gathered information over the years, and it's been confirmed that the Neighborhoods are correlated to this place and Liam, the headmaster. We had theories based off our historical records, but we weren't sure until now."

Whispers travel through our group, and Tessa waits for them to disperse before continuing.

"Your true parents were killed by the government in charge of the homeland. Unfortunately, I can't tell you anything else unless you join us."

The news isn't a complete shock, but it still shoots a pang of sadness through me. *This just confirms my nightmares.* I can no longer hold back my annoyance. "You've explained what you know, but answer me this. If you knew the Academy wasn't safe, why would you let K and me go after meeting us at the café? You wanted us to be spies, but how would we be spies if we didn't know our mission? Why not just take us straight there? Also, don't you think we deserve to know whatever you're holding back even if we don't join? It's our life." My tone is harsh, but I don't bother trying to cover it up.

"We wanted you to see firsthand what it's like there," Tyrus says. "You were also sort of experiments for Brayden to watch."

I'm about to shoot back a retort, but he puts up his hands. "Look, it isn't fair or ethical, I know. But we're in desperate times. I apologize for all the harm it caused you. Especially for Aviana. None of us expected any of you to get sent to REM before we brought you back here. I hope that in time you can see that we mean well. As for the information, there are too many risks involved in freely sharing everything we know. I'm sorry."

His response leaves me unsatisfied, and I lean back in my chair with my arms crossed. *I believe they aren't the bad guys, but it doesn't excuse the fact that Avi could be safe if they'd just taken us in. I hate how much lying goes on around here. But they aren't my enemy. I think. At the very least, they're the lesser of two evils.*

K stands, and I notice a vein pulsing on his neck as he says, "If you really are my sister's friend, Tessa, which I have a feeling you are, have you found what the hell happened to her after all this time? When I first heard your name, I never would have thought it would have been *you.* You were her best friend, and you both had all these secrets and never shared them with me. Now that you've brought me here, you better fess up."

My mouth drops open as I stare at him in shock. *I've never seen him so furious.*

Tessa's eyes widen, then soften, and she lowers her head. "Shouldn't we talk about this after?" She pleads with him through her large green eyes.

He doesn't respond, and I hear him choke back a sob. "You were the only person I know who June would talk to. You're telling us all this information, but all I want to know is why she just disappeared that day after she left our meeting spot. She said she was just going to grab something from her house to give to me, but she never came back! Where did she go? She wouldn't tell me anything because she didn't want me to follow, but I'm damn sure she told you."

Tessa seems to be on the verge of tears, and Tyrus must notice, as he moves in front of her, allowing her to take a step back. "Kieran," he says, "we put out several teams to find her. We were unable to find a body, leading us to believe any evidence of her life was confiscated."

K's fury turns to sadness, and he slumps. "Please tell me you found at least something." There's so much sadness in his voice that I can't help but feel for him. I want to comfort him, but I don't know how.

Tyrus says, "I'm sorry, but—"

A short older man with graying hair who'd been at the back of the group steps forward and exchanges whispers with Tyrus, then the younger man turns back toward us. "Harris just did a quick search," he says, "and it turns out there was some evidence found on what happened to June. It's not a pretty story." Tyrus looks at K gently. "If you want to know, we'll tell you. But it will hurt. And it sadly won't change anything. It might do you better to not know."

K is silent for a brief moment as all eyes turn to him. He has such a deep frown that it hurts me. "Tell me," he says, so quietly that I wonder if they heard him.

Tessa takes a deep breath, composes herself, and speaks. "The government must have found out she knew too much, so they disposed of her to protect themselves. They also knew that she had contact with her biological sibling, which is illegal."

My eyes widen. *So that's why I never knew Avi. But if I wasn't supposed to know her, then how do I have such distinct memories of us together?*

K turns silently, and I see pure pain in his eyes as he runs out the door we came through. Instinct tells me to follow him, and I shoot out of my chair to run out the door after him.

He moves quickly down several halls, and I lose sight of him. Just as I'm about to retreat, a small sob sounds from a room a few doors down. I slowly walk up to it and cautiously turn the handle, revealing a dark sitting area.

Kieran sits on a sofa against a wall, bent over with his head in his palms. I'm taken aback for a moment, wondering if I'm pushing my boundaries within our relationship. *He's vulnerable right now. What if he doesn't want me here? But I can't just leave him alone.*

The air is stiff and silent as I walk over tentatively and sit next to him. I reach my hand over and place it on his knee. He seems to break from my touch, and I hear him mumble.

"They just confirmed it's my fault. They killed her because she and I knew each other." His words pain me, and I place a hand on his arm, causing him to look up at me with puffy silver eyes.

"It wasn't your fault," I tell him. "You had every right to be with your sister, so whatever that resulted in, it's not your fault." I watch doubt cloud his vision and decide the best thing I can do is show him I care. I scoot closer and wrap my arms around him. The motion is extremely awkward, but he doesn't pull away from me. I feel a drop of liquid hit my shoulder as his head rests above mine.

"She was the only person I had," he says. "When we met, I was so happy to finally find someone who loved me for me. June was the reason I kept pushing on through my awful life at home. Whatever she and Tessa had been planning allowed her to link herself with me. I used to visit the borders of my Neighborhood and dream about the other side. There was a small hole that I discovered, and I would sometimes look through it to try and get a peek. One day, I found a small letter at the hole. It was from June. She explained that we were related. I wasn't sure how she knew, but I believed it. We would sit and talk there almost every day. That's also how I found out about Tessa. I was so happy with her that I never thought to ask how she found me. Or how she found the hole in the seemingly impenetrable fence that allowed us to meet. Ignorant bliss, I suppose. But I was curious about what the greater plan was that she would sometimes refer to. I never found out. Then one day, like I said, she left. And she never returned. I cared for her. She made sense, and I always wanted to find out more about what she was looking for."

I stay silent and hold him closer as he speaks.

"I haven't had anyone since she left and never came back. I guess I was hoping maybe she was still alive, but now that I know she isn't for sure, I have no one."

Something inside me breaks, and I pull back, looking him in the eyes. "K, I'm sorry. I can understand feeling unloved. Back home, all I had was Reginald, and now I don't know if I'll ever see him again. And I don't know how he's the son of the head-master. I'm lucky to have Aviana, and I'm lucky to have you. We understand each other."

Mentioning my old friend saddens me, and an ache pulses in my heart. *I need to find him. Once things are settled, I'll find a way to find him.*

K's eyes travel across my face, and tension passes through the air. Then, seeming to realize how intimate we're being, he pulls away. He wipes the tears from his face, and his expression turns flat. "Sorry," he says, his reddened neck showing his embarrassment.

I shake my head. "You don't have anything to apologize for." Pausing, I bite the inside of my cheek. "If you don't mind sharing, how did you meet Tessa?"

He stiffens. "I never physically met her until today, actually. But I knew about her through June. They would talk, I don't know how, and June told me about her."

Any further conversation is interrupted as the door is thrown open. We turn our heads in unison to come face-to-face with Brayden and Melissa.

"Ah! There you guys are. I was so worried!" Melissa exclaims, oblivious to the fact we were having a private moment.

K and I awkwardly scoot farther away from each other. Brayden looks between us and lands his eyes on me. "Callista, can we talk privately for a bit?"

A look of bewilderment crosses my face as I say, "Uh, sure." I stand from the couch, shoot a final glance at K, and follow Brayden out the door.

He leads me to a nearby room with a scanner and no door handle. He places his hand on the scanner. It buzzes and emits a green light. The door slides open, and he enters, gesturing for me to follow. I warily step inside, jumping when the door slams closed behind me.

The room seems to be an office of sorts. A few halls shoot off from a main room, and there's a sofa and two armchairs. He takes one of the smaller chairs and motions for me to take the other.

"I wanted to inform you that your parents used to be a part of our organization. Your biological parents. We weren't sure until today. Older members who knew them have confirmed that you look identical to the child who was in pictures with them."

I stiffen. "And what happened to my birth parents?"

He swallows. "They were killed. I'm sure you don't remember them, as your memory was likely altered with the Recall drug the Academy used to make you forget they ever existed."

My heart sinks as a lump forms in my throat. *I suspected as much, but now it's confirmed. And that Recall drug. I remember reading about that when we were escaping.*

I study Brayden, trying to keep my composure. *He knows information that I want to know. Even if I don't agree with what he did, I need his help.* I said, "I've had memories come back to me. In my dreams. I don't know why, but I remember being taken from them. It's also how … how I figured out my sister is Aviana."

His eyebrows rise, and there's a new fervor in his voice. "That's incredible. They said Aviana also matched the pictures, but I can't believe it's true. I wonder if your abilities being awakened was the cause. Or perhaps it's because you have three abilities and Recall wasn't strong enough to hold them back."

I raise my hand, stopping his train of thought. "The headmaster tried to alter my memories in his office, but it didn't work. Then, after I was knocked out for a week, K's memories were altered, but not mine."

"So you must be immune. That'll be very useful—" I glare at him, and he cuts himself off. "I meant, if you decide to help us."

Exhaling, I avoid his gaze, focusing on a point on the wall. "Aviana told me she was able to see some foggy memories after being in REM."

"Maybe being drained of her abilities messed with the drug's strength," he says.

I place my palm against my forehead, feeling a headache coming. *This is a lot. I don't know what to do.*

"I wanted to let you know that I really am sorry," Brayden says. "I didn't expect Aviana to be placed in danger like that. If I had …"

I stand, turning my back on him. "What's done is done. I'm going back to the others."

I don't give him the opportunity to say anything else and return to the hall.

TWENTY-THREE

I END UP SLEEPING AWAY the entire rest of the day in one of EMBER's bedrooms that consists of six sets of bunk beds. When I awake in the morning, I'm given a fresh set of clothes—a brown sweatshirt and jeans that are one size too big—and am shown to the bathing rooms, where I'm more than eager to clean up. The generosity of such amenities isn't lost on me, and although I haven't forgiven the dishonesty surrounding my being here, I can't deny that I'm not as angry as I was yesterday.

In the community dining hall, as others refer to it, K, Alec, Melissa, Avi, and I sit at a long rectangular wooden table. There are a few dozen others eating around us, all talking in low chatter. The room has little color. The walls are gray, and the floor is concrete. It smells like musty mildew. The food on the plate before me isn't as appealing as what was offered at the Academy, but it's more edible than what was offered at home.

"Do you all mind if I join you?" Brayden asks, holding his food tray in his hands.

I exchange a look with Avi, who shrugs. "Fine," I reply, not meeting his eyes. He slides in next to me and Melissa, a tight smile on his lips.

"How do you all like the food?" he asks. "I know it isn't much, but all we have is the left-behind food we found in the city's buildings."

I take a bite of the room-temperature fruit on my plate. It tastes exactly like the canned fruit K, Avi, and I found before, but not nearly as delicious. *I guess my tastebuds became too used to the quality of the Academy's food.*

"It's not the best, but it could be worse," Melissa says bluntly. Brayden seems to want to retort but thinks better of it. We sit in uneasy silence.

Fidgeting with my hands, I give Avi a worried look. *I need to know what happened to Lilac. And if there's any chance she's still alive.* "I'm sorry if it's hard to talk about. But I need to know. What happened? Did you see Lilac? We found a room—one like yours. With her name. It was empty."

Alec looks at me sideways, seeming to disapprove of my question. I ignore him, focusing on Avi.

She shifts uncomfortably, her eyes not meeting mine. "One of the guards told me they would bring me to the class," she finally says. "They said I wasn't allowed to know where the class was, since the training sessions were private and no other kids were supposed to know its location." Her eyes turn glassy, her mind seeming to go elsewhere. "I just remember walking for a long time until we eventually reached a locked door. The guard input a code, and then he brought me into this room. It was completely empty. Before I could ask any questions, the guard locked me inside."

I notice her hand start to shake, and tears glisten in her eyes. Then she continues.

"The room filled with some sort of gas so quickly, I didn't even have a chance to realize what was happening. I was knocked out. And when I woke, I felt like I was dying. I was suspended, tubes protruding from my skin. My mind was foggy, hazy. At one point, a man in a suit came into the room. I never saw his face. I don't remember what he said to me. I just remember screaming, demanding to be let go. Then he got close, and everything went black once more. Next time I woke was here."

Her eyes refocus, now filled with held-in tears. My stomach twists as I think about the atrocities she was subjected to. I reach my hand across the table to grasp hers. I feel as nauseous as I did when I first saw her in that room. Alec places his hand on her shoulder, his eyes filled with concern. "I never saw Lilac," she says. "But I don't think we'll ever see her again."

A lump fills my throat, and I swallow deeply, my breaths coming out shallow. *So that's it. She's gone.* "I'm sorry." I speak quietly, my throat too tight to make much sound.

"Aviana, I should have gotten you out of there sooner," Brayden says. "All of you. Then you wouldn't have had to go through all of that, and maybe Lilac would still be alive."

"Brayden …" Avi fumbles with her hands, uncomfortable.

"Yeah, you should have," K spits at Brayden.

Melissa frowns at us. "Go easy on him, guys. He clearly feels bad! It's not as if he directly sent Aviana or Lilac to REM."

"He still contributed," Alec whispers.

I cross my arms, giving Brayden a stern look. "We need some time to trust you again. Just please don't lie anymore."

"I won't."

A wave of silence washes over us. Alec rubs Avi's shoulder as she stares into the distance, her expression pained. I think of Lilac and our short time of getting to know each other. *She didn't deserve to die. Nor does any other person sent there.* A weight sits on my chest as I think about the pain Lilac must have gone through. *She was alone. Did she call for help? Or was she unconscious before she knew what happened?* I hope for the latter, even if both options are equally disturbing. I feel tears prick at my eyes and instantly raise my hand to wipe them. *Sitting here won't stop them. I need to take action. First, I need to find what they took from me.*

I sit up straighter, pushing myself up from the table. "I want to go look around the city more. Who's with me?"

"I'll come." Avi stands, her saddened expression fading from her face.

"Me too," Alec says. Melissa and Brayden agree as well.

I turn toward K expectantly.

He nods, joining the rest of us. "Where do you plan on going?"

"I want to find Emmy."

Avi's eyes light up at my kitten's name. "Do you think we can find her?"

"Well, that will be up to you. If you're able to connect to her, then maybe we will."

No one tries to stop us from leaving. Once we're outside the relative protection of EMBER, we move painstakingly stealthily so as to not alert anyone who may be watching to our presence. Eventually, we're able to make out the Academy in the near distance.

"Over there!" I point to the set of apartment buildings nearest the Academy. "That must be where Emmy is."

"Uh, that just looks like an empty building," Melissa comments.

"All the buildings here look empty," Alec says.

Brayden sighs. "That's because they are empty."

K ignores the discussion and turns to Avi. "Can you feel her?"

She bites her lip nervously. "Let me try." She closes her eyes, furrowing her brow in concentration. I watch her expectantly, tuning out the bickering between Melissa and Alec. As soon as her eyes fly open, a smile spreads on her face. "I can feel her. I can't connect to her right now. I'm too weak. But I can sense where she is, ever so faintly."

"So you can lead her to us?" I ask, holding back my excitement.

She nods. When she takes a step forward, her feet stumble, and she falls to her knees.

"Aviana!" Alec cries, falling to her side.

I crouch beside her, my stomach twisting in worry. "What happened?"

Avi's hand is against her forehead, her face contorted in pain. "It's just my head. It will pass in a little bit. Tessa said I'll have to get used to it but that it should ease up with time." She grits out the words through clenched teeth.

"Will you be alright?" Melissa reaches down a hand to help Avi up, her face filled with concern. Avi takes it and allows Melissa to lift her from the ground.

"I'll be fine. It's already easing up. Using my ability probably made it worse."

"Maybe this isn't a good idea then," Brayden suggests. None of us acknowledge his words. We're too focused on Avi.

"Lean on me," Alec whispers. Avi gives him a reluctant look. "Please." She gives in, wrapping one arm around his shoulder.

"Can you remember what direction without using your ability?" I ask, hopeful.

"I think so. I'll have to feel her out one more time when we reach the building. But I at least know which one to go to."

We slowly resume our earlier pace, Alec and Avi leading at the front. Brayden hangs back, tagging along from a distance.

Good. He's giving us space. Part of me feels slightly guilty for pushing him away. He seemed genuinely sorry for putting Avi in danger, and I can't ignore the twist of his face when we talked about Lilac. *I wonder if he blames himself for her death.*

The interior of the apartment building is not unlike ones we've seen before. It's eerily quiet and smells stale for a place that supposedly houses former Academy professors. I twitch my nose in disgust when I spot a cockroach dashing across the floor.

"Are you sure she's here?" Melissa asks, appraising our surroundings with distaste. "I thought she was with a retired professor or something."

Avi closes her eyes only for a second before she starts forward, pushing away from Alec's support. "She's here. Just upstairs." Her feet stumble once more, and Alec jumps forward to catch her. But she never falls. "I'm fine," she insists.

I exchange a look with Melissa, who shrugs.

Brayden and K stand in the corner in a heated, whispered discussion. I turn on them, raising my eyebrow. "Are you going to come?"

K shakes his head. "I wanted to have a moment to talk with Brayden about what he knows. We'll wait down here."

I side-eye Brayden and shrug. "Alright then."

Avi, Melissa, Alec, and I swiftly make our way upstairs.

"Shouldn't we be more quiet? What if someone actually does live here?" I ask.

"There's no way someone lives in this dump," Melissa notes.

"I wouldn't be so sure," I say.

Alec pauses. "Callista's right. It doesn't hurt to be careful."

"Fine. I'll mute our footsteps." Melissa activates her ability, allowing us to continue our path in silence. We go several doors down the upper-floor hallway before Avi abruptly stops.

"In here," she says.

Slowly, methodically, Alec twists the doorknob and opens the door. It doesn't resist, allowing us easy entry.

Avi and I creep inside first. There isn't a single sound. Regardless, we keep moving. Avi rounds the corner and stops dead in her tracks. I bump into her, not expecting her sudden lack of movement.

"Emmy!" she cries out, running forward. Yet her tone isn't joyful. It's full of worry.

I launch myself forward, my heart starting to race. My mouth drops open in despair when I see my small kitten curled up on the floor, her breaths shallow. Several dead rats are around her, their bodies half eaten. I run over and scoop her up, cradling her in my arms.

"She's still breathing," I say, reassuring myself more than the others.

"They just left her here?" Melissa remarks, disbelief clear in her tone.

Avi's voice is cold. "They're heartless."

Emmy looks up at me, her once vibrant green eyes now dull and sad.

"We need to get her back to the headquarters," I say.

The others nod, and we all nearly sprint back to the lobby. K and Brayden look at us in shock when we rejoin them.

"She was alone. They left her to die alone, but she was surviving off rats," I explain through rapid breaths.

"If we bring her back, she'll be well taken care of. I promise," Brayden says, his voice full of sympathy.

I nod at him. "Let's go."

Avi and I watch as Emmy eagerly laps up a bowl of milk, her tail twitching playfully. An elderly woman, who I learned is named Jamie, prepares a mixture of canned tuna and chicken for the kitten.

"I had a cat a long time ago," Jamie says. "Her name was Mittens. I'm so happy to be around one again, although I'm sorry for the circumstances." She speaks thoughtfully, her wisdom showing through her mannerisms.

"I can't thank you enough. I was so worried. She's my only remaining piece of home," I say.

Jamie brings the meat concoction over to Emmy and places it beside her. "Of course, dearie. My grandson and granddaughter have told me much about you and your sister here."

"Who are your grandchildren?" Avi asks, fixing her gaze on the woman.

"Tessa and Tyrus. My daughter, their mom, was an active member here since EMBER was founded twenty-five years ago. That is, until she passed. Since then, it's just been the three of us."

"I'm sorry to hear," Avi replies, frowning.

I take Jamie's words into consideration. *There are families that have grown with this group?*

"I know it's just an old woman's words," Jamie says, "but please give this place a chance. I think we could make a real change, especially with your help. I don't agree with all their methods, but I know everyone here means well." Her eyes crease as she looks at us.

She seems genuine. But was she just told to say that to try and convince us to stay? Or am I reading too much into it?

Uncomfortable with the current line of conversation, I give Avi a glance. She seems to understand and changes the topic, saying, "I don't think Emmy is safe with us anymore."

My mouth falls open. That's not what I expected her to say. "What?" I ask.

"I think we should allow someone here to take care of her. At least until things settle."

I glare at her. *She's my cat. Why is she telling me the best way to care for her?* I'm about to speak my thoughts but hesitate as I recall what happened to Emmy. *Maybe she's right. I can't use Emmy like we did without putting her in danger, and I have no space right now to have a pet.* My gaze softens, and I scoop Emmy up into my arms, cuddling her to my chest. Then I focus on Jamie. *She had a cat once. She won't hurt mine.* "Do you … Could you watch Emmy? Until I want her back."

Jamie's friendly smile puts my nerves at ease. "I would love to, dearie."

"This doesn't mean we plan to stay here, though," I remind her, not wanting to give her the wrong idea.

She lets out a rich, hearty laugh, then says, "I know."

Avi places a soft hand on mine, telling me, "This is the best thing."

We sit and play with the small kitten for a long while until we're summoned for dinner. I give Emmy one last squeeze, a lump forming in my throat as I hand her off to Jamie.

"I'll take care of her, don't you worry. And you can visit any-time," she says.

"Thank you," I whisper as I force myself to turn away from Emmy's gaze.

I see a little girl, the girl so familiar from all my dreams. She's dying, right in front of me, and I'm helpless. Tubes extend from her body in grotesque ways, and her skin is as pale as moonlight.

"Sissy, help me," she mumbles.

I run toward her, but she just grows farther away. I can't get close enough to touch her, to save her from her pain. Blood drips from her mouth as her eyes go black. I'm terrified, petrified, unable to move.

My parents come from the shadows, their faces bruised and battered.

"You can't save her.," They both say. "You can't save them. You can't save us."

Their voices echo in a melancholic way, sending shivers down my spine. I fall to my knees, broken sobs escaping from the hollows of my empty chest. I watch as my parents fade away, leaving me in the empty shadows, once again alone.

"Please, come back! Don't leave me!" I cry out, folding into myself. My heart races at an alarming rate, my fingers trembling in fear.

"Open your eyes!" Someone is shouting at me, shaking my frightened body. I can't escape my nightmare, the vision of my little sister dying before me.

"She won't budge," a low voice says. The words sound distant, too far for me to truly comprehend.

"How are we going to wake her?" Another voice, higher than the others.

"Like this." Cold water splashes over my head, and I shoot up, hair drenched and eyes wild. Melissa stands over me with a cup in her hand. "Sorry. You gave me no other choice."

Behind her, Alec, Aviana, and K stand, their faces twisted in various levels of concern. I push wet strands of hair from my face and push myself out of the soaked bed.

"Thanks," I mutter, embarrassed.

"Are you alright? What happened?" Avi's voice trills with her worry.

The images from my nightmares reappear in my mind, and I stiffen. Blinking them away, I shake my head. *She's okay. She's right in front of me, in one piece.* "Don't worry," I tell them. "It was just a bad dream."

They exchange unconvinced looks, but none of them question me further.

"Did I wake you all?"

"You did, but it's fine," K says with a shrug. "I would have woken up soon anyway."

Melissa places a hand on her hip, giving me a pointed look. "Well, now that you have us all up, what are we going to do? I can't stand to just sit in this place."

Brayden walks over to us from the other side of the room, where I hadn't noticed him sitting. "I've spoken to Tessa and Tyrus," he says. "While they figure out our next step, they offer you all shelter. But they hope you'll decide if you want to help our cause within the next week."

K nods at Brayden, and I take note of his lack of previously present distaste. *Just what did they talk about yesterday?*

"No need to rush the decision. There are still fresh wounds," Brayden adds.

"Yeah, I'd like some more time," Avi comments, shifting on her feet.

She's probably still wary after being put through so much.

"We should go to the outer edges of the city and explore the forest," Alec says. "If we do, I'll be able to create a more detailed depiction of the local area. We can see how far the woods extend." He speaks firmly, not revealing any slight emotion.

Avi's face lights up. "Maybe we'll find some form of civilization!"

"That would be nice," I mutter. *If we could find somewhere we're safe, we could leave all of this behind.*

"Then it's a plan!" Melissa states. "What are we waiting for?" Her tone is sharp, expressing her impatience.

Turning to Avi, I bite my lip. "Are you sure you can come? I know you're still recovering."

She raises her head, looking me directly in the eye. "Please don't worry about me. I'll be fine."

But you weren't recently. I keep my thoughts to myself and nod stiffly. "If you insist."

"I don't know. I really don't think we should go too far from headquarters," Brayden says with a frown, not meeting anyone's gaze.

"Why? Is there something else you're hiding?" I can't keep the snark out of my tone. When he meets my gaze, I feel a pang of guilt. *He's trying. I shouldn't be so harsh.*

"No one in EMBER has gone past the perimeter of the city in years," Brayden says. "I'm not sure if you're aware, but Eclium is an undisclosed landmass located thousands of miles away from any land. It would be near impossible to go anywhere but the places you see here. This area was supposed to be flooded, so its prior residents fled during the Climate Crisis War. Only part of the land succumbed to the ocean, and now the mass is so small that it's untraceable. The world's countries are too far away to ever find it, and anyone who knew about it believes it's underwater."

Alec seems surprised, and Melissa chews on her lower lip. I look to K and Avi, remembering the letter we discovered in one of the apartment buildings. *So it's true. That's why everything is abandoned.*

"Wait, then how did you or REMEDY or whoever find it?" Avi asks him, skepticism clear in her tone.

"That's classified information, I'm afraid. I want to tell you, but the council will have my head if I share important history with non-members."

Brayden's response is unsurprising but nevertheless bothersome. *Then they do have some information they're holding back.*

K looks at him and says, "Well, if all goes well, I'm sure you'll be able to tell us soon."

His words mildly shock me. *If all goes well? Does he want to join? This must have to do with the discussion he had yesterday.*

Melissa groans. "Let's go already. Enough of this chitchat!"

I roll my eyes at her and angle myself toward Brayden. "Even if there's just an ocean beyond those trees," I say, "I don't think it hurts to see for ourselves. We're going. You can stay here."

He starts to retort, then shuts his mouth. "Fine. I'll come with you."

TWENTY-FOUR

The luscious forest extends much farther than I originally thought. We've been walking for hours with only a slight sweat and muscle cramps to show for it.

The sun shines brightly overhead, its powerful rays beating down on us. If it weren't for the strong breeze, I'm sure we would all succumb to heat exhaustion. Every twenty minutes or so, we take a break so Avi can rest. She was initially against the notion, but after the first couple of hours, we all welcome the respite.

"This was a bad idea," Melissa whines.

"I told you there would be nothing," Brayden huffs.

She shoots him a glare, and he tightens his lips. I hang back, letting the others walk ahead. K stays back with me, giving me a sideways glance.

"What is it?" he asks me, his voice quiet.

"What did you and Brayden talk about? Why are you suddenly on his side?"

He chuckles, and I glare at him. "Sorry," he says. "I thought you were worried about something serious."

My mouth drops open. "Are you kidding me? This is serious. I'm very serious right now."

He sighs. "I just wanted to hear him out. I was mad at him too, you know. But I got to know him more when we were in the dorms together, separate from the group. Alec never spoke much, but Brayden always seemed like a good guy."

He pauses, looking at me intensely. I focus on keeping my cool and not letting the rising irritation in my chest overflow.

"He told me how EMBER really is just trying to put an end to the Academy. They've been working on trying to stop them for years. I could see the passion in him. I think this could be something good for us. We can answer our questions and put a stop to the people who hurt our friends."

Something about the way he speaks is strangely calm. He seems more at ease with me now, perhaps because of his earlier outburst regarding his sister. I can see a fire in his gaze, one that tells me he's sincere. Some part of the cold and standoffish boy I met has faded, giving way to someone more introspective and eager.

"I guess that doesn't sound completely awful," I say.

He smirks at me. "See? Not serious."

I roll my eyes, increasing my pace to catch up with the others. *I'll keep an eye out. If K trusts this group, maybe I should too.*

"Up ahead! I see something!" Melissa shouts.

"Be careful," Brayden says.

Melissa ignores him and rushes forward. K and I join Avi and Alec, watching intensely as Brayden follows Melissa. A speck of concrete peeks out from layers of overgrowth. As we get closer, the speck turns into a small cottage. It's made of brick and is almost impossible to make out. Much of it is covered in greenery.

"A house?" Avi asks the question that's sitting in my mind. Then Melissa locates the front door.

I reach out. "Melissa, don't—"

She ignores my plea, pulling open the creaky wooden door in one swift motion. Then she screams and falls back into Brayden, causing them both to thump to the ground.

Alec, Avi, K, and I run forward, joining the pair. In the doorway to the cottage, a man who looks to be in his late thirties glowers down at us. He wears jeans and a button-down top, his soft black hair falling in wisps around his face.

"Who are you? Who sent you?" His voice is raspy, his sapphire eyes narrowed.

A female's voice calls from somewhere deeper in the cottage. "Mason? What's going on?"

The man, Mason, ignores her. "I asked you a question. Where did you all come from?"

"We were trying to find a way back home and came across your cottage." K steps in front of Melissa and Brayden, speaking sharply and directly. There isn't an ounce of fear in his voice.

"This isn't a way home, boy. Now leave before I give you a reason to."

Brayden and Melissa scramble to their feet, brushing dirt off their clothes. As the man starts to shut the door, a woman pushes past his arm and reopens it. She looks at him and shakes her head.

"These kids don't look like students," she says. "And there's no way he would find us all the way out here."

Mason grumbles something indiscernible and moves aside. The woman turns her attention to us, looking each of us over.

"My name is Neena. What are your names?"

I hesitate for a moment, then speak. "I'm Callista. This is K, Alec, Brayden, Melissa, and Aviana. I'm sorry for, uh, disturbing you."

Neena smiles graciously, her cheeks dimpling. "Why don't you lot come inside for some tea?"

I look back at my friends, who all shift nervously. *This could be a trap. Or maybe it could be a resource.*

K makes the final decision, stepping forward with a nod. "Thank you."

"Of course, we never get company, so this is a welcome surprise. Right, honey?" Neena says.

Mason mutters something under his breath from beside her. They make room for us to go inside, and we all do so warily. I keep a mental hold on my ability in case we need to make a sudden escape. As soon as I set foot inside the cottage, the smell of fresh lavender and other floral scents fills my nose.

Neena leads us into a quaint living area with a fireplace and logs as seating. There are two bedrolls in the corner, and flowers line every inch of the walls.

"Please, take a seat. Would you like some tea?" Neena motions toward the logs, and we all shake our heads as we awkwardly sit on the wood. She shrugs and picks up a cup of something aromatic from a wooden countertop.

Mason sits across from us, studying each of us intensely. I notice Brayden squinting at the pair, almost as if he recognizes them.

"Brayden, what is it?" I ask, whispering to him.

"You said your names are Mason and Neena, right?" he asks, ignoring my question.

"Yes, those are our names," Mason huffs.

"This may be a strange question, but do you know anyone named Julies or Marshall?"

Neena drops her cup, and it shatters across the floor. I jump, startled by the noise. Her smile is no longer on her face, replaced by a deep, concerned frown.

"Did you say Julies?" she asks.

Brayden nods slowly, and both Neena and Mason look like they've seen a ghost.

"Did they send you here to bring us back? I told him we wouldn't ever return!" Mason's voice steadily increases in volume, his face turning red.

"Now, Mason, let's hear them out," Neena says, placing a gentle hand on his arm. He purses his lips but doesn't argue.

Looking over our group with new eyes, Neena sighs. "What do you know?"

I look to my friends, biting my lip. *So these aren't just complete strangers. How does Brayden know them?*

Brayden shifts in his position, clearly uncomfortable. "I remember hearing about you two," he says. "How you used to help out at EMBER. I'm a part of EMBER—have been for two years now. But the rest of them aren't, at least not as of now. They just recently escaped the Academy."

Neena and Mason watch Brayden intensely, silently taking in his words. His response seems to satisfy them, reassuring them that we mean no harm.

"I see," Neena says, then glances at Mason. She leans into him, inaudibly whispering something into his ear. His face tenses, and once she's finished speaking, he turns to her with a stern expression.

Wordlessly, they communicate, Neena winning as Mason lets out an exasperated sigh.

"My wife here would like to know if you all would like to know what we do. She believes we possess information your friend Brayden doesn't already know. Since you all know about EMBER and the Academy, we want to assist you so that you can understand what's really going on here. So you can avoid our mistakes."

"What do you know? How could you know anything of significance?" Melissa retorts snarkily.

I sit up straighter, crossing my arms. "How do we know if we can trust you?"

"Why are you living in the middle of the forest?" K questions, his expression serious.

Neena grins, folding her hands in her lap. "All reasonable questions. It will take a long time to explain. I don't want you lot to join EMBER without knowing our history. I imagine you've already been through a lot, and I feel for you."

"I trust them. I only heard about them briefly, but if they were accepted in my home, then I know they aren't to be feared." Brayden's words break the tension growing in the room.

"Well, your trust doesn't mean much," Avi mutters.

I glance at her, and she frowns but looks unapologetic.

"Fine. We'll listen." K speaks with finality, and no one argues.

I can't deny that I'm curious as to what they know.

Neena's face lights up. "Very well. To answer your questions, I have an ability, like I imagine all of you do. I'm a horticulturist and can control and manipulate nature to my whim."

Just like Lilac could. The thought of my old friend creates a lump in my throat. I stay focused on Neena, not wanting to get too absorbed in the past.

"I was one of the first abilitied children to be birthed. Mason is a scientist. His parents were both scientist assistants at the time abilities were created. We've both been heavily involved in this universe since birth."

Alec interrupts her, his eyebrows scrunched. "You were one of the first? What do you mean when they were 'created'?"

My mind scrambles, trying to make sense of it all. *I already knew not everyone has an ability. But I never knew why I have one. Am I finally going to learn why?*

"Of course you don't know. I'm sure EMBER has barely told you anything," Mason mumbles, more to himself than anyone else.

"Your abilities and mine are the result of a gene mutation experiment," Neena says. "At first, only a few newborns were experimented on. I was one of them. After the success of the project, now children like you are birthed already possessing the genetic sequence that allows one to develop an ability." She explains so matter-of-factly, as if she were only talking about the weather.

My mouth drops open. *So I'm an experiment? Or an experiment's product?*

K doesn't take the news well. He scowls at Neena, a dark shadow clouding his expression. "Did anyone ever think about whether any of us would want this burden? Or was it just a ploy for greedy politicians to get more money?"

"I can't answer that, unfortunately. But I understand your pain. I do." Neena pauses, allowing us space to speak. No one does. I look at K with worry, but he won't meet my gaze. "We were involved in EMBER during its early stages. We left due to the increasing corruption present in the organization. We wanted our own life and wanted no further part in their machinations. So we left. We had no way to access the mainland, which is why we made our home here."

"You should do the same. You'd be better off." Mason directs his words at all of us except Brayden.

"Things have changed!" Brayden exclaims, only to be waved off and ignored.

"What corruption?" I ask, mildly concerned.

Before Neena can explain, Mason jumps in.

"I'll explain things from the start. Don't interrupt me. If you have any questions, hold them until after, or I won't continue."

He pauses, and no one dares to utter a word. *He's tough. But if I can get the answers I've wanted all this time, then I'll deal with whatever comes my way.* I fidget with my fingers nervously, anticipating his next words.

"I don't know how much you all know. The country you come from used to be called the United States. After the Climate War, people within the government were at odds with one another. Too many of them had opposing views on how the government should still be run. To solve this, they fractured the country down the middle. Not much is known about the West, but it's said to be a land ruled by free choice. This is much unlike the East, or the 'New America.' That's where we all come from. After the Climate War, every country in the world separated into small units. Interaction between nations was cut off, leaving each government to do what it wants without fear of retaliation from the next. That's how the East grew. It created dozens upon hundreds of Neighborhoods, recruiting citizens to work for the government or sending them away to who knows where."

Alec interrupts, asking, "How—" But he's cut off by a glare from the rest of us. Mason narrows his eyes at him. He doesn't speak for several moments, and I wonder if he was serious about not continuing. Only once Neena has pushed him gently does he resume.

"EMBER's goal was to nourish and grow the new generation of children with abilities. That's why Neighborhoods were formed and why Spark Academy, now known as Remedy Academy, was founded. We wanted all the gifted children to thrive. Dozens of families joined our organization and raised their families within it, just as ours did. This mission was referred to as Project Spark, and it started thirty-one years ago, about seven years after the first generation of ability-bearers were born. The man you know as the headmaster, Liam, was a part of EMBER then, and REMEDY didn't exist. At the time, Liam was highly active in the Eastern government. He used his connections to convince government officials that Project Spark would be beneficial to them. It's with them that he got funding for Spark Academy. Yet that power wasn't enough for him. He was consumed by greed. He was so hungry for more that he and other government members gathered an army and overran Spark Academy. They disposed of anyone who got in their way. They were ruthless."

Mason's voice grows louder in octave as he speaks, his face turning red with rage. When he stands in a fury, my chest tightens in fear.

"Mason, please, sit down." Neena's voice is calm and firm. He looks down at her with a furrowed brow. Almost like magic, his rage melts away to sorrow as he thumps back down onto the log.

He places his face in his hands and whispers, "I'm sorry."

"I'll take it from here," Neena says. "Please forgive him. His parents were killed in Liam's conquest, so it's a sensitive topic for him." Mason visibly tenses at her words.

"It's okay. REMEDY has taken a lot from us too." Avi's words are gentle, her empathy shining through each syllable. I grab her hand, giving it a gentle squeeze. She doesn't return the gesture for several moments, making me worry that I was too forward. Then finally, she does, and I relax.

Neena continues. "As he was saying, Liam took over Spark Academy and turned it into REMEDY Academy. That's also when he formed REMEDY, an oppositional group full of tyrants. This all happened twenty-six years ago. He wanted to use the abilitied children for his own personal gain, to give him more power. Unfortunately, many EMBER members sided with Liam and his goals and left. EMBER was too weak to fight against Liam's forces and has focused on growing and regrouping ever since. Mason and I left during this time. We were young and vulnerable, but we had nothing in the group. We'd lived out of the old buildings until we grew old enough and I learned my ability. Then we came here and have lived here ever since."

Mason finally looks up with tired eyes, his expression sullen. "EMBER isn't any safer than the Academy. They can't protect you. Your safest bet is to leave like we did."

Several long moments pass as everyone absorbs the story.

So the government knows about this place. In fact, they orchestrated it. And it's just as I thought. Eclium is connected to the Neighborhood. Does that mean my parents definitely knew about Eclium? Did Reggie know? I push the thought aside as soon as I think it. *There's no way. He was probably at the wrong place at the wrong time.* Having suspected most of the new information ever since I got involved in this mess, most of it doesn't come as a surprise. Even so, I can't help but hate how my entire life was a setup.

I was raised for one purpose. To become Liam's toy. His pet. So were all my friends. That must be why I was so isolated. Why my parents were so secretive. It was all a part of a greater scheme. My stomach twists at the implications. *If everything wasn't real, then why would Reggie be real?* I shake my head, denial winning over my voice of reason. *It can't be possible, right? That the single good thing in my life was a figment of my imagination?*

My train of thought is broken by Melissa's voice. "What are we supposed to do with all of this? No offense, but I can't just live in a forest like a hermit."

"We'll do nothing." Brayden speaks coolly, an underlying irritation clear in his tone. He turns on us, facing away from Neena and Mason. "Please, don't be afraid. I promise you that EMBER has grown. We'll keep you safe. You won't be in any danger."

I can't help myself from chuckling at the irony. "Sorry, but it just sounds funny for you to claim we'll be safe with the same group that put our lives at risk."

Out of the corner of my eye, I catch Mason and Neena exchanging a confused look. I turn to them with a half-smile. "EMBER could have stopped us from having to go to the Academy. But they didn't, so Aviana almost died, and our other friend did."

Brayden looks to me in astonishment. "Callista, I told you I'm sorry. So has everyone else involved. What else do you want me to do?" He doesn't look like he's angry at me. He looks lost and has a genuine sadness glinting in his chocolate eyes that tugs me the wrong way.

"Not surprised," Mason scoffs.

"I have an idea." Neena's statement catches all of our attention. "Mason and I are quite knowledgeable about abilities. What if you all spend the next week training with us? We can teach you techniques that will keep you safe. That way, no matter what you choose, you'll have a fighting chance."

"The Academy already taught us how to fight," Avi says.

Neena grins. "Not fighting. Feeling. Being one with your strength. It's a whole different experience—one that I'm confident no one can teach better than I can."

"We'll be making our decision over the next week," Melissa reminds us.

K lets out a huff, his cold front still present.

I bite the inside of my cheek. *Getting stronger won't hurt us. And it will give me time to come to terms with everything I just learned.* "I'm in," I say. K's eyes widen as I shrug. "We have nothing else to do."

The others murmur agreement.

Neena looks out the wide window, her eyes reflecting the late sun. "It's settled then. Come back tomorrow. You lot should hurry off now. It's getting late."

We all stand and say our goodbyes. A strange pain settles in my jaw, my chest still constricted and tight. *Everything I've ever known was planned out. I never had any choice.* I struggle to accept the fact. *How could a group of people be so heartless?*

TWENTY-FIVE

THE NEXT DAY, BRAYDEN INFORMS the rest of us that he won't be joining us to visit Mason and Neena. He claims he has to help Tessa with something, but I think he was insulted by the couple's insistence on EMBER's shortcomings. So the remaining five of us hike into the woods without him. It's no easier than yesterday. Frequent breaks are still necessary, so we arrive when the sun has just hit its apex.

Neena and Mason greet us outside, Neena more eager than her husband.

"Come, come!" she says as she enthusiastically waves us over. Five cups of water are lined up on a tree stump. "I gathered some water for you all this morning. I figured you would be thirsty after hiking so long."

I quickly grab one of the cups and chug the liquid. It's the freshest drink I've ever had, even if it tastes slightly of dirt.

"Thank you," Avi says, drinking her cup more graciously than I did. K doesn't meet Neena's gaze, but he accepts the drink.

"We only have a few hours, so I'll be separating you all into two groups." Neena scans her eyes over us, a frown forming on her lips. "Where's Brayden?"

Alec wipes droplets from his lip with his sleeve. "He was busy."

"Oh, that's a shame." She recovers quickly from the news, placing a hand on her hip. "Before we begin, can you all tell me your abilities?"

We all share our skill sets, and I share last. When I mention three, her eyes widen.

"That's incredible!" she exclaims. "I didn't know such a gift existed." I smile sheepishly, something about her praise making me feel seen. She purses her lips, considering each of us carefully. "Alright. Alec, Aviana, and Melissa, please go with Mason. I want to work closely with K and Callista."

Mason nods at the trio and leads them into a nearby empty patch of grass. Once they're no longer in view, I'm forced to focus on the pair in front of me.

"Why us?" I ask, placing my cup back on the stump.

She smiles wildly. "You may think me to be crazy, but I have an idea. When I was younger, I searched through old research documents I carried with me that were left around by my parents after they passed. The papers were detailed reports of hypothetical scenarios that may be possible with future generations of abilitied children. One such hypothetical detailed how subjects with opposite abilities may be able to combine them to create a stronger version of their strengths. Seeing as you, Callista, are able to manipulate light and K can manipulate dark, I thought you may fit into this hypothetical."

Her words pique my interest, and I step closer. Even K looks more attentive, his expression no longer angry. "How would this work?" he asks.

"I'm not sure," she says with a laugh. "I lost the rest of the papers in my travels."

I deflate, disappointed.

"That doesn't mean we shouldn't try though!" she says. "It can't be that difficult."

K eyes her warily, crossing his arms. "What do you suggest we do to try?"

"Summon your abilities, and let's test it."

I do as she says, closing my eyes and summoning my orb. It sits in front of me when I blink them open, and I realize that I'm consumed by darkness. "K?" I ask, frightened. "I can't see!"

He lifts his shadow, shifting the ability to see from Neena to me.

"K, can you only allow for one person to see besides yourself?" Neena asks, not seeming concerned in the least by her lack of sight.

"Yes."

"Why don't you try to push your shadow into a concentrated area instead of an all-consuming blanket."

K furrows his brow, a frown tugging at his lips. I watch in awe as the shadows flicker, shifting and moving like feathers in the wind. K grunts, seeming to struggle with the effort. Then the shadow fades completely.

"It's pointless," he mutters.

"You almost had it!" Neena responds encouragingly.

K stares at her with an undiscernible look, then turns and walks away. "I need a moment."

I look to Neena apologetically and chase after K into the forest.

K leans against a tree, a sullen look on his face. "What's wrong?" I ask, approaching him cautiously.

"I can't believe everything has been a setup. Our entire lives. They were never ours. Even June. They probably set her up too. And these people act as if it's nothing. As if we should trust them when it's obvious that no one in our lives is trustworthy."

I smile sadly, leaning back next to him. *I didn't have to push the information out of him. He's more comfortable with me now.* "I feel the same. I always felt like something was off, but to hear it confirmed, it hurts. Even if I hated my old life, knowing it was all a sham for some greedy man makes it ten times worse. And I fear—" I stop myself, afraid to admit my thoughts aloud.

"What?" K looks at me with a raised eyebrow.

I swallow. "I fear that my friend Reginald was part of the lie. If he was, I don't know what I'd do with myself."

"I'm sure he wasn't," K assures me, although I can tell he doesn't believe it.

"This is too much. My parents. I never really thought they loved me, not really. I wonder if they were aware of what my purpose was. Or if they were blind too." K doesn't say anything. I peer at him with a curious look. "Why don't you want anyone to call you your full name?"

He seems put off by my question, his expression tensing. "I don't want to get close to people, like I told you before." A dark chuckle escapes him. "I guess it's too late for that."

I half-smile, letting out a sigh. "We should go back. Neena might be able to help us learn new skills. And I don't know. I think it would be pretty cool if what she said was true."

"You're right. Sorry for being such an ass again."

I laugh, punching him lightly. "It's fine, K. We're all asses sometimes."

The following week, Neena continues to focus on me and K. Brayden makes up one excuse or another to not join us each time we make the trek into the forest. None of us bother trying to convince him to come. I know I personally don't mind having a break from him.

Each day, Neena has K and me both focus on channeling our abilities into a single focus point. I have more success than my friend, likely due to having more experience using my ability. K initially struggles to control his strength, but he makes steady progress.

Working with K so intimately has definitely made me see him in a different light. He's no longer the cold and suspicious boy I once thought he was. He's thoughtful, just reserved. I can tell he's more comfortable with me as well. Conversation flows naturally between us, and not just about the serious things.

Today is our last day of lessons. We have yet to figure out if Neena's speculations are true. As we separate into our groups, I find my stomach twisting with nerves. *This is our last chance to figure it out. Then we have to decide if we want to join EMBER or if we'd rather be on our own.*

Neena's reddish-brown hair is tied back, her expression serious. "Today is our last day together. I want you both to put it all out there. Don't be afraid. Please, summon your abilities."

K and I listen to her instruction. My orb floats in front of me as a cloud of shadow sits in front of him. "Good. Now face each other. Think about what you've practiced with me. Make your focal point each other's ability."

I frown, unsure. "How—"

"Just do it," she says.

K and I exchange a look, both of us certain this won't work. Regardless, we push our abilities outward. The shadowy cloud and my orb approach each other, and I notice a faint spark as they touch edges.

"Push them closer," Neena instructs.

I try to extend my light farther, but it doesn't budge. "I can't," I tell her.

"Keep trying!"

K's face is contorted in deep concentration. A faint sweat beads on his brow. "Callista's right. My shadow won't move any closer."

Neena shakes her head, dismissing us. "We can't give up yet. Just focus on each other's strength. Imagine the light meeting the darkness, and the darkness meeting the light."

My head pounds from the exertion, my vision becoming fuzzy. Then the shadow slowly starts to absorb my light. My heart rate picks up, my hand starting to shake.

"It's working! Keep going!" Neena shouts.

I can barely see K anymore. All I see is light and dark. Something bubbles up inside me—an indescribable feeling. But it isn't good. The more fused our abilities become, the more the world starts to spin. Everything seems to be shaking. Spinning. My legs become wobbly, and I strain to keep my focus. *It's too much. I can't—*

I fall to my knees, and my surroundings refocus. Just before me, K is steadying himself against a tree, his breaths labored. Our abilities are gone.

We were so close. I reach up, wiping sweat from my face. *Were we not strong enough?*

Avi rushes over, her eyes wide and panicked. "What happened?"

Melissa joins her side, an apprehensive look on her face. "What did you do?"

Neena approaches me, her gaze wavering. "Are you alright?"

I nod, allowing her to help me to my feet. "I'm fine."

K slowly makes his way over, looking exhausted. "That was awful."

Alec and Mason walk up behind Avi. Mason looks concerned, his gaze focused on Neena. Avi and Melissa watch us expectantly.

"We were trying to combine our abilities," I say.

"You were what?" Melissa and Avi speak in unison, their voices high.

"I wanted to test something with them. I didn't expect this to happen," Neena responds.

Mason exhales. "That was reckless, Neena. Someone could have gotten hurt."

"We agreed to it," I say, not wanting Neena to take the blame when she was only trying to help.

"Did it work?" Alec looks at us with bewilderment.

"No," K responds, failing to hide his disappointment.

"I'm sorry, K and Callista," Neena says dejectedly. "I didn't intend to put you in danger."

I half-heartedly smile at the woman. "It's really fine. It was a nice thought." A silence stretches between us. No one seems to be sure if we should just go back to practice after the outburst.

"We should get back," Alec says. "Tessa and Tyrus expect our responses tonight."

"He's right," Melissa says. "I don't feel like training anymore anyway."

I frown. *What's the right choice? Run, or try and end the corruption?* I observe my friends and recall what happened to Avi and Lilac. *I ran before. Not anymore. I'm stronger now. I'll stop any more innocent people from being forced into the life I had.* I turn to Neena and Mason, resolute. "You two should come with us."

Mason shakes his head instantly. "Sorry, but we can't. Not unless there has been significant change. Which, based off the stories you've shared, there hasn't been."

"Whatever decision you make, just be careful, alright?" Neena adds, smiling sadly at us.

"Can we come back here?" Avi asks, her gaze darting between them.

Before Neena can respond, Mason shakes his head again. "It's too risky. If you decide to join EMBER, you can't. We don't need you accidentally leading them to us. If you don't join them, that's another story. Still, we wouldn't want you to come for a while. Just in case someone decides to follow you."

Avi's shoulders slump. I give the pair a bitter smile. "Well, thanks anyway." My mind is heavy, my body drained.

With one final set of goodbyes, we set off away from the strangely insightful cottage, on our way to make a life-altering decision.

It's dark out when we finally reach EMBER's headquarters. Tessa and Tyrus join us for dinner, along with Brayden. No one speaks as we eat. As I finish my last bite of chicken soup, Brayden breaks the silence.

"Did you make your decision?"

Alec, Melissa, Avi, K, and I all look to one another.

This is it. They may have their own corruption, but nothing can be worse than Liam. It takes one evil to fight another. I place down my spoon, looking up to meet Tessa and Tyrus's gaze. "We'll join your cause."

Brayden lets out a sigh of relief, his shoulders sagging. "That's great news!"

Tessa reaches out to clasp my hand, a hopeful glint in her eye. "I promise you won't regret it."

I glance back at K, who shakes his head.

We won't tell them about Mason and Neena. This is our group's little secret. I pull my hand from her grasp, giving her a half-smile. "I hope not."

Several days pass, and we're all acclimated to what life as a member of EMBER is like. Not much changes in terms of our life-style, but we're finally privy to more private information that was previously held back. Much of what Tyrus teaches us, we already heard from Mason and Neena, although he doesn't know that. One surprising thing we learned is that, apparently, Eclium was discovered by Liam when the former EMBER was financing a research project to find the perfect undisclosed location for Spark Academy. The New America government is the only government to know about Eclium. Furthermore, the same hypotheticals that Neena believes in are apparently sought after here.

Knowing that I have three abilities and that K and I are opposites seems to have given the group reinvigorated hope. Tessa insists that we'll be the winning pieces and that their success will be guaranteed with us assisting them. The pressure of these fantastical expectations has been weighing on me greatly. I think Tessa has noticed, as she hasn't mentioned her great hope since the first day.

As I'm walking down the hall toward the lounge area after lunch, Brayden joins my side.

"Hey, Callista. We've discovered some notes left behind by your birth parents. Liam never got to them. I believe there was a letter written to their future children in there somewhere."

My eyes widen, and I feel breathless. It takes me a moment to adjust to the news. A question I've yet to ponder pops in my head. Shifting on my feet, I ask, "Did my parents know Liam?"

He considers the question before nodding. "Yes, based on what Tessa has told me, Rosalie and Elijah were good friends with Marshall, EMBER's founder, and Liam." His gaze sweeps over me, leaving me with an uncomfortable tingling sensation.

"Brayden, can you show me the notes?"

I step back, needing space. He seems not to notice my uneasiness and moves toward one of the adjacent halls. I follow several steps behind at a slow pace. He walks into a small room on the left side of the hall, and I follow.

Inside, I see a large monitor on the wall with papers scattered on a massive wooden table. A piece of paper sits on the dark wood. I approach it, squinting to try and make out the cursive lettering. It's addressed to me, but the letter's content makes no sense. It's very sporadic, going from discussions on why science is the future to what the best food item is.

I chew on my lip, confused. Then I realize that certain letters seem to be more emphasized than others. They're darker, in black ink, instead of the deep navy blue everything else is. The difference is so slight that I'm surprised I even noticed. Biting my lip, I try and put the letters together. *Tone … rust … on? No, that's not right. Turn … on? That doesn't use enough letters.*

I ponder the letters for several excruciating moments before I finally realize what they say: TRUST NO ONE.

In my dream, my mom said to be careful who I trust. Now I'm being told a similar message. But why did they make it so hidden? I'm disappointed by the lack of an actual note and confused as to why my parents gave me such a hidden warning. I press my lips into a slight frown and am about to question Brayden when the monitor buzzes to life, showing a camera view of the room K and Melissa are in.

"Oh, I wonder why that turned on!" Brayden says suspiciously, then he moves toward the right. My eyes stay trained on the screen. I can see him fumbling with wires out of the corner of my eye. Static comes from a speaker mounted on the wall.

Finally, the camera's audio comes to life.

"I've been wanting to get you alone for a moment," Melissa says as she slinks toward K. He's sitting on a couch, a file in his lap. He looks up at her, seeming surprised.

"What is it?" he asks. Then he places the file on a nearby table and glances at her. The footage isn't very high quality, but I can decipher the smirk on Melissa's lips. For some reason, it irritates me. I can sense my heart rate shoot up as she slinks closer to K.

"You know, we haven't talked much, just you and I," she says. She sits next to K, placing a hand on his arm.

He seems perturbed, but it isn't enough to settle my growing angst. K is completely silent. I step closer to the screen, wanting to reach out and pull Melissa away from him. I'm not completely sure why I'm so upset at witnessing this interaction. My breaths come out noisily as my eyes bulge. I'm completely helpless as Melissa moves her hand from K's arm to the side of his head. He moves back slightly, reaching a hand up to remove Melissa's from his mouth. But as soon as he does, she leans in and kisses him.

⚸

TWENTY-SIX

A BURNING SENSATION TWISTS IN my chest, and my teeth clench. Just as I'm about to shut the screen off myself, Brayden beats me to it.

"There, that's fixed," he says.

Why do I even care whether she kissed him? I've never thought of him like I used to think about Reggie. My confusing thoughts race a million miles a second. I turn on Brayden, scowling. "What was that about?" I ask.

When he doesn't react, my anger diminishes. He stands still, like a robot, in the corner of the room. *What's wrong with him?* I hear distant footsteps and turn toward the door. I walk toward it, wanting to see who's approaching.

When I reach the door, I pause and focus on the sound of the incoming people. There's more than one person, and they're coming fast. I'm able to push the thoughts of what I saw out of my mind and instead focus on my surroundings.

Brayden still hasn't moved. I approach him cautiously, wary of him reacting. I stop as soon as I'm in front of him. He's still blinking and breathing, but his eyes seem empty.

This isn't right.

Just when I'm about to go call for help, the door flies open, and footsteps rush at me. Instinct kicks in, and I drive my foot back, resulting in a low yelp from someone as they thump to the floor.

I pivot and call for my light orb, letting it burst into flames. As soon as the next attacker comes, I push outward, and the flaming ball shoots straight into the person. It catches on their clothes, and as they try to put it out, it spreads, trailing flames down the hall.

Crap! I panic, dashing over to Brayden and running my hands through his pockets. My hands are clammy, not moving nearly as fast as I want them to.

"Where is it?" I yell. My heart feels like it will beat out of my chest as sweat drips down my face. I can hear more people screaming in the hall, presumably caught in the fire. Eventually, my hand touches a small metal object, and I pull it out and push the button. It buzzes, and Tyrus pops up, eyes wide with horror.

"Callista! You need to get out—"

"This place is burning, and this idiot won't move!" I motion to Brayden. "I could escape, but I won't leave Brayden to die."

The second sentence comes out desperately, and Tyrus nods. "There should be an emergency switch on the back of the object you're holding. If you flip it, your coordinates will be sent to me, but it will also self-destruct right after so that no one else can trace the signal. It takes thirty seconds to self-destruct. I should be able to make it."

After a moment's hesitation, I reply, "Hope to see you soon." *I just pray we have enough time.* Then I cut off the communication and search for the switch. I find it in a small section on the back, as Tyrus said, and flip it. A robotic voice speaks out of it.

"Self-destruct initiated. Thirty seconds remaining."

I pace back and forth as the countdown lowers. As soon as it hits twenty seconds, Tyrus appears, and I push Brayden's heavyset body toward him.

"Bring him first," Tyrus says. He looks concerned but nods as the countdown lowers.

I hear a woman's scream somewhere nearby and widen my eyes. "Avi?" I say. My sister flashes in my mind, and I look out into the flaming hall. She isn't there. I see a figure walking through the flames as smoke travels into the room I'm in. The screams seem to come from whoever is moving, and I call out again. "Who is—"

I choke on the smoke-filled air as the timer continues to lower. "Ten seconds."

Tyrus hasn't returned, and fear rises inside me. I pick up the device and throw it as far away from me as possible. Shutting my eyes tight, I prepare to try to brace myself against whatever explosion is about to happen.

"Five seconds."

More smoke travels into my lungs, and I feel woozy. As the countdown lowers to three seconds, I think of K, Emmy, Aviana, and Reggie. Even Lilac, who I never got to save. Sadness fills me, and I begin to fall over.

An arm grabs me as the device says, "One."

My eyes widen, and I heavily breathe in the fresh air that suddenly surrounds me. The air is cold, and I see Tyrus standing and breathing heavily next to me. We're now deep in the forest, surrounded by trees and shrubbery.

Melissa is standing nearby. When she sees me, she looks at me with wide and teary eyes. "You're okay! We were so worried."

I look at Tyrus warily. "Do you know what happened to Brayden?"

Tyrus frowns, shifting and looking uncomfortable. "I think Brayden may have somehow gotten his mind infiltrated. Similar to how the Academy alters memories, except they controlled his whole being. I'm not sure of the specifics, but we'll examine him to find out more."

I consider this for a moment. Although it sounds outrageous, so did the whole mind control thing until I was a victim of it. Knowing this, I decide that Tyrus's suggestion seems like the most likely answer. But I still don't understand why I was attacked.

"I … was the one who caught the building on fire," I say. "Before you say anything, it was in self-defense and an accident. A group of people attacked me. I thought we were safe in that place. How did they get in?"

His eyes widen, and his expression darkens. "I don't know. The only people who know about our headquarters are our allies, which means that for our enemy to get in, someone would have had to betray us. If Brayden was being controlled, that's probably how they found us. They must have found the location through him. We'll take action on this." He pauses, considering something. "As for you creating the fire, don't worry. With luck, it should have been quelled and didn't create too much significant damage. No one was hurt. Just don't do it again, alright?"

I nod, then pause. His answer doesn't help my suspicions of Brayden. *It seems awfully convenient that he wasn't in control of himself at the same time I was attacked. There must be some correlation. Or am I being too suspicious?*

I bite my lip. When I don't speak further, Tyrus shoots me a quick look and runs off toward Tessa. I make a note to find out later what he learns from his investigation, then I turn my attention back to Melissa. I remember the vision of her kissing K and frown.

"Callista, what's wrong?" she asks.

"Nothing. Where are the others? Where's Avi?"

She looks at me with concern, and I avoid her gaze. *She did nothing wrong.* I straighten, noticing her glance travel far off. Then she points.

"Somewhere over there, luckily no one is hurt."

I smile gratefully, then choke again and laugh it off. "Sorry, must have smoke in my throat still."

"We should get you some water. I think there are some scavenged supplies with the others. Follow me!"

She starts walking, and I follow. We head toward a forested area in silence, and I listen for any sound of Avi or K. I swallow. I don't hear them nearby.

Melissa stops, a puzzled expression on her face. She focuses on me, her eyebrows drawn. Biting her lip, she scans our surroundings. "Maybe they went to look for us? I told them to wait here."

"We should go back. Maybe Tessa or Tyrus knows."

She shakes her head. "I told them I'd meet them here. You stay. I'll go back and ask. That way, if they return, they aren't worried about where we are."

Her logic is sound, so I nod and watch her disappear into the trees. I hear leaves shuffling and turn. There's nothing. *Was it just the wind?*

"Hello?" I call.

The shuffling resumes, and I hear a piercing scream. *What was that?* Afraid one of my friends is hurt, I run toward the noise. I keep my pace steady, my chest constricting as my heart races. I don't pay attention to the ground below me, so I fail to notice a tree root blocking my path. As soon as my foot connects with it, I trip and land on a pile of leaves. Stinging comes from my arm, and I look over at it. Blood swells up from a new cut, then drips a thin trail down my skin.

Crunching comes from behind me, and I sit up to turn, only to feel something sharp prick my neck. The world becomes distorted, and I sway.

"Who—"

My voice comes out quiet as I fall backward onto the leaf pile, and the world fades to black.

I blink slowly as I open my eyes, and my senses all overwhelm me at once. The air is stale, and the lights are dim. I try to call out to my orb, but I'm unable to. When I close my eyes to search for it, it sits still as if trapped in a cage. I open my eyes and gasp.

I sit up in a small bed. My uniform is torn, and my wrists are chained together. I try to maneuver my hands out of the cuffs but am unsuccessful.

"Hello?" I call out to the otherwise empty room. I'm shocked by the hoarse sound of my voice. My throat is dry from dehydration, and I swallow.

I look around my room and am unable to see a door, becoming more claustrophobic with every second. Fear bubbles up inside me, and I crowd into the corner of my bed, hugging my knees to my chest. The only covering on my feet are small white socks. I can't help but feel sick.

A sudden glint of light catches my eye, and I look up to see a camera watching me in the corner. A light comes from a green dot at the top. I move out of my position to get closer.

"I know someone's watching me. Show yourself!" I can hear the trembling in my voice, and I shiver. When no one replies, I hopelessly move back to my bed.

I lie on my back and think. *What happened to Melissa? Did my friends get taken too? No, that can't be possible. They must have run away. Maybe Melissa got taken, but I have to hope that the rest didn't. It's the least I can do to settle my brain.*

The image of K and Melissa kissing flashes through my mind, further spiraling my thoughts. I lose my train of thought when my stomach rumbles. I look back up to the camera and scoff. "How many days has it been? Can you at least give me that?"

The camera blinks, and I sigh.

Just as I'm about to close my eyes and give up any hope I have, a low buzz comes from the wall. I turn and prepare to defend myself as a dark hall is revealed. An arrow glows on the wall, pointing down the ominous corridor.

I stand up slowly and move my shackled wrists closer to my body. I look down the hall with caution and search for any sign of movement. The end of the hall is shrouded in darkness, hiding whatever sits at the end.

Moving back to the bed, I reach down to feel its legs and find a loose one. I tug on it till it eventually comes out, causing the bed to collapse. I turn back toward the corridor and hold the leg in front of me, prepared to use it as a weapon if I need to.

The silence unsettles me as I head down the ominous hall. I move through it slowly and keep my ears open for any strange noise. Surprisingly, the hall doesn't last long, and soon I find myself in another white room with a metal door on the wall. Another buzz comes, and the door slides open. I prepare to attack but am taken aback with shock when it fully opens. I drop the metal rod from my hands and well up with emotions.

"Reggie?" My voice cracks and sounds even more hoarse than before as I stare at him.

He wears a dark suit, and his dirty-blond hair is combed back nicely. I'd recognize his familiar eyes anywhere. I was always sure they could make anyone who looks into them melt. He seems pained as his gaze meets mine, and I twist with a million different emotions. I'm utterly shocked, but I'm also infuriated. The heavy sensation in my stomach fights with the pounding in my ears.

Where did he come from? What happened to him? How can he just show up like this? Why is he here? How can he act like it's just another day? After everything I've been through …

I want to stay angry at him, to get answers to all my questions, but the feeling of missing him is too strong for me to ignore. I move toward him, reaching out my arms to hug him. But as soon as I'm at his side, he looks down at me and disappears. I look around in terror as the headmaster walks in.

"Callista, I'm sorry about that. I just needed to see if you're still susceptible to my son. I know you most likely won't believe me, but trust me when I say we need to stop him. He's out there somewhere and trying to hurt us. I have one of your friends here too. Maybe she can help you trust me."

As soon as he says this, Melissa enters, her eyes full of concern. I take a step back, my breaths shaky.

"How …"

"Take the cuffs off her!" Melissa cries, approaching my side. She furrows her brow, fumbling with my restraints.

"Why are you here?" I ask. "How am I here?"

Melissa is frowning at me as the headmaster steps forward and says, "My apologies. I put those on just so you wouldn't attack me as soon as you saw me. Also, if your powers aren't working, it's simply because we're in an anti-ability area. As soon as we leave it, you should be free to use them again."

He reaches out to remove my cuffs. I rub my wrists with my fingers and nod slowly.

Melissa gives me a sympathetic look. "Callista, I need to tell you something," she says. "I don't know what happened to the rest of our friends, but the headmaster has reason to believe they were double agents working for Reginald."

I step back, shaking my head. "What do you mean working for Reginald? Reginald isn't a boss. He's just a boy!"

"Just watch," the headmaster says, taking out a small controller and pressing a bright-red button.

❧

TWENTY-SEVEN

A SCREEN APPEARS OUT OF THIN AIR. I watch intensely as a video of Reginald appears. He says, "I'm going to end them all. I'm sick and tired of letting them push me and other people around. She put me in danger. They don't deserve joy. None of them do. They don't understand what it's like to be me. Now they will."

He speaks in a low mutter, seemingly to himself. His hair is disheveled, and he's wearing the same outfit I recall him wearing just a couple of months ago.

My heart hurts at his words. *Does he really mean that? Who is the "they"? Am I the "she"? Is he upset because I couldn't catch him? But we went through so much together ...* I feel a lump form in my throat as I turn to Melissa and the headmaster. "How did you get this video?"

"We have various operating cameras around the city. This video was filmed near the highway leading into central Eclium," the headmaster explains.

The highway? Does that mean I was close to him all along? My stomach twists into knots at the implication. Unsure what move to make, I step back and decide to let the headmaster propose what he wants. "What do you want from me?"

He grins and coughs low in his throat. "I wanted to propose that you become one of my leaders in my army to take down my son. You would be able to control all of my subjects and be in a position of high power."

Take down Reggie? I could never hurt him, even if he really does despise me so much. Unconvinced, I nod toward the blank screen and say, "That could be faked. Really, why should I believe you?"

"I know you haven't had much reason to trust me so far, Callista. And I'm sorry for that," he says. "I promise that all my actions up to this point were only for the greater good of all of the students at the Academy. I've been trying to prepare them to fight against my son."

I doubt that. You're just a power-hungry loser. I'd be better off anywhere else. I lean back on my foot, crossing my arms. "The Reginald I know would never hurt anyone." *And I trust K, Alec, and Avi.*

He drops his smile, almost looking genuinely sad. "I know you care about him. You wouldn't know just how much I've always wanted for him to have a friend like you. But he isn't the little boy he used to be. I have reason to believe he's been in cahoots with a more sinister organization, plotting against those he believes wronged him. And now that you're associated with me, he'll see you as someone who wronged him too."

You never even knew him as a little boy! I think. But his argument is almost convincing. I could sense some form of unfamiliar genuine rage in the video he showed me. But I can't ignore the obvious itch in my gut that he's holding back. I can't imagine that the boy I knew so long is a crazed psychopath. It's clear that I won't get any other information for now, as the headmaster has not given many direct responses. *I need to reunite with K so we can get to the bottom of this. By whatever means possible.*

I stifle a laugh. "May I please talk to my friend for a minute?" I fake my nicest smile, and he nods, grinning as he steps outside.

As soon as the door shuts, I turn to Melissa. *Keeping her with me may put me in more danger. But I can't just push aside all the good memories we've shared since we joined the Academy. I must believe that she had no idea this would happen. After all, if I'm to believe in the good I've seen in Reggie, I should treat her the same. I'll just have to keep an eye on her.*

Pushing my doubts and anger aside, I pull Melissa closer. "We need to get out of here."

She lets out a breath. "I've been thinking that this whole time. I just played along so he wouldn't lash out at me. If you just pretend to agree to his terms, there's a button we have to push in the hall he just went through that leads to an exit. I saw it when he brought me in here. If we're quick enough, we can escape."

I nod furiously and call for the headmaster.

He walks in and nods at us. "So, what's your choice?"

I exchange a final glance with Melissa and smile. "I'll do it."

"Wonderful! Just follow me through this hall."

I swear I hear him mumble to himself as he walks away. We follow closely behind. The door shuts, and Melissa watches the wall. The path goes on for ages until she eventually stops. I notice a tiny black switch on the wall. She mutters a countdown, then flips it, and a large passageway opens, leading out into bright light. I take note of her every action.

The headmaster yells as I turn and run through the passage, not realizing that Melissa is far behind me. As soon as I reach the end, I throw myself into the outside world and hear a thud. Turning, I see the door close and hear pounding.

"Help!" Melissa yells, and I freeze. Her screaming gets cut off, and terror fills me. *I just left her in there.* Guilt consumes me as I pick myself up and move away, realizing we're just outside the Academy gates.

"I'll come back. I need more help," I whisper to myself as I take off as fast as I can.

Once I reach the outskirts of the forest, I pause. My stomach twists in knots. *If something happens to her, I'll never forgive myself.* I take a moment to recount what just happened. *Why was it so easy to escape?* An unsettling chill crawls down my spine. Desperate to find my friends, I feel myself fill with strength. Instinctively, I close my eyes and call to my orb.

When it comes, I breathe a sigh of relief. I let it float above me and nearly fall over when someone taps my shoulder. Pivoting on my feet, I gasp as I come face-to-face with someone I never thought I'd see again. Before I act rashly, I step back. "Reggie? Is that really you?"

His dirty-blond hair hangs over his eyes, and he frowns. "It is. I know I have a lot of explaining to do. Please trust me, and follow me a bit away from here so I can explain."

I don't move. I can see the video in my mind from just moments ago—his painful words and cold, deadly expression. Crossing my arms, I eye him up and down. "How are you here?"

He shifts nervously, and I take note of his clear unease. "My father accidentally slipped and let me know in an argument that he was holding you somewhere. I knew he would be up to no good. I was just on my way to try and find you to get you away from him." He pauses, seeming to analyze me. "But it seems you already found a way out yourself."

His answer doesn't seem too unreasonable. Although I do wonder when they had a conversation, as the headmaster made it seem like they aren't in contact. I decide to trust him, for now. After seeing that image of him earlier, I don't feel as emotional seeing him again. Rather, I'm almost numb. I'm unsure what to feel. All I desire is an explanation.

"I'll follow you," I finally say. "But don't try anything."

He smiles slightly and nods.

I keep a steady hold of my light in case I need to use it against him or some other unforeseen enemy. When he turns, I follow him into the forest as the sun shines brightly above.

Eventually, we arrive at a small clearing several minutes away from where I left the headmaster. Reginald motions for me to sit down in the grass, and I do, waiting for him to explain himself.

"I promise you I didn't know Liam was my father," he says. "I'll admit that I've lied to you. You see, I was assigned to be your friend at a young age. I was never told all the details. I just knew that was my role. So while you couldn't be with other children, you could be with me. Your parents knew it too. However, as we grew older, I realized how great a person you are, and I forgot about that past role that was assigned to me. I guess now I know it was a part of something else. Trust me when I say no one else can be trusted. We can find the peace we've always wanted if we stay together."

It was a setup. Just as Neena and Mason said. And now my thoughts are confirmed. Everyone, every relationship I ever had was a lie. My chest tightens, a deep resentment settling in. I cross my arms.

"There are a lot of holes in what you just said." His expression falls at my stern expression. "Look, I'm not saying I don't believe you. In fact, I want to. But you need to explain more." *Like why you didn't try to find me. Why you let me be in all that pain without you.*

"I'll answer whatever questions I can."

I take a moment to observe him. He looks just as I remember, and his presence makes me feel vulnerable. I have a momentary desire to fall into him, to tell him all the pain I'm in. I lick my lips nervously. *I have to focus. I can't let the emotions overtake me.* I take a deep inhale and speak.

"If you didn't know Liam was your father, then how do you know now? When did you find out?"

He looks down, avoiding my eyes. "After what happened in the forest, I was teleported here. I didn't see you anywhere, and I was afraid something happened to you. I was near the city when I found the Academy. I decided to investigate it, and that's when I met Liam. He recognized me as soon as I said my name. I've been with him ever since—until I heard him talking about meeting with you. Then I knew I had to go. To find you."

I nod slowly, my mind scanning his words for inconsistencies. When I find no obvious ones, I move to my next question. "Fine. You say I can trust you, yet you just admitted you lied to me the whole time that we knew each other."

"That's not a question."

I roll my eyes and scoff. "But you know what I'm asking! Don't play coy with me."

When he meets my eyes, I'm surprised my heart no longer flutters like it used to. "Like I said, I didn't know why I was told to lie to you at the time. But I promise you, once I got to know you, it didn't feel like a lie. I genuinely pushed away what had been demanded of me and spent time with you out of my own free will. I was never supposed to leave the Neighborhood. I convinced my mom and the other people controlling me that if I was able to run away with you, you would never suspect me. That was just a lie I told them. The truth is, I was—I am—in love with you. I didn't know DETA was in the forest. I knew it existed, but not where. When I saw it, I panicked. I thought you'd be okay if I just went back to my original plan. That there was no way they would truly hurt you. But when I saw you fearing for your life, I regretted my decision. It was too late. I'm sorry. I understand why you may be wary about trusting me. Let me prove myself to you. Just give me another chance."

He seems so genuine, and almost sad. It makes me melt a little, and I have the urge to wrap my hand in his. But I stop myself. *He loves me?*

Shaking my head, I frown. "You can't just say you love me. Not after everything you've done."

"I can't just deny my feelings, Cal."

This is my chance to see if the headmaster's video was a lie. "Well, I can. That ship has long sailed. I saw the video, Reggie."

His eyebrows scrunch in confusion. "What are you talking about?"

"I believe you said, 'I'm going to end them all. She put me in danger. They don't deserve joy.'"

When his eyes fill with recognition, my heart breaks. *So it's true?*

"I don't know how you heard that," he says, "but I wasn't referring to you. I was talking about the people who forced me into the position of putting your life at risk. I despise them. I despise myself for ever listening to them." He speaks pleadingly, as if begging me to understand.

He never did mention me by name. It would make more sense if it didn't apply to me.

I resist the urge to melt at his despair, instead focusing on my final question. The most painful one. "Why didn't you try to find me?" Unexpectedly I start to choke up. I don't bother fighting back the wave of sadness and pain that overcomes me. "If you knew I was here, why would you let me think that something happened? That I would never see you again?" The tears welled up in my eyes start to fall, and I move my hand to wipe them away. I avoid his gaze, embarrassed.

He doesn't say anything for several long, excruciating moments. The only sound that fills the cool air is my sniffling. For a second, I think he has left. But then he speaks.

"I … I guess I was afraid to tell you the truth. Once I met my father and he shared with me, I was terrified you would hate me if you found out what he was planning. But when I found out his plans involved you, I knew I couldn't stay away, no matter the consequences."

I still don't meet his eyes, and I stare off into the grass instead. My tears have stopped falling, leaving me feeling stuffy. When his hand gently touches mine, I flinch. He pulls it away at my reaction.

"It's too soon. I still need time. This is a lot to process," I say, then turn back to face him. He inclines his head in understanding, then looks at me worriedly. I take a deep, refreshing breath to gather myself.

I need to find my friends. It may be risky, but I have to believe in the connection I had with him all these years. He might be able to help me locate the others. And I won't let him get too close.

I nod slowly. "Okay, Reggie. I'll trust you. For now." I force a small smile to my lips, a small bit of doubt still filling my gut.

He smiles back.

Desperately wanting to change the topic to more pressing matters, I stand up. "Can you help me with something?" He raises an eyebrow at me, and I frown. "My friend. She's stuck with your dad. We need to save her and find my other friends. I think we can do it if you distract him."

He nods and gets up, stepping away. "I'll try my best. I want to make up for my deception."

I incline my head, thankful, and we turn back toward the Academy. Walking together, we form a plan on our way. Reginald will go in first to distract his father for ten minutes. During that time, I'll go in and find Melissa. Then we'll all meet outside.

When we arrive at the Academy and I look up to face it, my nerves settle in once more. Reggie sends a reassuring grin my way, and I nod to him.

"I exited from that direction, so the entrance must be somewhere around here," I say as I move my hand to point to the locations.

We split off, and I head toward where I'd escaped while he goes to find the entrance.

I see the door I came from and move toward it, trying to ram it open. When it doesn't budge, I look around, finding a small window higher up. I grab a rock off the ground and throw it directly at the glass, hitting it head-on. It shatters loudly, and I wince, hoping no one inside heard.

I move over to a tree outside the window and climb my way up. It's not until I'm halfway there that I realize I'm high enough that a fall could result in me twisting my ankle if I land wrong. I avoid the glass pieces sticking out around the frame, slowly and carefully maneuvering myself through the small space.

As soon as the top half of my body makes it in, the rest falls, and I find myself tumbling toward the floor. I shoot my hand out to brace myself, jamming my wrist on impact. I can already start to feel the bruise forming beneath the skin. I groan as I hold my hand.

Then I hear footsteps and tense, only to realize they aren't coming from nearby. I lean my weight on my other hand as I push myself off the floor and look around.

The hall is empty. *I need to find the staircase.* Before I move, I listen closely. I don't hear any indicators that I'm not alone. *Reggie must be successfully distracting the headmaster.* The hall is eerily silent, and I know I still have to be careful. With a deep breath, I decide on a random direction and walk as silently as I can. The only light in the hallway comes from the small windows identical to the one I came in through. I find that the emptiness only makes it more unnerving.

When I reach the end of the hall, there's a sign. The top has an arrow pointing to the right labeled "Academy." The bottom has an arrow pointing to the left labeled "Research."

That's ambiguous. Doesn't the Academy also do research? I figure the right leads to the main school building. I turn down the left hall. It's a near copy of the first one I went down, except it's much shorter. At the end of it, there are two sets of doors. Two have small windows, which I peer through. One seems to lead to a dark room, and the other to a staircase.

Jackpot. I open the door as quietly as I can and slip inside. *Why are there no guards or cameras? Is this place really so top secret that the headmaster doesn't even have security?* I feel my mind fill with even more questions that will likely never be answered. A brief moment of curiosity as to where the stairs leading upward go makes me pause. *I need to find Melissa. Everything else isn't important right now.*

I push my curiosities aside and head downstairs. When I exit into the lower hall, I frown. It's full of various doors and connecting paths. *I just need to retrace my steps.* I picture the direction I followed upstairs and go back the way I came. It feels as if I'm walking blindly, and time passes excruciatingly slowly as I follow the walls.

Finally, I make it to a familiar opening. Seeing surroundings I recognize reinvigorates me, and I have to force myself not to run down the hall leading to the room I was imprisoned in. When I reach the eerie door, I push a button on it, and it slides open.

As soon as I adjust to the brightness in the white room, I freeze. Melissa is unconscious on the floor with a note next to her.

I hurry over and pick it up, my eyes scouring the ink splattered on the page: *They're all gone. They won't be coming back for you, Callista.*

TWENTY-EIGHT

MY HANDS SHAKE, AND I DROP the paper. Unsteadily, I kneel next to Melissa, feeling for her heartbeat. I push down on her chest with my palm, and my throat tightens when I feel no pulse.

No, this can't be possible. Panic swells in me, and I notice how pale her skin is. Tears brim in my eyes, and my breaths are quick and shallow. My eye catches again on the note I dropped, and I realize that are more words on the back:

She was no longer useful.

I let the tears fall. As I lean over Melissa's body, guilt and sorrow consume me. *How could I be so selfish? I should have gone back as soon as I left. I should have guessed the headmaster would retaliate.*

Then a cold hand touches me, and I flinch.

Reggie's voice is soft, but I hear an unnatural tone coming from him that causes me to get goosebumps. "I'm sorry, Cal. I'm here for you. I'm all you need."

My eyes widen in fury, and I stand. Nostrils flared, I glare at him. "Melissa never tried to hurt me. And who says that? I have other friends now too." I turn and stare daggers at him for being so insensitive.

Emotions I'm unable to identify flash across his face. "I'm sorry … I didn't mean—"

"We need to give her a proper burial," I say as I step away from Melissa. I wipe off my tears and motion for Reggie to help lift her. He does so silently, his face twisted. I freeze as soon as we get her off the ground. "Where's your father?" I ask.

He tightens his lips, then replies. "I'm not sure where he is now. I left after ten minutes went by. I didn't see you where we were supposed to meet, so I came here."

"Please carry her out of here," I say in a whisper.

He nods, gently picking up her lifeless body off the floor.

I keep a close eye on him as we walk down the hall toward the entrance in silence. I think of the good experiences I had with Melissa. *I didn't know her that long, but she wasn't the worst person. Sure, she could be a pain, but she was still my friend. We went through so much together, had so many shared experiences. She was one of us. And she helped me save Avi. Now she's another death on my conscience. A death I feel I'm responsible for.*

Along with the influx of memories, I think of her kissing K but push it away as soon as it enters, biting hard on my lip. *How could I think of that when she's gone? It doesn't matter anymore! She'll never take another breath because of my own selfishness.*

Despair wells up inside me, but I will myself not to cry in front of Reginald. Melissa and I were never best friends, but I'd bonded with her, even if it was less so than with the others. I think of Aviana and K, wishing I could be with them. *Would they be mad at me?*

Once we exit the building, Reggie directs me to a nearby field.

"I've seen a shed here, used for gardening to train those with nature abilities. I believe there's a shovel." He points, and I follow the direction of his finger to see a small wooden shed. "Find a place you'd like to bury her. I'll get the shovel."

I say nothing as he gently hands Melissa off to me. I struggle a bit but am able to carry her to a nearby flower pasture. Moments later, he arrives with a shovel in his hand. We take turns digging a hole deep enough for her. Once we've placed her body in it, I feel myself getting sick. I cover my mouth with one hand, and tears well up inside me.

I've never had to do this before. I close my eyes and turn away. Holding back a sob, I croak out, "Please finish this. I can't watch."

I then run off into the trees, not wanting to have to see the depressing sight. *I'm sorry, Melissa. I'm so sorry.* Once I'm far enough to where I can no longer see the field, I lean against a tree and let my tears fall once more. I'm filled with self-loathing and intense worry for my friends. Then my mind turns on me further, conjuring images of them facing the same fate as Melissa.

When Reggie appears, having already put the shovel away, I turn to him. "I want to go find my sister," I say.

He stops walking and turns to me. Then he hesitates, his hand reaching out briefly before he pulls it back.

Does he want to comfort me?

He swallows before speaking, his eyes narrowing. "Sister?"

I nod and start walking, pushing past him. "Yes, my little sister. I want to go find her and the others. They deserve to know what happened here."

He quickly catches up to me.

"I don't know how to find them though," I say.

"Where did you last see them?"

I stop, thinking back to before I was knocked out. *I know how to get back to EMBER, but would they still be there? I don't know how much damage my fire caused. Plus, would it be smart to show Reggie where they are?*

Darkness quickly approaches, and my heart sinks at the sight. "We were just on the borders of the city," I lie. *Well, it's partially true. EMBER's headquarters aren't that far from the border between the forest and city.*

Reggie scans our surroundings thoughtfully. "We should find shelter for the night. Then we can make a plan in the morning." He meets my gaze with sad eyes. "Is that okay?"

I nod, albeit reluctantly. "You're right." Instinctually, I summon my orb, used to relying on it for light. I realize too late that Reggie might not know about my new gift.

His emerald eyes shine with its glow. "Is that your ability?"

I nod, shifting on my feet. "So you've heard about it?"

"Yes, my father told me that some unique children have abilities, but he never showed me any proof. I guess he wasn't just spouting nonsense after all."

I wince, still uncomfortable with the notion that Reggie is related to the man who tried to kill my sister and killed my friend. *Does he know what Liam does to the children with abilities?*

We walk in silence toward one of the nearby abandoned apartments. A heavy weight sits on my chest—one that I'm begrudgingly growing familiar with. *Two deaths. Two friends, taken too soon. And I live freely. If something happened to the others …* I don't let myself think too much about the possibility of more suffering. *They're probably with EMBER. They weren't around when Melissa and I were attacked.*

Inside the apartment, Reggie and I sit on a dusty couch in silence. My orb dances in the space between us, illuminating the room.

The space is smaller than the ones I've previously visited. There are no separate rooms. The kitchen, living room, and bedroom are all connected, with no walls between them. The only separation is for the bathroom.

My nose twitches with the unwelcome but not unfamiliar scent of mildew. Unable to stand the quiet, I shift and angle myself toward Reggie.

"Do you know what your father does to people like me?"

"Do I know what my father does to people who have abilities?"

I nod, and he shakes his head. My head drops, as I'm not able to meet his naïve gaze.

"He kills them, Reginald." My voice is cold, unfeeling. Inside, I feel the opposite. A lump forms in my throat, making it difficult to speak. "He drains the life from them and kills them. He treats us as cattle, and his Academy is the slaughterhouse."

When I glance up at him, his mouth has fallen open, his upper lip curled back. "No, he never told me that." The pure horror on his face tells me he might really be as clueless as he claimed. I watch as he swallows, lowering his head in shame. "I'm so sorry, Cal. I didn't realize. I thought—"

"It's not your fault." My hand is atop his, and the words are out of my mouth before I can stop them. When I realize my actions, I pull away and stand up. My stomach feels sick.

"I'm going to bed," I say. "We'll talk tomorrow."

He doesn't speak, and I take his silence as an acceptance.

My body is stiff as I lie down on musty sheets. I close my eyes, willing my orb to disappear. In the darkness, I'm forced to replay in my mind the note I found beside Melissa's body. *How was she no longer useful? Useful for what? And what did it mean by 'They're never coming back'? Who are they? My friends?*

I'm exhausted, emotionally drained, and unsure about what's coming next. It seems like hours pass before I'm finally able to fall into a fitful rest.

I stir awake, groaning as light reaches my tired eyes. It feels like I got only a few hours of sleep, although the sun says differently. It's already halfway across the sky.

At the sound of shuffling, I turn, spotting Reggie rummaging through the kitchen cabinets.

"What are you doing?" I ask.

He glances over his shoulder, frowning. "Did I wake you?"

"No, I don't think so."

"I was looking for some food," he explains. He pulls out two cans and places them on the counter.

I stand, moving to pick up one of the cans. *Vegetable soup. How delicious.*

I sigh and carry the can over to the small kitchen table. Reggie follows, taking a seat beside me. I slurp on the can's contents silently, keeping my eye on the boy next to me.

If I want to locate the others, I have to go back to EMBER. But I don't want to show Reggie where they are. I ponder what the right move is. *Should I feel him out for a few days? See if he can be trusted? If nothing goes awry, then maybe things could get back to normal. Whatever normal is.*

"Do you remember when we were talking about our dream life?" His question breaks the easy silence.

"What about it?" I ask, finishing the flavorless broth.

He swallows, biting his lip. "I was thinking. After you told me about my father's atrocities. We need to stop him."

I raise an eyebrow, my curiosity piqued. "How do you suggest we do that?"

He hesitates for a moment. "We wait. Plan a long con. And in the meantime, we can fulfill our dream life. We can finally live peacefully together, Callista. Just the two of us." I start to refuse, but he cuts me off. "I know you need time to trust me. And I plan on proving myself to you. Just give it a chance. Think about it."

I purse my lips. *He wants to wait? And what, let all those innocents die in the meantime? What sort of plan is that? And did he forget about my friends?* I consider him carefully. *If I play along, then I can test him. He won't question my lack of urgency, as he'll think it's his idea.*

Eventually, I say, "If I were to agree with you, I need you to tell me everything you know about REMEDY and your father. And I want to make sure my friends are safe."

"What if I show you?"

"Show me?"

He nods, standing eagerly. "My father told me about an apartment he used to stay in. There might be old files there. Once we've located the information, we can find your friends."

But what if they aren't safe? I chew on my lip doubtfully. *It should only take a few days at most. They're strong. And I might be able to get something useful out of this.*

"How far is it?" I ask.

"He said it was right behind the Academy. He needed to live close to it so that he was able to help create the school."

I wonder if he lived there when it was still Spark Academy. Maybe old EMBER members lived there as well. Images of the old, musty apartment where we found Emmy flash through my mind, and I pause. "I'm surprised you haven't asked about Em," I state.

His eyebrows draw together. "Is she okay? I should have mentioned her sooner. I just forgot with all of the chaos going on."

I sigh, deflating. "She's safe with my friends." I can't tell him that she's with an EMBER member. "The Academy tried to take her from me, but she's safe now."

"I'm glad you've still had her for company, since I've been so regrettably absent."

I say nothing, unsure how to respond. Wanting to get moving, I shift anxiously on my feet. "We should get moving. Do you know which way to go?"

"I think so."

When we finally reach the set of apartments outside the Academy, I'm beyond relieved. The awkward silence that sat steadily between Reggie and me during our entire trek was extremely uncomfortable. I observe the line of buildings, taking note of the one I found Emmy in. *I don't think it would be there. It looked like no one had lived there in a very long time.*

"Let's check out the farthest one first and make our way back here," Reggie suggests.

I nod, following his lead.

The sun's rays don't pass over the building, creating a long, eerie shadow over us. The interior of the apartment looks much the same as the others I've been in. It smells stale, but it isn't nearly as dirty as its companion a few buildings down. The reception desk is barren, the couches covered in a thin layer of dust.

I frown, a sudden realization coming to mind. "Do you have any inclination what room it may be? This could take days otherwise."

He bites his lip. "I hadn't thought about that." Seeing my defeated expression, he visibly deflates. Then his face lights up with a new vigor, and he looks around excitedly. "What if we think of this as an opportunity to get ideas for our new home?"

I struggle to keep my doubt out of the look I give him. *He really is determined to go through with this plan.*

Shrugging, I step closer to the stairs. "I don't see why not."

The rest of the day and the following one go by in a blur. The apartments have at least forty rooms each. If it were on my terms, I know I could have finished our search in much less time. But Reggie's eagerness to thoroughly go through the abandoned rooms was unstoppable. He spoke, mostly to himself, about how it would be nice to have a comfortable space for us to finally relax in.

I agree with his sentiment, but not with his execution. *I won't let any more innocents die.*

We're finally on the sixth of eight buildings. As we enter the fifteenth room of the day, Reggie pauses, turning to me with a small frown. "You don't seem to be enjoying this as much as I am."

I freeze, taken aback by his observation. *I guess I wasn't as convincing as I thought.* Shifting uncomfortably on my feet, I sigh. "It's just a lot. Things aren't like they used to be."

He inclines his head, taking a deep breath. "I know. I'm sorry. I'm sorry about what happened to your friend, and I'm sorry about what my father has done. I wish I'd never put you in this position. I'll relax. I want to take things at your pace."

His words hit home, softening my reluctance. *Even if I don't agree with his plans, he is trying. I don't have to trust him yet, but I can't just keep dismissing his efforts.*

With a small nod, I return to shuffling through the desk drawers in front of me. I'm just about to call out that there's nothing here when my eye catches on a thin tablet and a power cord connected to it. I attempt to turn the device on, but it doesn't respond.

An idea creeps into my mind. I take a look over my shoulder to make sure Reggie isn't watching me. When I see him busily going through a bookshelf, I close my eyes. I picture my electricity like I have several times before, allowing the sensation of sparking vibration to shock through my senses. It comes to me easily. Reopening my eyes, I embrace the buzzing feeling that is accompanied by the flickers of energy in my fingertips. I move swiftly, not wanting Reggie to notice the humming. My hands wrap around the cord's metal end, and I push, willing the spark to leave me and travel through the cord.

At first, I'm not sure it's working. But when my nose twitches with the faint smell of burning, I catch sight of tiny particles shooting through the wire and into the device. The tablet comes to life, glowing faintly. I grin.

"Did you just—"

I jump, startled by Reggie's presence behind me. My electricity disappears, recalled into the insides of my being. The buzzing in my core diminishes, replaced by a tightening in my chest. "Geez, you scared me!" I turn to him with a scowl.

He ignores my comment, his mouth open. "Did you just create your own electricity?"

I bite my inner cheek. *No use denying it now.* Slowly, I nod. "Yes."

"So you have two abilities!" He doesn't form the sentence as a question, but rather as a statement.

"Yes, but that's not important right now." I scramble to get his attention off me, holding up the tablet. "We should search this."

He seems to sense my discomfort, allowing the topic to change. "Do you want to do the honors?"

I shrug. "Sure."

We head to the nearest couch, and, as soon as we sit, a cloud of dust explodes from its cushions. Both of us start to cough, and I wave my hand through the air to try and get rid of the floating particles. Once my reaction has subsided, I settle into the couch.

We have to sit hip to hip in order to both see the screen. Being so close to him, I'm reminded of the days we lived in the woods together. How he held me, and how I looked at him. I shake my head, willing the memories away. *Things were different. He wasn't a liar to me then.*

I swipe up on the tablet and am instantly greeted by a cracked robotic voice. A voice that's eerily familiar and unpleasant to my ears.

"Hello, welcome back. It's been a while. What would you like to access?" An animated diamond with a friendly expression stares up at me.

TWENTY-NINE

"DETA," I whisper. *Why is it here?* I feel Reggie shift beside me. "Access files," I say, my voice wavering.

DETA flashes red, the friendly expression shifting to a frown. "That requires an admin. Please try again with an admin."

My entire body tenses. *What if there's voice detection? What if it can tell that I'm not supposed to have access?* I push the tablet onto Reggie's lap. "You're related to Liam! He was probably an admin. Maybe it won't hear a difference in your voice or something." My voice comes out harsh and low, but Reggie doesn't seem to mind. He inclines his head, looking at the image on the screen.

"Access files." He alters his voice to sound raspier and deeper than it usually does. Its resemblance to the headmaster is uncanny, shooting a chill down my spine.

"Processing …" The diamond image blinks several times as we wait in nervous anticipation. Then it smiles. "Access approved." DETA's image dissipates, and I watch with a mix of awe and horror as the screen shifts to show a small list of names. "Which files do you want to access?"

Reggie looks to me, waiting for direction. I bite my lip. "Can you ask it more about itself?" I whisper, and he nods.

"DETA protocols," he says.

The screen shifts to display a list of sorts. I squint, trying to read the small print. Some of the information seems to have been deleted. Empty spaces litter the document where words likely sat previously.

"Do you want me to read this document for you?" it asks.

"Yes," Reggie says.

"Diamond Excellence Tortus Animosity, or DETA for short, is an artificial intelligence that was made to serve the _________ for _________. It has several functions, including but not limited to: Monitoring the climate of Eclium. Mapping the environment. Detecting new organisms. _________. Transporting _________ to Eclium. Sending information from _________ to _________. Monitoring all aspects of _________ _________ to ensure the success of _________. Providing desired information to its users. Allowing easy access to _________. And many other things that are currently in the process of being created."

Each time the AI reaches one of the deleted words, there's an empty pause.

Why was so much removed?

"Do you wish to see another document?" the voice asks.

I frown, unsatisfied. *So it has a multitude of functions. But all the more serious implications are inaccessible.* "Why are people transported?" I ask Reggie, who repeats the question to the device.

"I'm sorry, but the information you are requesting is no longer available. There seems to be some sort of virus in this device that has corrupted all files. I'm afraid I cannot offer any more."

Groaning, I throw my head back onto the couch. *So all of this searching for Liam's room, which clearly must be this one, was for nothing. I've learned nothing.*

Reggie shuts down the device and places it on the table in front of us. "I thought there would be more. Sorry, Cal."

I exhale, then sit up and meet his gaze. "It's not your fault. Do you really know nothing else?"

He deflates. "Nothing I haven't told you already."

I cover my face with my hands, feeling defeated. *I wonder if the others are worried about me. Should I just leave Reggie and go to them?*

A gentle hand rests on my shoulder, rubbing soft circles on my back. I tense, uncomfortable with the touch. I scoot away from Reggie instinctually, giving him a tight smile. He shifts in his position. "Sorry. Again," he says.

A broken laugh escapes my lips. He eyes me quizzically, and I shake my head. "This is too much."

"How so?"

A mania comes over me, my mind exhausted from everything I've been through so far. *There are too many dead ends. Too much pain and suffering that I didn't sign up for.* "Look at us. What are we even doing? I mean, I never thought the lies in my life ran so deep. I always thought you would be the one person who was honest with me, but I guess I was wrong about that too!"

He frowns. "I—"

Cutting him off, I stand. I wave my arms dramatically, gesturing to our environment. "I know you're sorry. But still. If I'd known all of what I know now, I would have never followed you in the forest. I would have just taken off on my own. I probably would have been better off. Maybe I would have even made it to the West! I'm sure the people aren't dangerous; it was just more lies fed to me by my puppet masters!"

My breaths come out ragged as tears prick at my eyes. An overwhelming wave of despair overcomes me. Choking on a sob, I cry out, "Why me? Why do I have to witness all of this? Be a part of all of this? I just want to be safe and secure for once."

I break, tears flowing freely down my face. Reggie watches me with his own sadness in his eyes. This time when he wraps his arms around me, I don't fight back. For a moment, I let him embrace me, pretending he never hurt me, that he's the boy I always thought him to be.

"It'll be okay, Cal. I swear I won't let them hurt you."

Reggie's voice is steady and warm, calming my racing heart. We sit together for an extended amount of time. He doesn't rush me. He doesn't say anything, allowing me to cry until my eyes can no longer produce tears.

I'm so weak. Drained and embarrassed, I push away from him and wipe my eyes. The action is meaningless, as my tears have long since dried on my cheeks.

"I'm sorry," I say, my voice hoarse.

"You have nothing to be sorry for," he replies soothingly.

We stare at each other for a long moment. *I shouldn't be so comfortable, right? He's a fake.* Ashamed, I avert my gaze and look at the floor. "What do we do now?" *I need to find my friends.*

"Two days. I want two more days with just you. We can catch up, maybe have a picnic like we used to. Then I promise we can go find your friends."

He wants me to wait longer? I hesitate, shifting in my spot. "You told me we could find them as soon as we found the headmaster's apartment. We have, and now you're telling me to wait longer?"

"Please, Cal. When I was distracting my father, he made no reference to having taken anyone but you and your friend. I'm sure the rest of them are fine."

"I don't know …" My words drift off as I chew on my lip. *Maybe it would be good to spend just a bit more time with him. I don't think I want him to meet my friends, at least not yet. And they weren't with Melissa and me when we were taken. They're probably fine.*

"Two days. No longer," I say.

I meet his eager eyes, seeing a glimpse of the boy I always thought him to be.

"Thank you," he replies.

The following days pass by slowly but joyfully. Reggie constantly goes out of his way to try and make up for his misgivings. Whether it be comforting words, lengthy apologies, or just showing me his genuine attitude, I'm hesitant to say his efforts have been successful. I find myself comfortable in his presence, yet I don't completely trust him. I suppose it will take much longer for me to completely forgive him. I can't deny, however, that I relish the familiarity of being with him.

"So, where do you think we can find your friends tomorrow?" Reggie asks, his mouth stuffed with crackers. A gentle breeze passes through the air, ruffling our stolen, tattered blanket as we lie out on the grass. The scene reminds me of the day Reggie presented me with Emmy and the nice picnic he prepared. Even though it isn't fresh, the food spread out before us today is much more delectable.

I ponder his words, a frown coming to my lips. *I still don't feel I should lead him to EMBER. It's too risky. And I might get kicked out for revealing an outsider to their location.* With this thought in mind, I lie. "I'm not sure. I don't remember where I last saw them. We never came up with a location to meet should we get separated."

His eyebrows knit in concentration. "What if we split up and search the forest and city? It's getting dark, but we can go out tomorrow when day breaks."

That would take forever. But still, it would give me a chance to find them alone without risking Reggie discovering EMBER. "How will we meet up or communicate?"

"We can set a designated spot once we arrive. There might be a communication device in one of the apartments."

He doesn't seem sure, but I don't see any better option. "We should go look now so we have it." At his frown, I add, "When we've finished eating, of course."

After cleaning up the picnic and searching several apartment rooms, I find two small, strange boxes in a kitchen drawer.

"I found something!" I call to Reggie.

He comes to my side and peers over my shoulder. "I think that's a walkie-talkie. I remember seeing a picture of one before in the old books. It's exactly what we need!"

I grin, handing him one. "Let's just hope it works."

When I press the button, a faint static buzzes in the air. And when I speak, my voice carries through to the device in Reggie's hand.

"Tuning in, this is Reginald Gray," Reggie says in a low, comedic tone.

I laugh, raising the pitch of my own voice. "This is Callista Tieron speaking!" He smirks at me, and I return the look. A moment of silence passes between us, then I look away, feigning a yawn. "We should go to bed. It'll be a busy day tomorrow."

"Do you want the bedroom?"

"Only if you don't mind."

"Of course not. I'll take the couch."

I glance at him, a warm appreciation humming in my chest. "Thanks, Reggie. Goodnight."

He inclines his head. "Goodnight, Callista."

As I exit the bedroom the next morning, I notice that Reginald is nowhere to be found. I pick up my walkie-talkie from the kitchen counter and press the large button.

"Hello?" I say uncertainly into the device. Then I wait for a response. Not long after the static starts, Reggie's voice comes from the other end.

"Hey. Sorry I left. I figured it'd be best if I started looking for your friends as soon as I woke. Can you describe them for me so I can get a good picture of who I'm looking for? I went south into the forest, so I figured you could head north, deeper in the city. This way, we'd cover both sides."

I cringe. *He couldn't have woken me? And I wanted to take the forest. That's where EMBER is located.* I hesitate before describing each of my friends to him, from their physical appearance to their names.

I can't go into the forest. If he sees me, I might give myself away. I'll just have to tell him later that I didn't find anything and suggest we switch search areas. Then I can find them.

The static stops, and I head outside the apartment. I make my way down the city streets, passing time more than anything. I doubt I'll find anyone, but that doesn't stop me from hoping I'll get lucky.

About an hour goes by with no word from Reggie over the walkie-talkie. I debate contacting him and suggesting the switch, but I decide against it. *It'll be fine. I just have to play this out. It's for the security of EMBER and my friends.* At this point, I've resigned myself to making a mental map of what the city looks like to pass the time.

But I'm startled when the walkie-talkie finally buzzes to life again. I pray he hasn't found anything and we can switch.

"I found something, Cal. It's a note, and it's signed by your friends. It was left near a pass in the woods, hammered to a crooked tree.

My eyes widen as a knot forms in my stomach. *That's where EMBER is located. But it's hidden enough where he shouldn't notice it.* I pause, focusing on his words. *Why did they leave a note outside? Avi knows I'm aware of the location of the headquarters.*

"What does it say?" I ask. The stretching silence makes me uneasy as I wait for him to reply. "Hello? Reggie?"

The device buzzes, and his voice seems more distant than before. "Your sister said they've moved on. Something about how after some debate, it has been determined you put their lives at too much risk. She mentioned someone named Lilac and being in REM. How it could have been prevented had you not been careless, and so they think it's better for you to go your separate ways. She says they wish the best for you."

I can't read his emotion over the device.

What? Why would they do that? I shake my head to myself in denial. *I already feel responsible for Avi's and Lilac's fates. But there's no way they would just ditch me, right? Not after everything we went through.* Then I recall how K and I attempted to escape without them. *I did it to them before. Who's to say they wouldn't do it to me?*

When I finally speak, my voice comes out pained. "You must have read it wrong. They wouldn't just leave me when I disappeared. They know Melissa went missing too."

"I'm going to find them."

The static ends, and I realize my hand is shaking.

"Reggie? What are you doing?" No reply comes from the device.

What does he mean, he's going to find them? An unsettling sensation weighs on my chest. *I need to find him. Then I need to find the others and get answers.* Turning back the way I came, I prepare for the hour-long journey ahead.

I finally reach the apartment, where I last saw Reggie, as the sun is in the middle of the sky. Grasping the device he left me, I push the button and speak.

"Reginald, what happened?" When I still get no reply, I fume. "Reginald, you better tell me what you're doing before I—"

I'm cut off by a loud buzz, and I drop the device to cover my ears. It lasts several painful moments and then abruptly stops.

Static comes, and Reggie talks, sounding as if he's out of breath. I lower my hands from my ears just as he speaks.

"They've been taken care of. I'm all you need, Cal. Don't worry anymore. They can't hurt you."

Goosebumps spread across my skin at his words.

"I'm coming back," he says. "Stay there."

What the hell? What does he mean, 'taken care of'? I'm leaning over to pick up the walkie-talkie just as someone grabs my shoulder and hoists me back. Instinctively, I throw back my foot, knocking the person to the ground. I pivot and gasp to see Melissa kneeling on the floor, muttering as she grabs her shin.

"Geez, Callista! That hurt."

I'm speechless as I stare down at her. *She's alive?*

She scowls at me. "Aren't you going to help me up?"

Snapping back to focus, I reach down a hand to lift her up. She accepts it and dusts herself off when she's on her feet.

"I … I thought you were dead," I whisper, still shocked that she's standing in one piece in front of me.

Her eyes fill with a deep fire that sets my nerves on edge. "I didn't die. Your friend Reginald poisoned me. After you left me with the headmaster, I had to act as if I wasn't aware you were going to escape. I expected to be punished, but I wasn't. The headmaster believed me and permitted me access to his library to think. When I was there, Reginald attacked me. He overpowered me and forced poison in my mouth. He placed some device over my heart so that even if I was somewhat conscious, you wouldn't be able to feel my heartbeat. When he left, assuming I was dead, I managed to spit out what I could of the foul liquid. But when my consciousness faded, I thought I was a goner. When I finally regained consciousness, I was lying in a pit."

She pauses, regaining her breath after speaking so rapidly. "I returned to the headmaster and told him what happened. He was right, Callista. Reginald is evil. I've been working with the headmaster to take him down." Her fists are clenched, fury radiating from her gaze.

I take a moment to process the bomb she just threw at me. *That doesn't make sense. She's hiding something. It doesn't line up. And Reggie has been good since we reunited. But then again, Melissa has also been a friend. Why would she lie? And Reggie has lied. So why should I trust him? He had every opportunity when we separated before finding Melissa.*

I step back, fervent denial pulsing within me. "He wouldn't do that." Pain crosses my face as I think about the strange things Reggie has done since I've been with him. *Melissa must be lying. She might have been my friend ever since I arrived, but Reggie was my friend longer.* "He's not like that," I tell her. *Right? I thought he was trying to make up for his lies. There's no way …*

I watch her face morph rapidly through several indiscernible emotions, then tears well up in her eyes. "He did, Callista. I would never lie to you! And he … he …" Her voice breaks as her tears flow in a slow and steady river down her face. "Callista, he killed your sister!"

I stare at her, bewildered, and laugh. "Is this some sick joke?" My voice rises in pitch as I speak, my doubt showing against my will. *Could she actually be dead?* I feel heat rise within me as my hands become clammy. *Nothing is consistent.* I attempt to think of the situation logically to no avail. *I don't have enough information. Why would he do this? Is this what he meant by taking care of my friends?* I stare at Melissa, hoping she'll laugh and tell me this is all a prank.

"I promise you," she answers, her eyes grave.

I turn and quickly grab the device off the ground. "Then I'll ask him myself."

When I turn back to face her, I swear a small grin flashes on her face, but it disappears just as fast as she showed it.

Paranoia. It's all paranoia. Pushing the button, I speak with pain, sadness, and anger flooding my voice. "Did you kill my sister, Reginald?"

Silence responds, and I wait expectantly. Then his voice replies in a cold tone. "Yes. I promised I'd keep you safe, and she hurt you. The others are next."

THIRTY

I⸏T TAKES ME A MOMENT TO absorb the message. At first, I don't believe it. Then all my doubts come flooding back in a flash of images in my mind. *He found me so conveniently. He lied to me about so much. He left to find my friends before I could form a proper plan with him. He set me up. He tried to kill Melissa. I saw her lifeless body before my own eyes. And I know he's manipulated me before. He lied to me my entire life, then manipulated me and lied to me again. I'm an idiot! He never was my friend. And now he took it out on someone I cared about, someone who was a threat to his manipulations.*

I drop the device and fall to my knees, my heart shattering into a million pieces. *She's really gone. I didn't save her. I just get everyone I care about killed.* I can't breathe. My throat constricts as sobs well up in my chest. I try to keep them in, try not to fall apart. *I haven't even had the chance to really get to know her. To know any of them. And now I won't.*

My hands shake as I let out a guttural roar. "No way in hell is he getting his hands on any of my friends," I mutter furiously under my breath. "Not K, not Alec, and not Brayden. That son of a devil is going to pay for this!" Pain from the loss of my sister and Reginald's betrayal wraps its tendrils deep into my veins.

Melissa stands in front of me, unmoving, with tears still flowing down her face. I sense her eyes on me as I cry. Moments feel like hours until I slowly stand up, my eyes dry and my soul empty. *Avi was the only family I had. That psychopath took her. I won't let him get away with this.*

I stare down at my hands, imagining blood coating them. *It's my fault. But what can I do?* I close my eyes, picturing what options I have. *I could run. Leave everything here behind and find a place to start a new life.* The picture of settling down somewhere peaceful seems almost impossible. *Avi wouldn't want me to ditch our friends. I can't leave. I must fight. And I can't go charging in without a plan or some way to get easy access to him. I have to risk it all. I must do anything and everything to find them. Even if it hurts.*

I pause, then open my eyes. *I'll do whatever I must.*

I look to Melissa with a new goal in mind. "I'm going to take the headmaster's offer. Reginald needs to be stopped." *I won't hurt any innocents. But I must make him believe I will. I'll figure out some way to avoid participating in their deaths.*

She wipes her eyes dry as she nods. "I'm sorry. I want to save them too. I know he can help. You'll see."

She motions for me to follow her, a solemn expression on her face. My anger creates a cloud over my mind as we walk back to the Academy in silence.

When we eventually arrive at the Academy, the building seems even gloomier than before. The sun is no longer out, and dark clouds fill the sky. Rain starts to pour in sheets. My hair soaks and sits on my shoulders in wet heaps. My normally light-brown locks are now dark, almost black.

Melissa leads me to the building we were in earlier, which sits directly next to the Academy gates. It looks equally as despairing next to its larger counterpart.

She has me follow her up the large, glossy staircase and through large metal doors, which shut automatically behind us. Water drenches our hair and clothes, and we soak the floor upon our arrival.

I follow her to a nearby sitting area with a digital fireplace. Although clearly fake, the flame still somehow emits heat. She takes one of the chairs in front of the flame, and I take the other, shivering slightly from the mixture of wet and cold outside.

"I'm sorry we couldn't stop him in time," Melissa says. "It pains me to know I failed. Liam really wants to help too, although it may be hard to tell. I promise you, his plan will work."

I force a smile and shake my head. "It's not your fault. I didn't save them either. I trusted the devil." I grit my teeth and shiver again.

Her face lights up, and she jumps from her seat. "There should be some extra outfits for us to change into in the closet down the hall. I believe there's a changing room there too. Want to come with me?"

I nod and follow her as she walks down the dimly lit hall. The closet sits a few doors down, and a rack of clothing lines the wall inside. Melissa walks over and grabs two outfit sets.

"These uniforms have a new technology that fits the clothing to your size when you put it on."

She holds two hangers with navy halter tops and white pants. I can see several pairs of navy boots paired with white socks. I hesitantly grab one of the hangers from her and spot the changing stall she mentioned in the corner. I move toward it, sliding the curtain closed behind me. My torn-up and soaked uniform slides off easily. I lean down to take off my shoes and socks, breathing a sigh of relief once my feet are no longer stuck in the buckets of water.

The navy top slides on easily, and as soon as it touches my skin, I feel it squeeze closer, forming to my body shape. It fits snugly, and I'm slightly uncomfortable with how tight on me it is. When I pull on the pants, the waistband quickly adjusts to my size.

I notice a choker on the ground and pick it up. It's made of thick navy fabric with a large *R* in the middle. I decide not to put it on and bring it out with the rest of my wet clothes.

Melissa is already wearing a new pair of socks and shoes, and her soaked uniform is in a basket sitting in the corner. When she notices me looking, she motions to it. "You can put your wet clothes in there."

I move toward the basket, drop my uniform in, then turn to her. I hold out the choker. She's already wearing hers. "I don't want to wear this. You can have it back."

She looks down at it, then back up at me. An unreadable expression crosses her face, then she frowns. She takes it reluctantly. I move toward the shoes, sit on the floor, and slide on the new socks and boots. I feel my hair soak the back of my shirt, and I brush wisps of it out of my face.

I look up to the sound of footsteps in the hall to see the headmaster peering in the door.

"Oh, I didn't expect you to be here," he says, directing the statement to me.

I shift uneasily. The fury within me reignites with his presence. *I can't let myself forget that this man is just as evil as his son.* I slip on the final shoe, push off the ground, and stand in front of him with false confidence. "I will help you if you do what I want in return."

"Hm? And what do you want exactly?"

I push back my shoulders, if only to make myself feel slightly taller compared to the man staring down at me. "You will help me protect my remaining friends. I will not stand and let Reginald hurt—" my voice breaks, and my bravado wavers. The remaining words come out in a whisper. I look down at the floor. "Hurt any more of them."

I swear I see him grinning down at me in my despair, but when I look up, he wears a mask of sympathy.

"Very well. I have a condition of my own too." He doesn't wait for me to reply. "You must do everything I say, regardless of whether you like it or not. If you don't comply, I won't help make sure my son doesn't get his hands on your friends. If you agree, they'll be safe."

I gulp low in my throat. *It's okay. I'll find a way.* My gut tells me to run, but it's no match for the anger fueling my thoughts. "How will you keep them safe?"

"I'll make sure our guard monitors their movements and Reginald's. If he gets too close, he'll be dealt with."

They'll still be at risk. But they have EMBER, even if they might not be trustworthy either. I have an urgent need to ask him one last risky question.

"Why do you hurt innocent children?"

He looks taken aback at my directness. Then he smiles sadly. "I wouldn't say we're really hurting them. We're just giving their lives a new purpose. Once each student has passed through REM, they exit as a new version of themselves. They're still alive. When we no longer need them, they're transported out of Eclium and given freedom. Some stay here to join our army. By being part of REM, they're helping us create a bigger, stronger force that will ultimately help us take down those, such as Reginald, who go against abilitied children. We'll be able to overthrow the government that has oppressed you all so long. We'll dispose of other groups that claim to want to help you but are full of liars. So yes, the students are dying in a way, but their sacrifice will help save many thousands of people like you. We almost have enough power to make our move. I believe that by the end of the year at the very latest, we'll be able to discontinue REM."

For a moment, I'm shocked. *They don't actually die?* A reinvigorated hope makes my stomach flutter. *Is Lilac still alive?*

"Can I see a student who went through REM?" I ask.

"Unfortunately, no. They wouldn't remember you anyway."

My heart sinks. *What does "new version of themselves" even mean? What really happens? And where's Lilac?* I have a sudden urge to attack him in a fit of rage but think better of it. *If I act out now, I'm only condemning my friends to death. If I participate in his plans, I can learn more about the students. Maybe I really can save them.*

With a deep, steadying breath, I process what he said. *I've never agreed with the practices of our government. I don't agree that kids should be unwilling sacrifices either. But I don't have much of a choice. Maybe, with my help, they can make the sacrifices even less.*

I feel like I'm being tugged in opposite directions. I don't agree with the headmaster's methods. They're disgusting and cruel, and to think my sister was a victim makes me sick. I don't even trust him. But my only other option would be to work directly against him. And without any support, I may end up putting even more people in danger.

In another universe, if I had more help, I would never agree to this. Yes, I do have EMBER. But I don't know them, nor do I know if they're ready to fight. I can't rely on them. I can't rely on anyone but myself. They might be just as untrustworthy as the headmaster. Even if they saved Avi, it could have been a ploy.

After having been lied to so many times, I'm confused about to who to trust. I must use as much logic as I can to make my decision. *The end of the year isn't that far away. If it seems that the headmaster is lying or won't be finished by the time he said, I'll leave. I can try to find a way to help the students when they're removed from Eclium. I sincerely doubt they're left with many resources. Even though I don't trust him, at least this way I'll have access to his deepest secrets. I can gather information, at the very least. I can be a spy for myself. Just for a few months. I won't think about the victims. That's all I must do.*

I use this reasoning as my way of not succumbing to the guilt over what I'll be forced to do. With a deep breath, I nod and put out my hand. "We have a deal."

He smiles and shakes my hand. I can sense Melissa's eyes watching me the whole time.

The next day, I wake in the small, confined bedroom on the cramped bottom of a bunk bed. Melissa sleeps on top, in a navy pajama set matching mine.

I play with the choker sitting tight on my neck and fall back, exasperated. Liam required that I wear it regardless of my desire not to. *Of course, it's a tracking device. I was right not to want to wear it.* The *R* pushes against my skin uncomfortably as I drop my hand to my side.

I stare at the bottom of the bunk above me, and a tear runs down my cheek. *I'm sorry I couldn't save you, Avi. Your death was all my fault. Mom told me to keep you safe, and I failed.*

I fling my feet up on the bed and curl up on my side toward the wall. I close my eyes, and more tears fall. *I don't want to hurt other people. I really don't. But I need to be with them again. They're all I have.*

I open my eyes and wipe the tears from my cheeks. Near the door to the bedroom, Melissa stares at me. *When did she wake up?*

She wordlessly throws me the same clothes I wore yesterday and turns so I can change in privacy. I groan, then push myself off the stiff mattress. I quickly slide on my new uniform and throw my hair in a messy bun. My choker buzzes with a shock, and I wince.

Melissa feels it too, and she motions for me to move faster. "He wants us to go to the kitchen, now." She throws open the door and walks out, expecting me to follow.

She's so nonchalant about this. How? I feel like a puppet on its way to its master as we walk through the narrow, dark halls.

Inside the kitchen, the headmaster—who requires that I call him Liam now—sits with two guards on either side. He glances up upon our arrival and motions for us to stand near the counter where he's perched. We follow his orders quickly and wait for his command.

"1845, you'll monitor 3265 to make sure she behaves. 3265, today I'm going to send you out to bring two more students to REM."

I wince as flashbacks of Aviana in that awful place crowd my mind. He must notice my hesitation, as he snaps to get my attention. "That won't be a problem now, will it, 3265?"

I shake my head and frown. *He's referring to us as numbers. As if we're specimens. I guess I'm "3265."* For a moment, I consider telling him to refer to me by my name but figure it's safer to stay silent. *I can't afford to anger him.* His old fingers tap something on the counter, and my choker buzzes.

"I just sent you the identification information for the two students," he says. "Push down on the *R* to pull up the hologram. One student has super strength, and the other can turn invisible. You both must be back here by sundown. 1845, bring 3265 to my office as soon as you get back. Now go!" He motions us off, and Melissa is already in motion.

I want to say something but think better of it, remembering his words from the previous day. *Never talk unless questioned.* I frown as I follow her out into the cold air. The wind brushes over my naked shoulders, and I shiver.

"Melissa, why are you helping him?"

She huffs and turns her head to look at me as we walk toward the main Academy building. "I told you. He'll help keep them safe. But I also have my reasons, just like you do." She looks away from me and speeds up. "Keep up. He doesn't like it if we're late."

I'm an animal trapped in a cage, lost and terrified. I don't think my jaw has unclenched since I got here. *I'm doing this to protect them. It's what Aviana would have wanted.* I know I'm just convincing myself so that I can hide from the pain of what I'll have to do. The wound from my recent loss is still fresh and stings inside me.

The main building is only a few yards away from where we're staying, and I gulp. "Melissa, did you know what would happen to Avi when she got sent to REM?"

She doesn't flinch as she responds. "No, I started working for Liam sometime after that. After we'd already left the school."

When could she have even been in contact with him? And why does she suddenly seem so cold? One look at her tells me she won't answer my questions.

Deciding not to bother pushing for further information, I speed up to match her pace. Eventually, we reach the front gate to the Academy, and I get flashbacks of our escape. *We were fighting together then.* A frown tugs at my lips with the memory as Melissa approaches one of the guards. They see our collars and move to open the gates for us, knowing what our role is.

Melissa goes over the rules for my mission in a hushed whisper. "We'll play the role of guards designated to escort the other students to REM. Don't show emotion. Don't flinch. If the students fight us, neutralize them however you need to."

How does she have it all memorized already?

The gaze of the other guards reminds me not to ask any suspicious questions. I nod and stare at the ground as we pass another guard checkpoint and finally arrive inside the Academy.

"I am only here to monitor," Melissa says. "He trusts me more than you, so he wants me to make sure you're reliable. If you have questions, you can ask. But there will be a penalty. Liam prefers us to be able to figure things out for ourselves." She stands still and waits for me to do my part.

I hesitantly press down on the *R*, and a hologram flashes right before my eyes, just as Liam said it would. Two separate files show a fifteen-year-old girl and boy. My eyes scan over their file information:

*Jessa Rosé, 8575 Invisibility—Neighborhood 37—Red hair,
pale complexion
Isaac Hess, 3742 Strength—Neighborhood 30—Dark hair, tan
complexion*

I'm overwhelmed, looking at the two kids the same age as
my sister. I close my eyes, using every amount of my willpower
to keep my breathing steady. *They're so young. They have so much
longer to live.* I hesitate, and Melissa notices, tapping her foot
impatiently. The action annoys me, and I walk off toward the
cafeteria, where the kids should be.

How does she stand to do this, as if their lives don't matter? Doubt
races through me, and anger rises in my chest. *I caused Aviana's
death. This is my punishment. This is the only way I can save my friends.
They're just necessary war casualties. And they won't really be dead.*

Melissa's footsteps echo behind me, moving as fast as I am.
The cafeteria isn't far from the front of the Academy, and before
I know it, I'm standing and staring into the large room. It used
to be a safe place for me to be with my friends, but now it looks
like a death trap.

A guard notices me and motions over to a petite girl who's
sitting alone with her face stuffed in a book. Her ruby locks stand
out like a sore thumb, and regret washes over me. I shoot Melissa
a final look, and her neutral expression stares back at me.

Reluctantly, I move toward the girl, dragging out the time as
long as I can. She must sense my presence getting closer, then
she looks up from her book and stares at me. Her wide eyes look
like little oceans, swirling into tidepools of fear.

I must use her ID number. No attachment. Order. Do not ask.

I repeat the instructions attached to the hologram in my
head. I adjust my posture to look taller and more confident than
I am before addressing the girl.

"Jessa Rosé, 8575, come with me. I'm your escort to REM." I nearly gasp in shock at the robotic sentence coming out of my lips. My mask slips faster than I expect, and I shake my head to snap out of it. I see confusion pass over the girl's face. Then she quickly jumps up and hugs her book close to her chest.

She stutters when she speaks, her voice coming out as a soft whisper. "C-can I please bring my book back to my room?"

I soften at the innocence of her reaction. *She's completely clueless that she'll never go back there.* I struggle between justifying what I'm doing and keeping my humanity. I hear a loud, forced cough come from far behind me, and I glance over my shoulder to see Melissa staring at me. I look back at the girl, who can only be four foot eleven, staring up at me. I force a smile.

"I'm afraid you can't, but I can bring it back for you." I say it quietly and softly, hoping to put the girl a bit more at ease without alerting Melissa.

Jessa lights up and nods, calmed by my promise. She hands the book to me. "Thank you. When you go back, could you place it next to the bear on my bed? I don't want to lose it." She shifts around with sudden childlike eagerness as she talks. Her innocence makes me feel even more inclined to protect her.

My heart breaks into a million pieces, and I must fight to keep my mask on. *No attachment.* I repeat the words in my head and risk stretching my hand out to her. *She's probably too old to want to hold on. But I can't help but want to reach out.*

Nothing happens for a moment. Then Jessa grabs my hand gently and speaks quietly to me as we walk toward the cafeteria exit.

Melissa shoots me a wary eye in warning. I shrug it off and think of the map I'd been shown to REM. The route is much easier than when I went to save Avi, and it makes for a short trip.

Just as we're walking up the final staircase, Jessa taps my arm and says, "I just turned fifteen before I got here. Life has felt so weird since I arrived. I wish I could go back home."

Your home never was a home. It was all a cage to keep you alive until you could be sent here.

She looks hopeful, as if I could help her. I feel the final parts of my mask slipping, and I quickly move again.

"I'm sorry," I mutter to myself, and I sense her wide eyes watching me curiously as I practically drag her along with me. Eventually, we reach the final hall, and I type in the door code. It opens with a low hum.

"By the way, miss," she says. "What's REM?"

THIRTY-ONE

MY MASK SLIPS, AND TEARS WELL UP in my eyes. I hear Melissa walking behind me. Then she unlocks my grasp on Jessa and pulls her away from me, toward her doom. I reach out, wanting to stop Melissa and tell her that we can stop this, but my feet don't move.

This is how I keep the rest safe. Not only my friends, but the kids of the future.

I become unaware of the amount of time I spend standing in front of the final door. Eventually, Melissa comes back with a scowl on her face.

"All you had to do was bring her in, and specified guards would have hooked her up. You were close, Callista, I'll give you that. Do better on the next kid, alright?" Her new persona, compared to the one I thought I knew, infuriates me.

"What the hell? You're just okay with sending them in there? After seeing what it does to them? After seeing them lose their entire life?" I whisper low and harsh, glaring at her.

She stiffens, crossing her arms. "We're at war. Sometimes innocents have to suffer for the greater good."

My mouth drops open. I'm utterly speechless. *I can't.* I want to scream and run and save all the rest of the poor students trapped here, but I know I have no choice. *This is for Avi and the others. If I don't obey, they and many more will die. At least this way, I can keep some people safe.*

I glance away from her, then follow silently as we head downstairs and back to the cafeteria.

"I'm sending some tips over to your messenger," she says. "Look them over while we wait."

I don't respond to her comments, zoning out with flashes of Jessa's innocent look in my mind.

After a short time, Melissa taps me on the shoulder. "3742 is over there. Don't hesitate." She nudges me forward, and I prepare mentally for round two.

Don't ask questions. Ignore him. Less communication makes it easier. I replay Melissa's tips in my head over and over as I get closer to the boy. Isaac sits talking to other boys who seem to be around his age, oblivious to his environment. His back faces me, and as I get closer, the other boys' chatter dies out, and they turn to stare at me.

"Guys, what are you looking at?" Isaac asks his friends. He turns to look at me. I see fear cross over each of their faces as they realize why I'm here.

"Isaac, she's going to bring you to that weird class! The one that makes ghosts!" one of his friends says, his voice slightly trembling.

Isaac seems to have a mask of his own and laughs off his friend's fearful expressions. "That's just a rumor. Ghosts don't exist. Just chill. I'll be back later." He casually stands and leaves his tray. As he does so, I realize he's close to a foot taller than me.

"Let's just go get this over with," he says, his arm hitting mine as he pushes past me. He then walks toward the cafeteria exit.

I process the moment quickly, then turn and hurry after him. Melissa watches, and Isaac stops moving to let me catch up.

"So, you're awfully quiet. Will you tell me what exactly this REM class is?" he asks.

I try to think of an excuse and accidentally stutter under the pressure. "I—I'm afraid that's classified information. My job is simply to take you there." I fake an authoritative tone and move toward the dreadful path I must take him on. When I realize he isn't following me, I turn back, only to see him staring at me with disgust. I see his mask slip slightly and rage seep through.

"I won't go until you tell me where we're going and why we're going there. I know I won't be going back to my friends anytime soon. My girlfriend had to go to this stupid class, and she hasn't been seen since."

It takes all my willpower not to give in and tell him to run and flee, that his girlfriend is probably gone from Eclium, and soon he will be too.

Clenching my jaw, I say, "3742, I ask the questions here. Now, follow me, or I'll have to force you." The words are toxic coming out of my mouth, and I turn, motioning for him to move. When he doesn't, I falter. *I don't want to have to use force.*

Looking back once more, I no longer see the calm and collected boy I saw before. Standing in front of me is someone who has faced so much loss that it tears at him from the inside. His image seems like a mirror reflection of myself, and it makes it even harder to do what I know I must do.

I notice Melissa in a dark corner, ready to step in if I need her to. I briefly close my eyes and summon my orb to my hand, easily lighting it into a ball of flame. *This should scare him. I won't have to use it.*

His eyes grow wide at the sight of the orb, and he backs away, looking for something to grab. I approach him slowly and methodically, not wanting to attack him but rather create fear.

He grabs a trash can and uses his enhanced strength to rip off one of the metal bars surrounding it.

He isn't going to back down. I need to make him scared. My powers surge, exploding the tubes of light that line the hallway ceiling. Shards of fallen glass slice my arm, and I wince, pushing through the pain.

Melissa still hasn't moved, and no other guards are in sight. *They want me to deal with him alone.* My thoughts make me deeply unsettled. Without the overhead lamps, my fire is the only thing lighting my way. It reflects in Isaac's eyes before me.

"What did you do to her?" he shouts, tears glinting down his face.

I stay painfully silent and watch as he approaches me, noting a shard of glass in his hand. Suddenly, he charges at me, slashing violently. I manage to dodge his first few blows, but he takes me off guard when he launches at my head with the metal bar. He manages to hit only the very edge of my skull, but his superhuman strength sends me flying backward.

My flame extinguishes, casting the hallway into darkness. My head pounds, and my ear pulses as a trickle of warm blood drips down the side of my head. Everything spins for several moments. I press my fingers against my wound, relighting my flame in my other hand.

Isaac is standing above me, his face streaked with tears. "You probably killed her, didn't you? And you're probably going to kill me next."

His words shoot through me like daggers, and I hesitate. "She's not dead, I promise." My words are barely audible and not even slightly convincing.

He moves to deliver another blow. I manage to roll to my side, narrowly avoiding potential death. The floor tiles shatter from the impact of his strength.

I lower my now bloodied hand to push off the ground while he steadies himself, dropping the glass shard he was holding.

"I don't want to do this. I understand you, Isaac." My mask is now gone, and I try to reason with him even if I know the end result can't change.

I seem to only infuriate him more with my words, and he glares at me.

"I'm not like you or anyone like you!" he yells. "You guys are all murderers. No one loves you 'cause you're so heartless! Your family is probably better off not knowing you! In fact, they're probably happier dead!"

His words stab into my still fresh wound, and rage pours into me like a waterfall. I forget myself, seeing only Avi and thinking of the pain she must have faced. A new sensation seems to take control of me, and just as he raises his arm to finish me off, I summon my light orb. It glows bright, brighter than it ever has before.

Isaac's eyes slam shut, temporarily blinded. As he staggers, I take the opportunity to charge at him with my flame, shooting it directly into him.

The impact of my hand against his clothing snaps me out of my rage-induced mania, and I stare right into his dark eyes as they widen in shock. Everything moves in slow motion as I look down at my hand now leaving his shoulder. His flammable clothes allow the flame to spread easily, and they quickly start to spread over him. Before they can kill him, he drops to the ground and rolls, extinguishing the flames. He has pain etched across his face as he looks to his arm, now covered in large burns. He doesn't even look mad. The pain is clearly too excruciating.

My stomach churns at the sight, and an overwhelming wave of guilt comes over me. I back away slowly, terrified of the sight before me and of myself. It's hard to get a clear picture of the damage, but the burns spread high, and he likely would have died had he not acted as quickly as he did.

That arm is probably gone for good.

He tries to stand but stumbles to the floor. Just as I'm about to try to help him, other guards appear from the shadows. Melissa is with them. She looks at the boy on the floor, sees his injury, and looks to me with a scowl.

I just hurt an innocent child. The impact of my actions echoes in my head. I find myself feeling like I'm falling into a never-ending pit as my head's pulsing fills my ears and everything goes black.

The next morning, I wake up with sweat on my forehead. Visions of Isaac and Jessa sit in my mind, taunting me.

I can't do this. I can't sacrifice anyone else for my selfishness. I have to get out of here. I already feel like I've lost part of myself. *Even if it was in self-defense, I still hurt Isaac. I burned him.* My stomach twists at the memory, and I cringe.

Slowly crawling out of bed, I remove the choker from my neck and place it under the covers. *If I'm fast enough, I might be able to find the others before Liam notices or Reginald goes after them.*

The sun is still rising, a faint glow illuminating the room. I glance at Melissa's sleeping form. *I must be quiet.* I consider my options. If I try and leave through the main hall, there are undoubtedly guards who will see me. My only other choice is to leave through the window and hope I can escape fast enough.

I move toward the glass, peering through its shades. I can see the forest beyond. The only thing separating me from it are the layers of likely impenetrable window. I bite my lip. *Even if this puts my friends at risk, they would understand. After all, EMBER is trying to save the students, right? That's what they claimed?*

I take a deep breath and open the shades as smoothly and silently as I can. As I scan the window for a latch, I feel breath on my neck. I pivot, instantly calling on my electricity. When I meet Melissa's tense gaze, I freeze.

"What are you doing?" she asks.

"I—Nothing," I respond, reeling my electricity back in.

She frowns and crosses her arms. "Were you trying to escape?"

"No!" I shoot back defensively.

Shaking her head, she looks at me with pity. "Callista. There's nothing for you to go to. You really think EMBER would accept you after knowing you willingly sent two students to REM? You made your choice."

"I was only trying to protect them." The retort escapes my lips and leaves a sour taste in my mouth. *I selfishly traded two innocents for my friends.*

Her eyebrows draw together. "And when they realize your friend was the one who killed Aviana, who took her from us all, why would they trust you?"

I swallow hard, my throat tightening painfully. "How could you say that?" My voice cracks, unsettled by the truth of her words.

She grimaces. "I'm sorry. I didn't mean it like that." Taking a deep breath, she continues. "They won't accept you. Whether it's right or wrong. I just don't want you to get hurt again, alright? Trust me."

My shoulders slump. *She's right. What was I thinking? I can't return to them. Not after I committed such monstrous acts.* When she places a gentle hand on my shoulder, I don't push it away. *I'll just have to find another way.* "It's just so hard. They don't deserve this."

"I know. I'm sorry for being too pushy. It'll get easier with time. I'm doing this with you. You have me, and you can trust me. We're doing this for the greater good. Remember that. It's not only for our friends. We can stop Reginald and his army if we keep pushing through."

She's right. These are necessary sacrifices. It might hurt, but we're stopping more people from dying. People like Avi and everyone else Reginald will likely hurt if he's successful. I'm doing the right thing.

I'm not fully convinced of the sentiment, but as Melissa leads me away from the window, I know I have no other choice.

Every day, I wake up with another part of my soul taken away. It's only been a week since I started working with Liam, but it feels like eons have passed. The only way I keep going is by focusing on my surroundings. I pretend to be the perfect little puppet, but the truth is that I'm watching. I'll find a way to save the victims I've punished, even though I can't find out anything about the students who are sent away to Eclium.

Melissa has been gentler on me and helps me gather the students when I'm struggling. We've grown closer, and I now know for certain that she's colder than I once thought. She has a one-track mind and doesn't seem to notice any flaws in our situation. Regardless, I know she's my only hope. *I just have to pray I can reach whatever humanity she has.*

During our lunch break one day, I approach Melissa cautiously. "Can we talk?"

She places her sandwich down on the tray in front of her. "What?"

I glance at the guards surrounding us. "Privately?"

With an exaggerated exhale, she stands. "Follow."

She leads me down a nearby hall, the smell of chemicals increasing as we near our destination. Then she pulls me in a side room, flicking a light switch to illuminate the dark space.

We seem to be in some sort of small lab. There are tubes and glasses spread out on high metal tables. Posters dot the walls with images of various formulas I don't understand. I note that the chemical smell is coming from a bubbling liquid positioned over a burner in the back corner.

My nose twitching in disgust, I say, "I need your help." She raises an eyebrow, waiting for me to continue. "What do you know about the students after they've gone through REM? Where are they sent?"

Her mouth twists down into a frown. "I don't know."

I watch her gaze intently, and she looks away. *She's lying.* "Please, Melissa." I'm aware that I'm begging, but I don't care. I can't stand to sit by and just force these innocents to suffer. There has to be a way for me to help.

She purses her lips and shifts on her feet. Then she meets my eyes with an intense stare. "There's nothing you can do, Callista. Even if you find them, it'll be too late. This is necessary."

Her words anger me. "You don't care? I thought you had the same goals as the rest of us. You saw what happened. You're just as selfish as Liam is," I spit.

My words seem to hit a nerve. Her eyes alight with a sudden fury. Stepping closer, her face directly in front of mine, she snarls, "I told you to trust me. You don't know anything. You don't know my reasons, what I've been through. You don't know how dangerous ability-bearers are." She steps back, her voice breaking for a moment as she adds in a low whisper, "How much they can take from you." Then she glares at me. "You want to help so bad? Fine. Every day at midnight, the REM students who have finished their class are taken in groups out the back of the Academy. There's nothing you can do to help. But go ahead and try." Taking a deep breath, she considers me with a softer look. "I pity you, Callista. You and our friends. You have too much misplaced hope. Maybe one day, you'll see the best path forward."

"I hope you will too," I spit.

No further words pass between us as she exits the room, leaving me to reevaluate yet another relationship.

The next night after dinner, I approach Liam with as much confidence as I can muster.

"I want to escort students after they've finished REM," I tell him. "I think it will deepen my understanding of your project and prove to make me better at my tasks." I keep my tone level, not portraying any sign of emotion. My gaze is steady, focusing right above his head, as if I'm so beneath him that I can't look him in the eyes.

"You can follow Hunter as he makes his rounds tonight," he replies. "Meet him in an hour where you usually bring the students. He'll be waiting. Don't think you can do anything untoward. You'll be watched."

I struggle to hide my surprise at how easy his agreement was. *And so soon? I expected him to make me wait.*

"Understood." I don't hesitate to leave, eager to be away from the awful man.

I pace back and forth in the halls for most of the next sixty minutes, too anxious to know what to do with myself. *I'll finally see where they go. I'll be able to get an idea of how I can help them.*

Other guards who pass by side-eye me, but no one questions my wait. When an hour has finally passed, I hurriedly make my way to the unsettling hall that I wish I wasn't familiar with. A boy twice my height and likely only a couple years older than me stands at attention, tapping his foot impatiently. When his eyes meet mine, he lets out an exaggerated exhale.

"Finally. Took you long enough."

"I'm on time," I respond defensively.

His eyes narrow. "Don't talk back, newbie." He pivots, starting down the hall. "Follow."

I scoff but listen regardless. We pass several rooms, some filled with victims of REM, and others empty. I find myself extremely thankful that there are no windows. *I don't think I could stomach seeing someone like Avi.* The thought of my sister creates an ache in my heart. *What would she think if she saw me now?*

"Where are we going?" I ask, not wanting to continue the silence.

"The others have already gathered the subjects. We'll meet them out back and escort them to the hub, where they'll be sent away."

I frown inwardly. *Subjects. That's all we are.* Then I ask, "The hub?"

Hunter looks back at me, his amber eyes intense. "You really know nothing, do you? I'm surprised Liam is allowing you to help." When I say nothing, he continues. "The hub is a monitored transport. It functions similarly to DETA, except on a much smaller scale."

So that's how the students are sent back to the mainland. "Where are the students sent away?"

"To the New America."

"And is there someone there waiting for them? To help them get adjusted to a new life?"

He pauses. "Of course."

"So they're safe?"

Before he can answer me, we reach the end of the hall, and someone opens the door from the outside. A chill breeze comes in, sending shivers down my spine.

"Ay, Hunter! Is this the newbie?" a young man calls out, his gaze traveling over me. I shift uneasily, not appreciating the unwanted attention.

"Yes, she's quite clueless," Hunter responds.

I roll my eyes.

The other man chuckles. "They always are! Come out here. We got a large batch today."

Batch? The word gives me pause. Hunter is already outside, and when he sees my hesitation, he shakes his head. "Come on out here!"

I take a deep breath and step out into the chill night air. At first, I only see other guards. "Where are the students?" I ask.

"Over 'ere, with Emera, Ollie, and the others," the other young man says.

I look to where he points and go cold.

The post's faint lights combined with the moon illuminate the site in an eerie glow. There's a large group of maybe ten or twenty students huddled together, heads bent, shoulders sagging. Each has skin that seems nearly translucent, lifeless, dull. They don't speak as the guards around them usher them into a line. They obey the commands, showing no sense of life. They're breathing, but not truly living.

As if sensing my stare, one girl, maybe about sixteen, meets my gaze. Horror threatens to consume me. Her eyes are dark and soulless. The blond bangs that frame her face hang limply. I can just barely make out veins underneath her skin, their darkness in stark contrast to her pale skin. Her lips are cracked and dry, and her expression is nonexistent. A female guard pushes her toward the rest of the group, and her stare is broken.

"How …" My voice comes out in a croak, my chest tightening. I can't breathe. *That was Lilac not so long ago. That could have been Avi. That could have been me. I'm allowing them to do this.*

Hunter has the gall to laugh. "What's the problem?"

I barely hear his voice over the pounding in my ears. My heart thuds rapidly in my chest. My hands shake, my vision blurring. *I can't. I did this. I need to save them. I need to do something. I'm useless. I'm a danger. This is my fault.*

I falter on my feet. *Focus. I have to focus.* My spiraling gaze travels over the group and the twenty guards around them. *There are too many. I can't do anything. There's too much risk. It's too late.*

Hunter says something else to me, but I don't hear him. Breathing is too hard. Tears I didn't know I was holding fall freely down my face. I turn and run, unable to stand the sight a moment longer.

THIRTY-TWO

"Callista, come here. Now."

I clench my hands as Liam calls my name. I barely slept last night. I couldn't get the image of the students out of my head. Their blank faces and dull eyes. I move slowly and deliberately to Liam's desk, where he waits.

Before he can get a word in, I snarl, "You lied. You said you weren't killing them. I will not be participating in this anymore! I'll find a way to protect my friends myself." I unclench my hands, sensing them twitch with nerves.

His unfazed expression makes me want to punch him. "I never lied. They aren't dead. If they were, then how did you see them? Would you like me to kill them? I can if you want."

My mouth drops open. *He can't be serious.* "They had no more life in them. They were dead. I will not help you do this." I turn away, my heart pulsing in my chest. *I need to leave. Now. Before he can do anything. I'll find another way to help them.*

"I wouldn't leave if I were you."

His words give me pause. Reluctantly, I turn and glare at him. When he pushes a button and a hologram appears with a video on it, I look at it warily. On closer inspection, the subject of the footage gives me pause. Two people are staring down at something as they make their way through the city. The viewpoint of the footage is from high above them.

"I told you I'd be watching your friends. I meant it. If you leave, I can easily turn my guard's protection into an attack." He pulls out a walkie-talkie and presses its button. "Please train your weapon on the pair. Prepare to fire on my word."

A static voice responds, "Roger."

My eyes widen in horror as I witness whoever is streaming the footage pull out a long gun. It looks identical to ones I saw used in old war footage at home.

"Don't do it." My voice comes out hoarse, panic swelling inside me.

He clicks the button again, and the hologram switches from the video to a control screen of sorts.

"See this? If I wanted to, I could send poisonous gas into each and every one of the rooms our subjects are kept in. I have this measure in case one of them acts out. But if you don't obey, I might just have to use it now." He raises a hand as if to activate the procedure.

Before I can think, I rush forward and slam my hands on the desk. My heart races wildly, my legs unsteady. "I'll stay! Just don't kill anyone, please!" *I'll trade myself, my own self-worth and soul for their safety.*

He smirks, closes the hologram, and eyes me. "You'll have to prove yourself after your incident last night and today. Now go." He waves me away with his hand.

As I drag my feet away, nausea overcomes me. *This is it.* I feel like I'm falling, my entire body numb and heavy. *What will happen to me now?*

I'm no longer sure how much time has passed. I'm an empty vessel being controlled against my will. I was unable to save anyone. Liam never permitted me access to the students again after my "episode." I don't know the last time I had a steady sleep. Mostly I feel outside myself. My actions aren't my own. My thoughts aren't my own. My words aren't my own. I'm a puppet. I have no say against anything because I know if I fight back, Liam won't protect my friends.

I'm not sure how many students I've led to REM, where they'll lose their humanity. After the first two, I stopped keeping count. All were just like I once was. I've condemned so many that nothing seems to matter. I do my best to be kind to them, to make them feel at ease. I'm not sure if it's any better to give them false hope, but it's the least I can do. Even after seeing the lifeless husks they turn into, I still have to participate in this game. *This is to protect them.* I repeat the simple sentence in my head every day, more to reassure myself of my reasoning than anything else.

I'm sitting at the counter eating my breakfast alone today. I had a nightmare again about all the faces of the students I've brought to their doom. I see them twist, contort, haunt me. They never go away.

It must be early because the sun isn't out and Melissa is asleep. I stare down at my oatmeal, moving my spoon around lifelessly. Creaking comes from the hall behind me, but I ignore it, dismissing it as typical early-hour noise. When Liam approaches me, I barely flinch.

"3265, you're finally ready to face orientation. Please follow me."

I push out of my seat, abandoning my food and following him. *I'm finally the perfect puppet.*

He leads me down several stale-smelling halls, not saying a word about what orientation is or where we're going. I don't ask questions.

When he leads me into a small open room with a few rows of chairs, my chest tightens.

"Take a seat," he says.

The sight of the students in the chairs causes bile to rise in my throat. The familiar lifeless husks sit stoically, their eyes focused ahead on Liam. They're all equally expressionless. My stomach twists, and I feel like I might throw up. I don't hesitate to take a seat, grateful for any excuse to not have to stare into their soulless eyes. I stare forward, watching as Liam takes his position on a podium in the front of the room. Four guards stand on each side of him for protection.

"Welcome, my new esteemed guard. I'm so glad to be able to finally recognize you all as my team."

The chattering guards quiet, and an eerie silence settles over the room.

"You may notice some of you are unlike the others. These are the best of our REM students who will be joining our guards."

So that's why they're here.

"I would like to inform you all on more history about our project and what roles you may have as a guard. As many of you know, our AI DETA transports students to Eclium. Said students are left in random locations. If you become a recruiter, you'll need to know this. The random locations are meant to create the illusion of choice. We don't want any incoming students to think we're forcing them to join the Academy. Our recruiters watch the children and have the responsibility of determining the perfect time to intervene and recruit. Should there ever be a setback, you must push back your recruitment to avoid suspicion."

Just like they did after seeing us at the diner. It's no surprise I had no choice then either.

"Our next role opportunity is the actor. Please turn your attention to this video." He presses a button on a controller I hadn't noticed he was holding, and a hologram appears before us. A woman with golden locks appears, standing with a jovial smile in an all-too-familiar setting.

A Neighborhood. It looks identical to my own.

"Hello, and welcome to the introduction of the acting path. I'm so pleased to inform you about this wonderful opportunity. Please, come along!" She waves at the camera, speaking as she walks. Her hair bounces behind her, curled to perfection. "As an actor, you must know that Neighborhoods are able to communicate privately. But subjects will be unaware. We must keep up the pretense that there's no connection between communities."

Her voice is trill and sends shivers down my spine. *I hate how nonchalant she is. As if she's not playing games with innocent fates.*

"Subjects also will be forced to attend mandatory annual appointments, where they'll have blood drawn so our scientists can determine how close they are to manifesting their abilities. They're also given a dosage of an ability controller that helps prevent their ability from manifesting before they arrive in Eclium. They also may receive other necessary drugs, such as memory-suppressors, ability-suppressors, and more." Images of a smiling doctor holding a needle appear and fade from the screen. "One way to know a child is about to manifest is if they feel an intense reaction to the ability controller, such as a rash. This reaction means they're about to manifest and should be prepared to be sent to Eclium."

I recall my last appointment with Dr. Isaac and the markings on my arm. *That's why he dismissed it. They all dismissed it because they knew what it meant.* A lump forms in my throat as I barely hold back a scowl.

The scene in the video shifts to one inside an all-too-familiar school. "It's not uncommon for subjects or students to wonder why they're unable to be around their peers while in their assigned Neighborhood. The reason children are allowed to be together at first is so that our guard can send the older children to Eclium and replace them with younger ones."

My jaw clenches. *Rotating us like cattle being sent off to slaughter.* I clench my fists, forcing myself to stay calm.

The woman continues, thrilled to be sharing the information. "During this early schooling time, actors also will monitor the subjects. If a child isn't presenting high enough levels of intelligence, you must send them to our high-security camps, where they'll become members of our New America military."

The screen shifts to show an image of what looks to be a prison. *I hate how easily she shifts between referring to us as children, students, and subjects. And high enough levels of intelligence? At the end of the day, they use us for our abilities. So why does our intelligence matter?* A lump forms in my throat, my despair heightened by the lack of concern in those around me. *They probably don't even realize anymore that this is what happened to them.*

The woman continues, discussing things that Reggie, Mason, Neena, and EMBER have already shared. *I guess this is the only thing Reginald didn't lie about.*

The video finally ends, and the woman waves a friendly goodbye to the camera. Liam clicks the device once more, and the hologram disappears.

"You may be wondering why students learn how to fight. We teach our students these skills so the best of them may be chosen to fight in our army. Most of them won't ever have use for these skills though, as they'll be sent to REM. This leads me to the final role you may have, besides the task of bringing students to REM. And that's escorting them to the hub. This task is only designated to the most reliable of guardsmen. Not only does it include bringing subjects out of REM and to the hub, but also sending them to New America. When the subjects arrive, they'll be left to fend for themselves. Their survival rate isn't high, but we can't afford to have them creating congestion for the Academy. Some of you," he meets my eyes, "have already lost your chance to participate."

I don't even register his directness. A rage I thought I'd long lost swells. *They're just abandoned? Discarded like trash? In that state? And what does he mean, creating congestion? The city is so empty, they could just stay here! But I guess that would create too much suspicion.* It takes every inch of my willpower to keep my mouth shut. *I can't do anything. He'll kill more of them. Why would he share any of this?*

Liam smirks, and I know deep down it's because he thinks he's broken me.

Maybe he has.

My mind wanders aimlessly as I drone through the rest of the day. *I can't do anything.* I know better now.

I make my way to my room, not surprised when Melissa isn't inside. She hasn't said a word to me since we last spoke so many weeks ago. She's been too busy to speak to me. In fact, she acts as if I don't exist. *I shouldn't exist. She's probably lost her humanity like I have.*

When my door flies open and Liam walks in, I don't flinch.

"3265, I need you to do something for me." I look up at him with a raised eyebrow. "Tell Kieran Erebus to stay here. Reginald has been getting closer to finding your friends, according to our monitors, and he would most definitely be safest here. I had him tracked down, and he refused to come with us until I told him you were here."

My heart stops. *K is here?* A plethora of feelings wash over me. My chest constricts, my breaths quickening. "Where is he?" I ask, trying to keep my voice steady and nonchalant.

"He's currently in the basement. You won't miss him when you go down."

I nod and move past him into the hall. It takes all my will not to sprint toward the basement door. It creaks loudly as I open it, then I move down the stairs. *K's here. He's here. He's safe.*

As soon as I reach the bottom and my orb lights up the darkness, I notice K behind bars in the corner. The sight sends my heart racing in alarm. *Why is he in a cell?* He seems to be asleep as I approach him, and the sight of him makes me weak.

"K," I whisper, startling as his bright-silver eyes flutter open to look at me. Recognition floods his features, and he jumps up and runs over to the bars.

"Callista! What happened?" His expression looks pained as he observes my appearance. "Are you okay?"

I keep my mask on and nod. "K, you need to trust me and stay here. I can't explain all the details right now, but Aviana is dead, and Reginald killed her."

His eyes widen in shock and confusion, and his lips dip in a frown. He considers me carefully, speaking slowly. "She's not dead. I saw her a few days ago. We've all been looking for you in separate groups. I'd been out for a while, trying to track you down, before I was brought here."

I stare at him in bewilderment. My throat constricts into tight knots. "Is this a joke?"

He looks hurt at the accusation and steps away.

He has to be lying. It doesn't make any sense, but he has to be. If Aviana isn't dead … if they aren't in danger … My mind starts to spiral at the implications of all I've done since that day Reginald told me he'd killed her. I start to feel sick, nausea swelling in my stomach. A sound echoes nearby and grabs my attention.

"Callista, I know you must be hurting, and I don't know what happened. But I promise you, she's alive. Something else must be going on here, and you're stuck in the middle of it."

When I look into his eyes, I don't see any hint of deception. My heart sinks. He has to be telling the truth.

"I'm sorry. I'm so sorry." My voice breaks. "He said he killed her, and Liam told me that I have to listen to him to keep you safe. I just couldn't have someone else die because of my mistakes. I've really screwed up, K. I—" I pause, taking a deep breath. "If she's alive, is there a way for me to see her?" I struggle to keep my emotions in check.

He seems briefly confused, and I tighten my lips. Much to my luck, he doesn't ask questions. "If we get out of here—"

A loud beeping sound from the hall cuts him off.

"Hold that thought. I need to go see what this is," I say.

I move away from K's cell. The only light is from my orb, lighting the dim space with a yellow glow. It pulses, almost as if telling me I need to go down the hall. *My own instincts must be causing it to act up like this.* The noise subsides, but I keep moving forward. I call flame to my hand, prepared to attack if necessary.

As I follow my orb, I realize I'm approaching an area I've never been to before. I notice a sign on the wall that says, "Do not pass this point."

Liam mentioned a certain hallway that Melissa and I shouldn't go down. I never bothered looking for it because I didn't want to get on his bad side. But if my friends are alive, I don't need to listen to him anymore.

The beeping noise blares again. I look behind me to make sure no one is following me, then quickly tiptoe forward. I go far down the hall, passing several rooms on my way. Eventually, the hall stops in front of a single wooden door. I call back my flame and slowly twist the doorknob, expecting it to be locked.

When it turns easily and the door creaks open, I freeze. *Maybe I shouldn't go in.* Uncertainty fills me. When I open the door and step in, I slowly nudge it closed so no one knows I came in here.

The room has a single desk with a computer, and there are papers scattered throughout. I walk toward the table and look through the papers. I take a mental note of their location, hoping I'll be able to put them back in their spot afterward so no one notices a difference. My hand brushes across a sharp object as I start to shuffle through the sheets.

"What?" I mutter to myself, moving the papers, only to reveal a pointy switch-like item attached to the desk. It hums quietly, then grows louder as the beeping that drew me here sounds again. I cover my ears, as the noise is unbearably loud. Luckily, it's only a few seconds before it returns to a low hum. I slowly remove my hands from my ears and reach out to the switch. Taking a deep breath, I flip it.

As soon as I do, the humming dissipates. *Why was it making noise?* I look around in anticipation and am about to sigh in slight relief when a low buzz emits from the wall to my side. I turn, only to see a large hologram glowing in a bright-blue hue. It shows several files on its screen, and I move toward it curiously. Warily, I reach out my hand and press on a file titled "3R." Suddenly I'm faced with a large block of text. I look up to the top and read.

About REMEDY

REMEDY Academy is a school formed to take abilitied teenagers, train them, then send them to REM. Our AI DETA monitors the students when they grow up in their respective Neighborhoods and continues monitoring them once they arrive in Eclium. It sends us a signal when a student is ready to join the Academy and alerts us if any unwanted people follow the students to Eclium. It is important to note that each student received their powers through a mutated gene scientifically implanted into them when they were an infant so they can join REMEDY Academy and become our subject. This implantation is connected to DETA and monitors students' locations, emotions, relationships, and knowledge of our project. In the case of subjects, each student is referred to as a test subject and lives in Neighborhoods full of control subjects. Every test subject will join a family of actors when they are young, and their birth parents are killed in order to protect the child from knowing they are different and acting out. Each test subject is assigned to another child, who is supposed to act as their friend so the test subject is less likely to suspect any strange occurrences. A child's power does not activate until age fifteen to eighteen. If activated before this time, the child must be disposed of, as they failed their test. The same occurs if their power has not activated by their nineteenth birthday. In REM, depending on the ability and strength in all areas of the student, they will either have their powers extracted and put into our ultimate weapon or be used as a member of our army, whose mission is to take control over the Earth and bring order to our destroyed societies. There is too much corruption on our planet, and we will fix this through taking control. However, there has been rumor of special individuals who have unique abilities that are opposites of another's. UPDATE: One recent example of this case is Callista Tieron, #3265, and Kieran Erebus, #8434, who possess light- and dark-related abilities. In these cases, the individuals will have their power drained and combined into a separate weapon if they do not agree to give their autonomy to us. We hope to use them as leaders of our new order.

I find myself reading the message over and over, hoping to see that it's just a cruel joke. Nausea rises inside me, along with the urge to flee.

It just goes deeper and deeper. This sick, twisted game. Now I know why that message about DETA had deleted parts. They didn't want people to know we're constantly monitored. We're their perfect little cattle. Anyone less than is removed, anything more than is more of an excuse to use. Nothing is safe.

Thousands of questions fill my head, and I tear off the choker around my neck. Tossing it on the ground, I smash my boot on top of it. It's satisfying to see the large *R* turn into tiny, useless shards.

A loud alarm blares, and speakers echo above. "3265 has initiated lockdown. Information has been breached."

It was a trap! The sound lured me here so I could get caught! Fear rises in my chest, and I panic. I move to leave the room and fill with anxiety when the door doesn't budge. "Come on!" I cry out. After trying to twist the handle with my clammy hands, with little success, I give up and search for another escape. I feel sweat coat my neck, and the room seems to be getting hotter.

I'm panicking. This is just a panic attack. I have to focus. I have to get to K. My efforts to calm myself are to no avail as I sense my reaction worsening. *Idiot. I did this. It's all my fault.*

The world is spinning, and my vision clouds further as each second passes. The alarm rings in my ears as a headache gnaws at my skull. "Please help me!" I cry as I fall to the floor in defeat. I watch the door handle twist, revealing Liam staring at me with a blank look.

"Well, I guess it's time for you now," he says. "It's a shame, really. I was hoping to get more use." He bends down and lifts up my chin with his finger. "Callista, are you willing to fully submit to giving your free will to our control?"

Even with my willpower slowly fading away and my head pounding, I manage to spit at him. "I will never submit to you."

I briefly see his other hand move to grab something, then a pain shoots down my neck. His finger moves away, and my head hits the floor, along with a now empty syringe.

"Goodnight, Callista."

I feel a large wave of nausea wash over me, and everything turns black.

THIRTY-THREE

DECEPTION IS OUR REMEDY. My thoughts cloud my mind, and part of me wishes I still believed the lies this place has fed me all the months I've been here. The deceit was like a protective blanket, keeping me safe from the unwanted truths and horrors of the real world. No longer do I have access to that remedy.

My consciousness comes back slowly and in small bits. My entire body is numb, and the walls around me are made of gray concrete. When my awareness fully returns, I look around, only to see that I'm locked up and connected to several tubes. A glowing liquid travels through them, and as soon as I realize what it is, I want to throw up. Instinctively, my body tries to squirm away, but I'm trapped in place. Sharp pains shoot through me where each of the tubes is connected to my flesh. As I look up, I notice someone hooked up several feet in front of me.

My eyes widen when I realize it's K. A dark, smoky liquid travels through the tubes connected to him, in sharp contrast to the bright substance in my own. When I go to speak, I'm partially surprised that my body allows me to.

"K? Is that really you?" My voice comes out hoarse, my entire body dehydrated.

His silver eyes drift up to meet mine, and he quirks a small, sad smirk. "Callista, I'm—"

"Stop. It's my fault you're here. I should have listened to you. I shouldn't have investigated further. I shouldn't have believed that Aviana died. I should have looked for you and the others. I let them get to me, and now we're here."

He frowns, his eyes sad. Before either of us can continue talking, a low laugh comes from our side. I turn to see Liam walking in with Melissa next to him. The sight of her by his side gives me pause.

"Ah, you two are awake." He grins maniacally at us as Melissa moves from his side and comes over to me, poking and prodding to check that the tubes connected to me are still working.

"Melissa?" My voice wavers, my stomach tingling.

She looks at me and scoffs. "You just had to fight back, didn't you, Callista? This wouldn't have had to happen if you'd just listened."

I raise my eyebrows in confusion.

She just rolls her eyes. "I've been working with Liam this whole time. Well, on a deeper level than you knew. I thought you may have caught on, but I guess you're denser than I thought."

My voice grows thick. "Why?"

She waves away my question as she walks away from me to check Kieran's tubes.

I should have known. How could I be so stupid? My hands shake, my rage barely constrained as I stare daggers at Liam.

"Let us go." I speak with more conviction than our current circumstances should allow.

"You know that's not possible," Liam says. "Since you didn't comply with my orders, you and Kieran will have your powers combined into a weapon. You two are a unique pair—complete opposites who create the strongest power when together. To be frank, you two are all we need to complete our domination. Your existence will speed up our goals. We've already gotten control of smaller countries, but we've yet to have enough strength to completely conquer every nation until today. Other students are like appetizers. You both are the main course."

I cringe at the comparison and sense anger emanating from K across the room.

Liam's eyes light up, and he tilts his head at me. "Want to know a little fun fact? We named ourselves REMEDY because we're curing all you children of your inevitable demises due to your abilities. We're saving you all by turning you into our weapons."

I practically laugh in his face. "You created us to be this way. If your intent was to 'cure' us by using us from the start, then you sure as hell aren't a true remedy for our pain. You're only creating more pain for every single student who goes here. You use the word *REMEDY* to hide the deception that lies beneath."

Liam frowns and moves toward me. He grabs a strand of my loose hair and twists it around his finger. "You're a smart and snappy girl, just like your mother was. What a shame she had to die. I would have kept her alive, but she just wouldn't give up on you or your father. All I wanted her to do was leave you and let me kill him so she could come live safely with me, but she wouldn't comply. I had to dispose of them both."

So he was the one who killed my mom. I swallow rapidly, overwhelmed by my emotions. I struggle against the tubes holding me aloft. I want to hurt him, to make him suffer for all the innocent people he's punished. *Who I've punished.* But, like always, I'm unable to do anything.

Liam turns to Melissa and smiles. "I almost forgot. Melissa, can you please bring Reginald in here? Oh, and June please."

K's eyes and my own seem to widen in unison. *Reggie? He's here?* I feel like I might throw up. *He didn't actually kill Avi. But he's still unforgivable.*

Melissa nods at Liam and retreats into the hall.

"June's here?" K shouts at Liam with more anger than I've ever heard him have before. "Why the hell is she here? I thought she was dead!"

Liam laughs, and it only fuels K's rage.

"Well, she was dead," the headmaster says. "But here at REMEDY, we have the finest technology. We were able to create an AI out of a scan of her thoughts and memories just before we finished her. I had a feeling it would come in use. Essentially, it is your sister, but not in a human body. I decided it's the perfect way to torture you for my own entertainment."

Before K can speak again, Melissa walks in with Reginald in chains, along with what I assume to be the AI version of K's sister. I glance at K's face, only to see barely restrained tears in his eyes. When I look back to see Reggie, I fume.

"Reginald, what's going on here?" I ask. "Why have you lied to me ever since we met?" My chest hitches as I cry out, hoping he has an excuse that would make sense out of this mess. When his eyes meet mine, they look so empty that it pains me despite my anger toward him.

"Oh, he's not really able to respond right now. That's my fault," Liam says.

I turn my head and stare daggers into Liam, who seems unfazed.

"June …" K mumbles to himself, and I wince at his pain.

"This is so boring!" Liam shouts. "Melissa, make it a little more fun, won't you? Entertain our guests in their final moments."

Melissa nods, then walks over to June's still form and presses something on her neck. June instantly starts moving and grabs something off a desk I failed to notice before. A needle glints in her hand, and she raises it above Reginald.

"What are you doing?" I yell, but it falls on deaf ears. Just as June raises her arm, I cry out again. "Leave them alone, you psycho! That's your son!"

Liam waves his hand, causing June to stop. "You're right. How about you and Reginald have a little chat. I'll give you privacy by waiting in the hall, but Melissa will stay here to make sure you don't act out."

With that, he walks out of the room, and June follows him.

Reggie just stands there for several moments, and I silently watch, hoping for him to speak. Just when I fear he's completely lost, he starts rapidly blinking, then stumbles. When he meets my eyes again, they're no longer empty.

"Cal?" His voice comes out in a croak. For a moment, all I can see is my friend in pain. But then his betrayal washes over me once again, and I spit on the floor.

"You have some explaining to do!" I shout. Out of the corner of my eye, I see K staring at the floor, seemingly oblivious to his surroundings. I find myself wishing I could at least hold his hand so we could deal with our pain together. Since I can't, I refocus on Reggie.

He grimaces, seeming lost. "I have so many missing spaces in my memory. I remember coming here with you and living with my father. He took me under his wing. I thought I might finally be forming a relationship with him. I hadn't thought to question why I felt myself becoming more forgetful around him. Then I found out about his plans and left him to find you. We spent time together again. But then I was attacked, and all my memories became shuffled and fuzzy. I don't know what else happened."

I stare at him, astonished. "So you're seriously telling me you don't remember all the suffering you've caused me?"

His expression darkens, and he shakes his head. "I'm trying to recall, but all I can see are fuzzy images."

"You don't remember telling me the truth?" My voice cracks, wavering in its inflection.

"I do remember that. I remember those few days we had together. Those memories were never forgotten. When you were more generous to me than I deserved. I know I lied to you, Cal. But I truly did find fondness in our relationship. I grew to like you, genuinely like you. I'm sorry I didn't try harder to figure out what was happening. That I didn't fight harder for you. That I never stopped their sick plan. I really thought for a moment there, after I found you again, that we could get back to normal in some way. But I was naïve. And now you're going to die because of me."

I can't believe it. Or I don't want to. It would almost be easier at this point to see him as the enemy. But I know Liam loves to play with people's thoughts and brains and to control everything he can. And I wouldn't be surprised if he did it to his own child. But I can't take the deceit any longer.

"I don't know if I can forgive you," I say. You might not remember what you've done. But you lied to me more. You tricked me. You manipulated me."

"But it wasn't me. It was someone in my skin. I'm myself now, and I don't remember it." His tone is pleading, as if he genuinely believes that makes any difference.

"That doesn't change anything! You could have been more careful. And one thing doesn't add up." I pause, swallowing. "If you truly didn't know anything, then why did you just accept us being here? Why didn't you push for us to leave? Why did you just want to make a home here, instead of any other place? Even if we're too far from any land, we could have at least tried."

"I …" He pauses, looking extremely guilty. "I was scared. I'm sorry. I understand if you hate me. Everything up to the point when we arrived was part of a plan I knew about. I didn't know where the plan was going, but I was still participating in it. I was afraid of what would happen to me if I didn't. I never knew the full extent of the plan, but I didn't ask questions. I know you told me what my father did to the students at the Academy. But I really did think I could stop him if I played along. That maybe all we needed was more time. I was willing to make sacrifices if, at the end, I could keep you safe. I was going to help you find your friends. I wanted you to be happy. But to keep you safe, I behaved like a puppet, just as my father wanted. I thought it would give me a chance to figure out what I could do if I was patient enough. After I was attacked, I don't know what happened. I just followed my orders. I guess my plan wasn't as foolproof as I'd thought. Had I known it would end up like this, I wouldn't have listened. Maybe I can help you get out of here. Maybe it's not too late."

Awfully convenient memory loss. I shake my head and laugh dryly. "Whatever. Your words mean nothing anymore." I motion to Melissa in the corner, then point to the door. "And she's not going to let us out. Neither is that psycho on the other side of the door."

Reggie looks genuinely pained, and he slouches. I no longer have the same remorse for him. All of this could have been avoided if he'd done something. He's the cause of everything. *Or am I for believing him?*

"Cal, please—"

"Don't call me that. We aren't friends. I don't know if we ever were."

This clearly pains him, and I avert his gaze, biting my lip. It's as if I'm being pulled in two separate directions. A part of me holds on to what I thought we had. I know that taking complete control of his own son isn't beneath Liam's psychopathic tendencies. But I also can't ignore what Reginald has done and all the lies he continues to form. His tendencies won't go away, so I may never trust him.

I look away from him, turning to stare at Melissa. She's unmoving, not even acknowledging the tension in the air. *And her. How could I believe her? Who else is a lie?* I look to K with concern. When he glances up and looks at me, I feel slight reassurance. *Reginald isn't worth my time. But I also don't wish death on him. I don't want to cause death for anyone else. If only to honor our memories.*

After several long, excruciating moments of silence stretch between us, Liam reenters with June. K jerks his head and snarls at Liam. Reggie turns, and when he meets Liam's eyes, I can see terror come over his face.

"What are you going to do?" Reggie asks.

Liam smirks. "You really don't remember anything. Well, I suppose I'm glad my plans worked."

He was under Liam's control. He didn't lie about that. But even after, he still lied to me again, even without the influence. It doesn't change anything.

Reggie says, "What did you do to me?"

"You performed your role as a conscious puppet, but you were clearly too attached to Callista here. I found you much more useful under my control."

Reginald lunges at Liam but is stopped by Melissa's grip. She holds him back.

Liam laughs and says, "Well, now you'll die without any friends. Was it all worth it?"

Reginald spits at Liam's shoes, still struggling to escape. He's clearly not in his peak condition, as he loses his strength quickly, breathing heavily after only a few moments.

Even though I no longer see him as my friend, the thought of Reginald being killed pains me.

"Don't kill him, Liam. Haven't you done enough?" I cry.

He turns to me and frowns. "But he isn't of use to me anymore. And I can't just let him go out and expose my secrets."

I laugh half-heartedly. "Can't you just use your memory eraser again? Make him forget everything and send him out into the world with a clean slate?"

Reginald looks at me with a glint of hope in his eyes. I don't meet his gaze, focusing on Liam.

K shouts, "Haven't you killed enough people? Just listen to reason for once!"

I'm surprised but thankful. *Reginald doesn't even deserve his plea.*

Liam seems to ponder our words before shrugging. "Perhaps I have. But listening to 'reason,' as you call it, would take too much work and precious time away from my plans. Plus, it isn't nearly as entertaining."

"Please, just consider—"

The words fall off my lips as Melissa tightens her hold on Reginald, Liam motions at June, and she steps toward him. Everything moves in slow motion.

I'm unable to speak as I once again see the glint of the needle in June's hand. I try to lunge forward, but the metal constraints around my ankles and wrists hold me in place. Reginald's eyes are pleading, not leaving my gaze for a second.

I yell out, "Stop!" as the needle plunges into his neck. He doesn't fall right away. I swear I hear the brief whisper of "I'm sorry" leave his lips as he slouches.

June and Liam step away as the life leaves his eyes. Melissa lets go of her hold on him, and his body falls to the floor.

I stare in shock at his lifeless form. It's as if all the lies no longer matter. I only see someone I once cared for, now taken from me forever. My lips start to tremble, and I feel a stabbing pain in my stomach as a tear falls down my cheek. I force myself to look up at Liam.

"You're a monster. He was your son." My voice comes out in a croak.

Anger flares up within me when he chuckles. "He may have been my son, but it doesn't matter. Plus, Melissa already agreed to become the next heir of REMEDY when I'm no longer alive. She's very obedient, and he wasn't."

He waves at Melissa. She moves to June, turns her off, and drags away Reginald's body.

"You have about twenty-four hours before your power will be completely drained and your body will become a husk of your former self. Thanks for helping our cause!"

With that, Liam walks away, leaving K and me alone.

THIRTY-FOUR

I'M NOT SURE HOW LONG WE sit in the deafening silence. When K speaks, it takes me a moment to register it.

"Callista …"

Still shaken from what just occurred, I don't say anything at first. But then I remember how he also just had to deal with something traumatic, and I attempt to recenter myself.

"I'm sorry. I can't believe he did that to you. To either of us. He manipulated our emotions just like he wanted to." I look to him with sad eyes, and he frowns. "Have we really lost?"

"It sure seems like it."

Uncertainty and numbness fill me. "K, are you scared?"

"I typically wouldn't admit it, but yes, I'm terrified."

"I'm sorry I couldn't save you all. And I'm sorry I didn't save you right away when you were locked up by that awful man."

He shakes his head lightly. "That's not your responsibility, and it never has been. In fact, I want to thank you for showing me I don't need to be afraid of relationships. When I lost my sister, I thought sharing and being with someone would be a waste of time. But you taught me otherwise." He pauses, then a hint of darkness crosses his face. "As for everything else …"

I gulp as he drifts off, averting his gaze.

"I know," I say. "I screwed up. A lot happened when we were separated. I'm just like Liam. I hurt a lot of people. Innocent people. I thought it was my only choice. I tried to fight back, but he threatened you all. So I gave in and became what he wanted me to be. I hoped that if I participated long enough in his sick plans, I could eventually find a way to fight back. But I shouldn't have done it. I don't know how I'll ever make it up to you. Or to all the people who were impacted by what I did. But I'm sorry. I'm sorry to you, and I'm sorry to everyone else I hurt. I don't expect you to forgive me. I don't know if I'll even be able to forgive myself. If these are our last moments …" My words drift off, tears welling in my eyes as I fully come to terms with our situation.

Silence drags on, and I fear he won't ever speak to me again.

"Callista, look at me." I turn and stare at him, tears still falling. He looks pained, but not angry. "It will take time. I don't hate you. I hate what you did in your desperation. It's awful. But you were also a victim in your own way. I know that. I still care for you. We've been through so much together, and you're important to me. I knew something was off when I saw you after all that time. I didn't expect something to this extent, but I'm not completely surprised. I know it can be hard to fight desperation. And you had little choice. It's obvious how manipulative Liam can be. If I were in your shoes, I'm not sure I can say I would have done differently from you. I'll forgive you. But more importantly, you need to forgive yourself."

My heart breaks at his words. *He's too good for me.* His kindness is something I've never felt before.

I choke on my tears and long for his embrace. "Thank you so much, K. You're more than I could have ever asked for or deserved." My words come out with a few choked sobs. "You showed me I'm not alone and that people do care about me. You allowed me to be brave and truly express myself. I used to think

Reginald was the only person who would ever like me, but you showed me otherwise."

How is he being so strong? I almost think I see the glint of tears in his eyes as well. The mood in the room is solemn, both of us slowly coming to terms with our inevitable death. Wanting to have some form of good news, I take a deep breath to stop my crying.

"Was Aviana safe when you saw her?" I ask.

He nods, and I let out a shaky laugh. The motion causes pain to shoot up my abdomen from the tube sites.

I bite my cheek as he speaks. "She's safe with the others. I'm pretty sure she's in a relationship with Alec now."

A small grin spreads across my lips. "I'm glad to hear it. I hope they can help take down this awful place." I pause, thinking about those I'm leaving behind. "Is Emmy still with Jamie?"

"She is."

I breathe a sigh of relief as silence fills the room again. My life slowly drains from me as my body loses energy. Images of the events that have occurred these past few months flash through my mind, and I decide to get one last thing off my chest before it's too late.

"K, I know it isn't important. And I know you're already being kinder than I deserve. But back before there was a fire at the headquarters, I saw a video of you and Melissa kissing."

I pause, allowing him to adjust to the information. He seems to want to speak, but before he can, I continue.

"And looking back at how I felt seeing that now, I realize I have feelings for you. You've been there for me through this all and are all I could ever ask for. I just wanted you to know before it's too late."

He's silent at first, seeming to consider me. My heart stutters in my chest, and I can't tell if it's from my nerves or the fact I'm getting nearer to death by the second. My mouth is dry, and I smack my lips.

When K finally speaks, he seems a mix of reassured and saddened. "First of all, Melissa forced that kiss. I never had an eye for her, as there was someone else who caught my attention." My eyes widen, and he smiles slightly. "Callista, I'll need time to accept what has happened. I think you need time with yourself as well. I still cherish you. If this really is to be our end, I also want to be honest. After learning what you've done, I'm conflicted. I hate knowing you helped Liam. Yet I know he manipulated you. It's a tough situation. I can't deny the way you've made me feel. I've seen your heart and believe you don't wish to create pain. And so I should tell you as well. I think—"

A loud yell from the hall cuts him off, and we both turn.

"Where are they?" a girl shouts, and it sounds like thousands of animals are trampling down the hall. The door flies open, and my eyes widen as Aviana stands there with two medium-sized deer, one on either side of her. Three other people come in behind her. I barely notice anyone except my sister.

"Avi?" I ask weakly.

She moves toward me with tears streaming down her face. "Callista, I missed you!"

Hearing my name come from my sister warms my heart, and tears fall from my eyes. The moment is ruined as a tingling sensation passes through my limbs.

"Wait, where are Melissa and Liam?" I ask in disbelief. I then take note of the three others in the room—Brayden, Alec, and Tessa. When I see Brayden, I stare at him. He looks down, avoiding my gaze. "And what's he doing here?"

Tessa moves over to carefully release the restraints from my body, and Alec and Brayden move over to K to do the same. When I finally regain control of my limbs, a shot of pain courses through my muscles from being stuck in such an unpleasant position. I'm unable to move my legs, as the tubes are still connected to my body.

Aviana answers my question as I flex my arms. "He said he would help. He claims he was attacked and that he doesn't remember what happened, as his memory was altered. Our medics confirmed there were, in fact, traces of Liam's drug in his system. The higher-ups insisted we not kick him out for being sloppy since they've gotten some help from him before and thought it would be a waste. He's on close watch and will be on probation after this mission so that no one has to worry about him putting others at risk. Don't worry. He won't mess up. Trust me."

So it really wasn't his fault.

I indicate that she can continue, and she eagerly does. "As for everything else, other EMBER officials are distracting them so we have enough time to escape with you guys. Alec managed to get a map of this place, and we've been trying to find you this whole time."

When my eyes travel to the large creatures next to her, she shoots me a reassuring smile. "Since I was separated from you," she says, "EMBER has been conducting experiments on samples of my blood and comparing its properties to samples from people who hadn't gone through REM. They still haven't found the perfect solution, but they did find a way to boost the remaining power I had left. It only works for a few hours at a time, but it is possible that if I continue using it enough, it will build up in my system and help restore my powers near completely. No one knows how long that will take or if it will happen for sure. I sometimes get dizzy from using my abilities, but other than that, it has worked great. I was able to compel these two deer to knock over some guards on the way so we could focus on finding you. Don't worry about any of that now. We need to leave, and fast."

I take a moment to process the load of information she just provided. *So it's possible to regain our abilities if they aren't completely removed?* The thought is somewhat comforting. *I'm just glad she's okay.*

I nod slowly and smile thankfully at my sister. Before I can say anything, both deer beside her move. I watch in astonishment as they bump their heads against Avi's leg. She lets out a startled laugh and places a hand on each of their backs, looking at them fondly. "I'm still getting used to handling such large animals."

Being close to the creatures should make me more nervous, but after all the recent events, I think people are more sinister than animals. I allow another moment of silence to pass before speaking. "I'm sorry, Avi. I'm happy to see you growing. I have a lot to tell you as well, but I'm so thankful for you."

She smiles at me, and it puts me at ease.

Before I can ask how they're going to proceed, Tessa walks over with a grim frown.

"We're going to remove the tubes from both of you now," she says. "Callista, you'll go first. Avi will release the latch connected to your body and try to pull each tube out as smoothly as possi-ble. We've been training her in the medical field, so I promise she knows what she's doing. While she does this, I'll heal your skin to prevent as much pain as I can."

My eyebrows rise, and I swallow my fear. *Any pain is worth getting out of here.* I glance at K, and he gives me a reassuring nod.

I take a deep breath, then nod at Tessa. "Just do it quickly." Avi looks at me with concern, so I force myself to smile. "It'll be okay. I trust you."

This seems to give her the boost of confidence she needs, and she approaches me, leaving the deer. When she's in front of me, she reaches down to work on the first set of tubes. I hold my breath as she prods at them, the latch tugging at my flesh. When she starts pulling one out, it feels as if she's taking out my intestines, and nausea overcomes me. I close my eyes, not wanting to see the gruesome sight.

"It's out," she says, and I open my eyes to look at her, surprised. One bloodied tube is in her hand. I expect to feel unbearable pain, but instead, I just have a cooling sensation on my skin. I find the site of the incision and see that it's already healed. Avi places a hand on my shoulder and looks into my eyes.

"Are you okay? Did it hurt?" she asks.

I shake my head, impressed. "No, Tessa healed me so fast that I didn't feel anything." *Except for that dreadful experience of the tube leaving my body.* I don't bother mentioning this fact, as I don't want to worry her.

She smiles at me meekly. "Only a few more to go."

I put on my bravest expression and bite down on my lip as she goes back to work. I manage to get reluctantly used to the uncomfortable sensation of the extraction, and the process goes by relatively smoothly. When Tessa closes the last wound, I'm instantly refreshed. My body is now completely in my control.

With some hesitation, I step forward on shaky legs. I touch my stomach where the tubes protruded moments ago. Then I take a few more steps, regaining more control of myself after each one. When I no longer feel like I might fall, I turn to Avi and Tessa, wrapping them both in a hug.

"Thank you so much," I say, tears pricking at my eyes. *I was prepared to die here. But now I still have a fighting chance thanks to them.*

When I pull away, Tessa inclines her head and says, "We still have lots to do."

I wipe my eyes as she turns to K. Both she and Avi walk over to him. I avoid the gaze of Brayden, who stands off to the side, and instead move toward K's side.

A frown is plastered on his face. "Is it really not bad?" he asks.

I shake my head. Then, wanting to be honest, I lean forward to whisper in his ear. "It's unpleasant when the tubes are being removed. Just be prepared."

He looks to me with concern, but before I can try to reassure him, Avi speaks up.

"We're ready," she says.

I nod and step back. When she begins to remove the first tube, I turn away, not wanting to watch the bloody process. A sudden jolt of pain passes through me, and I stumble. I'm able to catch myself before anyone notices that something is wrong. *Just ignore it. There are more important things going on.* I push away the pain and resolve to get some answers. Looking around the room, I startle slightly when I see Alec gently petting one of the deer. *They're so calm. Are they completely under Avi's control?*

Curiosity gets the best of me, so I approach him and tap him on his shoulder, making him jump. Surprisingly, the deer don't react to his sudden movement. Instead, they look at me. *It looks like they're staring into my soul.* I avert my eyes from theirs, focusing on Alec.

"They seem more like pets than wild animals," I remark.

He raises his eyebrows, then shakes his head quickly. "Sorry, I didn't expect you to come over here." A smile crosses his face. "It's fascinating. Avi's presence seems to calm any animal under her influence, so they're open to anyone they sense she doesn't deem a threat."

"What about when she's no longer controlling them?"

He shrugs. "They'll just go back to acting like wild animals. These deer, for example, would probably just take off."

That could be dangerous. Alec seems to sense my thoughts, answering my unspoken question. "Avi avoids predatory creatures for that reason. With her still weakened powers, it would be too dangerous."

I nod slowly. When I look to the deer again, they seem more inviting than before. "Do you think they'd allow me to touch them?" I ask, glancing at Alec somewhat sheepishly.

To my relief, he nods eagerly. "Of course. They're under her control." He motions to them, and I step forward cautiously. The deer watch me, their black eyes blinking. I slowly place one hand on the deer closest to me, and when it doesn't flinch, I move my hand in a petting motion. Its hair is coarse but not unpleasant. The animal doesn't react, and its companion only observes me.

"They really don't care, do they?" I say, although the response is obvious. *It's almost unnerving how calm they are.*

"I guess you could say Avi's power makes them more like mindless zombies than living creatures," Alec says. "Although they do seem to react to her with more liveliness."

That must be why they seemed more alive by her side. A chill goes down my spine, and I pull my hand away. I turn and face Alec, deciding to ignore the deer for the time being.

"So what's the plan once K is free?" I ask.

He pauses, seeming to think. "We shouldn't have too much trouble getting out of here. There were several guards in the halls and outside, but most or all were dealt with by us or the other EMBER members. However, some may be hiding out or called for backup. You and K are too weak to fight, so you'll have to hang back while we make sure it's clear."

I frown. "Can we really not help in any way?" I try to call for my ability to show him I'm still capable, but nothing responds. I have only the faintest sense that I still have some power. *I never thought I'd be so weak.* Other than that, I have only a faint pain that I work desperately to block out. *I can't let it control me.*

Alec must sense my defeat, as he puts a light hand on my shoulder. "You two have been through enough. As soon as we get to the headquarters, you two can take the medicine we've crafted. That will allow you to heal slightly faster. There will be plenty of opportunities for you to help once you've regained your strength."

K's voice pulls me away from our conversation as he says, "Thank you, Avi."

I turn and feel instantly lighter, seeing him standing and without the awful tubing. He looks to Tessa and inclines his head. "Thank you as well, Tessa."

She smiles at him and wraps him in a hug. He looks stiff for a moment, but then he slowly returns the gesture.

I'm glad to see he isn't still angry with her. I give them a moment, and as soon as they release their embrace, I hurry over to K's side. He looks at me wide-eyed, then a soft smile spreads across his face. I'm overjoyed when he pulls me in for a hug. Warmth spreads throughout my body from having my face pressed against his chest, and the weight on my shoulders feels lighter. When he pulls away, he meets my eyes, and they seem to tell me that everything will be okay.

He's too forgiving. I don't deserve it. Thoughts of all my awful acts resurface in my mind, and I'm grateful when Alec interrupts the moment.

"We must get going. It's getting late, and we have a lot to do."

THIRTY-FIVE

AVI CLOSES HER EYES BRIEFLY, and when she reopens them, she nods. "The hall's clear. It's safe to make our way to the exit."

K has already left my side and approached the door. I briefly catch him grimacing before he covers it up with a frown. He looks to Tessa, fully composed. "What should Callista and I do?" he asks.

"You two will stay in the back with Avi. She and Alec can both act as navigators and will be able to alert us to any danger. Brayden, Alec, and I will be in the front. All you have to concern yourself with is not getting in the way if we face danger."

"Let's head out," Alec says. I note that Brayden still hasn't said anything. *Not even an apology?*

Tessa nods, then she, Alec, and Brayden step out into the hall. I step toward K, ready to go after them, but he stops me with his hand.

"You go behind me. I don't want you to get hurt," he says.

I arch an eyebrow at him. "We're both equally powerless. Either of us could get hurt." *And it seems we're both dealing with these pains.*

He just frowns at me, and just as I'm about to argue with him, Avi steps between us.

"Just let him. I'll take up the tail." She pauses, looking at me with a gentle smile. "My deer will help protect us." Her eyes travel toward the door as she waves at the large creatures still waiting patiently nearby. I watch in a mixture of awe and slight terror as they move toward her, no longer seeming like statues. They stop beside her, and she places a hand on each one's back. I watch curiously as she briefly closes her eyes. As soon as she reopens them, she speaks.

"The others haven't alerted, so we should be good to go."

K nods and doesn't hesitate to step into the hall. I look to my sister nervously.

"Don't worry. We got this," she says.

I incline my head and step out into the hall. As soon as I'm in the long corridor, I'm met with seemingly endless darkness. I instinctively call out to my light, but once again, nothing happens. I'm unable to see K.

"K?" I call, reaching around in the darkness. I flood with relief when my hand hits his shoulder.

"Be quiet!" he says. I don't understand why our silence is necessary if it's safe for us to proceed. Then he tells me, "I thought I heard a yell."

I listen closely for a noise but am unable to catch anything. When Avi speaks from behind me, I jump.

"He's right," she says. I hear something too. It sounds like fighting."

I'm about to question how both of them can hear something completely mute to my ears when a loud yell echoes down the hall.

"There it is again!" K whisper-shouts.

"Can't we get some light here?" I ask, uncomfortable in the pitch black.

Avi pulls out a flashlight and shines it toward the floor in front of us. "Sorry," she whispers. "I forgot that you two can't see or hear as I do. I was using the deer. There's fighting. The others met trouble up ahead. I'm not sure how many guards, but it's not safe for you two. I need you to wait here while I go help them."

I turn to her, finally able to see her face.

"There's no way I'm going to let you go by yourself! I'm perfectly capable of helping," I say. My own body must have a vendetta against me, as a sudden wave of dizziness causes me to stumble forward. I just barely catch myself on the wall before I fall to the floor.

Avi looks at me with a raised eyebrow, her arms folded. "Clearly, you aren't well enough. I got in here without you. I'll get you out without your help."

I scowl at her. "That isn't fair."

Her expression softens. "I know how you feel. We've done research on what happens after being in REM. It can take up to thirty minutes for the side effects to fully register. For me, it was instant. I imagine if you just pay attention to your body, you'll see that you're in pain. You're going to need a lot of rest and time to heal."

Her words cause me to finally give in to the signals my body has been desperately sending out to me. I no longer fight to suppress it, and it doesn't take long for sickness to flow back in. A deep hollowness in my chest pulses, and I sense another wave of dizziness coming. I look to K and notice faint sweat droplets on his forehead.

"You can't push it away," Avi says. "I fear you both will soon succumb to your ill effects from the machines. Please, stay here. We'll fetch you once we've dealt with whoever is left." Just then, another shout comes from down the hall. "I'm going," she announces.

I want to fight her declaration but know there's no use. She hands her flashlight to me and takes off sprinting down the hall, her two deer by her side.

K has a hand to his forehead, his jaw clenched.

"What if we pass out?" I ask, my voice coming out weaker than before.

"I'm sure it'll be fine," he says.

Each moment feels longer than the last. I stumble down the hall in Avi's direction, wanting to be with her no matter the danger. But I don't make it far before K grabs my wrist and pulls me back.

"Just wait," he says. "We're useless like this."

I open my mouth, but no words come out. Instead, I just slump down against the wall and lay the flashlight down to light the opposite side of the hall. K sits down next to me, and we both stare silently forward. There's no more yelling. The pain inside me isn't steady. But I can sense it strengthening each time it resurfaces and passes, draining my energy. I have a deep urge to just sleep it all off, to ignore everything and simply close my eyes.

I have to stay awake. I need to stay awake. I turn my head, only to see that K's eyes have shut. *He looks so peaceful.* A faint smile crosses my lips as I lean back my head, giving in to my exhaustion.

Eyes. They stare at me from every angle, watching my every move. I see Melissa plunging death into Reginald on repeat. I feel angry, betrayed, distraught, and helpless. The boy who once held me in his arms lies crumpled on the floor. The girl I thought to be a friend doesn't flinch. I'm restrained, trapped, held against my will. I'm a monster.

Girls' and boys' voices echo around me. They tell me I deserve the position I'm in. They ask how it feels to be experiencing the fate I sub-jected them to. I try to apologize, to tell them I had no choice, but they don't stop. Their words become screams, horrified sounds that crawl over every inch of me.

The sound of conversation wakes me, and I slowly blink open my eyes.

I'm a monster.

An intense white light glares down at me, causing me to squint. Once my eyes have adjusted, I slowly sit up from my lying-down position. I observe my surroundings cautiously.

I seem to be in a lounge area of some sort, as several couches line the walls, and there's a coffee table in the middle of the room. There's a blank screen on one wall, and the other has a door.

The voices are coming from behind there. The couch nearest to me has a still form lying on it. With some difficulty, I stand and move toward the figure. I try to be as quiet as I can, but I must not be quiet enough, as the figure's eyes shoot open and look at me.

It's K. A slight bit of relief washes over me, and I sit back down on the couch I'd been resting on.

"We really did need rest," I say.

He seems to take a moment to adjust to our new surroundings. Before he's able to respond, the door opens, and Avi rushes inside. She has changed her outfit since I last saw her, and her hair is tied up in a ponytail.

"Thank God you woke up," she says with a smile. "I was starting to get worried we were too late with our administration of the medication."

I look to her with confusion as she takes a seat next to me. She wraps her arms around me in a quick hug, and when she pulls away, I notice a scabbed-over scratch across her jaw.

"Where did you get this?" I ask, concerned.

She smiles at me reassuringly. "There were a few straggling guards left at the facility. One of them managed to hit me, but we took them out. Although, in all honesty, they were stronger than we thought. If it weren't for our numbers, it could have gone worse. Luckily, no one was seriously injured."

I frown. *Whatever fight this leads to will be deadly. I just hope the death isn't on our side.*

Clearly trying to change the topic, Avi perks up. "After we defeated the remaining guards and returned to you, both of you were passed out. We brought you back here, to EMBER, as soon as we could. When we arrived, you both were administered the drug I told you about, but you've both been unresponsive for three days since the administration."

My eyes widen as I realize the implications of her words. "Wait, EMBER? Did you relocate?"

She nods quickly. "Yes. We're now located a reasonable distance from REMEDY. At least, that's what Tyrus told me. I'm unsure about the specific distance."

I turn to the door when someone knocks on it, watching as Tessa walks in and smiles gently at me. "I'm glad to see you two awake," she says. "I imagine you're still adjusting to your recovery. I know this seems like a lot, but nothing much has changed. The biggest news is that we've decided to incorporate a leadership council into EMBER. After the incident with Melissa breaching our walls under our misplaced trust, we decided our security measures need to be changed. Members are still being decided upon."

"Thank you again, Tessa and Aviana," K says.

Tessa looks at him fondly. "Of course."

A brief, somewhat uncomfortable, moment of silence passes, then Avi quickly stands.

"You two have been out for a bit now," my sister says. She turns to Tessa and grabs her wrist. "Let's give them a moment to chat?"

Tessa looks at her, confused, but doesn't fight as Avi drags her out of the room. As she exits, Avi shouts over her shoulder. "Find us tonight to discuss our next step!"

I watch the door shut, not understanding Avi's sudden departure. But as I meet K's deep-set eyes, understanding washes over me.

She knows.

I lean back on the couch and wait for K to make the first move, unsure of where we stand. *I don't want to push. He's been so forgiving with me.* Several silent moments stretch on. I find myself hoping that he feels the same for me as I do for him, that after everything that has happened, we can finally talk about what we could be.

He nods, almost as if agreeing to some unspoken words. When he stands and moves toward me with a determined look on his face, I'm taken aback. I instinctively move over so he can sit next to me. Once he has, he grabs my hands, and I turn to stare at him. I look on in silence as he presses his hand to cup my cheek.

"K—"

He shakes his head, and I stop talking. "I wanted to say this earlier." His breath is hot against my face, and my cheeks are warm.

"What?" I look into his eyes, which seem to be shining like moonlight.

"I think I love you, Callista. After everything we've been through, part of me wishes I didn't. But I can't ignore the part of me that does."

The words cause a million butterflies to flutter in my stomach, and goosebumps spread up my arms. "I … You do?" I'm hesitant, my voice coming out in a slight stutter. *I don't deserve that.*

My hair falls into my face, and he moves his hand to tuck it behind my ear. For a moment, I forget all the pain I've caused him and countless others. All I know is the here and now. But that feeling is broken when he abruptly leans back.

"I do. But I want to take it slow. So that we can both grow and deal with all the bad things we've been through."

He doesn't mention the atrocities I've committed and how he still needs to process it, but I know that's what he means.

"I think I love you too, K. And I'll give you all the time in the world."

He smiles back at me, then pulls me into an embrace. My heartbeat races, but for the first time, it's not in fear. Any worries I had before seem to melt away, and I feel safe in his arms. When the moment ends, I'm happier than I've been in a long time as I bury my face into his chest. "Thank you," I whisper into his shirt, which now smells of comfort.

He holds me tight, and his fingers twirl my hair. "Thank you too."

Time stands still as I enjoy the moment, allowing my mind to drift off.

I wake up with my head on his chest.

I guess I still needed rest.

The slow, rhythmic pattern of his breathing relaxes me as I adjust to my surroundings. As I lift my head, he grumbles but doesn't wake. A small white sheet of paper sitting on the wooden table catches my eye. Slowly, I fully sit up and lean over to grab it. A simple message is scrawled across it:

Callista and K, you missed the meeting, but we decided you both need rest. When you wake up, find Tessa, and she'll fill you in. I've also left you both some spare clothes. If you would like, there's a shower room down the hall connected to the room you're currently in.

~ Brayden

Underneath the note are two stacks of clothes and a towel with each. Placing the paper to the side, I grab the stack from the right, which seems more feminine. The outfit is simple—a tight black tank top and jacket, with black leggings and dark-orange wristbands.

I turn and easily spot the hall Brayden mentioned. I give a final glance to K's resting form before making my way to the shower room.

The door is clear, and when I step inside, I notice a button labeled "Blackout." As soon as I press it, the clear door darkens, giving me privacy. There isn't much inside the small room—only a single large shower with an area right outside it to place clothing.

Setting down my things, I strip out of my clothes and turn the faucet far to the right so I can have hot water. The room is quick to fill with steam, and I move over to lower the heat. When the temperature is to my liking, I cautiously step inside, warmth filling me as the dirt washes away. I find some products to clean my hair with and don't hesitate to use them, along with a brand-new toothbrush and toothpaste. I take a moment to close my eyes and enjoy the moment of calm.

I shiver as soon as I turn off the hot water, and I move swiftly to grab my new clothes and towel. Once I completely dry myself, I pull on the clothing. It slides on effortlessly and is snug against my skin. I feel a bump in the jacket and find a pocket with a comb with a hairband on it. Grinning, I pull out the small object and use it to comb my hair and tie it back in a braid. A small basket catches my attention, and I read its label: "Dirty Clothes Waste Bin."

With little hesitation, I throw in my old clothes and tuck the comb back into my pocket. I press the blackout button once again, and the door becomes clear, revealing the figure of someone outside. I open the door with caution and exhale with relief and surprise when I see K standing there, fresh out of the shower as well.

"Oh, hey, Callista."

He must have found Brayden's note, as well as another shower room.

A small flush travels up my face as I remember the previous night's events. "Did you rest well?" I ask, my hand instinctively reaching out to grasp his. He doesn't pull away as my fingers lace around his own.

He nods. "More importantly, did you?"

I return his nod, and we stand in silence before I recall our duties. "We have to go find Tessa."

A smirk teases at his lips. "I almost forgot because I was so distracted by you."

The comment is somewhat awkward, but its intent lands home. My face grows hot, and I stammer, struggling to form a sentence. *I'm surprised he feels comfortable flirting. I just have to follow his lead, I guess.* Eventually, my nerves settle, and I smile at him. "Oh, so you're a flirt now?"

"Figured I'd try something new. Before we go, I have to tell you something." I shoot him a quizzical look, and he grabs my waist, pulling me close. His expression turns serious. "Please don't leave me again, Callista. And don't keep any more secrets."

I hear pain in his whispered request, and I soften in his arms. *He must still be traumatized over his sister.*

"I'll stay with you forever, K. And no more secrets." I squeeze his hand tightly. "We should probably hurry."

He bobs his head, and I turn, comforted by his presence as he follows me down the hall and out of the lounge.

THIRTY-SIX

IT DOESN'T TAKE US LONG to find Tessa chatting with Brayden and Tyrus in a nearby hallway. As soon as Tessa notices us, she waves us over with a grin.

"Hey, how are you guys feeling now?" she asks.

We approach her swiftly, and K speaks for us. "We're better now, thank you. I appreciate the clothing and amenities, and I believe Callista does too."

He glances at me, and I take over. "So, what are we discussing?"

Tessa's earlier grin dissipates, and her tone shifts. "We have to talk about that in private. Follow me." She turns and strides down the hall at a swift speed, nearly leaving us in her dust.

My legs move fast to keep up until we reach a tight corridor. She stops in front of a wooden door and presses a few buttons, causing it to slide open. Tyrus, Kieran, Brayden, and I follow her inside.

The room seems to be a conference center, with its large dark wooden table and many chairs surrounding it. Tessa takes a seat at one end of the table, motioning for the rest of us to find a seat as well. As soon as we all settle in, she presses a button on a control sitting on the table, and a blank hologram appears before each of us. An outline of the dreaded school appears, and I wince at the still fresh memories of the place

"As you all are aware, this is REMEDY Academy," Tessa says.

"We at EMBER have been trying to devise a plan on how to take down their cruel system for almost a decade," Tessa says. "It has been hard for us to figure out a way to stop them. This is the first time we're finally able to make progress in our plan. Thanks to you, we no longer have to be stagnant. You've helped us gather valuable information. Don't fret. We don't plan on using you as a weapon like Liam did. We hope you'll agree to help us fight REMEDY and end them for good. You may not think you're any different than the rest of us, but what you have is extremely rare. Opposite abilities have never occurred, especially together in proximity to one another. It makes your abilities some of the most powerful out there. We believe that with you on our side, we can finally end this for good."

I take a moment to process the information and grab K's hand. I squeeze his palm, and he does the same to me, giving me the confidence boost I need.

"What has Aviana said about this?" I ask.

This time, Brayden answers. "Both Aviana and Alec have agreed to help us."

I nod slowly, running over any other potential choices we might have. It takes me only a few moments to truly realize this is our only hope. I turn to K and exchange a glance with him, hoping he's thinking the same thing I am.

"As long as you promise to not run things as cruelly as REMEDY does and specify what role we will have," I say.

Tyrus and Tessa exchange a look.

"We were going to wait until after you accepted to tell you," Tyrus responds. "But we would like to recognize you, Kieran, Aviana, and Alec with roles as full-fledged members of our team.

Of course, you'll need proper training, but we see potential in all of you and would be happy to be your mentors." He grins.

My eyebrows shoot up, and a sense of pride fills me. But the moment lasts only a second as I recall all the terrible things I've done. *I don't deserve that. The others do, but I've made too many mistakes.* Before K can say anything, I look up and meet Tyrus's gaze. *This is my chance to repent for my actions.*

"I appreciate the offer, but I can't accept that." Everyone in the room looks shocked, clearly confused over why I would reject such generosity. I inhale deeply, then continue. "I won't explain publicly, but the mistakes I made while separated from everyone here shouldn't be so easily forgiven. I can provide more details privately. Please still give the role to the other three."

K brushes his finger against the back of my hand, and I squeeze his back. My heart rate picks up a bit as Tessa and Tyrus whisper something to each other.

"We would like to know the story behind your decision, so please speak to us after this," Tessa says, then looks at K. "What do you say?"

I force myself to keep my gaze high, not wanting to look too shameful.

"I would be honored," K says.

Tyrus clasps his hands in front of him and says, "Wonderful. Well, if you wouldn't mind, could you and Brayden step out so we may speak to Callista?"

I turn my head to meet K's eyes one last time. Then he drops my hand, gets up, and walks away. Brayden follows him, leaving me alone with the twins. *I can do this.* When the two look at me expectantly, I take a deep breath and delve into the horrors I committed at REMEDY. As I progress through the story, careful to leave out any unnecessary details, I watch their expressions. They're clearly trying not to react, but I can see little cracks when I talk about the husk students.

When I've finished, my heart is racing, and I'm slightly light-headed. I force my body to calm down by taking several deep breaths. *It's going to be okay. I'm not going to be that person anymore.* My mind wars between self-loathing and reassurances. Once I've gathered myself, I attempt to stand as confidently as I can.

"I deeply regret my actions and understand if there will be consequences for them," I say.

To my surprise, Tessa looks at me sympathetically. "We appreciate you telling us this, Callista. And I believe you're regretful. You didn't have to share this with us. You could have just accepted our offer. But you didn't, and that shows you're learning and growing."

When she stops, Tyrus speaks up. "I can't condone what you've done. Even if you were manipulated. What you did is directly against what EMBER works toward." He takes a pause, allowing my chest to swell with emotion.

What did I expect? He's right. I'm just about to apologize again and dismiss myself when he resumes speaking. "In good conscience, we aren't able to allow you into our ranks as we would like to. We won't share your story with the others unless you give us permission. However, if Tessa agrees, I think we can give you a probationary period during which you can help us out with leadership as if you were a member. After all, we did the same for Brayden. And you do have potential. Quite frankly, we need you. Not only are you the only discovered person with three abilities, but you also have a connection with Kieran that will benefit us. You can think of this probation as a test and a way to make up for what you've done."

My eyes widen, and my mouth drops open, complete surprise washing over me. When I realize what he has said, I start to tear up.

"I think that's fair. You'll be closely watched, Callista. If there's any sign that you'll be acting against us, we won't hesitate to act," Tessa says, her voice stern.

"Thank you. This is more than I could ever ask for." My voice comes out broken as tears roll down my cheeks. I raise my hand and wipe them away, embarrassed.

"Prove to us, and more importantly to yourself, that you aren't who you were," Tyrus says, his voice gentler than before.

I nod vigorously and force myself to stand up straighter.

Tessa inclines her head. "Welcome to the EMBER team, Callista."

Later that afternoon, I pull Alec, Brayden, K, and Avi aside. None of them question my urgency, likely assuming my desire to speak to them has to do with Tessa and Tyrus's proclamations. My stomach churns with my unspoken words. *I have to tell them. They deserve to know what I've done. I can't live with myself if I don't tell them the truth.*

"I need to talk to you all about what happened when I was gone," I finally say.

Brayden puts up his hand, "Wait. I've been meaning to tell you how terribly sorry I am. It was incredibly stupid of me to let myself be put in the position where I put you all in danger. I'm sorry."

I look at him intensely, slightly annoyed by his interruption. I exhale. *What he did is nothing compared to what I did. I wasn't being controlled.*

"I forgive you," I say. The others murmur agreement.

Avi faces me, her eyebrows drawing together. "Is everything okay?"

I shake my head and motion for all of them to sit down on the couch in front of me. The fragrant smell coming from the floral arrangements in the corners of the room eases my nerves. Once they've all sat, I take a deep breath.

"I first want to apologize. To all of you."

All except K exchange uncertain looks. I hesitate. *What if they hate me?* I chew anxiously on my bottom lip as my friends watch me with anticipation. *This has to be done.* All of the past several weeks flash through my mind in rapid images. I swallow, forcing down the growing lump in my throat.

Then I tell them everything.

Their horrified expressions aren't surprising, but they still hurt me.

Avi's hurts most of all. She steps back, breaking eye contact with me to stare at the wall. "Even after you saw what they did to me, you still participated? Even though you knew?"

"I thought you were dead. I thought it was my only option if I wanted to keep everyone else safe. And when I wanted to stop, it was too late. Liam would have killed all of you," I retort out of instinct. "I—I'm sorry," I nearly whimper, ashamed of my defensiveness.

She frowns, seemingly conflicted. "Liam blackmailed you. But how long after you got there did he do it? How many students did you punish before trying to leave? Did you tell Tessa and Tyrus?"

I pause, remembering my fight with Isaac. My shoulders slump as I struggle to keep Brayden's gaze. "I did tell them. I'll be on probation, but they said they wouldn't kick me out." I lick my lips. "And. I don't know." The weight of their stares feels like it's crippling me. I fidget with my hands, my chest tightening.

"I can't believe you would do that. After everything!" Avi shouts, pain evident in her eyes.

I wince.

"It was selfish," Alec states, his tone harsher than usual.

"She was manipulated. I don't agree with her actions, don't get me wrong. But honestly, imagine yourself in her position," K says firmly, his voice unwavering. "Imagine if you thought that siding with the enemy was the only way to protect those you care about. All of that while dealing with the grief of losing someone close to you. She was vulnerable, and Liam took advantage of it. So did Melissa. Can you honestly say you wouldn't have acted the same way?"

My eyes widen at his words. *He's defending me.*

The others stare at him dumbfounded.

Alec grimaces, reaching a hand up to massage his forehead. "I suppose he has a point."

Avi turns on him, her mouth falling open. "You agree?"

My heart aches, seeing her so upset.

"I think we just need some time to think, Callista," Brayden adds solemnly.

I incline my head. "Of course. I'll leave."

I don't give them a chance to say anything further, exiting the room before the tears welling in my eyes have a chance to fall.

As the next few days pass, Avi refuses to talk to me. K assures me she's just coping in her own way and will come around eventually, but I'm not so sure. *Have I ruined our relationship?* I'm given little time to harp on the fact, as my every waking moment is consumed by drills. Tessa and Tyrus want to make sure everyone is in peak physical condition before we move forward with our plans.

"Focus, Callista!" Tyrus shouts as my fire nearly hits his shoulder.

"Sorry," I say, retraining my aim on the target just beside him. *I need to know how to aim. I can't risk having any unnecessary casualties.* I manage to take several steady shots, only to be distracted once more when Avi walks in the training room. This time, I hit the dummy Brayden usually trains with. Luckily, he isn't here right now to scold me.

Tyrus shakes his head at me and walks over to Avi. "Aviana, can I help you?"

I stop my drills to watch. Avi shifts on her feet, fumbling with her hands. "I actually wanted to talk to Callista."

My heart nearly stops. "Me?"

She nods.

Tyrus looks between the two of us, exhaling. "I'll leave you to it. Callista, when you've finished talking, go to the lounge. There's someone I think you should talk to."

I eye him warily as he exits the room, saying nothing else.

Avi looks up at me, her eyes filled with sorrow. "I'm sorry for what you went through. You were in a difficult position. I don't hate you. I want you to know that. I just need some space."

I frown. "I'm so sorry, Avi. I really didn't mean to hurt you. I hate myself so much for what I've done. I don't expect you to forgive me. I'll give you whatever time you need."

She opens her mouth briefly and shuts it again. Then she says, "That's all I wanted to say." She nods, then leaves.

I'm sorry.

When I enter the lounge, I'm surprised to see Jamie sitting on the couch, not another soul in sight.

"Hello, dearie," she says. "Come sit." She pats the empty spot next to her.

I pause. *What could she possibly have to say to me?* Sensing no ill intent from the woman, I slowly move toward her and take a seat.

"Before you ask, Emmy is in my room sleeping. I didn't want her to be a distraction, so I didn't wake her. I've heard you've been through a lot."

My eyes widen. *Did Tessa and Tyrus tell her what I did? Even though they said they wouldn't share?*

"What did they tell you?" I retort, more harshly than I intend.

Jamie doesn't react, her easy expression unwavering. "Don't worry. I didn't tell anyone else. You see, I've been around a long time. Over seventy years now. I've seen a lot. I know when someone's hurting." She places a wrinkled hand atop mine, her eyes filled with sincerity. "I know what it's like to loathe yourself. It's much easier to forgive another person than it is to forgive the person you see in the mirror."

I bite my lip. "I'm fine. Everything's fine." The words don't sound convincing even to my own ears.

"I don't want to pressure you. I just want to help. If it's too difficult to do it for your own sanity, think about your mission. Do you really think you can help with your full potential if you're too occupied thinking about what you've done wrong? If you want to change, you need to take action. How will you take action if you're utterly consumed by self-loathing?"

Her wise words seem to echo in the empty space. *I don't want to be a burden. I want to be better.* "I …" I can't put my swelling emotions into words. "I'm a monster," I croak, avoiding her gaze.

Rather than say anything, she wraps me in a tender embrace. I don't pull away. I don't cry. I let her hold me, unmoving.

"You're not a monster. Hurting people make mistakes. It doesn't define you. I'm sure if you knew exactly what happened to those students, you wouldn't have done what you did. And those you hurt, you can't unhurt. But you can use your passion to fight against those who continue to act in such vile ways."

I pull away, looking into her wrinkled green eyes. I can almost see a story in them, one of a woman who's seen countless horrors but still fights to live another day. *She's strong. I need to be strong.*

I swallow, nodding. "Thank you, Jamie."

She smiles. "I'm here for you. For everyone who's fighting this fight. You can find me anytime you need. Be careful."

I chuckle slightly. "I'll try."

THIRTY-SEVEN

I DART DOWN THE HALL THROUGH the bustling crowds of people, searching for Tessa. Murmurs of preparation echo around me, and my nerves excite.

Today's the day we'll finally execute the long-thought-over plan to take down **REMEDY**. It has taken us one month to fully prepare. Most of the preparations were made during my time with Liam, so it's only a matter of getting me incorporated into the plan. During this time, Tessa and Tyrus have held true to their word. I've noticed them watching me carefully, but I've made sure to not give them any reason to distrust me. *I have no interest in repeating my mistakes.*

Jamie's words have stuck with me, and I've worked intensely at channeling my self-hatred into action. I've been allowed to participate actively, as if I were a full member, but I don't have the freedoms that Aviana and K do. There are occasional meetings I'm not allowed access to, and when this occurs, I'm still given a short briefing afterward. Brayden, in a situation very similar to my own, also can't join these particular meetings. This has allowed me to ease into a mutual understanding with him. Out of all my friends other than K, he's been the most understanding of my plight. I assume his sympathy comes from knowing Liam's machinations on a deeper level than the others.

Avi was initially distant after we spoke, and Alec was always right by her side. But the past few days, she's acted somewhat normal with me, even if it's only for business-related conversations.

I don't know when Brayden's probation ends, nor do I care. *It's not my business.* The siblings haven't given me any indication that my probation is nearing its end either. This doesn't bother me in the slightest. I'm beyond grateful for them giving me a chance at all, as well as all the generosity and understanding they've shown me.

All the EMBER council members have been ordered to meet, including me. *Our last meeting before our final fight.* My deep-orange uniform clings to my skin as my feet move below me.

"Good luck, Miss Callista!" the voice of a child calls from behind me.

Instinctively, I turn, plastering on a friendly smile and giving a small wave before resuming my haste toward the office. I'm still not fully accustomed to being around such young, vulnerable souls. There are quite a few children aged ten and even younger, having been raised under EMBER. They aren't permitted to come with us on our mission, as they're not skilled enough yet. It never fails to be strange to me how my friends and I are only a few years older than them, yet we're considered capable of leading this important mission.

The murmurs dissipate the farther into headquarters I get, leaving me alone with my own thoughts. Fear and hope flow through me in equal measure, and I find myself trying to not doubt my skill as I get closer and closer to the meeting room. Just as I'm about to stumble upon it, the large door swings open, and K steps out.

"Hey." K catches me in my stride, pulls me in, and embraces me, placing a kiss on my forehead. We're still trying to find the perfect pace for our relationship, but I can tell he has started to forgive what I did, as have I. It's still hard for me to forget the memories, but I've slowly been able to accept them and use them as ways to grow.

I still haven't moved on completely though. As much as I'd like to believe I have, I still feel anger toward myself. The moment barely lasts a second before Avi interrupts us.

"Sorry to interrupt, but we don't have time for this." She motions between us, then she ushers us inside. We both blush and move into the room just before the door shuts behind us.

Tyrus, Tessa, Alec, Brayden, and the two other council members known as Harris and Mira sit at the table. The successor of EMBER, Julies, sits at the far end, watching us keenly. I incline my head toward Julies and take a seat next to Brayden.

Once we're all settled, Julies clears his throat and pulls up the hologram of our plan overview. The lights overhead dim to allow a better view of the screens before us.

"Intel has recently informed me that Liam seems to have become more aware of our plans against him in this past month since Kieran and Callista have escaped. Surprisingly, he hasn't tried to search for you both as far as we know, which has led me to believe he has other plans in store."

As second-in-command, Tessa speaks up in her usual, quick-to-lead way. "Will this influence our plans today, sir?"

Julies shakes his head and pulls up a new hologram screen. "This is a recording we received from Liam's headquarters thanks to Callista's information from when she stayed there."

I wince at the memory of seeing K locked up and finding the room that told of how we with abilities came to be. My eyes travel to watch as Julies plays the video. The footage is rough but clear enough for me to make out Liam and Melissa hunched over something or someone, along with thousands of papers sprawled about. The footage ends there and leaves me in confusion.

"Sadly, Melissa discovered we'd hijacked their cameras and shut them off soon after we gathered this clip." Julies swipes away the footage and hands the control over to Tyrus. As far as I've been informed, he and Harris have been put in charge of tactical maneuvers.

"I'd like us to go over our plan once more before we leave," Tyrus starts. "As Kieran and Callista are strongest together, they'll be paired up and sent to directly infiltrate and destroy DETA. Once DETA is destroyed, Liam will no longer be able to track any students, including those in our midst. They'll then be able to locate Liam more safely. While they're on their path, Aviana and Alec will lead two different groups, each using their abilities to find another way to Liam's quarters. Mira will stay with Aviana and Alec, using her telepathy ability. They'll gather information, and Mira will send it back to us."

He pauses, allowing us to jot down any notes we may need. "Harris and I will monitor the others in our army, along with Julies, as they free all the students in REM and those outside it. Tessa and Tyrus will report to us as they monitor from our headquarters. As soon as all of the students in the school have been freed, we'll join the rest of you. It's crucial that whoever finds the way to Liam first sends us their pathing through the device we've given you. Don't kill him when you first find him. You may render him unconscious if you must. Kill whoever tries to stop you. Once we've all arrived and interrogated Liam, we'll deal with what comes next from there."

I notice Tessa place a hand on Brayden's before she speaks up.

"Of course, there are smaller details, but I trust you all remember those. You'll be leaving at sunset. Any questions?"

Silence answers, and the nervous energy in the room puts me on alert.

After a few moments pass, Julies gives us a reassuring grin. "We'll meet at the front later tonight. See you then."

The day's preparations seem to flash by too fast. Before I know it, dusk descends. I call to my light for a final boost of strength, then pull on my black boots and rush out of my sleeping quarters. Aviana meets me in the hall, and we start our walk toward the front of the headquarters together.

"Are you scared?" she asks, her voice soft.

I stiffen, surprised by her non-business-related question. I hear an element of fear and summon all my courage in the hope of reassuring her.

"Honestly, I am. But I know that whatever happens, we're in this together, Avi." I have the sudden urge to give her what could be our last embrace, and I stop moving. She turns and looks at me with puzzlement. All of a sudden, my hands are on her shoulders. When she only stiffens but doesn't push me away, my heart melts. "You're only fifteen. You shouldn't have to be fighting like this."

She laughs bitterly. "You're only seventeen. Neither of us should have to do this."

A voice shouts from down the hall, and I reluctantly pull back from my sister's arms, only to see Alec waving her on. I notice a blush covering her cheeks, and I smile inwardly. "You should go."

She nods, giving me one last look, then runs off.

I follow her not long after, walking down several halls before the sounds of a crowd fill our ears. Hundreds of people stand in the main room, saying goodbye to families and friends. The room is simple, its walls barren. Its largeness would be overwhelming if it weren't for the people gathered inside it. There's no furniture except for a few chairs gathered for the older members.

Mira glances around the room before her eyes land on us, and she waves us over. Picking up my pace, I stride ahead of Alec and Avi to meet up with her. As I approach, she holds out a glinting silver object.

"Take this, just in case you need it," she says.

I glance warily at the dagger, then I take it from her and slide it into my boot for safekeeping. "Thanks." I'm waiting anxiously just as someone grabs the back of my shoulders. I startle, my entire body tensing.

"Are you okay?"

My eyes widen in shock as K moves around to stand before me.

I relax, giving him a half-smile. "Just nervous. Sorry—"

I'm cut off as silence descends over the room. Every head turns to face Julies. His silver-blond locks are combed back, adding to his intimidating appearance. He's followed by five other older members. I recognize one of them as Harris, EMBER's army general.

"Hello, all. I'm here to reassure you of our efforts just before we go," Julies says. "As you know, EMBER was established originally by my father, Marshall. Many of our older members here were around then. They helped form our organization. They know how my father was friends with Liam, the founder of REMEDY, long before either of them oversaw any organization of their own. Liam decided he wanted to be in charge and was unsatisfied with his status. That's why he created your abilities—in order to make an army to obtain complete control of our planet as a whole. This is why we'll stop him today. For our freedom. So that all of you who were blessed with an ability can grow and live as normal people, not as objects to be used and discarded. Some of you grew up here, but most of you grew up in the Neighborhoods. Your households oppressed you, trained you to be perfect, kept you under intensely tight watch. They raised you to be perfect and controlled. Today, we release that control. You won't be the perfect soldiers Liam wants you to be. You'll have your choice of life. You'll decide how you live. And that's what we fight for. We've had our ups and downs. REMEDY has tried to squash us. But we've prospered. We haven't given up. And now, together, we're the strongest we've ever been. There may be losses on the way. We've known this from the start. But I'm confident that, at the end, we'll come out with what we've worked so hard for. Freedom."

Cheers echo around the room after Julies's speech. Families dissipate, leaving those who will fight to do their final preparations. I'm surprised when Julies approaches me, motioning for me to follow him away from the others. I do as requested, my mind whirling over what he might want to talk to me about. When he stops, I prepare myself for the worst.

"Callista Tieron. I've wanted to talk to you since you first arrived here a month ago. But alas, we've been too busy doing our own things. Your parents were Rosalie and Elijah Tieron, right?"

I nod in reply, and he smiles.

"Based on my father's documentation," he says, "your parents were very close with Liam and my father. Here, let me show you something." He takes out a small device and places it on the side of my forehead. Some sort of vibration emits from its cool metal, sending pulses into my mind. It doesn't hurt, but it feels strange. "Close your eyes, Callista."

I do as I'm told and stand in darkness for several moments. Suddenly, I find myself transported into a new location, watching as two people seated on a couch laugh. They don't recognize my presence, and I realize I must be invisible to them. I recognize the beautiful woman as my mother, Rosalie. She chuckles and places an arm around the handsome man, my father, Elijah, next to her.

"Eli, what should we name her?" The woman places a hand on her large stomach, looking on at the man with pure love in her eyes.

Elijah places his hand over hers and grins. "Well, what were you thinking, dear?"

The woman ponders, and I notice a gold necklace sitting around her neck that reads "Rosalie" in shining diamonds. "Callista?" She speaks softly, and it fills me with warmth.

"It's perfect," he says.

The scene cuts away too soon. I find myself filled with disappointment when I'm left staring into Julies's emerald eyes.

"Those were my parents' memories," I whisper.

He nods sadly, then sighs. "My father had been testing a device to record people's memories, and your parents participated in his trials. These files were left behind, so that's how I was able to access them. They're stored in the device and are transported to your mind when connected to your frontal lobe. Once you close your eyes, you're able to access them."

Before I'm able to ask any questions, a loud voice calls from the other side of the room. "It's time to go!"

People scramble around us, and I frantically remove the device from my head and hand it back to Julies. He tucks it away as we both turn toward the speaker. Brayden steps down from a podium and controls the flow of bodies as they start moving through the front doors.

"We'll talk again," Julies says, then disappears into the crowd. I lose sight of him quickly.

I instinctually search for K. I see dark hair jostling against the moving masses and push that direction. "K!" I call. The figure turns my direction, and moments later, I'm in his arms.

"We need to leave now," he says in short breaths, and I nod quickly.

We follow the crowd out the door. Once everyone is released into the open outdoors, groups form and separate, heading in their respective directions. I bite my lip when I realize I didn't get a chance to say goodbye to Avi. *It's going to be okay. Stay focused.*

"According to our intel, DETA's control center is kept somewhere in the center of town," K says. I review the information in my head as we move toward the street. It takes only moments before we're alone and the air is eerily quiet. "If we continue to head north, we should arrive." Just as I pick up speed, K grabs my arm and wraps me in a warm embrace. "I wanted to hold you one last time, just in case," he says.

I smile sadly at him, then I turn away, tossing my braid over my shoulder. "It won't be the last time."

I hear an alarm blare in the distance and pick up speed. "We need to get moving," I say.

Little communication passes between us as we run toward the center of the city. Headquarters are only a couple miles out from the city line, so it doesn't take us long to reach the forest edge. Once we're no longer surrounded by trees, I turn my eyes to our coordinate tracker. It's supposed to lead us to the approximate location of our mission. Unfortunately, no one knows the exact place of DETA's mainframe, so the tracker will lead us as close as we can get. It hasn't started beeping yet, meaning we're still too far from the center of the city. With all the buildings being nearly identical, it's somewhat difficult to pinpoint exactly where the center is. I search the sky for any sign of DETA, but the towering buildings block any clear view.

"I guess we'll just have to go forward and hope we pick up a signal," I say.

K nods, and we continue powering forward. Much to our luck, after we pass several blocks of buildings, our tracker finally starts beeping slowly.

Good. A signal. We're getting closer.

Using the active tracker as a compass, we take several turns until the beeping picks up the pace. I start scanning the surrounding area but don't stop moving. No buildings look out of place, yet the beeping gets increasingly louder as we walk. When it starts to get quieter, showing that we're passing our location, I turn back. Walking to the loudest point, I look down and land on a sewer gate.

"Here." I wave K over, and he bends, letting out a grunt as he helps me lift the round piece of metal. We shove it to the side, and he uses his ability to see through the darkness of the seemingly endless pit.

"It's a short drop," K says.

Wanting to get moving, I push past him.

Just as I'm about to jump in, he stops me. "Let me go first. I'll guide us through the shadows just in case there are people who want to attack us down there."

He doesn't give me the chance to argue and hops down the hole. He lands with a splash. "It's safe!" he calls up.

I grimace and drop into the pit, water sloshing up around my boots. Shrouds of shadow envelop me, and I'm unable to see anything but K. Instinctively, I reach out and grab his arm.

"This is as close as the device can get us," he says. I drop my hand from his arm and tighten my lips.

"Hope it has brought us close enough to make this quick," I mutter.

We resume our earlier speed, and I find myself thankful that the sewer system seems to only have one main path. The fear for our situation finally settles in, but my striving to end REMEDY helps me not to focus on it. *This is my purpose now.*

Lost in my own thoughts, I don't notice as K stops moving.

"Here!" he says. Then he drags me into a room, and the shadows dissipate around me. The room contains rows of computers and various types of unfamiliar technology. I'm slightly taken aback by the masses of wires that seem to be ingrained into the walls around us. The cords glow a bright blue, showing through the walls like veins beneath skin. A massive screen on the wall reads "Current DETA Monitoring." Thousands of videos play, some monitoring what look to be Neighborhoods and others monitoring REMEDY.

Below the videos, a button labeled "STUDENT INFOR-MATION" calls to me. Curiosity overcomes my focus on my task, and I find myself reaching out, tapping the screen. The motion causes another screen to pop up, requesting a student ID. I hear K shuffling through something away from me as I type in my own ID.

The words that appear before me cause a tremor throughout my body.

THIRTY-EIGHT

MY HEIGHT, BIRTHDAY, EYE COLOR, blood type, ability, and parents' information, both birth and adopted, are listed. Below the basic information, an accounting of my personal life is laid bare:

> Assigned FR: Reginald Gray (Deceased)
> Current Location: DETA Headquarters
> Awareness: Knows more than should
> Current Emotion: Fear
> Device Status: Stable

I even see a small graph of what looks to be my heart rate below the rest of the information.

My body freezes in shock, only to be snapped back to reality when K gasps. "What the hell?" he says.

It's worse than I thought. I see him staring at the screen in just as much horror as I feel.

"I saw some files that said DETA can track lots of things, but I didn't realize it was this intensive," he murmurs.

My eyes train on the last words. *Device. Do we have some sort of implant that it uses to track us?* I gulp, my stomach stirring with the thought. *I need to focus on our mission. If it's destroyed, I won't have to worry about any possible device.*

"Have you found the switch to destroy it?" I ask.

He looks ashamed as he shakes his head.

"Well, I guess there's only one other way."

He tilts his head at me, and I push past him, closing my eyes and calling to my ability. It takes mere seconds for my hands to pulse with electricity, and I follow all the computer wires to what looks to be the motherboard for DETA. I sense K watching me as I get closer, close my eyes, and reach out my hands to place them atop the main circuit board. The metal is cold against my palms, and a sudden awareness of buzzing travels across my senses.

Just as I'm about to push my ability into the technology, K yells. I pull away and charge my hands, ready to attack.

As soon as I turn, someone grabs my shoulder and pulls me into them, the cold tip of a blade pressing against my neck. I feel blood seep from the small cut and trickle down. I wince from the pain and slowly wrap my hand around my attacker. I look on to see K fighting two men, fading in and out of his shadow in an effort to blind them. He manages to beat down one of them, and as he works on the next, I call to my fire. Whoever is holding me must notice it, as they press the knife harder against my neck, causing me to release my flame and drop my hand.

"K!" I manage to yell before the knife presses down again and I shut my mouth.

I watch K turn to look at me, and my eyes widen in terror as the man he's fighting takes his distraction as an opportunity to knock him over. A thud echoes as his body hits the floor, and the man tackles him.

"Callista! You know what to do! It's our only option!" he manages to shout.

I prepare one of the attack moves we've practiced so many times and call back to my light. I watch K summon darkness in his palm, and I mentally count down from three. When I get to one, I shut off all the lights in the room, and K uses his darkness to blind everyone, including me. My attacker's grip loosens, and I take the moment to strike with my light orb, turning it into fire midway. Heat emits from the now screaming captor, and I have to force myself to push past the smell of burning flesh. *It was self-defense. I had no choice. I can't think about that right now.*

I feel for my surroundings to find DETA's motherboard and resume the work I started. Closing my eyes again, I push my ability into the metal, and the buzzing resumes. It crowds my senses and seems to swallow me whole just before it stops.

I open my eyes, turning in the darkness with confusion. Before I give up hope on my barely formed plan, there's a sizzling and crackling sound. K calls away his darkness, and I look at him in relief as he stands above three fallen bodies. The noises in the room grow louder, and sparks start to fly. The computer screens flicker, and my gut screams at me to leave.

"I think it's going to blow!" I yell over the rising volume. I dash toward K, and we tumble out the door just as a burst of heat emits and a loud boom echoes through the hall.

Slowly, I crawl to my feet and pull out the communication device Julies gave me earlier. As it buzzes to life, I bring it up to my mouth. "Mission DETA is done. On our way to him now." I refrain from directly stating Liam's name just in case we're being monitored.

The ground shakes below us, causing me to stumble. The ceiling cracks above us, and adrenaline courses through my veins.

"We need to move!" K shouts as he leans over and grabs my hand, pulling me behind him as we dash through the halls to find an exit. We dodge falling debris, and panic rises in my chest. The mix of adrenaline and fear causes me to pick up my pace, and I nearly trip over my own feet. K's strong hand keeps me upright. I recognize the halls of the sewer and realize we're getting close to the entrance we first came through.

"I think we're almost there!" I yell over the surrounding chaos, so distracted by the situation that I don't realize when I drop his hand. He continues to run forward, and I follow, noticing a massive piece of debris hanging and slowly falling down from the ceiling. At our current speed, it will end up falling on top of K, so I speed up to move him out of the way.

"Watch out!" I scream just as the large piece of concrete falls. I lunge forward and manage to push K away from the death trap, only to end up trapped on the opposite side. I lie in the sewer water, staring up at the only thing blocking me from escape. A tiny opening catches my eye, and I stand. The gap is large enough to see through but not nearly big enough for a person.

"Callista?" K peers back at me through the hole in the rubble.

"I'm fine." I reach up and touch my throat, realizing the blood has dried and is no longer freely flowing. "Are you okay?"

"I'm totally good, thanks to you. I'm sorry I didn't notice sooner."

I shake my head even though he can't see my full face. "It's not important now. We need to continue our mission. I'll find another way out, but you need to find Liam. Hide in the darkness so he can't hurt you, then I'll come find you."

Silence passes for a moment, then I hear feet moving on the other side. "I'll update the others on what happened," K says. "You better tell us when you make it out."

I smile solemnly as more debris falls around me. "If I make it out," I mutter.

Running through sewers while the world is quite literally crumbling around you isn't an easy task. But knowing I have no other choice makes my growing exhaustion easier to deal with.

Aviana's and Alec's groups haven't made much progress, and K is still searching for Liam. It's been only five minutes since I separated from K, and while I've been reaching out with my ability, I haven't yet picked up on any light or electricity nearby. I've nearly given up when a sudden burst of energy catches my attention. I move toward it at a quick speed, continuing to dodge debris on my way.

The pulse gets stronger and stronger until I notice a bright light up ahead. Hope pushes me forward, and I nearly cry in relief when a single light bulb blinks ahead. It illuminates another sewer grate just like the one I entered from. My wet clothes stick to my body as I reach the ladder, and I climb up it faster than I knew I was able to. As I push aside the manhole cover, I grin at the sight of the night sky. *I'm out. I'm safe.* The heavy smell of smoke catches my attention as I pull myself out from the sewer and stand. Immediately, I tap on my communication device.

"I just got out. There's a strange smoke nearby. I'm going to investigate."

I follow the smell until the smoke becomes visible, trailing around buildings. Then I reach a collection of what seem to be recently destroyed buildings. Smack in the middle, the familiar diamond lies, sparks flying from it. Charred pieces are scattered next to its still form. It seems much larger than it did when it was suspended in the sky, and its size gives me unease. *It's finally gone. Liam can't monitor me anymore.* The awful smell of burnt rubber travels up my nose. I cover my mouth, not wanting to breathe in the stench. My communication device buzzes again, then someone speaks.

Julies's voice sounds from the small metal piece, and I pause to listen. "Good to hear you're safe, Callista. Please be cautious, and don't pursue any unnecessary danger with your investigations. We're just reaching the students so we can free them. Any progress with anyone else?"

Aviana speaks up, and I listen closely, worried for her safety. "Mira and I have been attacked by a squad of guards. We injured half of them, but we were forced to run to escape the rest. No sign of Liam yet though."

I exhale, relieved that she wasn't harmed. Then I press down on the comm button. "The smoke led me to DETA's remains. It seems to have fallen from the sky into this field. Would you like me to explore further?"

The device buzzes in response as Julies speaks. "There's no time. You need to catch up with Kieran. Just log the coordinates, and we can come back at a later time."

I'll just take a quick look. "Very well." I put away my comms unit and move cautiously toward DETA. The closer I get, the more enormous it becomes. It's about fifty times my size.

Swallowing the forming lump in my throat, I continue forward. I find an area where the glass shards have been thrown off, and I peer inside. Thousands of wires line the object, along with a bunch of confusing objects. I pull out my coordinate tracker and place a note so I can return after this is all over. *Maybe there's still more to learn.* I'm comfortable leaving it, as I can't detect any electrical presence, meaning it's fully disabled. The thought brings me comfort as I turn away, leaving the AI behind me.

The comm unit buzzes to life again. Tessa sounds far away as she speaks. "Callista, Kieran's vitals just went offline!"

My heart plummets at her words. I freeze in my steps, completely in shock and full of a million emotions. *No, not again. This will not happen again.*

My light orb is the only thing to brighten my surroundings. A rough breeze brushes by me as dozens of tiny droplets begin to fall from the night sky. The ground glistens with the water. I'm barely able to feel the cold, my inner turmoil heating me to the core. I pour my energy into my hands, holding on to it.

I hastily grab the communication device from my pocket and bring it to my face. "Do we know where he is?"

Brayden's voice crackles through, and I hear a slight bit of sadness in his words. "No, but I believe he must have found Liam or someone found him."

I rack my brain for anything that could be of use. *Come on, there has to be something!* Memories flash through my mind's eye rapidly, then focus on one particular image. I recall the strange unevenness in the ground I saw for a brief moment directly outside REMEDY's walls when we first escaped. *It's a far reach, but it's all I have.*

I push down the comm button once more. "I'll search everywhere for him." I allow my overwhelming emotion to take control of me. All I know is my intense desire to not let K get hurt. My boots splash in the steady rain, water hitting my face as I take off. I run toward the Academy, using my coordinates tracker as a guide. Wisps of hair fly in my face but don't faze me. My mind can only think of one thing.

K, I'll save you.

Before I know it, I'm outside the Academy gates. The darkness is foreboding, filling me with unease as I approach the uneven ground. Upon closer inspection, I take note of its square-like shape. *There must be something here. Inside is where all the others are. I should ask them for help.* I squeeze my eyes shut, clenching my fists. *Do I get help and risk something already having happened to him? Or do I go alone, risking even more?*

The emotional part of me pushes for the latter, but my logic wins out. I approach the towering metal bars, eyeing them suspiciously. *Now, how do I get through here?*

I reach out cautiously to touch them, trying to see if I can feel any electricity. When I feel nothing, I allow one of my fingers to touch the cold metal. Just the slight touch causes the gate to creak open slightly, and a chill travels down my spine. *This is too convenient.*

I shove my way through the gates and trudge toward the main building.

Inside, the building's lights are turned off. And, once again, no one stops me from entering. The awful metallic smell of blood travels up my nostrils as soon as I open the door and step inside. I glance down the hall to my right and see several guards trampled, stabbed, or killed by other means. My stomach twists, horrified by the sight. *They were on the enemy side.* I recall the guards I saw with the former REM students, and I grimace. *This was their chosen fate.* I plug my nose and resume my quick pace toward the REM area.

When I reach the end of the hall, I hear footsteps and turn off my light orb, pushing myself against the wall. I prepare to attack but nearly sob in relief when Avi approaches with a small flashlight in her hand. We fall into each other's arms and embrace. Only seconds later, she pulls away, seeming to remember her desire to be distant. I barely notice, too focused on her expression. Her face is contorted in worry as she chews on her lower lip.

"Where's Mira?" I ask.

"I lost her. Well, she just disappeared, and I can't find her anywhere."

I frown, looking into her ocean-blue eyes. "Avi, we'll find her and K. We need to get the others' help first. We don't know what we're dealing with."

She nods quickly and turns. "Let's go find them."

We stride down the hall at a nearly unnatural speed and stay silent along the way. *I knew that psycho had a plan. He made this seem too easy.*

The familiar halls are barely recognizable as I speed past them, solely focused on my goal. As we're approaching the staircase up to REM, a sudden burst of light explodes in our direction. We both manage to dodge the blast and run to opposite walls.

"Callista, I don't have any animals nearby to call to!" Aviana whispers from across the hallway, and I take the admission as a further need to protect her.

I practically toss myself in front of her and wait with fire in one hand and light in the other. I hold my breath, and, just as I blink, another beam comes down. It seems to come from closer than before, but I've yet to hear a single sound. *I know of only one person who has the ability to mute.* Just as her image appears in my mind, Melissa struts around the corner, a strange weapon in her hand.

"Ah, it's you again," she says. "And your equally annoying sister."

I sense Avi tensing behind me, and I grow increasingly protective. "Don't speak of her like that, Melissa. She never did anything to you."

She simply laughs, and I resist the urge to charge at her. Reggie and the husk students flash through my mind, further enraging me. *She's a monster.* I force myself to take a steadying breath. *I need to focus. She wouldn't come alone. She isn't that stupid.*

I glance around for other guards but am unable to see any. *There could be invisible ones.* The only light illuminating Melissa's form is a simple ruby necklace she wears. It glows brightly, allowing us to see her facial features.

"You're so funny, Callista!" Melissa says. "Liam told me your mom was actually just like you."

My face twists, and her grin widens. "Shut up," I practically growl at her. The reaction only seems to feed her sick and twisted ways.

"Anders, can you bring the little one over, please?" Melissa says.

A gust of air blows from behind me, and I turn just as someone grabs Aviana and quickly teleports away. Barely a second later, a man standing next to Melissa has a knife pressed against Avi's neck, and I catch a glimpse of blood trickling. I step closer, and Melissa shakes her finger.

"Get closer, and he kills her," she says.

I snarl at her and debate attempting to attack anyway. She seems to notice the intention in my features, as she laughs again.

"I have more men than you know," she tells me.

"What do you want, Melissa?" My words are filled with venom.

"I want you all to back down. Let Liam finish his plan and offer yourself to be his creation's host. As you know, you and Kieran are the most powerful. If Liam drains the powers both of you have into a mass weapon, he can inject it into you so you can become the weapon's host. You'd still be alive, although I doubt you'd have much personality to you." She swings her weapon over her shoulder. "Losing your powers can do that to a person. But you would know that, wouldn't you?"

My breath quickens. The students' faces flash through my mind once more, with their empty, hollow eyes and faraway expressions. *She's a monster. And I am too.* My self-hatred creeps back in, threatening to consume me.

Aviana's eyes catch mine, taking back my attention. She moves her lips ever so slightly, mouthing two simple words: "Distract her."

Uncertainty travels through me, but I trust in my sister and listen to her command. I call on the mask I utilized while under Liam's command.

"Hm, can I think about it for a moment?" I ask, shifting my weight and posing as if I'm bored. She sneers at me, and I fake a giggle.

"No," she says. "This is your last chance."

I ignore her and twirl wisps of my hair in my fingers, looking away from her gaze. "So, Melissa, why did you even start working for Liam?"

"Don't ignore me."

Good. I'm getting to her. "Did something happen? Perhaps he took you in through his pretty lies as well?" I peer up at her and feign my most innocent look. My words only fuel her more, and I fear that she might take it out on Avi. Instead, she moves toward me with a frightening look in her eyes, Avi still in her grasp.

"You don't know what you're talking about," she sneers.

My mask nearly slips, but after looking at Aviana's weak but reassuring smile, I manage to regain my composure. "Maybe he hurt someone close to you? Or convinced you that you were protecting someone?"

She continues moving closer, and I tense. Somewhat reluctantly, I continue my prodding. "Was it a sibling you weren't supposed to have? Or another relative? Oh, wait. Was it your family?"

Those words seem to trigger something in her, and she tosses my sister to the side. I watch as Avi thumps against the floor and notice a small trail of blood at her neck. Melissa swings the weapon from over her shoulder, her lips in a tight snarl. I see tears forming in her eyes, and my stomach flutters uncomfortably.

"Shut up, shut up, shut up!" she yells with her voice clouded in pain.

Before I can prepare, a laser fires at me from her weapon. I dodge the shot just in time, but the laser grazes my arm, leaving a burning mark. My new pain drives me to attack her once again, firing up my hands and jumping toward her. She pivots away before I can reach her, a scowl forming on her lips.

"You don't understand. I had no choice. Liam said that if I helped him, if I became part of his team, I wouldn't have to see anyone else I care about get hurt."

Her words make me pause, and she takes the moment to strike. *Just like me.* I come back to my senses and sidestep her before she's able to land a blow.

"Melissa, Liam did the same thing to me. I understand. I wanted—"

"I watched my family die in a fire," she says, rage oozing off her tongue. "I thought it was just a regular fire, but it was caused by someone just like you, like me. Apparently, some kid manifested their power early and escaped their Neighborhood, setting flame to everyplace they could. They were burning every Neighborhood they touched. And mine was one of them. I lost my everything. My parents, my home. The kid was taken down, eventually. But it was too late. I'd already lost all I cared for. I couldn't stand to let people like that exist, unmonitored and a danger to everyone around them. When I got here, I was infuriated. But then I met Liam. Unlike you, I believed in Liam's project. He promised to make sure no one with these powers would be able to lash out the way I witnessed. That we would learn how to perfect our abilities."

Before I have the chance to respond, she aims at me. When she fires, I realize I won't be able to dodge it in time. As my mind scrambles for what my next move should be, I'm shoved out of the way of the laser. I fall to the floor with a thud, and when I look to my side and see Avi, my eyes widen.

She was somehow able to reach me before the laser could. I quickly scan her body and realize that the shot grazed her arm. Blood trickles from the wound, and when I meet Avi's eyes, she seems distant. *She saved me?*

"Avi!" I cry out, and out of the corner of my eye, I see Melissa aiming again.

"You're both foolish," she announces. "This wouldn't have happened if you'd just joined us."

But before she can fire a fatal shot, shouting comes from behind her, and I notice Alec, Julies, and Brayden. Melissa turns in shock, and I take the moment to stand and fire up my hands with electricity. With her back toward me, I jump at her, connecting my current with her shoulder.

At first, she doesn't react. But when the tendrils start spreading across her body at a rapid speed, she screams out in agony. Her body shakes as she tries to fire at me once again. But her rapid movements make her unable to pull the trigger. Not wanting to have her image scarred in my mind, I have to force myself to look away as she crumples to the floor. When she goes silent, a heavy weight sits on my heart.

I killed her. Even though she was just manipulated like I was.

Brayden steps forward, placing a hand on my shoulder. "She was too far gone. This had to be done."

I stiffen, doubting his words. I force myself to concentrate on everything she's done, how she tried to kill me and Avi and how she killed Reggie. *It was self-defense.* I justify her death with the thought, focusing on my friends. *Just as she once told me. There are necessary casualties in war.*

THIRTY-NINE

THE SMELL OF BURNT FLESH sickens me. An unwelcome lump sits in my throat as I continue to consider the girl I once thought of as a friend and everything that happened to her. *I don't know if I can ever get used to this.*

Pushing away the emotions to deal with later, I hurry over to the others. Brayden has gone over to Julies to fight off some of the remaining guards as Alec tends to Avi on the floor. It takes mere moments for all the guards to be lying lifeless on the ground. There are far more than I thought there were.

"Thank you for coming, but how—"

Alec cuts me off and motions to Avi. "She told us."

I look quizzically at my sister as Julies wraps her neck and arm with a bandage to help with her bleeding.

Although she was nearly unconscious mere moments ago, Avi manages to explain. "I lied when I said I didn't have any nearby animals. I had a feeling someone was there and figured if they thought I was powerless, they would think of us as weaker. I was able to control a nearby rat and catch the attention of the others before leading them back. That's why I wanted you to distract her."

My eyes widen, and I process the information. Then I crouch down and smile at my sister. Tears prick my eyes as I consider her carefully. She nods, answering my silent question. I wrap my arms around her in a gentle embrace.

"You really are amazing, Avi. Thank you for saving me."

She smiles weakly back at me, but the moment doesn't last long, as Brayden grumbles nearby.

"Harris is bringing the last of the students to safety," he says. "We need to get moving. K's vitals are still offline."

I stand back up and nod at him. "About that, I believe I know where they are. Just outside the Academy walls, I saw a strange unevenness in the ground. It could be a trapdoor, and since we aren't supposed to know about that specific location, Liam might hide there."

Julies stands up and nods. "That sounds like it will be our best bet."

Alec helps Avi to her feet, and we all turn back toward the front door. Determination fills me, and I clench my fists. "Let's end this."

As soon as we open the door, I note the pouring rain. The others wait for me to guide them. I take a deep breath and step forward. Chills travel up my spine, but I push forward, driven by my desire to find K. Luckily, the uneven ground isn't far, and we have to trudge through the downfall only several feet before we reach the area.

"It's here," I say, motioning at the spot. Rain continues to fall over my hair and clothes, soaking me completely. Most of the water soaks into the ground, but a small area near the square outline begins to collect the liquid. I move my light closer to the spot and see a small indentation. I place a gentle hand on it and hear a faint clacking noise. Where the grass once was, a handle is revealed. I wave over the others, pull upward, and slowly lift the hatch.

Julies moves over and takes the weight from me. "Go with them," he says. "I'll go last."

I hesitate but then give him a respectful nod. Brayden and Aviana make it to the bottom first, and I scurry down after Alec. My feet hit a concrete floor, and I move away from the ladder so I don't block the way for Julies. A loud bang echoes through the room, and I look up only to see that the trapdoor has closed. Brayden sprints over and bangs on it, but it doesn't budge.

"Crap," he mutters, and I frown.

Julies can keep himself safe. He's the head of EMBER, after all.

Alec and Aviana are already looking around for any clues. I observe the room, noting its three halls branching off in different directions. Brayden strides down the frontmost one, and I decide to follow him, leaving Alec and Aviana together.

"Where do you think they are?" I ask.

He scoffs in response, glancing back and forth as we move. "Knowing what I do of Liam, this is probably a trap, and we're just pawns in his game."

I freeze, unsettled by the thought. "And you came in here willingly while knowing that?"

He turns and nods at me. "Yes. He most likely wouldn't come to us, so the only way for us to get to him is to do what he wants."

The hall is eerily quiet as we resume walking, and I resist the urge to run. I hear a scream that sounds just like my sister's and instantly turn, sprinting like I never have before down the hall toward where I last saw her.

"Aviana, I'm coming!" I yell as I hear Brayden's feet echo behind me. The simple concrete walls seem like an endless labyrinth, and fear rises in my chest. *What if something happened to her?* I nearly fall several times with my increasing speed, and soon enough, Brayden is running right next to me, his long legs allowing him to run faster.

It feels like hours have passed by the time I round the corner, finally going down the path Avi last took. It's not soon enough when I stumble across Alec, who's standing in a doorway. Brayden stands next to me, and just as I'm about to ask where Avi is, I notice her in the room. I push past him, hurrying toward my sister.

Aviana turns to me, terror in her eyes. "They killed her."

My eyes widen, and I step to her side, my heart nearly stopping as I look at Mira's dead body on the floor next to a dark door. Nausea swells within me as I snap my head away from the sight. A simple arrow painted on the wall points to the door, and I freeze. *K might be dead too.* Logic fades from my brain, and I sprint toward the door, throwing it open.

As soon as I step inside, I start to fall. Each second feels like eternity. I let out a scream, and my life flashes before my eyes. I squeeze my eyelids shut and prepare to hit the floor and die, only to be surprised when I land on my feet.

"What the—"

I hear commotion from above and move out of the way just as Aviana jumps down. After her, Alec lands, then Brayden.

"Why would you come after me?" I ask. "I could have been dead!"

Avi shakes her head. "It's only a short drop. We didn't hear anything, so we figured you were okay."

Only a short drop? I feel momentarily embarrassed by my dramatic reaction. Just as I'm about to respond, I hear clapping from behind. I watch as their blank expressions shift to rage and fear. I slowly turn, and my heart sinks as I see Liam standing in front of us. Too many guards to count surround him. My eyes land on one with a person in their arms.

"K!" I have the urge to run at him, but Brayden grabs my arm and hoists me back.

Liam grins maniacally. "What a coincidence that we're all here!" He turns and nods at the guard holding up K. "You can let him go."

"Yes, sir." The guard practically throws K in the space between us and Liam. His body lands with a dull thunk. Brayden releases my arm, and I hurry to K, searching for his heartbeat. I nearly cry in relief when I feel a steady pulse vibrating through his chest.

Liam looks down at me and sighs. Then he snaps his fingers, and three guards disappear, only to reappear with Brayden, Avi, and Alec locked in each of their arms. Brayden struggles, but even with his strength, he's unable to escape the guard's grip. I stand and defensively move over to K just as Liam hands me a flask.

"This will wake him up. I disabled the thing you were using to track his health to lead you all here. I guess it worked," he says with a smirk.

"How did you know we would come here?" I ask him, unconvinced that our turn of fate was a mere accident.

"I suppose I can tell you. It isn't a coincidence. You see, I wasn't completely sure. I was in the process of implementing several carefully plotted trapdoor systems when you escaped. I wanted them to be obvious, but not so obvious that you would suspect them of being a trap. Knowing I couldn't guarantee which one you might discover, I designed them so they all lead here. Luckily for me, you managed to spot one of the ones already built."

He speaks nonchalantly, and I glare at him. *He's smart. But not in a good way. I'm a fool for not suspecting anything. Just another fault on my list of mistakes. I'll make sure luck won't be on his side next time.*

Brayden, Alec, and Aviana stare at me but know better than to say anything. I don't speak, not wanting to give him the satisfaction of my response. Cautiously, I grab the flask, prepared to lash out at any sign of an attack.

"Go on, use it," he says. "Or I'll have to punish one of them."

As soon as the words leave his mouth, more guards move next to each of my friends, each one holding a gun to a head.

"Let them go, Liam." I force my voice to come out stern and unwavering. But inside, my nerves light up.

He laughs in my face. "Do what I said, and then we can talk about how you'll all help me."

Reluctantly, I open the flask and turn to look at K's resting face. *Please don't kill them. Don't kill my friends. I won't cause any more innocents to die.* I slowly tip the container, letting a single drop splash on him. As soon as it does, his eyes shoot open, and he sits up instantly. When his gaze lands on mine, he pulls me in for an embrace.

I mutter into his ear, "Not now, K."

He looks up from me, and, as soon as he sees our friends' situation, he pushes me away and stands. Before I can stop him, he uses his ability to turn off all the lights in the room. Chaos erupts, and strong arms wrap around me, causing me to wince. Then I call to my flame. I manage to light my attacker on fire just as a gunshot goes off, and I fall to the floor.

My eyes widen in shock as I fall over, my hands flying to wrap around my leg. Pain consumes every inch of my body, and tears prick my eyes. I watch as blood gushes from my thigh. I nearly vomit from the gruesome sight, but I try to focus my attention on my surroundings instead.

To my right, Aviana and Alec are battling unsuccessfully, completely outnumbered. Brayden screams as Liam launches a dagger into his gut, and I wince. We're steadily losing an imbalanced fight, and my heart sinks as my hope fades. I watch helplessly as K gets pounded to the floor by a guard with superior strength. A sob escapes me as the sounds of his bones shattering reach my ears.

As all of us lie crippled and severely wounded on the floor, Liam moves to me and bends over. He puts a wrinkled finger under my chin and forces me to look at him. Tears continue to fall from my face, and he frowns.

"Callista, it's really a shame. I would have made you the host for my greatest weapon yet. You know, I didn't ever understand why your parents fought for you and your sister so hard. I only ever thought of Reginald as a tool. Such a shame that I had to kill him once he caught feelings for you." The mention of Reginald's former self pains me, and my crying increases. "My wife was a pain too. That's why I got rid of her."

I manage to call to my flame, but he notices, putting his hand in his pocket. In my moment of distraction, I fail to notice a guard come behind me and hit me with a stun gun. Sparks shoot through my body, and I fall to the floor, forced to stare at Liam as he towers over my body.

"You never give up, do you? I tried to be so kind to you, and this is how you repay me. I'm quite sad I can't have you and your boyfriend help my cause, but I guess I can still use you once you're dead. Your power is stronger if you're alive, but you're too much of a liability."

Although I can't do anything, tears continue to stream from my eyes. *I'm sorry I failed you, Mom. I couldn't find a purpose. I couldn't save them. I'm sorry.*

I close my eyes and prepare for my inevitable death. Time passes by slowly, and the only feeling I have is the steady loss of consciousness from blood loss. When a loud explosion sounds from above, I open my eyes.

Surprise overwhelms me as hundreds of former students flow in. Fighting resumes. Lights flicker, and a small girl rushes to my side. I watch as she places a hand on me, and all my senses come back, along with a steady ease of the pain in my thigh. All around us, the guards are fighting with fellow members of EMBER and the former students. It's almost magical seeing so many abilities activated at once. *If only it weren't in such a dangerous situation.* Some students are kneeling over Brayden, Avi, K, and Alec. When I sense the girl lifting her hand, I look down and realize my leg is healed. Before I can thank her, she's gone, and I notice Julies moving toward me.

"Did you do this?" I ask.

He nods and reaches down a hand to help me up. As soon as I'm on my feet, I hug him quickly in thanks.

"We don't leave our people behind," he says. "These are all the students who hadn't been sent to REM class. The ones who were in the class and needed to heal have been sent to headquarters. I'm sorry I didn't come fast enough."

"We can talk later. More importantly, where's Liam?"

"He went through there." He turns and points to a hall opening that used to be a wall, then grabs my hand, forcing me to look him in the eyes. "I got information out of one of the guards. Liam has his first prototype—a weapon he made out of the REM students' abilities—with him now. I know you and Kieran can stop him together. Now hurry!"

He nudges me away. Just when I'm about to ask him to explain further, I realize he's already fallen into the crowd of bodies. *I have no time. I need to find K.* My heart races as I scan the crowd of faces for him. I struggle to focus with the various sounds of each student's abilities reacting with the guards' weapons. Some of the students are also shouting, making it even harder to discern anything.

When my arm is grabbed, I startle, prepared to call for my flame.

"It's just me!" K shouts, and when I meet his gaze, I relax, if only for a brief moment. I pull him toward the hall Julies pointed out so we can have some silence. The walls of the tunnel can't completely block out the clanging and grunting of battle, but they at least allow me to hear myself speak. Before he has the chance to ask any questions, I fill him in with the information Julies told me.

His eyes widen as I speak, and when I finish, concern fills his gaze. He grabs my hand and squeezes it. "I thought I lost you."

"I thought the same." I pull him closer, needing to feel his chest against mine. I want to stay with him like this forever, but when the sounds of screams reach my ears, I know I can't. I pull away and look at him sincerely. "We have to go."

His focus shifts, and he nods down the hall. "Let's do this."

I send him my best smile, and we turn, running down the hall and leaving the others fighting behind.

FORTY

THE PASSAGE GROWS INCREASINGLY dark and narrow, and our footsteps echo as we run. It's surprisingly lengthy. Once the sounds of fighting have faded, we're left in eerie silence.

The walls have gotten so narrow that K and I can no longer run side by side. I let him take the lead, hoping it will help me defend his back once we arrive. My heart beats rapidly in my chest, not helping my anxiety. I call out to my light, not wanting to continue running in the endless dark shadow. *I don't even know what we're going to do. K and I never succeeded in combining our abilities. What if the moment comes when that's what we need to do, and we fail? We also have no clue how powerful the prototype weapon is.*

A thousand thoughts rush through my mind as I struggle to focus on the path ahead. It seems like hours have passed when I finally spot a glimpse of light at the end of the tunnel. We slow down our pace as we get closer, and I let go of my ability.

"Do you see any way we can sneak up on him?" I whisper, trying to scan what I can see over K's shoulder. He shakes his head, moving over slightly so I can see what lies ahead.

The hall opens up into an expansive space, giving us little room for cover. There are two ledges on the sides of the opening, and K quickly moves to flatten himself against one. He motions for me to take the opposite side and puts a finger to his lips. I stand as still as I can against the ledge, straining to listen for any hint of Liam's location. At first, there's nothing. *Are we too late? Did he go somewhere else?* As I fill with doubt, I hear a low muttering from inside the room. I turn my head to look at K and pick up as much as I can.

"My plan … foiled … not … yet …"

The muttering abruptly stops, and my breath quickens. Then there are footsteps. I push back on the wall, trying to make myself as hidden as possible. As the footsteps get closer, I call out to my flame. I expect Liam to catch us and attack, but instead, the footsteps pass us and go deeper into the room. I take a deep inhale and let it out, settling my nerves.

K peers over the edge and then nods at me, pointing. He then dashes into the room, surprising me. I hesitate, then follow him inside.

We crouch behind a desk, and I realize that we're in some form of laboratory or research area. Papers are scattered across the floor, clearly shoved off one of the multiple desks in the midst of a rage. There are tubes on tables and other unfamiliar devices lining each surface.

When I risk a peek over our hiding spot, I notice Liam hunched over some strange object. The room smells strongly of chemicals, and the longer I sit in it, the more my nose stings. My brain scours the room to find the best angle for us to attack from. None of the tables or desks are positioned where they would allow us to sneak up on Liam. We would have to expose ourselves no matter what, even if just for a moment.

The muttering resumes, but now Liam is too far for me to make out any of it. *We need to make a move.* I tap K on the shoulder, then point to one of the desks closer to Liam. He nods, and I scramble toward it. I don't notice the tiny shards of glass on the floor surrounding the desk, likely from a shattered vial, until one of them slices through my palm. I bite my tongue to hold back a yelp. I bite too hard and mutter a curse under my breath. As the metallic taste of blood fills my mouth, I realize I may have given up my position.

My heart rate increases once again, and I make every effort to be as quiet as possible. When K follows me, I motion frantically at the glass, and he manages to avoid it. He grabs my palm and observes it as blood drips onto the floor. It's a clean cut but not a deep wound. He doesn't seem to realize that I made noise, which gives me a small hope that neither did Liam. I pull my hand away from his and use one of the glass shards to cut off a piece of fabric from my shirt, wrapping it around my palm to stem the bleeding.

When the stinging begins to numb, I peer up over the desk. Liam's not there. K notices it too, and we exchange a panicked glance. Before we have the chance to react, I hear the sound of something charging. We both turn our heads at the same time, only to see Liam smirking at us. Now that he's so close, I realize he seems to have armor of some sort atop his clothes. It's somewhat translucent, explaining why I failed to notice it earlier. He's holding a massive weapon. It looks similar to a gun, but something seems off about its shape. There's an extra attachment that looks unnatural.

"You stupid children! Why do you insist on getting in my way? You must have a death wish!" His eyes are wide and vicious as he shouts at us. "I'm going to end you now! Then I'll end your friends too!"

K and I exchange a glance, and, just as he fires the weapon at us, we split apart, dodging its blast. A strange purple energy connects with the floor, wrapping its tendrils around the legs of every surface it touches. Now on the opposite side of the room from K, I feel slightly more vulnerable.

"I didn't want to have to use this yet, but you obviously aren't going to back down." Liam reaches into his pocket and places a small device on the weapon in a swift motion. Before I can react, he aims at me. I see K rush at him just as I prepare to dodge, but to my horror, Liam pivots and fires the weapon right at K's chest.

When the blast hits him, K flies backward and hits the wall. He's wide-eyed and alive but motionless. I instantly run over and kneel beside him. His eyes meet mine, but he can't speak.

"What did you do to him?" I shout, glaring daggers at Liam.

"He's disabled. One of my lovely students had the ability to demobilize people. I thought it strange at first, but it really is quite useful." He pushes something else on his weapon.

My mouth drops slightly in horror. I look back to K, unsure what to do. *I need to get that away from him.*

I stand, ready to face my enemy. "If you let him go, I'll do what you want." My voice comes out empty and cold.

Liam raises an eyebrow as he takes aim at me. "You really expect me to believe that a second time? To be fair, you did help me move my plans ahead quickly. All those students you took to REM, all the power you gave me, saved me a few months of work."

His words cut like a knife and crack my resolve. I take a step forward, baring my teeth at him. My hands warm as I call to my flame, and the sound of crackling fire fills my ears. I push out my hand just as he pulls the trigger ever so slightly, and the purple energy shoots out again.

I throw my flame aimlessly as I try and dodge it, running and jumping onto one of the desks. But much to my horror, the energy spreads up like vines, and its tendrils reach me. I look and see that my flame managed to hit Liam, but his armor seems to absorb it. Before I can even try and escape the frightening energy, it climbs up my legs, hissing like a snake. Liam smirks as I panic, my skin feeling as if it's about to melt off. When the tendrils wrap around my neck, my head starts to pulse.

"This one is one of my favorites. I combined the ability of telepathy with one of the students who was able to control electricity, much like you. Except they couldn't also create flame and light. That, my dear, is your specialty."

As seconds tick by, my mind seems like it's being torn apart. I don't know if it's Liam's doing or just the fact that my thoughts are being infiltrated, but I can't stop the images of all the innocents I hurt from flashing across my vision. *Come on. I can fight this!* I can no longer see the room I'm in, only the images of my past. Liam flips through my memories as if they're a picture book, and the further back he goes, the more I swear my brain may explode.

When he reaches the last time I sat in the field with Reginald, the day I got Emmy, I feel myself fall backward onto the desk with a thud. The sudden impact clears my mind, and I blink rapidly. The pain in my head doesn't subside, but I can finally see. I glance down at my body and see that the tendrils have retracted. When I lift my head from the desk, I see Liam angrily pushing buttons on his weapon.

"I guess you aren't such a mad genius after all," I spit, getting up slowly, as I fear I may pass out. My mind feels like it was shredded. Liam fumes, and his hands shake as he frantically tries to fix his weapon. I take advantage of the moment, using my remaining willpower to charge up my hands and fire a blast of flame at him. I aim for his face, the only place not protected by his armor. But before it can impact, he disappears. Seconds later, he reappears behind me.

"This came from one of the first students you brought to REM," he says. "I think her name was Jessa?"

My heart nearly stops as my broken mind recalls the innocent girl I hurt. I'm once again overcome with feeling, destroyed by what I did. I struggle to stay focused as Liam pushes me forward from behind, causing me to stumble toward K. Already in a weakened state, I'm unable to keep myself from falling atop K's still body. When I sense him beneath my palm, I feel recentered.

I can end this. I'm not alone. I look up, meeting K's gaze. *I need to free him. But that weapon is too strong.* I take a deep breath, then push myself to my feet once more.

"Liam, if you're so powerful, why do you feel the need to disable one of us? Shouldn't you be able to take on both of us at once? Or are you too scared?" I ask, turning slowly to face him with a menacing stare.

He frowns, clearly bothered by my statement. "My weapon, this armor, it's stronger than both of you. As long as I have it, I'll win. It may have some flukes, but no one, not even the strongest of ability-bearers, can stop it. I'm not scared."

I smile, looking at him condescendingly. "All your actions up to now have shown your fear. You have to manipulate others to do the hard work for you. You had to manipulate your own son! You act like you're so tough, but you're afraid of your own creations."

When he snarls at me, I can tell I've gotten under his skin by mentioning Reginald. He aims at K. As soon as he fires and the blast hits, my heart stops. For a moment, nothing happens. Then, much to my relief, K's leg twitches.

I got to him. He freed K. He stretches out each of his limbs, and I find myself thankful that he wasn't in a still state for too long. *Had it been longer, who knows if he would be able to move so quickly.* As soon as K stumbles to his feet, he joins my side.

"I'll show you who's scared!" Liam shouts, pressing another button on the gun.

"We have to get that weapon out of his hands," K whispers, and I nod.

"He'll expect us to charge together. So let's come from opposite sides. It may be risky, but it's all we can do," I suggest, speaking as quietly as I can.

When Liam raises the weapon, K and I separate and rush at him. He flicks his aim between us, clearly unsure which shot would be more advantageous. When I'm almost in front of him, he fires at me, and a strong wave of energy throws me against the wall. I hit it with a thud, the sound of the wall cracking echoing in my ears. The corners of my vision start to blacken. My head pulses with more intense pain than before. I blink rapidly, trying to regain focus. *Come on, K!* My vision doubles, and the world before me spins. I can barely make out Liam and K fighting over the weapon, and I can't tell who's winning.

Liam abruptly shoots himself in the arm with the device, almost like it's a needle he's injecting himself with. K goes in and out of shadow, and Liam is trying to keep hold. Then, an object comes flying toward me. It spins across the floor, slamming roughly into my legs. Moments later, K follows, and the sound of him crashing through the wall echoes around me, further intensifying my headache.

I slowly reach down my hand, wrapping my fingers around something metallic. My pulse quickens as I realize what it is.

The gun!

The realization that Liam is now weaponless gives me a boost of energy. I wince as another sharp pain shoots off in my skull when I move to stand. I steady my hand against the crumbled wall, using every ounce of my remaining strength to push myself off the floor and onto my feet. K is on the floor beside me, and I notice blood oozing down his forehead. For a moment, my heart stops. I step carefully over debris to get closer to him. When I reach his side, I let out a gasp as he looks up into my eyes.

"I'll be okay," he mouths, but I can tell he's just saying that.

We don't have much time left. We need to finish this. I offer him my shaky hand, and he shakes his head, staggering as he pushes himself off the ground. He moves just as unsteadily as I do, and when he joins my side, we wrap our arms around each other.

"He used the gun to give himself more strength. We won't stand a chance at close distance," K whispers into my ear.

I grimace, unsure if either of us has enough strength left. My vision stabilizes just enough for me to make out Liam seething from across the room.

"I killed my wife for this! I killed my own son! Don't you understand? This is what has to happen!"

We stay silent as he becomes more noticeably manic as each moment passes. I look away from Liam, meeting K's gaze. *This is it. We have to try and combine our abilities. We have no other choice. Even if it didn't work last time, this is our last resort.*

I call on my light as K pulls on a shadow of darkness. Both of our abilities are flickering, clearly as weakened as we are. I push all my rage, despair, and sadness from the past several months into my power. The light grows larger and brighter, greedily eating up my emotion.

"We'll no longer feed into your deceit!" I shout over Liam's hysteria.

He turns and stares directly at me, pure and utter malice in his eyes. Before he has the chance to try anything, I fire out my light. It moves forward at an increasingly quick pace, and seconds later, K's shadow is beside it. When it's finally directly in front of Liam, I let out a cry and let my ability take control. I watch in horror and amazement as the light becomes absorbed by the darkness and the darkness is absorbed by the light. My body is shaken, drained of any remaining power. The sight before me is indescribable; color ceases to exist and words are useless.

It worked. It actually worked. The combined mass grows and grows, something never seen before but clearly full of power. Liam's eyes widen in horror. Before he can attempt to do anything, the large sphere-like cloud explodes and lets out a large blast of heat. The impact is larger than I expected. When the excess mass comes flying toward us, neither K nor I have enough willpower left to fight back. We exchange one last meaningful stare before falling into endless black.

FORTY-ONE

I WAKE UP WITH A GASP, FEELING AS if my heart may pulse out of my chest. When I open my eyes, I'm met with an intense light that causes my head to pound with unbearable pain. My breaths come out short and quick, and my vision spots. I start to panic, my body shaking violently. A cold hand rests on mine, and my body calms. A pair of gentle eyes look down at me, and a soft smile greets me.

"It's okay. It's over. You did it," Avi says.

Just the sound of her voice makes me feel at peace. "Liam's gone?" I ask, my voice coming out hoarse.

"Yes. He is."

I look down, noticing a tube protruding from my arm. The sight ignites my defenses, causing my panic to return. Just when I move my hand to my arm to remove the unwelcome device, Avi grabs it.

"Don't. You and K were both severely injured in the battle. You've been unconscious for almost a week. We had healers work on you, but none of the ones we have are skilled enough to deal with internal damage. This tube is just to make sure you're getting proper nutrition. I promise."

I look at her with concern, but I know she wouldn't lie. "Where's K?" I ask, forcing myself to settle back against the mattress. *This must be the medical wing. We're back at base.*

She frowns. "He hasn't woken up yet."

I sit up abruptly, but she pushes me back. "His vitals are steady. You need to worry about yourself right now. The others are taking care of him."

"Can you at least fill me in on what happened since I last saw you? To keep my mind busy." I move my free hand back to prop my pillow, allowing me to sit up more.

"After you and K left, there were hordes of guards coming down on us. Liam must have called in reinforcements. They outnumbered us two to one. We were able to fend them off well at first, but they just kept coming. Even though we had abilities stronger than their weapons, their numbers were too much. Some of the students who were helping out got severely injured. Quite honestly, for a moment, I thought we might have lost. But I think the anger we all held helped fuel us. Eventually, the guards stopped coming. They had no more supply. And I think they weren't prepared for our resilience. It wasn't easy, and it was horrific."

She wavers, grimacing. I recall the smell of blood and the sounds of violence, imagining what it must have been like.

When she speaks again, her voice is steady. "But we reduced their numbers. When they saw they had no winning chance, the remaining guards fled. The students regrouped, and Julies guided the rest of us to meet up with you. As we were running down the hall, we felt the blast that must have knocked you out. You and K were both badly injured, and Liam ..." Her voice drifts off again, leaving the words unspoken.

Her battle was no easier than mine. I place my free hand atop hers. A swell of love for my sister and joy that she's safe cloud up inside me.

"Thank you, Avi. I'm so glad you're safe. I don't know what I'd do without you."

She glances away for a moment, chewing on her lip. "I want you to know that I forgive you. I think I understand better now what happened. I don't blame you. I saw how hard you fought back there. I know you care about this fight."

I chuckle, pulling her in to wrap her in an embrace. At first, she stiffens, but eventually, she relaxes and returns the embrace. I have an unfamiliar sense of calm, knowing this battle has been won. I would be happy to stay here, with one of my favorite people.

"Kieran has woken," a voice calls in from the door, breaking up the moment.

My eyes widen. "Avi. Please go check on him, since I can't." She nods, hurrying out. My nerves flare, and I wait anxiously for her to return. Seconds tick by, and the only sound I can hear is the dripping of the fluid going into my body. When I hear a knock at my door, my heart stops.

"Come in!" I call, praying for good news. When the door flies open and a medical bed is pushed inside, I strain to see who its occupant is. When my eyes meet K's, a smile spreads across my face.

Avi comes in behind, pushing the bed and a pole with a tube system like mine. "I was able to get permission for him to reside in the same room as you."

I grin widely, eagerly watching as she moves K beside me.

"I was worried about you," I say, reaching out my hand across the distance between our beds.

"The first thing he said when he woke was your name," Avi says with a playful smirk.

K looks to her, his cheeks flushing with embarrassment. "I was just concerned about her," he says, reaching his hand out to meet mine. He gives me a squeeze, and I return it.

Avi looks at both of us cheerily. "You two should rest. Julies wants to have a meeting, but we've been waiting for you to wake. I imagine that as soon as he hears that you two are well and alive, he'll want to continue with business. I'll ask him to give you until tomorrow."

I mouth one more "thank you" as she exits the room, leaving us in silence.

"I can't wait to leave this bed," I say with a stiff laugh.

"Me too."

I observe K, taking in his current state. His forehead, bloodied only a few days ago, is unscathed. He looks tired, and I realize I'm exhausted.

"Even after all that time, I guess our bodies still want more rest," I say with a sigh.

K smiles gently at me, then leans back his head. "I know I just woke up, but I feel like I haven't slept for days," he says.

"Probably just a side effect of all the tension we went through." I lie back as well, squeezing K's hand one more time before letting go. "Let's get some rest. I'm sure we'll be busy tomorrow."

I close my eyes, finally at peace.

The next day, K and I are finally able to leave the medical wing, only to be ushered by one of the healers to one of the many small living spaces.

"Meet Julies in the main office in forty minutes. There are clothes for you on top of the dresser!" the girl calls, leaving the room in haste.

"You can clean up first," K offers, and I don't argue. I instantly go to the bathroom and turn on the shower, dying to wash off the grime that's built up all over me. When the hot water hits my skin, I instantly relax. I swiftly wash my hair and body, then exit the shower so K can use it. Then I realize I left the change of clothes outside. My cheeks flush in embarrassment as I slowly creak open the bathroom door, sticking my head through the crack.

"Can you pass me the clothes?" I say, my voice slightly unsteady.

K lifts his head from the paper he's reading. When he sees me, his eyebrows shoot up. "Oh, of c-course," he says, clearly as embarrassed as I am. He grabs the clothes off the dresser and brings them over, briefly meeting my eyes as he hands them to me.

"Thanks," I reply, shutting the door more quickly than I mean to. I swiftly change into the form-fitting uniform, then braid my hair as I step into the main lounge. K has already gathered up his belongings. "I'll wait for you here," I tell him.

He nods, then disappears behind the bathroom door. When the shower turns on, I take a seat, picking up the paper K was reading. As I scan the pages, I realize it's an old document from a time decades before I was born. Before the country was fractured, and before abilities existed. *It's strange to think about all the things that have occurred. I once would have never thought I would contribute to the seemingly always changing future of this world. Now it's hard to say exactly what's next. I'm sure the people back then never could have predicted what has occurred these past months.*

I become absorbed in the paper and my own thoughts. Time drifts by, and soon enough, K steps out of the bathroom, fully changed and prepared.

"Are you ready?" he asks, hanging his towel on the nearby rack.

I place the paper on the table and stand, giving him a half-hearted smile. "As ready as I'm going to be."

As we walk to the door, we take one another's hand. We don't leave each other's side as we go to the meeting spot. No words pass between us, recent events being too heavy for light chatter.

When we arrive, Julies greets us at the door, saying, "Welcome to our main office. Right this way, you two."

I exchange a glance with K, then drop my hand from his. I stuff both my hands in my jacket pockets.

Julies leads us down a hall I've never been through before and then into a small office. The room seems more elegant than the rest of EMBER, its floors pristinely smooth. There's a pleasant aroma in the air, the exact smell unplaceable. A large polished dark oak table is in the middle of the room, adding to the refined appearance.

My stomach quivers when I realize it's only the three of us here. *Where are Avi and the others?*

Julies takes a seat in a small white armchair and motions for us to sit across from him on matching seats. We do as ordered, and I fiddle with my fingers anxiously. Julies sends us a friendly grin that puts me slightly more at ease.

"I know we have a lot to discuss." He shuffles in his chair and settles in, folding his hands on the table. "And you must be wondering where everyone else is. First, I'll assure you that we'll meet with them soon. When we do, I'll have you debrief us on what exactly occurred when you went to face Liam. But before that, I needed to meet with you privately. I have an offer for both of you."

My pulse quickens, and I fight off the nervous urge to bounce my leg. He turns to look at K.

"Kieran, how would you like to be trained to be our future leader of affairs? We would like to work with you so you can get more experience under your belt before we give you the position officially. You have potential, and with our help, I think we could shape you into being perfect for this role. You would be a major contributor toward our future projects and help us lead our reformation. If you accept, you'll be briefed further on your position at a later time by our new current leader of affairs, Tyrus."

K looks shocked, his mouth slightly agape. I try and read his expression, but he seems to be fluttering through several emotions. He takes a deep breath, quickly regaining his composure. With a nod, he replies. "I would be honored, sir. Thank you so much."

Julies extends a hand, and K shakes it.

I grin at K with excitement. "You deserve this," I mouth, and he smiles at me. I then wait for whatever Julies wants to propose to me. When he finally turns, I straighten and feign confidence.

"Callista, I would love the honor of having you trained to be one of my commanders. Just as I said to Kieran, I think you have potential. I know you're on probation, so you wouldn't receive any hands-on training for a while. However, you would still be trained in other ways. I want to see more from you. Correct me if I'm wrong, but I think you want to improve upon yourself. I can help you do that. I think in time, you could thrive here. You've proven yourself to be willing to do anything to protect those you care about, and I greatly honor that. In this role, you would be trained under Tessa, who's to be my first in command."

My mouth nearly drops to the floor as I stare at him. I feel emotional as I consider everything he's just said. *I can have a fresh start. I can learn to move on. I can't take back my mistakes. But I want to grow. I want to become better.* I flush in slight embarrassment and wipe a tear from my eye.

"Of course, I'd love to have that honor!" I tell him. We shake hands, and as soon as we finish, he stands.

"Well, I'm glad to welcome you both as our new trainees. The work won't be easy, but I have no doubt you'll be able to handle it. Tessa and Tyrus will brief you further at a later time on what your job will entail. The other officials would like to meet to discuss what happened with Liam and our next move. Would you mind if I escorted you?"

K reaches down and grips my hand. "We wouldn't mind at all."

The familiar conference room is more crowded than I've ever seen it. At least ten different council members sit in a cluster at one side of the long table, while Alec, Aviana, Brayden, Tessa, and Tyrus sit on the other. I take a seat with K next to Avi, and she smiles at me. Julies stands at the far end of the room and addresses everyone with his classic smile.

"We've won the fight, but the struggle isn't over. Liam wasn't the last one in our way. His roots run deep, just as ours do. So he still has supporters. There will be another battle to end it all. We have Eclium, but not yet the New America. This is our first step to victory." He pauses to allow us to take in our success. "Additionally, our plans to replace REMEDY Academy will take time, but they're not impossible. But first, it's important for us to discuss what occurred last week." He turns to me and K, motioning for us to take a stand. "Will you two fill us in?"

"Of course," I say, getting up and hoping I look more collected than I am. K and I take turns informing the others on what occurred, from Liam's weapon and its abilities to his armor that deflected our individual attacks. I struggle through the recount of how Liam tore up my mind, invading my thoughts and memories. I can still feel the pain, especially when he recounted the students whose lives I destroyed.

K serves as my rock throughout it all, having experienced his own share of suffering. It's evident that no one expected such power from Liam, especially considering the weapon was only a prototype.

When we've finished, K grabs my hand and gives it a tight squeeze. I close my eyes for a moment, grateful that the weight is no longer on just our shoulders.

"That wasn't exactly what I expected," Julies says, uncertainty clear in his voice. A few whispers pass around the table as everyone takes in this new information. K and I take our seats. A sudden realization sends chills down my spine.

"Do we know if there were other prototypes that may have been given out?" I ask.

The council members exchange glances, and Julies frowns. "I'm not sure. We weren't able to find the remains of the one

Liam had in the wreckage, so at least that one is destroyed. But we can't be too careful, if it's as powerful as you say."

If there are more of those weapons, then someone else could try and finish Liam's project. But most of the guards died in the battle, and so did Reginald and Melissa. Who else was on Liam's side?

"For now," Julies comments, "we should be on alert. I'll have some of our people look into any possible connections to Liam who may possess potential prototypes." The other council members murmur agreement. "In the meantime, I would like to discuss something prevalent to the future of our organization and home. Please join me in welcoming our newest command members—Tyrus, the new head of affairs, with Kieran as his trainee, and Tessa, my new first-in-command, with Callista as her trainee!"

Applause erupts throughout the room, and I smile, feeling more hope than I have in a long time. Avi looks to me with delight, and I lean over to wrap her in a quick hug. "I couldn't have made it this far without you," I say.

"I've never been prouder as your sister," she replies. When she pulls away and meets my gaze, she looks wiser than her years.

Everything that has occurred has aged all of us. I give her one last grin, then observe the rest of the table. Tessa and Tyrus don't seem surprised by the announcement, but they take the congratulations with pride and dignity.

Once everyone has settled down, Julies claps. "Now, let us celebrate our success and plan our next steps. First, how we'll demolish that god-awful building." He chuckles half-heartedly, and I sit up straight, ready to conquer our new future.

FORTY-TWO

May 10, 2125

It took us nearly a whole year to completely demolish the old Academy and build the new one, but it was well worth it. In the few months since, we've managed to get the new EMBER Academy up and running. There's no longer a gate preventing students from entering and leaving the Academy. No one is trapped, and everyone may do as they please. In my new training position, I've observed Tessa as she monitors every sector of EMBER, ranging from war councils to architectural discussions.

In the past month, I've finally been removed from my probation. Tessa sometimes allows me to monitor sessions alone when she has other matters to attend to.

Aviana is now an instructor for the youngest kids at EMBER Academy, helping them learn how to use their abilities. We decided to make EMBER open to all ages so that any child with abilities can learn how to use them.

Alec works with the Intel Committee. Brayden has continued working in his position with war planning, and Tyrus has been thoroughly working with K in their position.

K and I have grown even closer than before, and I think we've finally reached a place where he has forgiven me and we can comfortably express our feelings for one another. I'm still forever thankful for his generosity, and I'm so fortunate that I can love him.

When K and I killed Liam, what was left of the REMEDY government in Eclium had little to no choice other than to submit to EMBER. All of Liam's known weapons were destroyed, and a proper memorial was created for all the students' lives that were ruined. Remaining guards and teachers have reluctantly joined us. Any dissenters are sent to be locked up until we can decide what to do with them. We've created a new program to provide adequate living arrangements for any remaining husk students. They don't ever speak, but at the very least, they won't die.

Eclium's various empty buildings are now functioning as extra housing for students, and new jobs are popping up for the older ability-bearers. The cat Reginald gave me, Emmy, has become a sort of mascot for the new Academy. She lives freely among its halls and is adored by all the students.

We even have new transportation systems that can bring us anywhere in a matter of seconds. It has taken time, but slowly we're turning Eclium into a safe and welcoming home for all ability-bearers.

We don't know if the government is still strong in New America without Liam. We don't know for certain that there isn't someone out there with Liam's technology. Our only way of learning is from our limited number of spies positioned in the country. We're no longer able to return to New America after destroying DETA. According to the spies, the Neighborhoods have been becoming more restricted. Julies believes there's a rebellion forming in the country. Now that the government can no longer send children to Eclium, we worry about what they'll do. That's why we've just recently released our first prototype of a teleporter to the New America that only we can access.

I close my journal and stand from the park bench on the forest's edge. Placing my pen and book in my bag, I smile at K.

"Let's go check on the Academy, shall we?" I motion for him to follow me, and he reaches out to grab my hand. Our fingers interlock as we walk together. The only sound in the air is the wind brushing through the trees. I embrace the silence, glad to have a peaceful moment.

"We've come so far, but there's still so much to do," K says wistfully.

I look up to meet his eyes. "We'll do it. Together. Like always." I squeeze his hand, and he squeezes back.

When I look ahead, I see the familiar steps to the Academy. As we approach them, I'm confronted with my memories of my first days at the Academy. *It's different now. That place is gone.* My chest tightens as I recall all the deceit I've been fed, and I find myself filling with doubt just as a young girl runs out and hugs me.

"Miss Callista! I missed you!" she exclaims.

Her presence snaps me out of my near pitfall, and K rests a hand on my shoulder, giving me a concerned look. I shake my head at him, assuring him with the motion that I'll be fine. I run my hand over the girl's dark locks and smile down at her. "I missed you too, Mari. Now, why aren't you in class?"

Her bright-blue eyes look up and meet mine, and she gives me a sheepish smile. "Miss Aviana told me you were coming to visit, and I really wanted to say hi!"

I lean over and lift her up, carrying her back inside. K follows me inside with a small smile on his lips.

Mari chats my ear off as we walk down the hall, eventually landing in front of Aviana's classroom. I walk inside and put the small girl down, a giggle escaping me as she runs off to play with the other kids.

I'm still working to show how sorry I am for what I did to the former students. Most students don't recognize me directly, as they likely just piled me in with all the other monstrous guards with no names. They just see me as Callista, someone helping our new world. Not a monster. But the few who do recognize me look at me with fear or disgust, making sure I never forget my mistakes.

Avi walks over and hugs me, taking me out of my thoughts. "Are you going to go visit Mom later?" I nod. She reaches into the pocket of her overalls and gives me a small pressed-flower keychain. "Can you give her this?"

I take it and slip it into my own pocket. "Of course, Avi. You're still free to come if you want, you know."

"I know, but Alec and I made plans to go out later. I'll visit another time."

I shrug and turn to leave. "Have fun, but not too much!" I shoot her a wink over my shoulder and notice a tiny flush on her cheeks.

"Oh, shut up!" she replies.

I laugh as I walk out of the door. I turn and look at K with concern as we walk. "You good, K?"

He startles, and I realize he must have been deep in thought. "Yeah, I'm fine. I just wish June could have seen this."

I rest a hand on his shoulder. "She's still here with you even if you can't see her."

"I hope so."

We begin our walk around the Academy to check in with all the classes in silence. The routine checkup takes several hours and goes smoothly, without any need for long discussions. When we finish and step back out of the building, I exhale. The sun is already setting in the sky, and the heat starts to lower in its intensity.

"I'll meet you at home, alright?" I say.

K nods at me and places a soft kiss on my lips. Then he heads toward the tele-tram. I stride toward the opposite tele-tram, which heads toward the recently built Eclium town hall. The soft breeze in the air calms me, and I smile to myself.

We've done good.

When I eventually reach the tram and step inside, I tap my destination into the waiting keypad. The machine counts down in a robotic tone from three, and nausea overwhelms me as it speeds ahead. Only a few moments later, the tram comes to a stop outside the town hall.

I've gone on that thing so many times, but I'm still not used to its effects from the speed. The nausea doesn't last long, and within moments, I'm steady once more. Straight ahead, the tall, seemingly glowing building waits for me, and I move toward it without hesitation. I smile when I see that no one else is in the large building and head right to my parents' memorial area. The smell of fresh flowers creates an airy lightness in the space.

"Hi, Mom and Dad," I say to the portrait of a young and beautiful couple hanging on the wall. It doesn't bother me when there's no response. I reach up and trace the outline of their figures. *Rosalie and Elijah. I only knew them for a short while. But my memories hold strong. I know I would have loved to have them as parents.*

I drop my hand and take out Aviana's gift, along with a bouquet of daylilies from my backpack. I place each on top of the long table just below the portrait.

"I heard these were your favorite flowers, Mom. And Aviana made this for you guys."

I step back and stare into the large photo. *I should ask Julies if he has any other memories he can give me. I haven't thought of it since everything has been so hectic.* Whenever I see my parents in my dreams, I wake up with puffy eyes and an incomprehensible lightness in my chest. Noticing the stars glinting in the night sky through a nearby window, I decide to take my leave.

"We're turning EMBER into a burning flame made of passion and community." A sad grin spreads across my face, and I sigh. "I love you guys. I'll be back next week."

I wave at the photo, then walk to the exit, hoping the door's automatic locks haven't activated yet. When I press the open button and it works, I sigh in relief and head out. I hear the lock activate behind me. *Just in time.*

I let my orb guide me to the tele-tram. Once I step in, I enter my new home address. Again, seconds later, I arrive at my destination. K and I live in an apartment at the Council's estate. The estate is expansive and brings great comfort when I see it.

I yawn as I walk toward the door, sluggishly pushing the button and walking through.

Tessa waves me over as I pass by. "Callista, we've received new intel from Neena. Come here."

My heart stops. *What new intel?*

Nervously, I approach her side. She pulls out a hologram and shows me the message. Neena has a panicked look on her face, her eyes darting back and forth.

"They're tightening restrictions. There must be someone who's controlling all of this, but we've yet to find out who. The children, we've seen them through the gates. They don't even bother separating them anymore. All of them are dragged around and herded like cattle. All these innocent children. They can't even fight back. I don't know where they send the ones who develop their abilities, but I can't imagine it's good. Mason has told me he's intercepted reports. They want to reclaim Eclium. Whoever is running this is up to no good."

The message cuts off, leaving Neena's horrified expression to stare at me. A lump forms in my throat, and I swallow, my mouth suddenly dry.

"Have you told the others?" I ask. "What does Julies say?"

Tessa's eyes are sad and lost. "I have, except for Kieran and Julies. I haven't seen them yet. We have to increase our training. We need to recruit as many of our willing students as we can. We can't let this go on for long. I fear that Liam had more connections and plans for his demise than we expected. It no longer seems like the government was as dependent on him as we thought. Tomorrow we'll start drafting our next plan."

I chew on my lip, considering her words. "Alright. I'll tell K when I see him."

She nods solemnly. "Thank you."

I move toward the elevator, which works similar to the tele-tram and teleports me to my floor as soon as I type in the number. I nearly fall over due to the inevitable nausea but manage to gain my composure. Then I stride down the hall and unlock my room door. When I see K sitting inside with Emmy on his lap, I smile softly, taking off my shoes and walking toward him.

"Hey," I say.

His eyes light up when he looks at me, and I frown as I take a seat next to him on our plush couch. "Are you alright?" he asks.

"Tessa just showed me a message from Neena."

"What did it say?" He sits up, attentive. Emmy stretches, disturbed from her nap. I inform him of what I just learned, and my frown deepens at his distressed expression.

"This is awful," he says.

"Those poor children …" My words drift off, my shoulders sagging. I lean back on the couch and take a deep breath. Emmy cries, and I place a gentle hand on her, pulling her onto my lap. As I pet her, she falls asleep once more. "We'll start drafting plans tomorrow."

He leans over to wrap his arm around me, pulling me close to him. "We'll stop whoever is running this. Together." I lean my head on his shoulder, closing my eyes. "EMBER will continue to be a great place as we continue to build it up. I know it. Even if this is terrifying. We'll fight through everything that crosses our path together. I promise to always be by your side."

He gently places a warm kiss on my forehead, and I smile ever so slightly. "And I'll always be by yours."

The steady rise and fall of his chest as he breathes calms me. Through thick and through thin, we've been there for each other. We've grown together, and now we'll continue on to our next stage. Our lives may have been full of lies, but one thing holds true. More now than ever, I know that I must surround myself with honesty. That will be the remedy for my life full of deception.

Acknowledgments

Writing a book has been a dream of mine ever since I was a child. I remember time and time again trying to create a story only to give up after a few pages. And now I've done it. I've written a novel. And I couldn't have done it without my amazing and supportive family.

To Heather, the most incredible "mama" in the world. Thank you for being there for me throughout this journey. You were one of my first editors and readers, encouraging me to continue even when I faced writer's block. Without your eternal support, I could have never reached the finish line. I love you to the moon and back, and I will never forget how you helped me on this journey.

To Ken, my wonderful father. You have helped me through this entire publishing process and have been incredibly kind in helping me get here. I would only be here and able to proudly say I published my first book before the age of twenty with you and your assistance. We can both proudly call ourselves authors, and I am eternally grateful to you for that. I love you so much and appreciate everything you have done for me.

To my cats, Babyboo (Booboo) and Bigkitty. I may be silly for thanking my cats, but you both have been two of my rocks throughout this process. Booboo, you always sat next to me (or on me) as I wrote and provided a welcome respite whenever I needed a break. Bigkitty, your little "mehs" always cheered me up when I was stressing over if I was doing a good job. Thank you, my sweet babies, for I love you more than you'll ever know.

To everyone I have told about my novel and who has shown me excitement and genuinely cared to know more: I once would have never thought that I could do this, so your eagerness pushed me when I lacked my own. I am so thankful for your words; I carry them with me.

Finally, thank you to my editors. I learned so much from each of you and have grown in my experience thanks to your critiquing of my work. I can't wait to continue my writing journey and will never forget how you influenced me.

About the Author

ALEXANDRA GAVRANOVIC lives in Georgia where she is studying Public Relations. She has been writing and crafting stories since she was a young girl, and enjoys the process of being creative.

When she's not studying for her college classes, Alix enjoys spending time with her two cats and her dog, reading dystopian novels, and playing video games. She is also an avid pianist with 12 years of experience.

Deception Is Our Remedy is her first published novel.